WINNERS

WINNERS

A NOVEL BY

Judith Green

Alfred A. Knopf   New York   1980

Library of Congress Cataloging in Publication Data
Green, Judith H   Winners.
I. Title.
PZ4.G7958Wi 1980 [PS3557.R3727]   813'.5'4
ISBN 0-394-50387-2   79-3484

Manufactured in the United States of America

FIRST EDITION

For Willie, God bless

WINNERS

1

As I'm driving home, I'm thinking about why, for the past year, she's made me so happy and what's going to happen to that happiness now. I'm wondering, too, after how many minutes of marriage does the humdrum wipe out the freshness of beginnings. When do you suddenly know that what you're experiencing is mostly a good memory? Five years? Ten? Never? Is never better?

I'm also thinking about the meeting. It's driving me crazy driving to it. I'm rushing to where I don't want to get to. Isn't the decision made, anyway, before we meet to make it? No. I can still decide. And I don't want it. Just thinking about the hands to pump and the asses to kiss makes me sick. Sixty-two counties of clamoring slobs believing any bullshit as long as it comes out smelling like: "Ask not what your country can do for you."

Automatically, I press the tape deck, but now the blare of "Dolly" makes me sad and uneasy. Yet just this morning I couldn't get it loud enough. Just this morning, like so many mornings for the past year, I pressed the rewind button to listen again, to try and catch it at the top, because it's Maria's favorite song. I loved to picture her dancing to it, going faster and faster as the beat grew wilder, the music louder.

Like the buildup of wave upon ocean wave, she'd crash through me as I'd watch her skirt flare, her mouth open slightly, and her soft lips shine under the russet gloss she uses for summer. I'd see her on tiptoe leaning forward until their cheeks met. And as they moved, her long hair, tied back in a wisp of chiffon, would fly from side to side. It would make me crazy wanting to be Latham, wanting to hold her close, thinking about whether she was thinking about bed when she danced with him. Sometimes, I'd stretch and agonize so far I'd almost be him.

I'm at a stoplight now and the syncopated part of "Dolly" is on. It's punishing me by not letting me turn it off. It's really blaring, "Amanda! You can't turn off so fast without being punished. No way, Amanda."

My windows are open and I'm creeping ahead as the cross traffic slows. I want to get a jump on the Volkswagen. Little cars always challenge my Mercedes. I press my foot way down. The tape is screaming. I feel dizzy.

I feel the room swayin', for the band's playin'

They're all singing and she's dancing faster and faster. The tiniest drops of moisture are visible in the creases of her forehead. The band stops for a break. Holding hands, they go back to their table.

But why should I be punished because something's over? I didn't push her out of something wonderful into me. We both were bored, lonely. Just because I started it, why can't I finish it? I've got to convince her without hurting her that she isn't any more that way than I am. It's not where either of us lives. She only thinks it is because he's unbearable. Yet to reduce it to mere Lesbian chic is too cruel. Curiosity? Need? A love, yes. But, Maria, sufficient unto the time. The time is over, Maria. Isn't life's law of gravity that all things run down?

I'm doing eighty and I don't feel it. I look into my rear-view mirror and push on. No smokeys behind and on my CB someone called the Big Bamboo assures me "it's clean and green ahead." I still hate Latham. I hated his calling her a "sleeper." What's that supposed to mean? Because she rode with the hunt, her body should ride to the rhythm of his horseshit? Tight in the saddle. Tight with the booze. Extra tight in the cooze. That's all he's ever known. I hate the cop, too, but differently. Imagining I was him used to be a turn-on.

"How did it happen?" I always asked, and she always answered. She knew it excited me.

"My security alarm went off. It rings at the station. If you call and say it's a mistake they check anyway. You could be dialing with a gun at your head."

"He came and checked?"

"Yes. I asked if he wanted something soft to drink. He said he'd worked all night and needed a real one. I made him a Scotch. Then I asked him to sit down."

"Why?" I watched her eyes not watching mine.

"He was tired. He looked exhausted." She laughed as always after a half-truth. She's not capable of lies and wants to be caught in the halves.

"What did he look like?" If she answered, I didn't hear, because I saw him anyway. He was a linebacker with a stud's sneer. Then I heard myself ask how old he was. "I don't really care." I cared a lot.

"I don't remember exactly." She seemed to be trying to remember. "He was before Latham. It must've been seven years ago." She spoke slowly. "About my age then. About twenty-six."

My words were fast. "Nobody's about twenty-six. Nothing costs about twenty-six dollars. How long before he undressed you?" I could see everything.

"He was married." She was uncomfortable. I was going crazy.

"Don't married men undress women?" I hugged her closely, covered her mouth, and thought of his lips where mine were. "Did he excite you?"

"He was so different."

"Like us?"

She got red. "No."

"What did he do?" I had to know.

"He went to the blinds. He started to close them. I didn't stop him. Then he loved me."

She always said "loved me." It was sweet and I could have killed him. "Did you come?" Inane question. She always comes.

"I guess I thought I did. Then."

"How often did you see him?"

"A lot for a little while."

With every grain of hate for him, I loved her more. "Did he ever do anything to you with his gun?" I knew the answer. I could feel it where she had.

"Yes."

"Dolly" plays into other songs and I let the tape run out. I switch to the news and "If you give us twenty-two minutes we'll give you the world." What I really want is the time, because the car clock runs wrong. I don't know why, but it annoys me that announcers pronounce *Concorde* like the hotel. Only that woman on the NBC nightly news accents the last syllable. That gives her credibility. She's there because she's smart, not only a libber like those punched-out, rip-and-readers with their campus casualness and their eyes leaning toward the teleprompters, "In front of the Capitol," or "Live from Reykjavik, Iceland." Even when the sun shines, their raincoat lapels flap into their wispy, all-American hair. I wonder how many people are offended by their inoffensive looks?

I love spring and it's just beginning. The calendar is wrong. It didn't start six weeks ago. "April is the cruelest month," but not because of "mixing memory and desire." I expect it to be spring and it isn't. That's not nice, Mother Nature! There were four inches of snow this April and only now is there some green fuzz showing. I don't count forsythia as spring, or cherry blossoms. I don't live in Washington. I live one hour north of Manhattan and reach as they will, only the weeping willows pop before the beginning of May. Like the patient camera in a nature film, one can see the daily progress as leaves start to hide the setback homes that winter opens. I like the trees when they're flat like Corot caught them. It won't be long now. "It's May! It's May! The lusty month of May." I forget whether I gave her the *Camelot* tape. But I told her about all the openings. First-nighters fighting the crush. The overture splitting the silence. New York at its climax.

"How fabulous, Amanda." She said. But did she feel it? Don't you have to be born in New York? I wasn't boasting about an evening, I was bragging about a city. Did she understand? When I lived on Sixty-eighth Street I used to play just musicals. I even bought duplicates not to have to turn them. I don't understand how kids get meanings from the explosions of today. I can't even get the words.

My radio is beginning to tune in and out of the New

York stations. I hate the local ones. "A brindle and white English bulldog answering to the name of Mary Alice has been lost in the vicinity of Mount Holly Road. Generous reward. The Parents Without Partners' meeting has been changed from the Methodist Church to the Boys' Club in Katonah, still at seven o'clock. And Alcoholics Anonymous has asked us to pass along these words, 'After you've recognized your problem, don't be afraid to be recognized. Come to the meetings.'" They'd never make Bob and Ray. They shouldn't be making fifty megacycles.

A couple of months ago. I needed that station badly. God, was it only a couple of months ago? There was an almost blizzard. I couldn't drive. I was listening for school closings. Endlessly, the announcers recounted their own hells about getting to the studio. Ruggedly, in the morning darkness, they'd hooked plows onto their magical front-wheel drives. Who gave a damn? Let that moron station give them a citation, but on their time. Then again about the public schools, the parochial schools. More about their driveways. Come on. Come on. Come on. I had to know. I had to get to the city. We had never loved in the warmth of the snow. Finally. Yes. Open. Hooray. By the time I was on the train, the children were on the bus. By White Plains, I had read the *News* and some of the *Times*. By Grand Central, I had finished the puzzle.

The flakes were small and close, making the air under the gray sky white. People walked hunched over, watching their footing, their hands shoved deep into their pockets. The icy flakes clung to my hair as I raced along Vanderbilt Avenue looking for an empty taxi. I jumped into one whose light went on before the passenger was out. Mumbling through a shaking head, the man slammed the door and got his change in the street. The cab, a new Checker, had so many "Please Do Nots," I was surprised Myron Appleman took it out in the street. Nonstop, I heard how if trucks made deliveries at night and private cars were taxed the minute they crossed the bridge, the traffic problem wouldn't be. "And something else. Get *me* in Gracie Mansion for a year and I'll hand this city back to the white man." Suddenly, I found myself wishing for the singing cabbie who prays I'm a talent agent.

The light turned red across from her apartment. Unable to wait the hours for it to turn, I stuffed too much money into the palm of the misbegotten and got out. Holding my hand traffic-cop style, I ran wildly in front of Allied Movers and into her overheated lobby. As the elevator door closed, I know the light still hadn't changed.

My finger seemed to press through the bell. She laughed as she opened the door. Before it closed we kissed. And there it was. That clean, wonderful smell under the perfume. I bent my knees and my arms circled the blue flannel. Between Suzy, William Safire, and *"Pequod*'s captain in four letters," I had pictured it all. The robe, the square pillows, the thickly quilted comforter that waited in front of the drawing fire.

The first feel of cool sheets is one of life's great sensations. It can't be memorized. But like everything with her, it was unique. I've held other people as tightly, many, but none as tightly as I'm holding her now. She folds into me with all angles melted. Watching her eyes close, I whisper about making a tent and getting out of the storm. We pull the covers high and slide down. I raise my knees and warm my feet on her legs. They move slowly up and down until they rest past hers. I love her being little. My arms bring her into me.

"I'm glad we came in from the cold." Her voice is soft and she sounds about eight.

"Were you very frightened?"

She answers on my lips. "A little."

Her hair is loose and soft and the dark brown strands fall upon my neck. She's beginning to move, rocking slowly, pushing into me. Her lips open just enough and my tongue circles under them. She makes the tiniest sound as her movements become stronger. I hold her down with my body and I kiss her nose, eyes, ears. The ears make her wild. My tongue is all over them. One arm is under her head. The other reaches between us and I put my fingers there. It's wet. She's moving so fast. I can't stand it. The bed is hot. She kicks the covers, but they stop at my ankles. I finish them all the way and then I pull back to look at her. I never remember her eyes so strong. I spread her legs far apart with my knees. She pushes the rhythm faster and faster. She stiffens. Her mouth is half open and contorted. There is only the slightest relaxing. "Oh, God. God, I love you," she says, remembering to keep her fingers flat on my back. She eases a little more. "I love you so."

"I know you do. Do you know I love you?"

"Yes." She is breathing hard.

I love my power of making love to her. I'm still on top and our bodies are slippery. We kiss and I wipe her forehead with the edge of the pillowcase. That pained look of orgasm is still there and it's driving me crazy. Suddenly, my body is slapping up and down against hers. It's moving faster than ever and as I'm coming, I put my hand there and wipe it over her face. It's more than a moan. It's loud, uncontrolled, unexpected. Her head is twisting back and forth as my fingers push her mouth open.

"You love this. Don't you? Don't you?"

"Yes. Yes."

"You'd have made a great whore. Do you know that? Do you?"

"Yes. No. Only with you." The tears fall from under closed lids. I move on my side, pull up the sheet and pat the dampness on her stomach, breasts, and thighs. She smiles. Her eyes are closed. She rolls toward me, embarrassed, wonderful.

I get sick thinking of her with Latham, thinking of his sleeping where I am now, touching her where I've just been. I see his pushing her head down and making her go there. That's the one. That's the thought that grabs and twists. Her body demeaned by that drunken, nonperforming flesh taunts me to such a peak that I suddenly find myself humping the air. And then, almost as if I were operated not by me, I put my hand there and maximize my overwhelming revulsion.

There are pictures of Latham all through the apartment. In frames of gold, the smile freezes at the Oval Office with Nixon, at the Jerusalem Museum with Kissinger, and with Carter when he was still a Jerry Rafshoon invention. There was once talk of posts in Spain or Italy, but only during fund raising. All that ever developed were a lot more eight-by-ten glossies.

Although Marr Electronics carries Latham's signature beneath the chairman's letter in its annual report, he has as much influence with daily directives as he had with the writing of that letter. Most things that pass Latham's desk have been passed before ever reaching it.

The multi-use minitube developed by his father and two Japanese electronics geniuses he'd hired at the end of the war was America's first big step into the tiny world of transistors. But that unwanted over-the-counter stock,

whose first public offering in 1948 was a broker's nightmare, has since split more times than its original offering at
nine.

Up until money, Latham lived in Flushing, which he
now recalls as Oyster Bay. Although the resources came in
time for boarding school, boarding schools had not quite
swapped the old school tie for the new arts center or science lab. Only with the most discreet tips to "chums" at the
Racquet Club and with promises of more to come did
Latham, Sr., manage to trade some points on the big board
for three undistinguished years at Choate for Latham, Jr.
Yet no matter how many overseers, Lowells, and Leveretts
the old man mustered, Harvard never gave the nod.
Though the turndown did creditably at Brown, Senior
never again saw him without betrayal daggering from his
eyes, or so it seemed to Latham. From then on Latham's
life seemed programmed by a series of self-destruct buttons. By the time Maria came along, it was too late.

I don't know how many times I've asked her how they
met. It kills me, but I keep wanting to reconstruct everything. I detest skiing, but that winter, six years ago, I picture myself in Klosters. At night, when I can't sleep, I'm at
the Chiesa Hotel sitting with her and one of Saudi Arabia's
richest rebuilders of Babylon. I know if Latham hadn't seen
her with him, there would have been no Latham, no meeting, no prison.

"My five-year marriage to Taylor had become a matter
of paperwork."

"How did you know the sheikh?"

"I didn't."

"Why were you sitting there?"

"He asked me to."

"Did you have an affair with him?" Just saying it, I
saw it.

"Yes." She smiled. She knew I knew and I loved it when she answered my thoughts. She raised her glass. "He *also* taught me Somerset Maugham's greatest personal weakness was in being incapable of enjoying 'that communion with the human race engendered by alcohol.' Obviously, a liberated Muslim. Good?" She asked the word "good" like a lessoned child questing for the compliment.

"Very good. Did you ever tell Latham?"

"Yes. He didn't mind."

Naturally not. Not only was he a boozing Muslim, but suddenly Latham, with his blown-dry hair, ascots, and instant crest ring became the Exxon tiger.

After Riyadh, she told me about the dissident Pole and then it was home-again, home-again to dismantle the Georgetown house and claim one small boy from that faultless amalgam. She and Taylor—two corporate inheritors, reared together amid the rich sounds of tennis balls, hunt cup weekends, proms exchanged at Princeton and Wellesley, and finally marriage vows. The deadening effect of habit had ambushed them into what no man could rend asunder.

After the divorce, a freedom year to study photography in Paris and an undisciplined apartment in Manhattan were sufficient to distort Latham's appeal. Solid, she thought as he avuncularly slipped in and out of her life. Comforting, the way his grown sons wrestled with hers. And then came Christmas. The clang of corner Santas, crowds rushing with packages, people becoming families. Desire goes unreal at Christmas.

Latham had spoken of marriage, but she heard it only as a distant reassurance. The same way she heard his insistence that she continue her photography—no matter how remote the assignments. But now, as they walked past the lighted trees on Park Avenue, his words became immediate, and she linked his arm with a closer closeness.

Before the New Year ended they were married. It was a small wedding given by his mother for her redeemed "boy." The apartment at the Waldorf Towers still sparkled of Christmas. Above the laurel-trimmed mantel a Cézanne self-portrait watched no less than a Supreme Court justice perform the law-book ceremony. Buckshots of caviar and magnums of Dom Pérignon deluged the well-chosen guests who proffered lifetimes of joy to the newlyweds.

Her parents had arrived the previous morning. After the wedding, they would return to Lake Forest where they would relive their daughter's marriage with the mirror images they had known forever, seen forever, needed forever. Suddenly, the vulgar abundances and the all too uncontrolled effusiveness of today would become more graceful, even enviable. From those descriptions I could see how her parched, Midwestern wellspring had made her lovelessly elope with Taylor, mistaking his Washington transfer as her salvation. And now, here she was again with Latham, sculpting still another life with the same illusions of contentment and security.

Wasn't it only an hour ago I was looking at that six-year-old day captured in glorious Kodacolor and caged in Cartier gold? Only sixty minutes since I taught her O'Neill wrote, "Love, honor and obey till love do us part" into his first wedding ceremony and I learned she wanted to leave Latham? Leave Latham for me. Of course it was love, Maria. Of course we said "forever." Those are the rules for breaking the tedium. But wanting to leave is breaking the rules. Maria? Sweet, wonderful Maria? I promise you where you want to go is where neither of us wants to be.

Around the next curve is my exit, Reader's Digest Road. There, in that huge red-brick building on the right emanates the world's most popular soporific. I still can see those pastel covers piled beside my parents' bed. Mother, a constancy of self-improvement, would monthly wend her way to a "more powerful vocabulary." Sometimes, I would quiz her, reading definitions and nodding at her answers. Later I would hear her on the phone pushing those new words into conversations.

There was one time when that magazine actually excited me. It was when my brother found some articles on German tortures. I still feel a twitching when I think about the Gestapo officer's burning the young girl's breast after tapping the ash from his cigarette. You couldn't read anything that good in there today. Now the people's opiate is ruled by the paying page; the wholesome guzzlers of Campbell's soups and the Kraft addicts who all-year-long save on "Lenten specialties." The only place I ever see the *Reader's Digest* is in a doctor's waiting room.

Pleasantville, even the town bearing the *Digest*'s postmark, is a sellout. It doesn't live there. No matter how nice it sounds. The *Reader's Digest* is actually alive and sick in Chappaqua.

I'm just in time to catch the drones pouring out of the heavy brick building. Antlike armies of Datsuns, Toyotas, Pintos, spawned by the four o'clock whistle, are making room for the night shift. It couldn't matter less that the policeman raises his hand in front of my windshield. They can all flood past.

As I wait I'm seeing her light a cigarette in that tentative way of a nonsmoker who looks at the end, never quite sure it's lit. Now she's out of bed showing me a dress. She loves the unfamiliar freedom of being naked. My eyes, like those before an ophthalmologist's light, follow everywhere. She cinches the dress to her body. It and she look so tiny. Maybe because I'm so tall.

"Halston," she announces.

God, how I hate that second-city label syndrome. "Did they say Jackie bought one?"

She smiles with the smile of someone who knows what she's being caught in is love. "Do you like it anyway?"

"I like it while you hold it. I won't like it on, when you're off, without me."

She lets it crumple to the ground and comes back into bed.

To me one of the great fascinations of love is in not being able to recapture, even fleetingly, the intensity of a particular moment's passion. Tauntingly, it seems to ricochet from an excitement I can't ever quite claim. It's the Central Park carousel when I was little. No matter how far I stretched, my arm never reached the brass ring. Maybe I didn't want it to. When I got big enough, I never tried.

I still can see that pockmarked boy who strapped me in before the music began. Then, after he gave the signal to start, he'd weave between the bobbing horses and collect the tickets. When it turned really fast he would jump off, always just missing the high round wall. I wonder why people who work in places like that always have that kind of skin.

As her new fervor grows into swift spasms, I pull my arm from under her, moving it as far back as I can without interrupting the rhythm. Her closed eyes give me time. I hit her hard. Twice, three times. "Don't stop," I command. "Fuck me! Fuck me!" Miraculously, she continues. When I relax upon her, I kiss her cheek and move my fingers along the redness. Holding hard, we stay hushed in fast breaths and silent conversation.

The policeman is tapping on my window. I didn't hear the horns. I start with a jerk as the driver behind me holds up his hands in exasperation. Will I soon see WELDON stretched across his dented bumper? Will other cars tear off their Mammoth Cave and Carlsbad Caverns stickers for Weldon?

I stop at the Mobil station. I'm surprised some energy czar doesn't jump from the pump and grab my credit card. Why should I be sentenced for keeping those illiterate, tree-swinging Arabs in Rolls-Royces? What about my two thousand shares in that undug petroleum lode? Why the hell don't they drill that into their energized heads?

I ask the guy to fill it with unleaded, please, and "check the oil and water too."

He slides the stick in and out. "Next time it could take a quart, Mrs. Weldon."

"Thank you." I feel through the glove compartment for my Mobil card. After finishing the charge, he rests the clipboard on my open window. As I start the ignition, he starts to talk. Since he doesn't move, I rev the motor and turn toward him, hoping he'll see my shrug of impatience. He doesn't.

"That's really great about Mr. Weldon getting the Olympics for New York." He's leaning into the car. "Nobody thought he'd carry it off. I mean get it away from Los Angeles. My folks say the Olympics, thanks to Mr. Weldon, are gonna bring New York back again."

"Thanks, Paul. I'll tell him." Get away from my car.

"Being head of the committee and everything maybe he could get me some tickets. Not him personally. I mean his secretary or someone."

"It's a little early. Remind me a little closer." I try to smile nicely. "He may have a different secretary in five years."

Paul laughs through his nose as kids do after they've realized their own stupidity. But why is he still stuck in my window? "My family, we never knew Mr. Weldon was once poor. Boy, he's sure done a lot and has a lot left when you think of all he's done."

Maybe my new look of "what the hell are you talking about" keeps him glued so he can explain.

"My dad heard him at Legion Hall. For Senator Crane?"

Now I've got it. Those parade-marching poppy sellers were lucky enough to hear the Evita Peron number: "I didn't come from money, but I came from the smell of it. So strong was that smell that it immobilized my senses into mobilizing my brain. And now that I've got it, I don't want those bureaucratic U.S. of A-holes in Washington taking it away from me in order to maintain an army of lazy louts. Idle with welfare, healthy on Medicaid, and fornicating on child support. And that's why I'm for Ed Crane. He's shown he's a leader for the doers, not the dreamers; for the people who want their own money in their own hands, not in the paws of politicians. Ed Crane's got more than insight. He's got vision. And as the Bible says, 'Where there is no vision, the people perish.' "

There's enough rhetoric in them thar words to tarnish the Cross of Gold.

"My dad said he really got those guys going. That he really makes a lot of sense."

"Thanks, Paul." His words get farther away as I roll up the window. I never noticed before but he must have at least ten thousand freckles. Except for one redhead, I don't know anyone who's grown and has freckles. Where do boys' freckles go when their teens go? Back to the palette to be reapplied by another Norman Rockwell? Again, I press my foot for those six hundred horses to *Vrooom!* these last few miles.

Thinking of the meeting my stomach feels gutted. I wonder exactly how long Albany takes door-to-door—or would it be lawn-to-lawn—via chopper? If ERA goes through, would I be called governess?

Turning into our road, I'm constantly reminded of all the runover dogs and red-taped pigs needed to install that DEAD END sign. And even though NO TRESPASSING is attached to every pin oak along our bump-inserted drive, browsers still find themselves "lost" in front of that massive porte-cochère.

Pedro, our most recent butler to "know for sure" he and his wife want this job "for permanent," opens the door.

"Anybody home?" I ask.

He shakes his head as he takes my coat. "No children yet. Mr. Weldon call and say he'll be a little late."

2

I'm thankful for the minutes alone, for the privacy of silence. I crave the solitude of my hot, hot tub. Endlessly, I let the water stream through the scented oils. The heat is relaxing, tranquilizing. Leaning against the curved marble, I feel my hair damp against my neck and push the stray wisps high under the cap. I need to have streaks desperately. The roots are now almost the ends. Time. I need some time. I never have time to do anything.

I had more time when I worked, wrote, went out every

night. What happens to clocks after marriage? Do they stop ticking while you do? While the children grow and you don't? I used to remember individual years. Now they cluster into bunched celebrations—birthdays, anniversaries, Mark's successes. Successes built by us both, but accepted as Mark's.

The hemlocks and the red maples, planted when we moved, are full and tall. Everything and everyone has grown. Isn't it my turn? Time. I need some time.

But I made time for her show. It was a big hit. Wasn't it? I didn't take the pictures, but I took the time to make her have the show. Tons of it. It had to be a success or the Whitney wouldn't have approached her. No way.

The high spot was seeing Truman there. Truman in his torn topsiders and Sonny and Cher sweatshirt. "I loathe Latham Marr," he said. "And I loathe portraits, although these aren't too hateful. But I'm here because Marr's faggot son wants to make *Tiffany's* into a black musical."

One of the joys of Truman is his roaring laugh. And when he laughs, people look at me to see who's being so funny. Even when Truman stops laughing his face looks like the smile sticker.

His body was thinner. He'd had his face done. He looked great.

"You look great."

"I'm marvelous." He spun around. "And you? Still year-round at the summer palace? Didn't anybody ever tell you the country was for first wives? That 'promise' means production and not that 'love and cherish' shit?"

Suddenly, I wanted to be home, to splash words, scenes, acts across the page.

"Busy being busy?" he singsonged. "With what? A menu marriage?"

The tub is finally beginning to drain a little of the day's shock. I think people say "forever" only when they know it isn't, but know, too, it's too soon to be over. Leave Latham and me leave Mark? God, the shock just shot through me with Sing Sing volts. Dazed, I reach for Doctor Zolta's roughened sponge and his eight-dollar soap. "Upward strokes on your face and neck." But that's not Zolta's voice. It's Mother's. "Otherwise, all you're accomplishing is tearing down the muscles." It's a voice of disbelief that *her* daughter is not only careless but unconcerned about the proper removal of makeup. The same "stupid for yourself, smart for others" daughter who at thirty-eight still exposes her "soon to be ruined" face to the sun. Until I die, I shall live between those arched eyebrows of incredulity.

I never did tell her about the move Zolta made. "Doctor" Zolta, in his long, white coat and elegant offices. "Yes. Yes," he said, shaking his head from side to side as I lay on the reclining chair in the "examining" room. I went directly there from the train the day vacation began. Yes, Mother, I know the world's richest and most glamorous go to him, that you pay over a hundred dollars and still wait six weeks for a consultation.

"I think I can save it," he said. Then he sighed heavily. "So much sun. So little care. You see, I see underneath. Underneath is almost destroyed." Maybe he meant "soon to be ruined."

"Really?" I noticed the "nurse" was no longer in the room.

"You know, it is impossible to see what skin is really like

when all you see are the areas which have been exposed to the elements. You know when you die your behind will be the same soft as when you were born?"

He was wearing one of those miner's headbands and he kept staring at me. My heart was clumping where he was staring.

"It is necessary that I see your breasts."

I was so startled I almost said "Yes." It would have been easier. I'm sure he counts on that. Somehow, I managed to slide from the chair and abort his conscientiousness. Instead of outrage, I felt a dumb guilt quickly pacified by buying his products. Products I still use. For a long time, I used him, thinking of what he would have done to me, of how he would have felt my breasts and where else he would have gone. For years, I saw him slip into one of those thin, disposable plastic gloves. I'd open my legs wide so he would see he didn't need any cream. Thanks, Mom. Having your juices flow *is* good for the skin.

Stepping out of the bath, I feel dizzy from the heat. Wrapping myself in a towel, I sink between the sheets on my bed. But before I can begin making believe what is isn't, I'm stopped by the reality of Mark's car crunching onto the courtyard gravel. Sightlessly, I watch his routine. Turning off the ignition, he places the keys under the mat and leans across the seat for a pile of papers. Shoving them under his arm, he grabs the handle of his briefcase. Turning sideways, he pushes the car door closed with his shoulder.

Going straight to the library, he spreads the papers on the oversized partners' desk. God, let everything be emptied and puffed. His scrutiny is not that of an aesthete, but of an inexorable perfectionist. "Aesthetics went out in the fifties under the FHA. Where dough is concerned ugly is more than tolerated. It's obligatory. How else did those veterans get sixty-nine-hundred-dollar homes? Levitt deserves a hundred yachts."

Mark's continued success has sufficiently buttressed his security to allow him to flaunt his sole semester at Georgetown prior to Korea. He's now able to revel at the government's typical "thoroughness" in sending him through the Harvard Graduate School of Business without authenticating the forged college diploma. "Strengthen the strong so that when we inherit the earth we can look after the meek."

From my bed I can see the open magnolia blossoms blowing against the broad windows. How nice to know the days are growing longer. How stupid for Daylight Saving not to spend each day with us. Mark's right about the small farms, to whom we give the sun, being antiques. "Progress" should foreclose them. What guilt *are* we assuaging by shortening our days to elongate their ends? And why does guilt attack only when it's too late?

The buzzer buzzes on the intercom. "I'm home. I'm in the library."

"Oh. You're home. When did you get home?"

"A couple of minutes ago. What's going on?"

"Nothing."

"Mandell and the group will be here any minute."

"You mean Max?" Certain people Mark calls mostly by last names only. I hate it. It's the kind of thing my mother did with service people after Daddy made his money. Her manicurist is just "Mullins." The ladies who wax her legs are Stone and Fleischer. Never "Miss." I've been with her there. Nobody else calls them like that. I wonder what jollies Mark and Mother need?

"Will you want tea or coffee or anything?"

"This meeting is vitally important. Just some peace." I know he means the children. He means the dogs. As we talk, the dogs are already yelping at the bell.

The phone rings and I pick it up before the ring finishes. "I'm sorry about today, Amanda." The voice is tiny. It would carry only inches across the room. "Do you know that? Please say yes, Amanda."

"Yes." I'm hesitant, without much conviction. I'm suddenly too embarrassed to answer this too personal question.

Mark buzzes. I tell her to hold. "Mandell's here. Come on down before the others come." He doesn't wait for an answer.

"I have to go. Mark wants me in on the big power powwow."

"Latham's driving up with the senator."

"Naturally."

"When will you call?"

"As soon as it's over." I feel like I'm talking to a stranger about things we shouldn't talk about.

As I hang up, I'm absorbed by loneliness, like some empty theater waiting for an audience. Mindlessly, I pull any dressing gown from the hanger. Makeup base, blusher, lipstick—I apply them all as if automated. I bend my head over and brush, brush, brush upside down. When I throw my head back there'll be some body to the mess. Mechanically, I shape it into shape. As I look into the mirror, I see her. Please don't be upset, Maria. I care so much, so very much. That's why it's over. Thank God Maria never stays angry. Although inside it kills, she's able to file her hurts and angers into some mysterious book she will never open again. Please, Maria. Don't let me be your exception. Pressing my arms close to my sides, I gladly realize I don't have time to think now. I grab a pair of flat gold thongs. "Stand up tall. Be proud of your height. People take you for what *you* think of yourself." But Mother, it's tough at fifteen.

For me, the library is the room I like best. Its coziness doesn't demand the exuberance of flowers that decorators substitute for warmth. When I go through pages of *Architectural Digest* or *House & Garden,* I love to cover up the flowers and watch the rooms grow cold. But here, the high bay windows let the outside in all over. Constant sunshine warms the old woods, the leather volumes, and the ornate Victorian frames. This would have been the definitive room for Thackeray's *Book of Snobs.*

Mark gets up from behind his desk, from behind his papers. Together, we kiss the air. If I had to extract Mark's singular passion for me, it's the one that goeth before a fall. Always, I see him see me as a goddamn oakleaf cluster. Needed for the same reason as his constant quotes, making up for what they can never make up for.

He looks at his watch. "They should be here any second. I said six." He looks back at his watch and shakes his disciplined head. "Maybe I'm fast. Amanda? What time do you have?"

As usual, Mark speaks to that undefined slice of space somewhere out there. It's as if no one is good enough to be addressed directly. Endlessly, he will talk to the air, even blink at it. Too often I've tried to meet his eyes. Impossible. As impossible as tossing a ballerina from her twirling spot. I hope the pols can topple his eyes, make them see human-to-human.

Max stands and stretches to kiss me, slipping his tongue between my lips. "You still must be growing," he says, his eyes feeling my body. "Not that my size hasn't been big in my fucking success and vice versa. People expect outrage from Napoleon."

" '*Pourvu que ça dire.*' Let's hope it lasts," Mark translates happily.

"Our Marcus is also a linguist."

"Napoleon's mama wished those words for her boy just before the shit hit the fan."

"I guess we are quoting Mom today." Although Max has no accent, he sounds as if he's speaking with an inflection one can't quite pinpoint. It's an intonation probably designed to make one never quite sure if he's farce or fact. "By the way, Marcus," he once said with this impenetrable duality, "I forgot to tell you, I balled the Morgan Guarantee chairman's wife after that dinner you thought was too grand for me to attend."

Max epitomizes all that screams guilt to Mark. Long ago, Max dismissed the puritan ethic as "a crock of shit from some runaway slobs who couldn't hack it where they were. I'd be ashamed to say I was sown from the seeds of the *Mayflower*."

Walking to the bar for some wine, I hear Mother telling me to be sure Pedro pours just to the middle of the bubble when he serves the table. "Not like last time, dear." The "dear" is to convey her love, even though it's to an idiot. Max pats my knee as I sit beside him.

Mark gets up and moves some ashtrays, making sure pairs are on the same table. Then he pushes the Miró a centimeter to the left, steps back, and moves it a centimeter more. Going to the mantel, he reaches for the clock, opens the back, and imperceptibly changes the hands.

Max leans his cigar against the ashtray. It's always against. Never in. Although he appears unconcerned about its status, he always manages to prevent its imminent extinction by a perfectly timed inhale and to avoid its sudden collapse by a seemingly last-minute tap of the ash. This is his self-styled amusement, watching his hostess' silent, well-bred mouth grow grim as she anticipates the inevitable. Now Max is watching Mark watch. It seems each time he goes just a little further to annoy him just a little more.

The fat Montecristos, numero two, and the yearly Mediterranean charter are the only extravagances in which Max indulges. How could he acknowledge the carefree hours that luxury demands? Where could he find time to pamper them? To amortize their being? Anyway, that kind of time takes two.

The undeclared defiance of smuggling the cigars through customs is only part of the pleasure imported with those Havanas. Equally satisfying to Max is the habit of flicking his finger across his tongue and feeling for that usually nonexistent trace of tobacco. As with the British stutter, it provides him with that extra moment to locate that extra thought.

Not only doesn't Max adapt to his surroundings, he seems totally unaware of their existence. Even now, with his city pinstripes hanging on him like some commuter disaster after the air conditioner quits, Max appears totally comfortable and compatible with the environment.

So different from Mark whose correct cloth for the occasion always seems cut without comfort, suited more to the tightly tailored world of the establishment, that wonderful world whose emotional seismograph registers more on performance than passion.

Max and Mark, each but a left and a right without the other. A contradiction that works no matter which one makes the bullets, no matter which one fires them. It is Tinker to Evers and nothing to chance.

"So, Marcus," Max says, finally tapping his ash. "I think Lanacola can do a good job on you. After all, look what that wop Michelangelo did for David."

Max would really laugh if he could uncover the statue-cover in my mind for *Time*'s Man of the Year. It's Mark. He's naked except for a large, tripartite fig leaf clustered on his parts. My face, amorphically suburban, smiles from the leaf that covers the cock. The face of each child adorns the leaf that covers the glorious orb from which each sprang.

"And," Max continues thoughtfully, passing his finger over his tongue, "after we glorify the outside, we'll mold a little clay for the inside. Maybe even a lot."

Mark's eyes darken to disapproval. Max is always half making fun when I'm around. He loves pricking the pomp so safeguarded by Mark, so overly protected, like something one's always wanted, but only recently acquired, and still can't believe he's got.

"Definitely a lot. My smooth-over tool, please, for Mr. Weldon's perfect timing in scooping up worthless slums, empty shops, and even emptier air rights."

"Who matched me dollar for dollar? Who plotted the stadium site, the monorail route, the mall of hotels so easily convertible from Olympic Village to Convention City?"

"I'm only mentioning things not to mention."

I don't know what Max is getting at, but I do know what he's gotten to. It's always the same. Mark.

Mark and Max go back far, meeting first when Mark's law firm was "saving" Zeckendorf's skin and Max's real estate firm was "rescuing" his land. Soon after, they became Maxweld Realty. Though together for years, with Mark now well past forty and Max well past that, there still exists an atmosphere of Max the mentor keeping Mark the menace from trouble. Mark is not to play with things little boys don't understand, especially very smart little boys, because they're the ones who have the biggest gaps. They're the ones who need the most protection. Or is it surveillance?

I like Max. I liked Max when I hardly knew him. I like the spunk, the spirit, the mischief that cuts hard or soft. I like its shock value. I like the day we first met aboard his charter in St. Tropez, "even though," Mark warned, "it will probably be filled with whores." Some half-bikinis did happen to pass drinks as Max talked land with Mark. And while Max talked, his arm crossed my back and his fingers began to manipulate my breast, his eyes never straying from Mark. He never not noticed a nuance, never neglected a beat. I pressed my elbow hard against his knuckles, hugging his hand in place. I wanted him to take my nipple between his thumb and index finger and squeeze it. I looked at him, but he didn't look at me. Mark noticed nothing. I felt my muscles tighten and open, tighten and open. His features were thick. His sizable stomach hung low beneath his trunks. He had no age. He had no looks. Yet he made me feel like a whore and I wanted him to fuck me like a whore.

That night, in bed with Mark, he did. I've often thought of telling him how thinking of him made me come. That was almost six years ago, on my sixth anniversary. After not coming for so long I wanted it again, and again, and again. . . .

The horns and the dogs go off simultaneously. "I'll get them," Mark says, jumping up.

Max takes a deep, thinking puff of his cigar. "Bailey, the lawyer, he's the big one. He's the real head of state." Max's voice is quiet, definite. "There are two governments, you know? One runs the state and the other runs for elections." His words are slow as if he's figuring rather than informing.

"Joe Bailey's supported every fat cat regardless of party for twenty years. But you've never heard of him. Right? But he's got more clout than any politician I know. He spreads more patronage than pigeons do shit. Nobody even knows what he looks like. Ask anybody who Bailey Park's named for and they'll swear he used to pitch for the Dodgers." Max fans the smoke from his face to mine.

With a loud clearing of the throat, Mark leads the back room boys to the parlor. "I know you all know Max," he says, "but I think only Latham and the senator know my wife, Amanda." Huge pride.

Hello, Latham. How's your money? "Hello, Latham." I stick out my hand as he bends to kiss me. Eagerly, I kiss the senator. Next, Joe Bailey gives me the firm shake and the big, Irish smile. Mother, why aren't you here to see the pinky ring, the too-high tie clip (tie clip?) and the capital class of that maroon initial stretching across that white-on-white in his breast pocket? Whatever, I like Joe Bailey. I know what I see is what there is. The face opens when you play his way and shuts when you don't. He'll share the Cracker Jack with anyone so long as anyone doesn't share the prize.

"And this, Amanda, is Sandy Lanacola. Sandy is probably, no, I take that back, no probably about it. Sandy *is* the best P.R. man since Barnum. And that's a long since." He doesn't deny it. He just shakes his head wearily. He looks hassled, rushed, and sweaty. I'm sure he lives at home where he gets even sweatier when his momma tells him "stop rushing—who's so important you're killing yourself for?"

Is he the fellow, this P.T. or P.R., is he the S-H-I-T who's going to tell me how I feel about abortion? Is he the one who's going to let me in on my ideas about the death penalty and transvestites performing at the White House? And after he's accomplished all that, will he dress Sara and

Sonia in matching gingham pinafores (McCall's pattern
476) for the hype in *People* magazine?

The last one Mark pushes in front of me is somebody I
could have liked. I can tell, just from his looks. I like his
brown shoes, his skimpy glasses, his in-the-background
manner of not needing up front. Mark grabs his shoulder.
"You've certainly heard me mention Brad Howell."

Brad is the only one who could laugh at this. I know he
will. Won't you, Brad? "Brad Howell?" I say the name
slowly, my voice in distant recall. "No, Mark. I don't think
I ever have." Brad? Good. Thanks. I knew I could count on
somebody.

"See? I've overdone you already," Mark recovers. "But
why not? Why not brag about snagging the best creative
head in the country?"

"Because it's untrue," Brad answers. "The reason I *know*
it's untrue is because I wrote it." Again, the untricky laugh.

Mark is looking between the space where Brad and I
are standing, still clutching the glen-plaid shoulder. "Don't
believe Brad's horsht. Believe the facts. Believe the
speeches he wrote. Believe the television spots for all those
big mouths whose bodies are now in capitols and Senate
seats."

I can see Brad is sick of returning any more "shit kicking" answers. And as Mark continues to praise the faceless
air, Brad moves away. It's fun watching Mark refocus after
the surprise of having his arm flop to his side.

Everybody has a drink of some sort. As the smoke thick-
ens, it spreads into rising layers and holds in a pattern just
below the ceiling. Pedro was told no interruptions. That
meant to add telephones to children and dogs. The broad
library doors look strange all closed up. I don't think I
knew they even had moldings.

Before I sit, Mark motions to me. "Amanda." His voice

is almost inaudible. He looks toward the doors. "Tomorrow, make sure Pedro polishes those brass handles." Aye, aye, sir! Then you can be the fuck-ass ruler of the Queen's Nav-ee. Instead of just your old, ordinary *fuck-ass* self.

As head of this unformed Republican committee assembled to select this nongubernatorial candidate, Max starts this apolitical meeting. But not before leaning back into the sofa, stretching his legs onto the coffee table, and taking a long, confident inhale. "Maybe we're not the best or the brightest, but we've got what it takes to get our job done. And tomorrow we'll settle with Darcy on when and where we'll announce."

All at once, the best and brightest turn on:

"I can get the state committee to deliver the nomination. Our problem is not to split the party."

"The primary's not till September. Carey only had six percent recognition in September. The Olympics have already made you a household god."

"Nothing ever begins till the World Series ends."

"Ask the people what they want. Let them tell you. Then tell them what they want."

"Six months of barnstorming isn't worth six seconds of prime time. But it takes dough to create the image, package the profile, send it into the streets."

I'm thinking I saw Bela Lugosi do that once. First he pressed a button in his library so the books could swing around and the stairway could appear. Wickedly, it curved to his underground la-BOR-a-tory where test tubes bubbled and syringes burped before the final stabs. Then suddenly, the "guv" (no offense, fellas, just our figure of speech) would break from the table's leather straps and tramp the shiny, wet cobblestones of London on his bloody campaign.

Sandy Lanacola's hands are waving. I bet he's sweating all over. "Politics is Hollywood except Hollywood's real. Hollywood comes right out and says it's fake. We've got to convince them that our scenes, our wardrobes, our loose ties are real. Women have got to believe Amanda Weldon really disagrees with her husband on the death penalty, that she's enough woman to disagree on any crucial issue. There's a big woman's vote out there that we've got to catch. And with this issue we've got two things going. The sympathy of no one should die and also her appeal to ERAers as she defies her husband, the candidate."

Not one person is looking at me, at the woman's vote. "I happen to believe one hundred percent in the death penalty." A few heads turn at the intrusion. "I said I am completely in favor of the death penalty."

Exasperation wipes Lanacola's face. "So am I. But I don't tell my Catholic mother that."

They all have that look like they're going to wait until I'm not around to discuss me. All except Brad. He's smiling at me.

Suddenly, no more talk about me. More about districts. Upstate. Downstate. Thirty thousand employees. The primary. Twenty thousand signatures. "What's twenty thousand signatures? Since that's all we need for the ballot, consider it run and won. Our asses will slide into home before they know we're in the ball park. Or more to the point, before they know they're out of it." Not laugh-laughs, but snorty laughs, meaning "great point," "brilliant point." It's all decided. All decided before it's all decided.

Are governors' wives "protected" by the Secret Service? Will some dark-suited, ambitionless thug stand outside my door, his arms folded and his jacket puffed over that bulge? Maria? You can be court photographer and ice the hypocritical ingredients of the political cocktail. And after you've "caught" Latham kissing babies and rubbing Indians you can send the evidence to Cartier for the final solution.

Why are they all standing? Don't tell me they're going. Maybe they really haven't been here, after all. "Good-by." "Good-by." "Good-by." "Good-by." "Good-by." Only Max stays. Only Big Daddy lingers with the smoke. He's got to tell the "kid" more. Get to your corner, kid. That was only round one.

As I stare at Mark now, unruffled, excited, pleased, I'm struck by how little he's changed from the air-brushed piano portrait taken at our wedding soon after we were "introduced" by television. There we were, two of the guinea-pig panel who had "left security to seek success."

The camera light turns red. A guy with earphones points to the moderator. Oh my God! We're on the air. We're talking about success to the preselected audience who's told to "Look interested. You never know when the camera will catch you." Thank heavens it's taped. I keep reassuring myself that if I happen to say "fuck," and I know I will, they can bleep it out.

The first "success" talks and talks. He was the youngest vice-president in Macy's history. He got there by "pre-guessing the public, anticipating what they didn't know they had to have." And here he is, still only twelve years old, heading his own hundred-million-dollar business, selling blah-blah-blah. . . . "But if denim dies, it's mahoolah for me."

The Jewish emcee laughs. "For all of you who think 'mahoolah' is a Moroccan village, it isn't. It's Seventh Avenue for bankrupt. And so you attribute your success to spotting the trend." She isn't asking. She's finishing. "And now, Amanda Horne."

Me? Who, me? Don't look at me. Don't ask me. Don't you know I'm going to say "shit" and "fuck"? A sour taste jumps into my throat. I try to swallow it away, but it stays. And I'm hot. So hot.

"What made you walk away from twenty-five thousand a year on Madison Avenue to the possible zero of off-Broadway?" I don't have to say anything yet, because she's looking away from me, continuing into the red "eye." "I saw Amanda Horne's play *The Cause* over a month ago, and I must say its impact is still inside me. It's a devastating statement about people we all, unfortunately, know too well . . . the valueless do-gooders whose life is consumed by championing anything from panthers to pot when their true mission is themselves. Is that a fair statement, Amanda?" Her voice is tentative, interested.

I'm on. I'm hotter. I go. "It's not only the unknowns. It's also the big-name writers, directors, and politicians of the West Side's great unwashed. The geniuses who made radical chic so welcome are now terrified to walk their dogs. Just let one of the Chicago Ten into their living rooms or have one Mario Savio or Angela Davis teach their 'unusually bright' monsters and you'll see them pushing Rosey Greer and Rafer Johnson right back, fast back, to the back of the bus."

During the commercial the moderator tells me she not only lives on the West Side, but washes there. "Maybe that's because I'm not a genius." She laughs. She's nice. She tells Mark she is going to open the next segment with him.

Again the cameraman points. She begins. "Mark Weldon, my notes tell me, left a six-figure salary, the presidency of a real estate company listed on the New York Stock Exchange, and enough future options to guarantee a seven-figure future."

While she speaks the "eye" is on Mark. I watch his icy control on the monitor. " 'If life is not good enough change it . . . and damn the consequences.' I went with the advice of H. G. Wells."

"Being a millionaire isn't good enough?" she asks.

"Not if it means working for somebody else." I hear him monopolize the time. He speaks easily. He makes me feel I'm learning. He discusses R.E.I.T.s, mortgages, depletions, depreciations. It sounds like we could all make money.

When the time is almost gone, she asks for a summary, "Just a line. Why success? Why the risk to get there? Mark Weldon?"

"I agree with Emerson. 'The path of escape known in all the worlds of Gods is performance.' I guess I'm an escapist." I like the intimacy around his eyes, the boyish looks surrounding that brain.

"And you, Amanda Horne?" She looks at the clock. "Why success?"

"Freedom."

Two months later Mark and I were married.

3

They were already "gathered together" waiting for Uncle Peter and for me. We were waiting for Wagner. The baby chapel, adjacent to the big stained-glass mother, is filled.

Faultlessly, the flowers duplicate the delicacy of spring. But as with so many things Mother does, she does them for those key few whose acknowledgment is her accomplishment. "And don't forget," she ordered the florist, in the same tone she told me to walk tall, "immediately following the ceremony the altar pieces are to go to the reception." Of the three florists considered, Mother chose the most expensive, just for that reason.

"The bride carried cymbidium orchids and stephanotis . . ." I would read tomorrow. Why have I heard of stephanotis only in connection with weddings? I wonder how many brides know what stephanotis looks like after they've tossed it high into the air?

Silence. The organ has stopped. The fuzzy conversation along the pews dies down. Everyone must be in place. Sweet Uncle Peter in his rented splendor takes my arm. I don't think I've ever missed Daddy more than this minute. I hope he sees me. I see him.

I see him in the rented summer houses on Long Island's North Shore. The houses Daddy found too small and Mother found because the mailboxes read right. I see him pacing off my croquet wickets and twisting his pipe cleaners into animals and flowers. I see Paula—my old nurse— and me riding in his new, funny-looking Studebaker. I hear Daddy's soft southern laugh and Mother's sardonic mimic when Paula and I thought the back was the front.

Daddy should have been a country writer instead of a city lawyer. I can still see those people I never met, the ones he cared so much about who lived and worked on the farm where he grew up. The farm Mother never cared to see. But then how could she look at clapboard and chicken wire after describing a plantation? Just as she could never go to her reunions at Barnard, having only taken courses at Columbia.

I see Daddy winking at me during Mother's lectures about the right people and my wrong friends, about how much she's tried yet how little she's succeeded. And now, suddenly, I see Daddy two years ago. He's being carried to an ambulance. The doorman's tilting a huge doorman's umbrella to shield Mother from the rain. A red spotlight whirls around on the ambulance roof. Silent men lift the stretcher through the parted doors and scramble up after it.

Daddy looks frail and tired as they strap him in. I smile hard and exaggerate my lips to form, "You are going to be fine, Daddy. I love you." As the silent men pull the doors shut, I see the wink and watch both eyes close. The picture is peaceful. Maybe he's back on the farm. . . .

A photographer clutching his F-2 Nikon rushes in front of us, kneels. *Flash!* The organist begins to pound it out. *Da . . . da . . . da da.* Slowly, sanctimoniously, we step into step. God, white shoes make my feet look big. "Look *up.* Smile."

Da . . . da . . . da da. We are in view of turning heads. There is a rustling from both sides as people stand. Think something beautiful. I'm thinking how remarkable, when I think of all the people I've fucked, I feel so virginal. Clothes make the man. Pomp makes the empire. Bride means untouched.

Keep in step. Smile. I remember feeling flattered whenever a bride smiled directly at me while going down the aisle. Now I see the eyes you catch are accidental. I'm looking for Paula, whom Mother called my governess. She came from "Frankfurt am Main." She always said it that way, like that was the name of the city, not the city *and* the river. I don't know why, but I used to make her swear to me her family never liked Hitler when I knew they did.

I can see her letting down the hems on my school uniforms and sewing name tapes on my socks. It's a rainy Saturday afternoon. Milton Cross is explaining what will take place during the last act of *Die Meistersinger*. I'm on my bed putting my British Colony duplicates into my stamp book. Where *is* Paula? Why isn't she where I can see her? Why isn't she up front?

We are at the altar. Mark is at his handsomest. He is the only good-looking man who has ever attracted me. But even now I look through his looks. I see a detachment, a strength. It's saying, "Buy part of this rock." No one ever said that before. The others, all the others, seemed to see in me what I see in Mark. Mark's my first time not wondering what he can do for me. Yes, Mother, I know the others had money and names. Lots of names all strung together, names like your new friends or like you would like your even newer friends to have. But I didn't want their names. And I didn't want the Village poet or the Kafka disciple either. Not for this long walk. I'm going to buy part of that rock, Mark. That's why I'm here. I'm taking out the policy right now. And it's on my life.

Uncle Peter gives me a kiss before the final letting go. His eyes blink tears away. Tears for me. Tears for the happiness inside me. I smile and watch him sit beside my mother. Her lace-trimmed handkerchief is dabbing her tears. Tears for her. Tears for her bravery in watching it all slip away . . . far away.

The first time she saw Mark she knew. I knew she knew. There's a dreamlike terror that underlies my mother's voice when she's surrounded by situations about to escape her hold.

"You're not thinking of marrying him, are you?" It would be a long time before she would refer to Mark as anything but "him."

"If he asks me."

"If *he* asks *you*?" The look, the tone, the stiffening—she rose; a much grander, more dramatic movement than getting up. She made herself a drink. She stood angled at the bar, enabling me to watch the dissolution. The drink was not to calm her nerves, but to establish her martyrdom. Mother doesn't drink in the afternoons. Mother says she doesn't drink. "Well, just a little something over ice, please." Her father was an alcoholic. No, he was not "just a heavy social drinker," Mother. He was an alcoholic. That's only one of her reasons for hating "the filthy, superstitious, ignorant, know-it-all Irish."

Though she grew up in New York, Mother never felt she grew up right. For her there was no immunization for an Irish heritage and convent schooling until the partial antidote of Daddy. Then with a mixture of pride and resentment she stretched to give me the advantages she'd missed, the advantages of society's high hedges, the right schools, clubs, and watering spots; all geared toward today, to make me not marry a Mark.

Even after Daddy made money, I could feel Mother's discomfort entering rooms she had longed to enter. She was never convinced that only she was singling her out. And the only time I remember her really crying was when Daddy left the austere names of his law firm, those heavy swells who sounded like so many trunks falling downstairs. But when he founded his own firm with his name only, she was pleased. Because Horne, Horne and Horne loomed like some ancestral deity, even though it was born like a multi-generation novel in a flash on the title page.

Although Mother's Brannigan background was finally eviscerated, it was never gutted from her guts. And here she was again, spiked and digging in, living in her glass house and throwing stones. The green was on. *Go!* Sally forth, Mother, and pour that drink, that signal to me of the devastation I'm causing you.

"What do you know about him?" Her voice sought a control she hadn't lost. "Who is he? Who knows him?"

"I do," I said solemnly.

"Then what God hath joined let no man rend asunder."

Miraculously, the flowers arrived before the limousines. The same black line of limousines that years later, during my drives to the city, I would see strung out along the parkway, their headlights beamed into daylight, following the same hearses. Although Mother would have preferred the reception at the more prestigious Colony Club, Daddy's money came too late. But having only a few of Mark's "people" come from Rochester affirmed Mother's hope that neither her energy nor her money was misspent. Anyway, how could they be? Wasn't this all for me?

Just a handful of the assorted ladies, in their understated jacket dresses, remembered me when. They were mostly new old friends. And the men who went with them were those archetype soldiers of *Fortune* who seemed forever noosed in their regimental stripes; those country club perennials who rubbed their unused cocks against "the younger set" at Fourth of July and Labor Day dances. I'd like to see their Madras trousers when they threw them into the corner. No. I really wouldn't. But it's another wonderful thought for Hallmark on this special day.

The frizzy-haired director of my play is my only attendant. I don't have any floppy-hatted bridesmaid-type friends anymore. I left them at college, on graduation day, when we all swore we would stay together forever. Mark used the chairman of his old company as his best man. His choice was a "pleasant surprise" for Mother since several of the "thank goodness *they're* coming" guests knew him well.

Mark's mother never took her eyes from her son, the son she raised in the company town after her husband died, leaving behind the minimal company pension for her and her teenage boy. Proudly she watched him charm and flatter as she had seen him do so many times when mortgage money, car money, or food money was needed from Uncle Ned or her horrible sister, Florence. She believed Mark could do anything, be anybody. And wasn't she right? Here she stood, between Uncle Ned and Florence, in a thickly pelted mink stole, a three-strand necklace of real pearls, and a dress from Paris, watching her son marry a girl who loved him almost as much as she did.

We stood on the receiving line. *Flash.* We stood as a bridal party. *Flash.* We stood dancing. *Flash.* Mark stood and raised his glass, speaking to that space, that air out there. Ask me as I'm looking up at him, is he looking at me? Yes.

" 'Remarriage,' observed Samuel Johnson, 'is the triumph of hope over experience.' " Pause. Poise. *Flash.* "And, in this instance, love, too."

I can't feel his eyelashes as he kisses me. His eyes must be wide open. Mine aren't. We each whisper, "I love you."

Mother couldn't wait. She had to lean across the table. "Why did he have to bring that up? Why even mention a previous marriage? If he's as smart as you say, why didn't he wait for experience?" Mother would never understand my saying Mark needed to be married to a model and that I was lucky the model had been first. One thing about Mother. She was honest. Only her concepts were fake.

So was the bottom of the cake. "Don't press too hard,"

the caterer warned, taking us into his little conspiracy. "The last layer is cardboard." Hurriedly, he backed away. *Flash.* That's the best in the book. The smiles are really smiling. Imagine. A fake cake.

After it was wheeled, carved, and left uneaten on most of the plates, Paula managed to rescue the plastic bride and groom from their precarious height. As a surprise, she had it pedestaled and plaqued and presented it to us when we got home from our honeymoon. Whenever I look at it, it reminds me of baby shoes dangling from the windshield mirror of a fin-back Caddy. But what it really is, is the ultimate prize in the ultimate carnival.

"Don't go yet." "Dance." "Dance some more." "When you leave it's over." "The bride and groom are what the people want to see." "This is *your* day." "Enjoy it."

I don't want to drink. I don't like champagne. I don't come good when I'm high. I don't want to "do-si-do" to any more tables with Mark, spreading sweet-smelling shit-chat to people who want to go too. I'm looking at the "make sure it's low enough for conversation" centerpiece and suddenly I see that lady in front of the Plaza Hotel. I'm about eight and Mother is hurrying me along because she is cold. The lady is carrying a centerpiece. Mother wears her superior sound. "It will probably be dead before she gets it to Newark." She didn't have to bother to explain anything further to me. I always knew exactly.

Like now, hearing her say "Harvard Business School" and "his father was a giant with Kodak for years." I must remind myself to ask Mark how tall his father was. Ha! Ha!

Finally, I can start to go. I can change from my wedding dress. I watch Mother's maid, Anita, the miracle of survival, put more and more, and still more, tissue between its folds. When she finishes is looks like a fat capital **Z**.

When she finally lays it to rest, in the box of its beginnings, the lid barely fits over the mound of stuffed silk. With a slipknot I've watched her make for years, on packages of clothes "goin' to family in Charleston," she secures the day forever.

"*Your* daughter will wear that at her wedding." Mother's eyes are full. Her neck looks tired under the single strand of Oriental pearls that I don't want, but "someday will be yours."

My eyes are also full. "I hope it will be just as beautiful."

We hug each other closely. We kiss. For just a moment I wish I were that little girl suffering from that big, terrible strep throat. Mother was so worried and so nice. Whenever she looked at me she cried and she cared.

"I love you," I said.

"I hope so," she answered. Her voice was far away. Maybe she was waiting for the doctor. Doing something for *me* again.

I hoped so too.

Maria and I are sitting in bed, naked. The gently floraled sheet is pulled high around us. The white leather album is opened flat, sharing our laps.

"Wait. Not so fast." She flips the page back. "Who is that with the frizzy hair?" The small tip of Maria's index finger doesn't cover even half of Lorna's face.

"It's Lorna. I've told you about Lorna. She's the one who directed my play."

"That's Lorna? And she was your only attendant?"

"Are you jealous?" I laugh.

"Not if you stick to type." She laughs.

"Don't forget hair was in then. Picture her bald. Bald she's not bad."

She looks again. Then at me. "You didn't, did you?"

"Did what?" I love it. I have a lunker on the line. It's taken the bait and I'm playing it in and out. In and out.

"You did. I know you did. It would have to be someone like that. Someone smart and different and nobody." There's the thoroughbred, ears back, quickening the pace before the jump.

"Like you?"

She looks at me. Her expression said I wasn't funny. "No. Not me. But *you*. Like you, then. I know I'm right. It doesn't matter. But I am. Right?"

"Wrong. Wrong. Wrong as rain." I wet her ear with my tongue. She scrunches her shoulders, but she doesn't look at me or close the book. She continues to turn.

"It just gets worse." Her voice is almost a whinny. It's a picture of Mark's toast.

"What's so horrible there?" I ask.

"Not *him*. You. Look how you're looking at him. God! Like he's some god."

"He was."

"See? I'm right."

"Wrong. Do you know what 'was' is?"

"I've seen you look at him like that now. When he's explaining something. I see you look like that."

Why did I bring these fucking pictures? I move to slam them shut. "It was your idea to see them. It was supposed to be funny."

She pushes my hands from the album. "Just promise you don't feel like that anymore? Say, I swear I hate Mark."

Repeat after me, children. "I swear I hate Mark."

"Nothing crossed counts?"

Repeat after me, children. "Nothing crossed counts."

She flips through the remaining ten thousand dollars in about as many seconds. But that last "memory" along thirty-five millimeter lane, the very last page, is too much to flip by too quickly.

"This really makes me barf."

"Baar-rrrrf? Barf where? In the loo at Foxcroft?" Teeny is the kiss I give her cheek.

"You're right. Vomit." She tries but she can't make the right sound. I adore her.

Actually it makes me "barf" too. There we were, department store dummies, our heads touching, our future framed through the car's rear window on our way to the airport, on our way to fuck.

Listening to the propellers of the twin-engine Beech roar into takeoff, all I really hear their revving into is *You're married! You're married! Married!* Faster and faster and faster. Looking at my left hand, at the shiny round evidence, I suddenly feel an overwhelming circle of protection echoing from that skinny band.

"I'm afraid it's just too thin for an inscription," the disappointed salesman told Mark and me, shaking his head at all the beauties with baguettes that were spread on the velvet tray. Mother was slightly more blunt. "That's the sort of ring you change into when you play golf or tennis." Where's the boy from the carousel? He'd understand.

The co-pilot takes off his headset and turns toward me. "Is your safety belt on, Mrs. Weldon?"

Mrs. Weldon? Who's Mrs. Weldon? Which safety belt are you talking about? Is it ever. And how. "No. It isn't. Thank you." Click.

"The Keys? Tarpon fishing?" Mother was horrified at the plans for "her" honeymoon.

"Yes. We love it."

"He loves it. What is tarpon?" Only she could manage to say "tarpon" like an illness.

I wanted to tell her it's what they roll over a baseball field when it starts to rain. I wanted to tell her it's Go Fuck!, that old card game I used to play with Paula and my friends. Never once with you, Mother. But it really wouldn't have mattered much in either case since she was already preparing it like Scotch salmon, anticipating her friends' questions.

I never told Mark I'd never been in a small plane before, that before him I was too frightened. "It could be a little bumpy," he warns clicking his seat belt shut. "Since we don't go much above twenty we may get into some stuff we can't climb out of."

"Why no higher?" Didn't all my other captains "level off at an altitude of approximately thirty-three thousand feet"?

"For the same reason I told you to swallow a lot. We're not pressurized."

He always said "we" like that. "*We* can't climb out . . . *we're* not pressurized." Is that "we" a part of the action? A part of the owner? Where does "we" see him?

I reach for his hand as we taxi. He's looking out. "We don't need much runway. Two thousand's plenty to take off and land. That strip at Marathon is just perfect for us."

"How much does a jet need?" I really don't care.

"It depends on size." He's still talking to the window. "A Saber liner, a little one, needs a minimum of three." I squeezed his hand. He knows everything.

Bounce. Bounce. Up through the clouds. I wipe the creases of my palms on the seat until I see the blue, lots of it, all around. After a few minutes of all blue, Mark moves front and crouches between his old buddies, flying his old plane. I'm thinking about Mr. Henley, his old chairman, at my old wedding. "Don't thank me for the plane. It's a thoughtfully selfish gift. I want Mark to miss these little *necessities* big business can have, so I can have Mark."

He stood between us, his hands on our shoulders. "Only one thing I can't fathom, Mark. Why the hell you're flying all that way to fish, considering the catch you just made?" His tone was unusual. It sounded like congratulations, all right, but office congratulations, transaction congratulations.

Twenty thousand feet below, I see the geometric parcels of browns and greens mesh into the total puzzle. And as we pass the shore, those once massive waves merely trim the sand with the slimmest sliver of chalk. I'm always surprised at how blue the gray Atlantic appears from here. Looking down into its flat patina, I'm watching all those stewardesses slip into those yellow vests, making all those signs and then blowing into those cloudy tubes. They always remind me of apathetic teachers facing an equally uninspired class of deaf and dumbs. All they've taught me is I couldn't inflate one of those things on my life.

Now Mark and the head pilot are in passenger seats. I love to hear Mark's laugh. It's big and responsive. "Just like a salesman's," said Mother. It's easy to know those men have been together a lot, put in lots of hours, formed a lot of good times. Even bad times make good memories when you remember them with someone you like.

Help! Oh, my God! I can't stand it! The drops. Bumps. Oh, God! Help me! I'm soaking wet, clutching my seat like some stiffened soul on the electric chair, right before life and limb separate forever. Stop! Why are those bumps? Help me! Mark!

Finally, the pilot turns. Why is he still sitting in *that* seat? Is he crazy? He doesn't expect me to smile back, does he? Fly the fucking plane. Idiot.

"It's always kinda bouncy when we get off of North Carolina. Just no getting around Hatteras."

"Kinda bouncy." Is he insane? Stop smiling, hyena head, and fly the fucking plane. Oh, my *God*. That drop. We're not high enough.

"We'll be out of these pockets in a couple of minutes." He continues not to fly the plane. He turns his smile away, back to the laugh, back to his old buddy who doesn't turn at all.

I wonder how many brides died on their wedding day. Did Eva Braun? Did they crunch the capsules on the same day they got married? I forget. How old do you have to be before *The New York Times* writes your obituary and keeps it on file? Is it how old or how much you have done?

I think I feel my body feeling a little looser. Body to brain—body to brain. Over and out of it. "When you walk through a storm keep your arms up high . . ." and then open the air vent all the way and direct it there so you can air out. The next voice you hear may be that of your husband. My husband? Where did he come from?

"Oh, good. It's already fastened."

It never wasn't.

"We're only about five minutes out." He clicks again. At least his old buddy is bringing us in.

"It was pretty rough for a while there, wasn't it?" I take his hand again.

He looks at me illogically. "Maybe. For a minute." He doesn't believe what he said.

. . .

"That's our *Town & Country* special. How many copies would you like. Any wallet size?" I wonder how many years photographers keep negatives? If they gambled right, they could throw out half the weddings. I close the book and slam it to the floor. I move us down into the bed and hold her to me. I whisper-sing into her ear, very slowly, very softly, "The party's over. . . ." I move my voice from one breast to the other, along her stomach. I slide way down. "It's time we started to love. . . ." My toes push into the rug. I put my hands on the sides of her knees and push them wide apart.

I spread her with my fingers. "This is what I want a picture of. Will you take a picture of this for me?" I'm opening and closing. Opening and closing. "Will you take a close-up? Really close up?" I hold it open and my tongue licks it lightly, gliding back and forth. "But don't take the close-up until I make it hard and big. Big enough to fit into me. Promise you'll take it? Promise?" My tongue circles the sides and goes back to the middle, around the sides and back to the middle. Imperceptibly, patiently, it moves faster, stronger. I feel it growing under me.

Her arm is over her eyes, closing it all out to shut it all in. Her neck is back. Her head moves from side to side. "God! Oh, my God."

I nip it between my teeth. I let it go. "Promise?" Her knees try to find each other. Quickly, hurtingly, I push them apart again and anchor myself between them.

"I promise. Promise." Her voice is low and heavy and shaking.

I'm looking at it go in and out, out and in. "It gets like a little cock. Do you know that? Do you? It's just like a little cock. It's like fucking a cock."

"Make it a cock. Make it bigger! Harder!" The words are grunts. They sound like suppressed screams.

"It's getting hard. Feel it? Feel it getting hard? It's so big. Your cock is so big." I move my body up on hers until our mouths are together and my lips and tongue are wiping her taste onto her lips and into her mouth.

Urgently, forcefully she pushes her body into me. Again. Again. Again. "I love you. I love you so. Don't ever leave me. You can't. Ever. Never." She is so hard. She is almost into me.

I wedge my hand between us, fingering us both. I dig my nail into where she's hard, where she's about to explode. She yells. It's the sound at the top of a nightmare. I turn my body around and put myself on top of her stiffened lips. "Bite it! Bite it." I'm almost, almost there. Hurry. Hurry. Get me there. "Hurt it! Now! Hurt it! Bite it!" Don't make me lose it. You fucking cunt! God. Please don't let her make me lose it.

"I can't if it hurts. Does it hurt?"

"Don't talk! Move!" I'm making my own rhythms between her teeth, tiny movements so she doesn't think I want out. It's coming. Oh, God! Come on! Come on! *God! Thank God!* I stay rigid, letting it swell. A giant pulsation takes over my body. My breaths are the kind the doctor demands when he listens to my back. I squeeze my thighs tightly and stretch my legs up beyond the headboard. The wall feels cool to my feet. My God. It's still there. I can't believe it. I can't believe me. Suddenly, I'm aware of air sliding across our wet bodies. My muscles begin to open a little. Slowly, little by little they start to ease. The tears come, uncontrollably, deliveringly.

She is afraid to move. She is afraid to spoil anything for me.

"Was it good for you?" she asks.

"Couldn't you tell? Just a little?"

"Yes." There was the small proud voice. The little girl, so pleased to please, so unself-conscious.

I kiss her toes. Each one. One by one, then back again. "How come your feet are so little?"

"It's good everything isn't." And there it is again, that ferocious innocence, so embarrassing, so strangely compelling.

No one gets up. We cool off on each other. Slowly, the rhythm runs down—78 to 45 to 33—never not touching, always tiny-kissing and teasing-talking in our special world, our inner space.

"Is your mom sending you back to camp?" I am almost inside her ear lisping on all the s's as good as I can.

"She said 'No.' She is not going to. Not if they are still going to call me 'midge.' "

The blanket is on the floor. We are under the sheet, inside the tent. It's all very secret. I whisper very quietly. "I won't tell a single person. I mean it. Nobody. But are you really ten?"

She is very angry. She squinches her eyes meanly. "Do you know you are a giant already and you are going to grow much more. Look at your hands. The doctor will tell you that's how he can tell. Look at them."

"No wonder the kids don't like you." I push my lower lip far out.

"None of them?"

"Maybe one. Just maybe. And that's all."

"Who? Nobody ever writes. Nobody ever gets in touch."

I push my middle finger deep inside her. "Like this?" I move it around slowly, slowly. The friction begins to fade.

It's moist enough now to rev to 45. Faster. Faster. Around and around. More and more. It's never enough. Never.

Mark kisses me nicely, happily. "It's not too many brides who are lucky enough to spend their wedding night at Bob's Marathon Marina." He gets up and pats my naked back with that light tap-tap of finality, the tap that always decodes into "That's it . . ." "That's all for now. . . ." Later I would get to know this act as the afterbirth of the four-minute fuck, enough to sustain Mark for too long.

No, Mark. Not yet. Please. Shit! Why did I drink that stupid wine with Bob and that stupid guide. Fuck the backwater, the tides, old times. Why did we stay there so long? Mark, I love you so. But I didn't come and it's my wedding night. When you come back, please make me come. I don't want to do it myself. I haven't done that since you.

I don't move or get up when he gets back between the dank wrinkles. I want to stay slippery so it won't take long. It won't, Mark. I promise. Why do I feel his impatience? Mark, I just want to rent this hand for a minute. I take it and put it there. It's heavy, lifeless. He doesn't move it away. He doesn't move it at all. Why do I feel a feeling that is even more than embarrassed? I lay my hand on top of his and press his middle finger between me. Ask him! I can't. You can. Ask him!

"Please, Mark. Please?"

His hand starts to move. Clinically? Romantically? I don't care. Just keep going. He's saying something. What? Please don't talk, Mark. His voice, his words are completely detached from his hand. "On her wedding night, Juliet warned Romeo, 'I should kill thee cherishing.' Any similarity?"

I don't want to think. I roll onto his practiced fingers.

He works them over and over the slippery part, as if he's playing four next-to-each-other notes. The metronome races double time, triple. . . . Cymbals! Timpani! I'm all of them together. After lying there a moment, I say happily, "thank you, sweetheart. Mark? I love you." Softly, I kiss his sleeping cheek.

4

It's hard to believe that picture of Mark is almost twelve years old. I wonder who'll take the hot and harassed look we'll see plastered over billboards, in railway stations, on the outsides of buses, in the windows of empty storefronts. It won't be easy to naturalize Mark to the point of lugging a rumpled jacket over his shoulder. I'm convinced the minute he wears something it automatically becomes immune to dirt and wrinkles. Maybe special effects can do it. They can do anything. Just ask my children. Sometimes I believe their whole world was cloned from the rib of special effects.

I open the windows wide and ring for Pedro to remove the debris from headquarters. Right now, I'd gratefully settle for the noxious muguet of Daisy Air Freshener. But unlike Mother with her Airwick, I'd never remember to hide it behind the dictionary before "they" came, and pull it out after "they" left. As the cars roll from the gravel, I hear the front door slam shut. I'm sure Max hasn't gone. Before I call, I'll ask him to dinner, to occupy Mark.

Even now, as I look at Mark from the doorway of the porch, he's still locker-room fresh. He's watching and listening to Max, the perfect blend of mouth and motion.

"And don't forget, Marcus, the rich will always get a

push from the poor. And don't you confuse it with a pat on the back. It's a shove for you to fall flat on your ass, preferably on the side with your wallet."

"For Christ's sake, Mandell. Why do you always play the frustrated surgeon looking for the goddamn lump that's never there? Isn't five thousand years of persecution enough for you?" The faster Mark went at Max, the more wind he got, like a quick-hoisted jib before the big blow.

"Don't convince me, Marcus. I'm saying prepare for the pressure. You think Noah waited for the flood? Invent questions. Postdate answers. Fortune's got a funny way of getting unfortunate." Max tilts his head and blows four tight, perfect rings. So fascinated are they with themselves, they don't see me standing at the door, watching the thick gray circles bump into each other.

"Ahem. Governor?" They both look up. "Governor, would you ask your campaign manager if he would like to stay for dinner?" I must say "governor" sounds sort of appealing.

"Don't ask him to ask me. Maybe he won't. I'm staying."

"You're right. I wouldn't."

"See how the players always make wrong decisions? Amanda's the only right one you ever made in your life."

"What about you?" Mark asks Max.

"Me?" Max says as if confronted by a retard. "Me? Lucky the day *I* decided to pull you from the sewer."

"You know? He believes that." Mark's tone is marveling. "You know, Max, sometimes even 'success has to portray a certain humility. ' "

I leave as Max screams he doesn't want to hear one more word from some "La Rouchefafucking frog" or he'll croak. Going up the stairs, I can picture Max's hands flying. I feel guilty tiptoeing past Sonia and Sara's rooms, but, then, they have their homework to do. I'm sure they have homework to do.

I lie on the bed too lethargic to pull off the spread or turn on the lights or telephone. Especially telephone. "Hello? They're gone. All but Max. He's staying for dinner."

"What's happened? What's happening?"

"They're all playing with themselves about Mark for governor." Tell her it's over, Amanda. Tell her! It's easier on the phone.

"Governor? Governor?" She sounds as if our connection is slowly tearing away. Right now, I want to hold her, comfort her, but that kind of holding isn't possible now.

"What difference, Maria? Don't you understand that will be great for us down here when he's up there? And Latham will be completely immersed as head of the State Liquor Commission." God, Amanda. You're a coward. No. I'm not. I want to go to her tomorrow, to face her to tell her. Face it, Amanda. That's what you don't want. Coward! "Whatever, Maria. It won't matter." Keep forcing it. After all, it's only until tomorrow. You have to do it for her until tomorrow. "Anyhow, the primary isn't until September."

"What does that mean?" she asks. I can't stand her voice so small. I should get in my car and go to her now.

"It means I'll come in to see you tomorrow."

"You mean it?"

"I mean it." But, Maria, what you mean and I mean are too horribly different. Please don't make me talk anymore.

"Do you love me?"

Abruptly, I switch tones, using the voice I always use when somebody's listening. "You're absolutely right. Right. You couldn't be righter. I'll call you later." I push the phone far away. God, it kills me to think of her joyless

evening with Latham thick-talking the senator into promises he wouldn't keep even if Latham were sober. But she
can't leave Latham for me. She's had men before me. Serious ones. She told me. I'm sure she threatened them, too. No
you're not, Amanda. Down deep you know she didn't.
Coward!

Suddenly there really is somebody stomping toward me
in an extra-short ("everybody wears them like that")
school uniform. It's an angry, impatient ten-year-old. Here
goes. "You're absolutely right. You couldn't be righter. I'll
give it to you tomorrow—about ten thirty. Will I ever. Absolutely."

The wound-up body is seething as I hang up. "I hate
her. I hate her so. She is so gross and so sick." Fury furrows
everything.

"Hello is one word. Mother is the oth—"

So annoyed. "Hello." Followed by a quick, distracted
kiss for which I should be whatever is more than grateful.
"To think anyone is as sick as Sara, and you and Daddy
don't do anything about her."

I am so not listening that I shake my head into almost
dizziness showing her I'm hearing every word.

"But now you've *got* to do something. To think I have
to live in the same house with someone so gross." All the
words are one and the screechy tone never varies. A pattern
that always accompanies the same theme. I don't *have* to
listen to hear.

"What now?"

"It's easy for you to say it like that because you don't go
to school with her. If you did you wouldn't say 'what
now?'" Pause. Inhale. "Sara, my wonderful sister, is a
whore."

A fast flash as an eleven-year-old in bright lipstick and

high heels stumbles across my mind. "Sonia. That's gross."
What should I yell about first? The language? The hate?
The sibling horror of it all? Geneticists do say at least three
years should exist between children in order to avoid
rivalry. Of course, they are assuming you'll still be fucking
after three years.

"It's not as gross as what's happened. Sara's a pig and I'm
the one who has to live with her and I can't stand it any
longer. She'll have to go away to school or I will." The
nonstop words race out like a double-time Xerox competing
against its own output. "I can't live in the same house with
a whore."

"Sonia!"

"I didn't start it. They're all saying it. Tim MacIntosh
saw her kiss, really kiss, Jamie after assembly." (That's his
name? Jamie-after-assembly?) "Jamie's the one she's always calling a faggot." Her face is scarlet and her breathing seems to be searching for air.

Do children have heart attacks? During a trauma of this
magnitude, what are the actuarial statistics on cardiac ar-
rests for ten-year-olds? This must be what John Marquand
meant about when you get right down to it life is just a
matter of taking the dog in and out. These hugely important minutiae. These titanic tinynesses. The ones you've got
to solve now. It's called coping. I'm too old to cope. I've
always been too old to cope. She's staring at me. She's waiting for me to cope. "Where is Sara now?"

Aha. The furrows unfurl slightly. Maybe Mommy's regaining a little of what she really doesn't have. Her mind.
"She's in her room. On the phone per usual."

"Tell her I want to see her."

Again. The telling look about my incredible stupidity.
"Then she'll know *I* told you."

I can assume that look too. "Who else could have told me?"

"Maybe a school mother. I would call if I had a child in school with a—"

"Shut up!" I'm screaming the two words I hate most in the world. The two words I forbid the children to use. But I can't keep them in. I've had it with this creep. I don't even know why I'm angry at Sara. What did she do again? She kissed a faggot? She kissed a faggot and now she's a whore. Is that the counterculture fairy tale of the frog and prince? Sonia's little hands fasten onto her hips. I've redirected her rage. "Let me think a minute, Sonia, about how I'm going to handle it." (Handle what?) "Let me think what I'm going to say."

"What are you going to say?"

"I said let me think about it. Now, get out!" That settles it. *I* am going to have the heart attack. There's no space left between the hard thumps in my chest. "Your uniform's too short," I scream. "*You* look like some goddamn whore in that uniform. And wash your filthy hair. It's in filthy stuck-together pieces." The back doesn't look back. I'm my loudest. "Do you hear?" No answer. "*Answer me!*"

"Yes."

"Yes what?"

"Yes. Mother."

The defiant slam of the door undoes it all. Like a wild woman, I pull it open. "You come back here. Don't you ever slam this door at me. You come back here. Do you hear me?" She better be able to. They can hear me loud and clear in the Oslo Institute for the Deaf. I know my heart attack is at its peak as I watch her slowly, carefully, hatefully reclose my door. No. I am mistaken. As I hear her seal herself into her own room with a force that simple things like paint and hinges and solid oak can't endure, those speeding thumps begin to burst through.

I think I'll have a drink with Mark and Max. Anything's better than any should-do alternatives.

Mark and Max are not too dissimilar from Portia and her life. Six weeks later and you're back where you were. Max, weary-wild, is about to expel his prize prodigy. "How many times do I have to spell it out? Why make the SEC c-u-r-i-o-u-s?"

"Amanda. Max is showing off again. In fact, to the letter of the law." Mark waits for the no recognition. Undaunted, he continues. "You have curiously ambiguous morals, Max. Remember how you even used to quote Thomas Gray? 'Too poor for a bribe and too proud to importune. He had not the method of making a fortune.'"

Max shook his head. "Don't defend you to me. As a future governor, just remember about worthless leases not being too worthless. Shouldn't be anything too ambiguous about that, even for you, Marcus."

Maybe not for him, but what about for me? Mark gets up and puts a fresh napkin under Max's glass. With the old, damp one he wipes an ash that has blown onto the table.

"Don't forget, Marcus. It's never public opinion. It's public emotion. You know what emotion is, don't you? You've never been cold-assed about getting where you're going, have you? It didn't mean much, not much, to you to get into this wonderful community, did it? How many illusions do you think you've cold-assed manufactured to make yourself believe you really belong? That they would never want to see anything but good happen, like becoming governor, to one of their very own, like you?"

As my thoughts nod to Max's words, I'm back at that

party when I think it all began. When I first thought I couldn't last. I can almost set my mind on that date. How many years ago? Five? My God.

5

COME FOR COCKTAILS

TO MEET: *Amanda and Mark Weldon*
ON: *Saturday, the twenty-seventh of April*
TIME: *Six to eight*
PLACE: *Muffie and Jay Van Sandt's*
RSVP: *Regrets only*

We arrived early just as we were supposed to. The double-story frame house was almost a replica of the saltbox they owned in Edgartown, the tiny New England enclave where they met, grew up, married, and returned each summer.

Mark adjusted his tie, patted his hair, and smiled at his teeth in the rearview mirror before getting out. "This will be painless," he said matter-of-factly. I made no move to open the door. I felt like idiot baggage that somehow got lost between takeoff and landing.

"For whom?"

"Join. Why fight?"

"Why do I have to do either?"

Mark gave my hand a "there, there, now" pat. "Just think of it as something for Sonia and Sara. They'll want to be where their friends belong. And Davis is the best tennis pro in Westchester, especially for kids."

I pushed my nails into my palms. What am I doing here? Am I going to be reintroduced to my old college roommates? Who is Mark? Is he one of their husbands in his blazer and plaid pants? I never even saw those pants before. But where are his needlepoint slippers?

A child who "belonged" pushed open the screen door. "Mom's coming." Then he let it slam shut. How lucky could Sonia and Sara be? Mark had his arm around my shoulders as we went in and waited for "Mom." It was cool and dark inside, a combination of twenty-five-watt bulbs and early awnings. Obviously, Muffie was one of the careful types who saw the sun as an enemy, a fader of those sunny, bright fabrics she bought to brighten the house. Antimacassars covered arms and backs along the long body of the living room. On the over-grand Steinway, frayed velvet frames with carved jade inserts held black-and-white family groupings on long lawns and flat beaches. The squinting children kneeled in front while parents and grandparents pyramided behind.

A teenage boy in an ill-fitting white jacket and tilted bow tie asked us what we wanted to drink. We followed him to the dining room where a had-to-be-inherited sideboard served as bar. Stacks of thin plastic glasses and half-gallon bottles of unknown brands crowded the surface. Unknown brands—that was the authentic benchmark of the established. So established they outlabeled the labels. The soda and tonic bottles were the biggest I had ever seen. They looked as if they belonged on water cooler stands so one could just push-button them into use.

"There you are," Muffie boomed, as if she'd even looked under the beds. "Oh. Good. I'm glad Eric has fixed you up." The sloppy bartender looked down, not up. "Eric's a Whitethorn. He belongs to Brownie and Jack."

"Oh." Mark nodded meaninglessly. "Glad to meet you, son." Brownie and Jack's possession wiped his hand on his apron before extending it to Mark.

A Whitethorn, eh? I wondered if they were part of the Chippewa Whitethorns or the Amawalk Whitethorns. Or were they possibly a branch of the Ottawa Whitethorns whom Pontiac led to Detroit after Ford settled in Dearborn?

Is that really a red grosgrain bow on the back of her head? The child who slammed the door must have stuck it there when Mom wasn't feeling. Bully for him!

"This is such a drag. Isn't it?" Muffie asked excitedly. "But we're lucky. We've got the whole committee coming so you'll only have to go through one of these. You probably know most of them, anyway." She knew we didn't. "Parkhurst. Junior Parkhurst? The president? He's coming, too. What a character. Sometimes I have to go along with Boop. He really *does* believe he's the club. Really."

She said "really" like the brook and the stream—rill-y. And fast. Very fast I answered. "Rill-y?"

She answered. "Rill-y."

This could go on forever. Rill-y. It could. Mark to the rescue. "How many on the admissions committee?" he asked.

Slowly, thoughtfully, Muffie tapped her fingers. "Eight. And thank heavens they're finally getting some younger blood like Jay Van Sandt."

Muffie was one of the infinite breed who always calls her husband by his complete name. "Jay Van Sandt." I'm sure Boop says "Junior Parkhurst." They are throwbacks to when familiarity, especially with husbands, bred unwanted children. This was part of the same breed who summered and wintered at half places. "We'll be at Hobe." Without the "Sound." "We'll be at Fishers." Without the "Island." "We're going to Lyford." Minus the "Cay."

"It's really great you and Jay are doing this," Mark said. His hand pressing against my waist.

"It rill-y is, Muffie. Great," I echoed. What's great is, the fucking club is getting *us*. What's great is that that Dutch dummy and that fucking Muff can sponsor *us*. You've got it bass ackwards, Mark!

Muffie shook her head as she spoke. "You know, Jay Van Sandt couldn't believe you and I were in boarding school together?"

Neither can I. "Why?" Let puffie Muffie dangle.

"I mean he could. He just couldn't."

I wonder if I should tell her her fat is sticking out through the side of her wrap-around dress, through the part where the pull-through sash hasn't covered the hole it's pulled through.

Muffie looked at the chiming clock. "Speaking of Jay Van Sandt, I wonder why he's not back. He went to the Fowlers' and the Cranes' to get some extra ice."

What a wonderful picture. The heir to Van Sandt Copper hauling his Scotch cooler for free ice. The ice-age they live in . . . that's not America for me.

"Speak of the devil and the devil arrives," Muffie said as Mighty Ice, mission accomplished, raced through the door.

"Amanda. Mark. I'm sorry. Gosh. I've been gone longer than I thought," he said to his wrist, blaming his watch. "I'm so sorry. Well, anyway, I see Muffie didn't let you dry up." He forced a laugh through his nonjoke.

Mark raised his glass. "Before nobody can hear anybody"—his voice was strong and warm.—"I want you to know Amanda and I were just telling Muffie how great we think you two are to do—"

"Do what? Nonsense." He spots Eric. "Hey, Eric. How are ya, fella?" He clomps him hard on the shoulder. "How about a little gin and tonic for an old man? And don't forget, just let the tonic whisper to the gin." The same laugh. "He's a wonderful boy, that Eric. One of the Whitethorn kids. You know Brownie and Jack, don't you? He's Lehman Brothers."

All of them? Or just one?

"Hey, here comes somebody you've just gotta know." He yanks somebody by the jacket. Somebody spins around. "Hey. Craig. Whoooa, boy. Before you get to the oats say 'Hi' to the reasons for the feed. Hey, Mark and Amanda, this is good old Craig. He's our executive head of our Road Review Board."

He took the introduction more like "Hail to the Chief." He was all teeth and one skinny, skinny, skinny tie as he generously shook hands. Oh, come on, Jay. You're putting us on. We couldn't really be meeting the head head, head on. Of what? Listen, fella, maybe a little later I'll ask you why you don't review those little holes in our big roads. I mean just before they become wells. Okay, Craig, old boy? Very ugly boy. Listen, Craig. Know the story of the three holes? Well! Well! Well! Big curtain raiser in vaudeville, Craig. But then, life upon the wicked stage was not the life for progenitors of Road Review prexies. But it's a helluva story to start a board meeting with when you discuss holes. Assholes like you.

Only a slight guffaw came out of the hole in his mouth before he left us to fill it with anything more substantial.

It never fails. Everybody at once. The awkward emptiness is suddenly teeming with the whole tribe of Amawalk Gold and Tennis. Some have the totem crest on their blazers, some on their ties. All of them have it sewn in their speech. I feel the same identification and desire for continuity with them as I feel with people streaming by in an airport.

"So this is Amanda," I hear him say. When I look up my immediate impression is of a goat. Maybe because those few remaining white strands are too long. But they're not a beard. They're back-of-the-head, down-the-collar too long. And the goat is also a crest wearer. My God, even on his cufflinks. Mark and Muffie are flanking him. Maybe propping him up is more accurate. "Welcome, Amanda. Welcome." The goat just sounded like Saint Peter right before the gate swings open.

"Sweetheart. This is Mr. Parkhurst." Mark raises his eyelids. Meaningfully? Of course, meaningfully. It means go into your act, Amanda. Should I faint? No. Not good enough. Swoon? Better. Let him keep pinching my tit with his eyes? Better yet. I've got it. Let him cop a feel. Perfect. And then can I laugh, really belly laugh, that this is "Junior"? Fuckget it. There's nobody to laugh with here, nobody to roll on the floor with at the thought of "Junior" turning out to be Peter the goat.

"What a pleasure, Mr. Parkhurst." I extend my hand.

"Junior. Please. It's Junior."

"Oh, rill-y. Junior. Thank you." The stringy-haired paper eater leans for my cheek. I watch his eyes open meaningfully at my low-buttoned blouse. My God! What is that smell? God! It's got to be the whole Puerto Rican perfume counter. Hey, Junior. I think I'm going to throw up on your crest. Maybe that's how he overpowers the Amawalk squaws so he can feel their dry little papussies. I'd like to pull up my knee and make him keel over like he's making me do. I don't know Boop, but poor Boop.

"Van Sandt just justified my recommending him for admissions," Junior says in praise of himself and really to himself. He looks at Muffie. "Has Amanda, here, met Betty?"

"No. Not yet. I'll find her," Muffie volunteers eagerly, happy to be able to be of service to Junior. President Junior. President of the Amawalks. Who kills all blacks with tomahawks.

"You'll love the wife. Wonderful girl."

Oh, no. This is too much. Wife? Betty? And they call her . . .

"Boop. This is Amanda and Mark," Muffie announces proudly.

Sometimes, the expected can throw you more than the flyer from left field. Like now. My preset image of the reservation's first lady and the act I see before me are harrowingly interchangeable. I must admit, however, I didn't see the sweater set in green, but then again I also didn't envision its coordinating with those pop-eyed frogs leaping across the completely predictable ass-spanning skirt. But I saw the short gray hair, easily styled, so all it ever demanded from the world of hairdressers was the occasional trim. It's not that she would frown on "others" coloring their hair, but her mother hadn't, neither had her grandmother, and why should she be a slave to . . . blah, blah, blah. The eyes are perfect, a wrinkle-lidded determined blue that got things done just the way "wonderful girl" wanted them done. And her natural ruddiness naturally precluded any artifice except for the thinly drawn lines of lipstick applied without a mirror. There are no stockings under the blue and green tasseled flats, but then her legs are probably tan all year. Probably from Hobe.

The jewelry pins the final accent on the déja vu. First, the lifeless engagement ring, a scratched sapphire surrounded by thickly pronged diamond chips. Its heavy Edwardian setting maintains the proper disregard for contemporary "fads." Doubtless, Mummy had given that ring to Junior. You remember. That was right before they wrapped Mummy in all that gauze. But to really show off the no-need-no-care-for-jewelry, the watch takes first prize, folks. Just like you, ladies and gentlemen, I can hardly believe my own eyes, but there it is. That glorious little Waltham face is being held on that fine, sun-spotted wrist by a no less than gen-u-ine, ex-pand-able *Speidel* . . . you heard me right . . . I said *Speidel* band.

"Jay and Muffie told us such wonderful things about you two. I'm so happy to finally meet you."

"Thank you." I like the way one front tooth crosses a tiny bit over the other. It makes her look like she's smiling when she talks.

"I understand you're a playwright?" She says "play-wright" like "freak." "What have you written?"

Perhaps the whimsical tooth triggered me. I wrinkled my forehead in a maximum effect to achieve total recall. *The Tempest, The Cherry Orchard, Streetcar, Oh! Cal-cutta!* She's staring. I can't see that tooth anymore. Oh Calcutta, you'd better weep for me. My stomach's in a flut-ter and I rill-y have to pee.

"Rill-y."

How do you say I'm only kidding to someone you don't know but know enough to know it's going to sound like I'm making fun of you.

Mark doesn't miss a beat. He goes right to the phone booth, changes into his cape, and takes charge. "Darling. Not the plays you adapted for television. What I think Mrs. Parkhurst—"

"Call me Boop. Please. Boop."

Superman smiles at Boop. "What I think Boop wants to know is about your own work."

No she doesn't, Mark. But thank you, Mark. And please don't yell at me later, Mark. I began talking about *The Cause*. Muffie leaves to get another drink. Junior's eyes start to roll around the room. Boop tenses every muscle in her throat stifling a yawn so she can continue flattering me with her interest. A little girl who "belonged" shoved three scraggly deviled eggs between us. Their tops had already hardened on still another unrefilled tray of child-passed hors d'oeuvres.

"Dee-licious." Boop says to the midget as she wipes her thumb and index finger on the edge of the stained doily. "I'm ashamed to say that's my fourth," she boasts. "But that will probably be dinner for me."

I'm sure it will. The noise is so thick and the smoke so heavy I can't believe I am listening to so many people laughing. What at? A little unsteadily, Muffie returns to lead me away. "Everyone wants to meet the guestess of honor," she says to Boop. Boop laughs appreciatively. Oh. Now I see. That's the kind of thing. I laugh out loud just to see if I can just in case I have to.

Muffie laces her arm through mine, more for her than for me. Or were the floorboards that uneven? Another one of the discomforts of early American "charm" that always escapes my chauvinism. "I'm dying for you to meet the MacIntoshes," Muffie says charging ahead.

"Are they from the Big Apple?" Ha. Ha. Ha. Ha. Ha. Right?

I feel her shake her head. "No. No. From here. Mattingale Hill? His mother was a Mattingale. Her family owned it all. It was a land grant from the king. Mattingale Hill?"

What does she want me to answer? "Oh. Mattingale Hill." I sound all-knowing. I promise I won't discuss any more fruit, even blueberry.

"Exactly." She is so relieved.

"God!" I take his name in at least five syllables. I can't possibly sound any more impressed than that.

"Exactly." Am I detecting the tiniest trace of boredom at my stupidity? I do believe I am. "It's been Mattingale Hill as far back as the Revolution. It was a *very* famous battle site."

I don't know whether to say "God" or "rill-y" or get down on my knees and beg forgiveness for ignorance. But I am saved.

"Amanda. These are the MacIntoshes. Marcie and Mac." Mac is not a blazer-crested warbler. He's a patch-on-the-elbow warbler. And Marcie? One day she, too, will be "wonderful girl."

"Great to meet you," Mac says exuberantly. "Just had a great chat with the other half. Great guy. Just great."

"We understand one of your little girls is going to Amawalk next year. We must tap you early for our Parents' Council," Marcie says hopefully.

Muffie nods agreement. After seeing how solidly entrenched I am, she goes back to the bar. Hooray. But here's what I suddenly hear myself asking. "Where do you live? Near here?" I am so ha-ha-ing inside, I just pray it doesn't come out.

"Mattingale Hill." They both press the buzzer at the same time.

"Mattingale Hill?" I try to manage equal parts of recognition and reverence.

"We've got the gatekeeper's cottage of what used to belong to the family."

"You grew up in the big house?" Now it was curiosity.

"Father did when he was a boy. Grandfather was forced to let it go during the Depression. But he held on to the guest house. That's where we all grew up."

I'm afraid to ask where the guest house went. I just try to keep looking at them importantly.

"We don't even know the people who live in Grandfather's house now." His tone is proud. "And from what I hear, I don't think we'd want to."

Marcie shudders. Even the thought is anathema. "They've got nothing but money." She shudders again. "It's all so gross."

"I don't know if you realize it, sweetheart, but just the way you said that was great." He laughs and kisses her cheek. "They've got nothing. Absolutely nothing. The only thing they've got is money. Great. Not that I wouldn't want to have it. But not when it's only that. There's too much of that around here already."

"Do you know they've paved their entire driveway?" Marcie says disbelievingly.

"With what?" I ask. "Gold bricks?"

Now Mac bestows his bourbon-and-water acceptance on my cheek. "Great. Just great. Marcie, you've got to remember that. Muffie and Jay said you were great. That's just too much." His obituary is going to read that he committed a sort-of suicide—death came at cocktails from his own enthusiasm.

Suddenly, there's a great roar for silence. After all, you can't clink plastic. Jay Van Sandt yells through a rolled magazine for quiet. He isn't able to get above the noise by standing on anything, thanks to the "charm" of the low ceilings. The roar rolls to a rumble. Go, Jay.

"Some of the guys planned a little surprise for the Weldons, or should I say in honor of them?" As he speaks, "some of the guys" move toward the piano. Bodies push together and a cavelike closeness seems to cork the air around me. Jay continues. "I don't know whether you're aware that we bulldogs outnumber you crimsons, Mark." He looks for Mark in the mess. "Even the 'onery tigers stand at bay when we bark. And that's just what we're about to do."

Mock hisses and boos are followed by applause, sufficient encouragement for the overwilling octet to curve around the piano. The fifty-year-old preppie on the end leans forward and blows a little hundred proof into his pitch pipe.

"Can you believe they're all Whiffenpoofs?" Marcie asks with a pride that could only indicate having suckled each one.

"Hmmmmmmm . . . hmmmmmm . . . hmmmmmm." They nod. They're in tune all right. Spanning fifty years and four wars, they're in perfect tune. All one nation indivisible. Or is it invisible?

> *To the tables down at Mory's*
> *To the place where Louie dwells*
> *To the good old-fashioned bars we know so well*
> *Stand the Whiffenpoofs assembled*
> *With their glasses raised on high*
> *While the magic of their singing casts a spell.*

A spell? More like a pall on this sea of becalmed wives. Those are the poor lambs, these hapless mimeographs each only herself away from welfare, with her benign acceptance of only room and board for her educated labor. Conditioned and conventioned, they move like stalwart atavisms pacing their widow walks, never questioning the bounty. Performance is a far, far better thing than dissension.

And chanting up there, in anachronistic harmony, the hilltop inheritors back in their forefathers' shirtsleeves, but without their forefathers' arms to fill them. Baa-baa black sheep, secretary jocks, studs of the playing fields who peaked long ago on the short-lived vine of the Ivy League.

Holding their glasses and swaying nostalgically, they remind me of the no-one-can-touch-us camaraderie of the British only hours before Singapore fell into the go-getting arms of the enemy.

And we'll die and be forgotten with the rest
... hmmmmmm ... hmmmmmm ... hmmmmmm.

Big hoot-and-whistle applause gives thanks as the group disperses and generously joins us mortals. I would have had a lot more wine by now, but "believe it or not we ran out of ice." What I can't believe is Jay Van Sandt handing out hard American wampum to go "buy" hard American water. Poor Jay, having to assume such a profligate spirit.

"In Xenia, Ohio, and Bad Axe, Michigan, he drew crowds far, far larger than double the towns' populations." It's Tonto's father holding forth. "They came from all over."

They came from all over. All over where? Could you please repeat those towns for the West Coast? Xenia, Ohio? Bad Axe, Michigan? Mark is among the group listening. I am the fringe of the rally.

"I don't believe polls." Tonto, Sr., continues. "What are polls? A couple of people phoning a couple of people and that's the country? I believe in seeing and hearing the country for myself; in seeing the people come out, in hearing them cheer and yell. What does a secret call or a TV hookup mean? Hoke-up's more like it." Pause. The laugh. "It's a goddamn, excuse me, shame Mitchell and Stans resigned. The country went crazy then. I can't believe the James Buckley I once voted for actually suggested that a

presidential resignation would be 'an act of statesman-
ship.' " His voice, all these years later, is cruel and wild. "I
tell you a moral paralysis gripped this country when the one
great President of our lifetime had to expose himself to a
guy like Rodino. Some wop who loses his Godfather head
and wins some demented decision from some cop-out committee to subpoena history. That committee, every last one
of them, they're the ones who should've been cited for con-
tempt."

I watch Mark. He can't look at me. Not while he
doesn't talk, he can't look at me.

Muffie weaves around the circle toting a large plastic
bag. "More ice? More ice? Anyone for more ice?" Needed
or not, full or empty, she drops the smooth, new cubes
into the group, splashing the remains of the glass, more often
than not, into the air or onto a dress or jacket. "What's so
serious?" Muffie asks, making still another splash-drop. "Oh.
I'm sorry. I see. I wet you. Oh. I probably did that before.
I'm sorry. Better wet than dry, though." There are a few
smiles. But this time they don't have any sound. Muffie moves
her offerings to new victims.

"It's most unfortunate," Boop says sterilely, "that today's Americans possess so strong a sense of guilt as to
make them reveal what our ancestors were taught to con-
ceal." Her force is in her quiet, taut control. "We are
being taken down by ourselves. And marked down by others." The thin, tight, painted lines hardly move as she speaks.

" 'He that is without sin among you, let him first cast a
stone.' " A new voice and guess whose. Not Luke or Matthew. Oh, no. They're not spreading the good word today.
Today it's Mark quoting John.

I see the heads nod approval. They are as if they
are in church, programmed by God into responsive nodding. Their eyes are on the Good Book following His

gospel in silent speech while their fingers trace His words.

But what about our apostle? Amawalk's newest Billy Graham leading the flock? How can he? If he can, I can. And Mark, sweetheart, I'm doing this just for you. You are making me so sick with your interchangeably fluent lizardry that I want to see it work now. Here I go.

"I firmly believe Billy Graham wasn't any help to Nixon back then. Personally, I always believed Billy Graham gave God a bad name."

"You mean Rabbi Korf." Mark smiles at me, showing the others the silliness of my mistake.

"I mean Billy Graham."

"I don't understand." The smile freezes. Oh, yes, you do, Mark.

Boop's head cocks to one side as if that will aid her comprehension. "Why do you say that, dear?" She sounds as if she had genuine concern for my sanity.

Mark doesn't even perspire in bed. But that's not Muffie's splash around his hairline. Explain me, Mark. Hurry up and whitewash your black cloud.

"I think I know what Amanada means. I guess I should after all these years." Smile. No serious tone in his voice. Obviously, nothing to worry about. "Are you aware that he's probably sold more books than any author in the world . . ." Pause. "Except for the real God."

"What?" It's the Whitethorn.

"Except for the Bible. What Amanda resents, and for that matter I do too, is the commercialism that seems to build houses for Graham instead of for God."

He's getting them. Boop has stopped dialing Payne Whitney. "His personal wealth is staggering and his life-style has certainly been a contradiction to the cloth but noticeably not to his nature. While he crusades against public squalor he is enhancing his private wealth. When you're not among the people you lose them. You can't just talk down from the pulpit. You can't only hold private audiences in the West Wing. They have to be on the West Side, too."

The heads nod again. Not a hundred convinced, but not unconvinced. Once more would do it. Next time they would clap hands, leave their seats, and go forward.

Almost abruptly, I am shaking hands, saying nothings, and watching the room thin out. Having raped the hors d'oeuvres, drained the firewater, and set sufficient smoke signals, the Amawalks leave. When our turn comes, only Jay is at the door begging off any "thanks" for whatever. "I tell Muffie all the time," he says, holding the brass door knocker to help steady himself, "white goods are poison for her. I've managed to get her off the juniper berry, but she can go pretty hard at the vodka." I wondered if he would fuck her or hit her. I don't know why. I just wondered.

The door finally closes behind us and Mark shuts off his smile. As his hand clutches the shift, his knuckles look like X-rays under his tight skin. I'll bet he'll want our next wagon stick shift. He pushes into "D" and presses down and out of the short driveway. My gears are still at the party, locked into reverse.

The holes in the dirt road are only adding to the contamination. If they keep this mud for the "good" of the horses, how many have to be shot each thaw for broken legs?

The bones in Mark's cheeks are clenched. His chin juts out like an under-the-helmet goose-stepper's. His voice is agate. "What in hell were you trying to do in there? I want to hear all about that little ego trip? I don't get it. You know these people. These are your people. You're one of them. Tell me."

"Knew, Mark. Past tense. Were, Mark. Past tense. I don't want any part of them. I'm not about to take one giant leap for mankind into yesterday. That frightens me like today terrifies them. For them, progress is marrying somebody who's not a virgin."

Mark turns off the motor. His eyes are like their eyes. Cold. Set. Missing tear glands. "You're always stupid when you're drunk. Stupid drunk."

"And that's always your answer when I don't yes you. Well, no no no no *no no no*. No, these are *not* my people. And *no no no*, this is *not* my place. Watered blood. Watered genes. The next generation won't have chins. No chins, Mark."

"Yell a little louder since you're not drunk." He is cruel and chinless.

"They won't have chins!"

Mark starts the motor. "You're not stupid drunk. You are stupid *and* you are drunk. Aren't you the one who always says never say no to a group of anything? Look for something good for *your* good. Take them one by one."

"You take them, Mark. Take them one by one and shove them right up your hypocritical ass." My words are a little heavy, a little slow, but a lot sure. "Mark, I have a feeling you and I are engaged in a great Civil War and you are testing me to a point I can't long endure. I better have a new birth of freedom or I shall perish from the earth."

"Drunk or sober, nobody's ever accused you of not being verbal, not running off, like some raging Harlem hydrant."

"What's the matter with Harlem? Do you hate 'Nigras,' too?" Better tight than right like you, uptight asshole! Ha. Ha. Ha. Ha.

When we get home Mark makes himself a Latham-sized

piece of whiskey. I pour a pretty good piece of Stolichnaya and only after that first glorious harshness do I add some ice.

"Tell me, Mark. Let me in on the big favor you're doing for me and my children by burying me and my children. Where's the guy who took the chances and made it because he took the chances?"

I love to watch Mark control his distaste for liquor. But that's Mark's secret weapon, control. Cunt-roll? Ha. Ha. Ha. Ha.

"I don't need chances anymore, Amanda. I'm there. I can spit or smile as I please."

"Bullshit, Mark! Here is not there, and you know it. Here is just the beginning of whatever you want. But whatever you want, you want it all. And you'll be fucking well careful to say 'fuck off' only to those slobs who can't say it to you."

"You cunt. You lousy cunt!"

"Thank you, Mark. Thank you very much. At least you've given me a value. Cunts are useful, Mark. Do you know that? Do you? Do you?"

"If you think I give a shit for that seedy, two-bit slice of AHmeerica they call a club, you're even sicker than your mother. Screw them. Screw you. I couldn't care less about belonging. I'll tell them all to shove it."

He lights a cigarette from the wrong end and crushes it down as if the cigarette did it on purpose. "Great decision, Mark. I can't wait to hear you tell them."

One rrrrrinnng. Two rrrrrinnngs. "Answer it." His tone says, When a phone rings, that's woman's work. "Answer the phone. Damn you."

"Has your mind crippled your body?"

On his way to the rrrrrinnng, his glass barely misses my head. "Who? Can't you talk up? Louder?" His voice is irregular and impatient. "Oooooh. Oooooh. That's *much* better. Yes. That's fine now." His tone has become normal, conciliatory, patient. "When? Really? I don't believe it. Great. Just great news. She'll be just as thrilled, naturally. The girls can? Right away? Great." Laugh. Fucking forced laugh. "I can't tell you how pleased we—it's terrific to hear. Thanks a million." Ass-kissing voice, hang up the phone. "Please thank them. One by one. I will. Right. You bet I will. Great. Good-by."

At the same moment that Mark puts down the receiver, the hypnotist removes the last trace of trance that tented him before the ring. With his spell gone, Mark sits beside me, snuggling into a small corner on my chair. He puts his arm gently around my waist and kisses my cheek.

"That was Junior Parkhurst. Never in Amawalk's history has there been a meeting right after a party to accept anyone. But they did it for us. We're in."

The word "in" emphasized years of work, dogged direction, need. I feel sad looking at this operative genius, this tough tycoon whose only hurts have been inflicted by non-functioners. So still the child—another Sara, another Sonia —living by rules, not sufficiently here or there or anywhere to live by the guts of his own values.

Where are you running, Mark? I squeeze his hand hard. For him.

6

The following day's mail confirmed the phone call with our very own stamp of belonging, Audit # W-21. I wonder who the lucky twenty are who preceded us in the "W" computer? How wonderful that the kids can now belongingly scribble their names for the nourishment of uncooked hot-dogs, or mostly celery tuna salad, spread gappingly between day-old slabs of styrofoam. And now Mark can roll with the guys for the round of drinks after the game. He, too, can shake the worn leather cup with all his available good humor and then feign foul play when the liar's dice come up untrue.

Leaving the bundle of bills still peeking through their glassined windows, I decide I must get to that book to get out of this mood. Yet while driving to the store, all I keep hearing are Mark's words, reinforcing my antagonism.

"You're no writer. You're a bullshit conversationalist about writing. You're a fraud who puts 'author' on her passport. Writers write. Why did Sinclair Lewis stomp out while teaching his class at Harvard? 'How many of you want to be writers?' he asked. Every hand shot up. 'Then get out and write.' "

Fuck you, Mark. Fuck your fucking quotes, Mark. Fuck this food and fuck this house. All you see is what you see. You're a bottom line, net after taxes fella. You're the financial statement. What about the guts statement? What about the statement that can't be stated statement? You can't read what isn't in black and white. Sometimes, why not play the red, Mark? Sometimes there's more to win by backing a loser whose time is coming. That's the big bet that says, Hang in there, it's coming. Try it, Mark. Try me.

Double damn! The fuel needle is wobbling between E and there-ain't-no-more. Double shit. Nothing burns me more than the ashtray full and the gas tank empty. How much macho do I have to put in my *"por favors"* before those fritos fill and empty where *they've* emptied and filled?

Airplane glue and gasoline have always done for my

olfactories what Chanel does for most women. As I consciously breathe way down and listen to the ring-ding-ding of the disgorger, something is getting to me. I feel a prickling of distraction. Involuntarily, I look out of the side window, across the island of pumps, into two deep, black eyes. My eyes stay fixed as if anesthetized before undergoing a test for glaucoma. I know as soon as I'm able to look away, I'll want to look back. And not with fear like when I'm on a bus and I think some degenerate is casing me and I keep looking at him until he isn't looking at me anymore. Not at all like that.

I know when I look back what I saw is going to say it to me again. I'm right. It's not quite a smile that's slanting his lips, but whatever it is, it's taking me out of myself. I see a lot of dark hair on his hand as he pays the attendant. I'm not going to use my credit card. And you, attendant, please don't use my name. I hold a ten-dollar bill out of the window. Thank goodness. He's just taking it. The black eyes are smiling more. My God! I want those thick, rough fingers. Yes. I want the dirt under them, too.

He's nodding. I nod. He tilts his head back in an ever-so-slight, follow-me motion. I shake my head, yes. Along wherever we're going, he now and then looks into his mirror. Don't worry. I'm still attached to the tow. You won't lose me.

But will I lose you? Am I going to awake and see Mark beside me stretched into dreamless sleep? If I am, please not yet. Inside me is going all crazy. Every machine is set to pay off at once. The lights are signaling madness.

His blinker says left. We turn and keep going. Now the blinker says right. We slow way down and turn into a narrow driveway where weeds stick up. He moves his hand under the raveling sisal in front of the back door. Finding the key, he springs the bolt to the kitchen. I never thought I'd be glad to see what I'm seeing on the living room walls. Not one, but two exaggeratedly carved and ornately painted crucifixes, each flanked by Palm Sunday palms. I feel equally blessed by the sepia-colored photograph, of all of whoever they are, at somebody's communion.

He holds out his hand and leads me up the narrow, uncarpeted stairs. We go through a door at the end of a small hall. A plastic Christ stares like some Playland prize from the middle of the heavy, dark dresser. On top of the dresser, a long embroidered cloth is secured by a brush, comb, nail buffer, and mirror, all in chipped blue cloissonné. I'm thinking not to think any inside things, just outside things. Like the bentwood rocker in the corner. Somebody needlepointed hard on its mustard yellow cushion. Too hard. And those slats on the back must hurt when somebody (maybe the same person) leans and rocks.

He's unzipping his jacket. "Hello." There's more black hair at the neck of his open shirt and over the white of his undershirt.

"Hello." Like Christ on the cross, I can't move.

Let's neither of us say any more.

"This is my mother's house. She's in Jersey visiting Ramona, my sister."

"Does she visit your sister a lot?"

He nods as a glaze fixes my mind. My what? I watch him pull his shirt from his pants. "She helps with the babies. My brother-in-law, he's on the road a lot."

"That's good."

"That he goes so much?"

"Yes. No. That she helps with the babies."

"You have babies?" His undershirt is the kind construction workers wear when they sit on pilings chomping early

lunches of heros and submarines. It doesn't have the bulge
of beer, but then he's young. Why do his shoulders have so
much hair? Why is hair obsessing me?

"I have two girls. Yes. How did you get that tattoo?"

He laughs. Another, thank God. As black as is his hair,
as white are his teeth. You're a nice guy. Boy? Man? What
are you? Whatever, please come here.

"With a needle. It's a pineapple. See?" He's coming
toward me. The pineapple reminds me of a hand grenade.
I am the hand grenade. I'm going to go off.

"It was done in Hawaii. I love Hawaii. I was there two
years with the navy." He is smiling happily. "I don't have
room for all the names that said 'Welcome,' but the pineapple means welcome and it reminds me of them all."

I want to ask how many. I want to know if he'd have
room on both arms for them. "How many babies do you
have?"

He pulls the belt from the loops of his pants. "We just
have Joey. We are trying for more."

Show me how you try. Show me. *Show me.* "We have
Sonia and Sara." I'm saying their names because I'm not
afraid. I'm trusting you. I want you to know it. And Sonia
and Sara, I want you to know I'm not jeopardizing you.

White sport socks. More hair on the ankles. His ham-
strings are work-hard. So are his chunky calves. Please!
Don't let it show through the opening in your jockey shorts.
I don't want to see it. It's to do, not to see.

"Not Italian names." He says. "But nice. Nice for girls."
He must be hearing my head because he pulls the spread
off the bed. Only after he's under the sheet does he take off
that underwear and toss it to the rocker. I can't wait for
those unwashed hands to be where I'm going to soap myself into virginity.

Coming out of the bathroom, I'm wrapped in more mustard yellow. I've scrubbed like a whore and powdered with the innocent smells of a baby. I made sure to brush the powder from there so he wouldn't think it was gray. The harsh texture of hotel-quality carpet startles me as I tiptoe toward us.

I am almost the length of the bed. I'm pushing close against my tucked-in side. Why is all this happening so slowly when I'm going so fast? Hurry! Take this towel off me. Smell me. Fuck me!

"Are you trying to play games staying over there? You're not here to stay over there, lady." His voice is low. He jerks the sheet to the floor. He's on his knees next to me. It's high and stiff between his thighs. It's thick and it's hard. It's ugly. It's uncircumcised. *Make me put it in my mouth.* There's a burn across my back as he strips the towel to the floor. He locks his thumbs under my knees and pushes them out. Out more. He wedges himself between me. His thumbs open me up. He takes one away and with the force of his left hand keeps me wide. His other hand takes his cock. Pushing me even farther apart, he guides himself down the ridge, to the soaking hollow.

"Don't tell me, lady, you were waiting to be invited." Holding his cock, he starts forcing it through the wet. There's no way he's not going to push it far enough so when he lets it go it'll stay locked. God! It can't go any farther, can it?

Suddenly, his body takes over the shoving. As he drives it even farther it starts to hurt like labor. Will I have to be sewn? I begin to wail as if in primal-scream therapy. I put my hand there to feel if there's blood. He's prone and pumping and he's rubbing against what's inside those in-side folds. Every neon on the strip blows a fuse. Bastille bombs crash in crossfire. I'm shaking into craziness. He's coming more and more. It's down the tops of my legs. Even soft, he's hard. God! Another thrust. I feel the veins. I tighten against the throbbing. He raises on his palms and looks at me. He's still hot and moving in there. A Madonna, hanging from a thick silver chain around his neck, hits my cheek and falls onto my neck. Thank God her eyes are closed.

"Tell me you've been fucked better."

"I can't." I feel him ever-so-slightly easing out.

"Do you think you will be?"

"No."

"You're wrong." He gets up. "Don't get up. Understand?"

"Yes." I don't.

He's stretching for something on the top of the closet. His voice is strained with reaching. "Do you belong to a country club?"

"No." I feel over-undressed lying there. I lean to the side and move my hand around the floor for the thin piece of terry.

"Are you rich?"

"No." I wipe my legs and thighs where they are sticky.

"Are you afraid?"

"No." I don't know if it is the staggering intensity of what just happened, or just the loss of the real world, but I feel the detachment of a lodger who's found his bed includes the barmaid. It might be a tuppence more, but I'll take it. He's reaching in the closet. What for? I wonder if he was born in this bed with his mother hollering for Jesus while his brother, the priest, turned his head in repugnance as the water broke.

Is some Father around here going to know about me?

Do you always tell the same one? If you do mention me, please don't do it around here. Go to some church in Portchester. Portchester is full of Italians who fuck long, blond Junior Leagues from Rye.

"Lie on your stomach." He's holding something. "Lie on your stomach. Don't be afraid." His voice isn't nice, but better.

"Thank you." I say it into the pillow after turning onto my belly. I could easily hump a bump in the mattress and come.

"Did your mother ever do wash?"

They say when one sense is overly acute the others suffer. Sex has definitely damaged my hearing? "What?"

"Put your hands together. No. Not like that." He puts them over each other. "Did your mother do wash? You know. Clothes? Hang them out to dry?"

All I can think of is, "Four and twenty blackbirds baked in a pie." "No. She didn't." But wait. I'm not going to tell you, but she did do her underwear and sometimes a sheet when she got "under the weather." You see, my mother never had "the curse." Never. How could a childbearing gift from God be a "curse"? Your momma would have appreciated that about mine. Probably only that.

He's kneeling on the side of the bed opposite to my face. I don't want to turn. He readjusts my wrists. "Hold them like that." With a bosun's deftness, he knots them together. "This is clothesline. My mother doesn't want a machine. I ask her all the time."

I'm sure you do. I'm sure you're a very good son. I'm sure you know you're a very good husband. I know I'm a very good wife. He rolls me onto my back. My hands are prisoned between my spine and the sheet. With one end of washday between his teeth, he anchors first my left, then my right ankle to the bedposts. The expanse spreads me wider and he's looking into where I'm helplessly open.

From the floor at the end of the bed, he puts one hand firmly under me. Raising my head as much as I can, I see a dirty, calloused thumb push deep inside me. My neck hurts. I let my head flop back onto the pillow. I'm wild down there. I keep trying to push together. It's so naked. Now both dirty thumbs are pushing in there. He leans down and staccatoes his tongue on and off. On and off the beating bump. Now he's licking it and making wet noises. His thumbs are working fast. Fast and hard and plunging. Suddenly, something so alien is down there attacking, hurting, killing.

"Don't. Don't." I'm yelling. "What are you doing?" I push so high into the air and pull and twist so fiercely I think I'm going to drag the posts from their moorings.

"This is what we put on the wash." The voice is heavy. Panting. "Ever had a clothespin here?"

"Oh. My God. *Owwwww!* My God. *Owwwww!*"

"Should I take it off? You want it off?" He shakes it while it's holding me, squeezing me, pinching the inner folds. And what's inside those folds is pushing to come out. The more it grows, the more unbearable the pain.

He gets up and comes to the top of the bed. He puts his knees into the pillow and wipes his cock over my eyes, ears, nose, back and forth across my lips. "Open your fucking mouth. Open it." With his free hand he squeezes the pinching clothespin even tighter.

My screams are like sirens spiking the air with an emergency. He forces himself into my mouth, my throat. Again the squeeze. I can't control my spasms.

He doesn't take it out of my mouth. It's huge. Huger. "Take it! Take it! Swallow! Take it! You'll never get this where you fuck, you fucking fucker." He's wild. With his fingers, his tongue, his cock, he's in every place he can be.

The final release is so strong that its finality stays there shaking inside of us. Unwilling to leave. Unable to.

That evening, still completely undone, yet competing as usual with Cronkite for my Home Box Office share of the audience, I try to get through. "Mark? Mark!" His turn to me is not quite enough to lose Cronkite. "Mark? Do you know there are not enough jobs for Harvard grads who have majored in Asian studies?"

Now it's a one-eighty from the screen, because I can see both his eyes saying he didn't hear right. "What did you say?"

I repeat my fascinating news.

"What's your point?"

"Well, you yourself say Asia is our country's biggest issue. Yet there's twenty times more work for plumbers. In fact, plumbers are in demand."

It's his I-don't-want-to-bother-now-with-your-craziness voice. "I'll tell the dean of graduate studies to put in a plumbing course. Judging from our bills, it should be well received."

Net after taxes turns back to net after Nielsen. I continue. "I heard that fact from Joe the plumber right after he fucked me. Today. In fact, he told me that just a couple of hours ago. Right after he fucked me."

"Shssh. I want to hear this."

7

"You see, Marcus, your five years of living here are not quite enough to make you belong. To be one of them, God forbid, your great, great, great dust would have to be reborn."

I'm thinking about the time Mark upgraded us from Presbyterian atheism to Episcopalian atheism. The time he had us dunked into that last cesspool of this stinking community. Our final devotion into the holy trinity of right club, right school, right church.

Sitting on the edge of the cushion, Max points his cigar at Mark. "Marcus, you've gotten all you can from these practiced freeloaders. You can be through being grateful for their lapping your booze. Their future is their fucking past. Forget them. All you gotta remember is when they say, 'I wish the old man hadn't left the trust fund so tight,' there ain't no trust fund. There ain't no bread. And Marcus, if there ain't no bread, there ain't no dough." Max keeps staring at Mark, knowing Mark can never completely dismiss their seeming acceptance, but hoping he'll at least recognize it a little more clearly.

Through the Windexed glass, past Mark's head, the fattest robin I've ever seen is pulling what has to be the fattest worm from the soft spring ground. Furiously, he shakes his head while clamping his wriggling prisoner in his beak. The more he jerks the more he moves back, always managing to keep just the right amount of tension. Wow. I'll let it all fly on the robin to pull it out whole. No way he got that big halfway.

"Why do you Jews think you see everything better than anyone else? Why do you figure everyone else for tunnel vision? How come only you can catch the rail to see what's coming up to close you in? Trust me. I know these people. And what I'm looking for is what I don't want. And what I don't want is any kind of tough time."

Wow! Robin! I knew you'd get it. And all in one piece. God almighty! It's gone. How in God's name did you swallow it so fast? Will you do a big bird-do the minute you fly away? You'd better do a big one, fatso. Do birds do more do-do when flying than when grounded? Dial your local ornithologist, dummy.

"Don't worry, Mandell. The worst bad they can say is that I bought my heirlooms. Just like I bought that shit of yours, about, 'Don't shit where you eat.' My slate is *fucking* clean."

Suddenly, I have this feeling that I've awakened and today is the day of the operation. My stomach is thick with fear and it's making me hot and fuzzy. I see myself spread on page one of the local press. I mean really spread, legs apart and everything. It's a big smear campaign. I'm a huge smear cartoon. I'm hanging on a clothesline. An oversized clothespin is pinning my thing on the line. A strong, hairy man is squeezing the clothespin with all his might. The caption is headline size:

PLUMBER PINS POL'S WIFE

"That's *not* shit, Marcus. Or if it is, they'd gladly swallow it. And then they'd congratulate themselves that they really had this funny feeling about you all the time. But being so open-minded, they gave the outsider a chance. But all they need is just that prick of blood to hound you from your booze-bought security. You won't hear the locker-room whispers, but you'll see them. That's when they'll seem like roars. And when they stop, when their cupped hands leave their mouths, the silence will sound even louder."

"What about when I'm in Albany, Max?" Mark's tone spans the months ahead. His voice comes from between the flags on either side of the stately desk overlooking the Hudson.

"Then they'll pat each other's asses like faggot full-backs."

Joe. That was his name. Joe. Joe what? I can see the black lettering on his mother's dented mailbox. But I can't make out the name. It ended in an O. I can always drive past. I hate my thinking he'd try anything just because he's a plumber. Didn't he give me that dashboard Pietà so no harm could catch up with my speeding? More than I got from Wilmington's best. ("One says Du *Pont*. Never *Du* Pont.") I'd better not play what can so-and-so do. I'll die the coward's death before Max gets the Teamsters to put them in cement.

"Mandell, listen. We know the Olympics is dynamite. Without a dime out of pocket, I've already got a name it would take millions to get. And not only did we grab the Olympics, but we plunked them on top of the city's biggest open sore. We're cleaning up what no other administration could wipe out. And before we're even an administration."

"Cleaning up *on*." Jiminy Cricket made "on" sound like thirty years with nothing off for good behavior. "It talks good, Mark. But keep looking over that newly-square shoulder. Keep looking for that close pal who can't wait to turn your five-ring showplace into a three-ring circus."

Mark stares hard into Max, but his tone is soft, almost playful. "I will fear no evil for thou art with me! Ev-er-y step of the way."

My head goes back to Max. Somehow it seems the ball

is returned before it's caught. "I'm talking us," Max says. "But it's you they'll be after."

Mark moves his neck as if to free it from too tight a collar. An action that helps him find the thoughts buried under exasperation. "For Christ's sake. So we thought of Times Square?"

"Just stumbled on it. Right?"

"No. Wrong. You can't stumble unless you're moving. And we were moving to a site in the city. It's called upward mobility. But not for us. For the city. The state."

Max, thinking his own thoughts, nods slowly, but not at Mark. "My grandmother was right," he says. "You *can* learn from a fool." He grabs the pad beside the phone. He draws five interlocking circles. Three above, two beneath.

"Clean and selfless like the Olympics. That's Weldon." Max holds the pad so Mark can see. "That's your campaign logo. Your face in one of the circles, triple-enlarged. It'll be on buttons, banners, posters."

Baubles. Bangles. Bright shiny beads.

"It's a fucking natural. What do you think, blondie?" Max brushes his hand against my breast. Not waiting for an answer, he stands up and addresses the crowd. "There he is, folks." Max points to a circle. "The next Republican governor of the Empire State. None other than Miracle Mark of Olympic Park. Ladies and gentlemen, I give you the man already in your winner's circle—*Mark Weldon.*"

Max is wild with his own eagerness. It's catching. I can hear real cheers. Wrap-around cheers from real people after the loudspeakers have blared Max's introduction.

Mark applauds. "Great timing, Max. Perfect to present at tomorrow's meeting."

"What meeting?" Do I really care?

"We need Amanda, tomorrow. Don't we, Max?"

I care they're not answering me. Using me. Talking around me. I care enough to feel a pulse in my head.

"Are you kidding? You'll run but she'll win."

As if there were no conversation since my question, Mark presses the memory button on his computer. "Tomorrow we meet with Darcy, State Republican Chairman, to decide when and where to announce my candidacy."

So it really is all decided. Their voices sound like Higgins and Watson after Eliza pushed out her *h*'s. Whatever worried Max seems back in its box between some Alps. I like that "Miracle Mark . . ."; and here's to all you ladies who hate to look at stiff, or as "they" say, in-repose cocks. Remember this consideration when you cast your vote.

> *Miracle Mark of Olympic Park*
> *He'll only pitch woo in the pitch, pitch dark.*

"Is that really true, Mrs. Weldon?"

"Yes. It is."

"Has it always been like that, Mrs. Weldon?"

"Yes. It has."

"Could you stand there one minute, Mrs. Weldon, holding that sign with those words while we get a picture? Thank you. Thank you so much."

And here's to all you courageous gays who are proud about who you are. My husband will be thrilled at this turnout. And believe me, I know from whence I don't come when I tell you:

> *Miracle Mark of Olympic Park*
> *Equates each cooze with jaws in a shark.*

"Is that really true, Mrs. Weldon?"

"Yes. It is."

"Has it always been like that, Mrs. Weldon?"

"Yes. It has."

"Could you stand there one minute, Mrs. Weldon, holding that sign with those words while we get a picture? Thank you. Thank you so much."

Max is shouting his wisdom at Mark. "You *are* Kennedy's balls, Marcus. You're that kind of high-class hump. That's why you need a lieutenant governor who's come up through the hard boot ranks. That's why you'd be so lucky with someone like Merebaum, who's been in the system for years. Just so long as it's not a dame. Never been one who couldn't do your job better. No such thing as a political Ms. who isn't some tortured dike torpedoing her way with boobs she wishes she didn't have."

My God! Maria? Tomorrow? That means I can't. And I can't the day after. And the day after that is the weekend.

"Hello, Maria? Of course I didn't know when I talked to you. You don't believe I did?"

"I don't think so."

"What do you mean 'think'? Would I have made plans?"

"Latham didn't say anything about a meeting."

Why would anybody tell Latham anything except where to sign. "He didn't know."

"You sound different."

Her voice is tiny. Not adorable tiny. Guilt-making tiny. "I'm not." I answered as hard as I could to sound the same.

"What are you wearing?" she asks.

"Just some robe."

"I wish you were wearing what you didn't today. Wearing it here. Now."

I can't reconcile what I feel. I don't want to believe I'm so embarrassed even though I am. Holding the phone with my shoulder, I'm rubbing my arm. It doesn't itch. The rubbing distracts me. *Stop it.* "I'll call you later or as soon as I can." Good. That sounded like it should.

"When later?"

"After dinner?"

"So long?"

I'd like to overlook those words as a question and mistake them for good-by. "If I can before, I will."

Max is still on a high. "You gotta balance the ticket. Not all city. Not all white. And easy on the Knesset."

"Why don't we wait for Darcy to—"

"I'm just saying you don't have to give anything away. You've got a drumroll of credits that'll—"

"But Darcy may want his—"

"You're Darcy's insurance to keep him there!"

Mark is listening with less and less pleasure as Max keeps interrupting.

"Your announcement's gotta be *wham!* We need network and local coverage. There's never a second chance to make a great first impression." Max waves his cigar like a wand. No doubt turning strategy into precluded victory.

"Can't somebody get the goddamn door?" Mark yells over Max and through the frantic barks of what United Parcel still thinks are attack dogs. Oh, my God! That voice. Hasn't today been enough? Please, dear God. Not that voice. Oh. Wow. I am too old to cope. And as far as that shit of yours goes, Mother, about "A girl is still a girl while her mother's alive." That's just exactly what it is. Capital S. If I weren't already so guilt-riddled, I'd believe the absolute reverse would be wonderfully rejuvenating.

"Did you forget I was coming?" Mother asks, almost hopefully.

How reassuring to have constants, no matter how momentarily disquieting. Mother would love to wallow in rejection while watching baby squirm.

"The extra place is not Elijah's," I say flatly. Thank goodness I told them about Max. I must remember to ask Max in front of Mother, eyebrows arched in subversion, if he'll *please* stay for dinner.

"Darling. Please tell Andro I have some things in the car for the girls."

"Pedro, Mother."

"You've had so many." Or, translated on the UN earphones, how inadequate a housekeeper can you be? You certainly didn't learn that at home. Of course, if you'd let me help . . .

"You don't have to bring something to the children every time you come. You know that, Mother."

"How would I know that? The minute they see me they look around."

"That's because you're always too generous with them."

"I'm sure you're right. It's my fault they're spoiled. But I always want to be assured a welcome."

Did I ever tell you they've always hated what you've given them unless I've told you what to get?

"Where you want these packages, Mrs. Horne?"

"Oh. Thank you. You can put them right on the chair, Andro."

This is definitely one of the evenings for the pneumatic drill. "Would you like a drink, Mother?"

"Well, just a little something over ice, please. Well, maybe today, a Scotch. That golf took a lot out of me. There's nothing worse than the aging process. You think it's never going to happen, but it does. Not to a young girl like you, my darling. But you'll remember these words like I remember my mother's." She continues talking as I hand her the glass. "You look tired. Are you, Amanda?" She presses her forehead to mine. Doctor is Mother's finest role. She shakes her head sadly. "You just do too much and for what and for whom? I certainly never see you." Stepping back slightly, she inspects the decay and inserts the large bore into the drill. "Now's the time you should play tennis. Your father and I never could get you off the courts. Now's the time to get rid of that winter waist."

Now's the time to preempt the star. To step on her next lines. "It's just bloat, Mother. Just drinking too much." You see, Mother, lots of times Maria and I had bloodies before we made love. Sometimes, as early as eight or nine in the morning. And going down doesn't take it off like humping.

"You're too young to need the false buildup of liquor. It's not only stupid. It's cumulative. I hope you recognize that. I hope something is sinking in besides the alcohol."

How "lucky" I still am to have Mother unchanged. Maybe that's why, when she isn't with me, I never picture her as she is. Treated little, I still see her in my childhood. I see her rushing home, late. Her face is red and icy cold. I'm in feet-pajamas. She kisses me with her cheeks. Then, looking into the foyer mirror, she turns her head from side to side and takes two long pins out of a hat that always slants onto one corner of her forehead. A veil, with unevenly spaced black dots, ends just below her nose. After she takes off her hat, she shakes her high hair and lets it fall loose. Her lunch-box purse of black alligator matches her ankle-strap shoes. "Accessories should always be the best, because most people pay them the least attention."

"Would you like a little more, Mother?" You don't have to chew the ice. She can hardly bear to look as she hands me her glass.

"Just a little, since your father isn't here. He cared. Whose voice is that I hear with Mark?"

"Max's."

"Oh. Yes. Mandell. I should have known by the cigar through the house."

After twenty years, I'm thinking of Airwick twice in one day?

"Why is Mandell so loud?"

"Can't you call him Max?"

"I'm *not* calling him anything. I'm asking *you* a question."

"He's enthusiastic. And with great reason. It's all unbelievable, but they're planning to—"

"Where are the girls? Do they know I'm here? Why is it whenever I'm here they're busy with homework? Yet, whenever I want them in the city, they're skiing or something because they have no homework?" Poor Mother. No one has the conspiracies life has layered on her.

As if responding to some Pavlovian bell, the girls rush in. "We didn't know you were coming, Grandma," Sara says, looking around.

"Of course not. Why would you?" I catch the look from the tone. "How are you, girls?"

Collective. "Fine, thank you."

And thank you, girls. I won't forget the "thank you." Together, they spot the packages.

"I see you see them already," Mother says, grimacing her genius to me. "I have never forgotten. Nor would I? After all, what are grandparents without presents? Or really, old age without money?"

Perfunctory kiss. "Thanks, Grandma." They exchange quick smiles as they tear off the wrappings. First Sonia, in the uncertain voice reserved for Grandma's gifts. "This looks like fun." She pulls some limp plastic from the box.

"Aha. You have the panda. Bring it here, Sonia, with the box. What won't they think of next?" Dutifully, Sonia carts the five-cent piece of plastic. "You first fill this plastic container with water, then place it between these special brackets, put it in the freezer overnight, and tomorrow you'll have a panda ice mold."

I don't blame Sonia if she's thinking she should probably still be calling her grandmother "Ga-Ga."

"And Sara, that must mean you have the giraffe. He's a little trickier with the long neck. But you're both so clever, you should have no trouble. I wish I were staying over to see them."

"Sonia. Sara." It's my catch-my-eye voice. "Put them neatly in the box if you don't fill them right away." They nod, knowing we all mean they go in the "present" closet. I have a strange feeling they will remain there until I meet some caterer who's doing a zoological fund raiser. "I just don't know where your grandmother finds such unique goodies."

She accepts the compliment with a sigh of heavy achievement. "With children like yours, who have everything, it's not easy. I assure you. Why don't they fill them now?"

"No. That's okay," Sara answers. "We'll wait till we have more time and they can really be good." Before they explode, they run out.

"Why is Mandell still here, Amanda?"

"Max, Mother."

"It must make you feel good to correct me. I just hope, for your sake, your children don't do the same to you."

Why didn't I just put Perrier in her glass? The bore is too big to be in so far. I go to the bar and make sure I stand hiding the anesthesia I'm fixing.

"Is that all vodka you're pouring?"

That's it. Right through me. "No, Mother. Sorry. It's mostly water."

"Since you're married, you've changed so. I never really know what to believe anymore."

"Must we? Every time?"

"It's not that often. And my time is short."

I know that, Mother. I know you've been dying since I've been six. I also know you're the only woman alive who hasn't "evacuated" in thirty years. "Mother. Nobody has any more than today."

"Forgive me, Amanda. I don't mean to begin, but I see you so rarely that I feel it's my duty as your mother. You'll think of me when I'm not around."

"Where are you going?" I can't believe I'm hearing this again.

"I can understand it's not edifying or stimulating to fill your life with the Mandells of the world, but don't let that be sufficient reason to resort to that false stimulation." On the word "false" her eyes crack through my glass. "It's different in my case, darling. My life is over. Yours is still ahead. And no one should deprive you of it."

Here's her tally so far. Revolving servants, a product of a poorly run home. Spoiled, ungrateful grandchildren. Her daughter's house, turned into a conference chamber for vulgarians. And a daughter who's turned into a lying, unproductive alcoholic. Little wonder the poor woman's life is over.

But don't fret, Mother. Even when you're gone I'll think of you. Just like that old record told me to. The one Grandma gave you when you were a child? I can just see the red Victor label with the grooves only on one side of the thick shellac. I wish I could open my Victrola, push in the winder, and wind until it couldn't anymore.

And after blowing the dust off the needle, I'd lift the arm and put it right at the beginning, right past the smooth border. At first, the words would almost bump into each other:

Always/think/of/mother/No/matter/where/you/roam

Then they'd space into perfection about how friends are really rotten. And finally the grind-down message.

A-l-w-a-y-s t-h-i-n-k o-f m-o-t-h-e-r . . .

No doubt she would remember all the words and once again explain their wisdom.

I can't believe I've downed that whole vodka. I think, though, it may have made the burr a little smaller. Fuck. Fuck. *Fuck!* Why did I have to catch that shake of her head. Suddenly, the mad woman from Con Ed is drilling past my guts and trying for the pavement of my skull.

"That's no answer," she says, staring, drilling. "It hurts me to see it. I hate to repeat myself. But it's cumulative. It creeps up on you."

First, I'm thinking how I can refill my glass. Next, I want to thank her for explaining "cumulative." And finally, I'm thinking what a good priest she'd make. Single-handedly, she could arouse so much guilt in need of absolution that the churches would overflow. Oh, yes. Father. I mean, Mother. I have sinned. Peace be with me? When? Not until the cord is cut? I thought that happened at birth. No? At death? You mean final absolution doesn't happen until it doesn't matter anymore?

It's strange she should hate the church when she's so much the church. Maybe one of those sissies at Saint whoever-the-hell-she-was-at gave her "supreme unction." Then the guilt. Then the money changes hands. Maybe it was the Mother Superior. "Always think of—"

"Mother Horne. What a surprise." Mark bends over as Mother turns her head away.

"I'm *sure* it is," she says to me.

"You know Max?"

I'm so glad for once Mark said "Max."

"Not only does she know me, she loves me. Right, Matter-Horne? That's how I see you. Strong. Superior. That will be my new name for you."

I love you, Max. Did I ever tell you I love you?

"I guess that's a compliment."

"You bet, Matter-Horne. And the governor's going to need that strength of yours."

Mother was confused, but she wasn't upset at being confused. Why would she be expected to understand someone like Max?

"You see, Matter-Horne, your good-for-nothing, semi-gloss, wife-abusing son-in-law is going to be the next governor of the state of New York."

Even my pouring the whole bottle won't distract her now.

"Mark. Darling? What is Max talking about?" Mother is using her best voice. She must use it almost all the time now, because she hardly ever slips out of it anymore.

"Max is leaping a few hurdles and flipping a few months, but I do plan to run. We hope to announce it soon. Until then . . ."

"Dearest Mark. If there's one thing I'm not, it's a talker." Wearing a wonderful platform smile, she hugs and kisses Mark, first on one cheek, then the other. "What thrilling news. Congratulations seem so inadequate. How lucky we all are to be such a wonderful family. That includes you, too, Max." She raises her glass in his direction. "Amanda. If you don't mind 'Matter-Horne's' interference, ask Max to stay for dinner. It's a celebration. Tell Pedro to put on an extra place."

8

"Remedy."

"R-E-M-E-D-Y."

"Excursion."

"E-X-C-U-R-S-I-O-N."

"Separate."

"S-E-P-E-R-A-T-E."

"SepAHHrate. Try it again."

"I forget. What is it?"

"Try it. SepAHHrate."

"I can't. Tell me." Not only is she irritated, but at me.

"Here's a good way to remember. I always used to get it wrong too. Just think of *a rat* in the middle of it. See? *Sep,* now *a rat,* and *e.*"

First she mumbles something. Then supreme praise. "Neat-o. S-E-P-A-R-A-T-E."

It's already a glorious morning. The sunshine is streaming through the windows crisping the ruffles on the newly washed eyelet curtains while the cut-glass syrup pitcher throws endless rainbows across the flowered kitchen paper. All are good omens. We're lucky today is so beautiful, for the crowds as well as for the cameras.

"What about your diet?" Sonia asks, pulling her plate

out of reach before I can stab the carefully cut piece of French toast.

I firmly (not so firmly at the moment) believe good figures are in direct proportion to bad mothers. They are completely dependent upon the number of breakfasts one does not sit with one's children.

"Why are you on a diet, anyway?" Sara asks. "You don't look fat."

"Because Mom is always on a diet," Sonia answers logically.

"Right. But please hurry and eat so you don't prolong the torture of my having to look at what you're not eating." I take an unsatisfying swallow of almost cool coffee.

"Icchh," Sara says, shaking her head. "I hate milk with syrup. It's like milk with grapefruit. It's bitter. Do I have to drink it?"

Leaning into the middle of the table, Sonia empties her glass. "I like it. I like that taste."

"You would. Nurd. Double nurd."

"*Stop!* No. You don't have to finish it. Sonia, you are wonderful to have finished. But you'll both be supernurds if you miss the bus. Hurry. It's almost eight." I'm able to figure that out only by deducting twenty minutes from our newest wizardry in kitchen clocks that "times the most delicate soufflé within a minute." The trouble with all these goddamn catalog come-ons is that I never remember to which Granny-looking New England mail order menace my mistake should be returned.

"Sara? Just two more before you go. Likable."

"L-I-K-A-B-L-E."

"Good. All right. Separate."

"S-E-P *a rat* A-T-E."

Even Pedro and Francesca laugh. I hand her her wrinkled list for a last check on the bus. "You're a hundred and so get a hundred. I love, adore, and detest you both with all my heart." I clasp a hand of each and squeeze my signal. Our signal. Eight squeezes. Each squeeze a word, translating into: I-love-you-the-best-in-the-world. Two squeezes come back from each not-so-little hand, translating into: Me-too. They've told me how they'd discussed with each other that I'd promised each I *really* loved her the best. It's true. I really did. And each believing I lied to the other makes it all work. Actually, each is right.

Watching them now, holding their hands, never wanting to let them go, I suddenly feel a mean loneliness shooting through the sunshine. I don't want the heels on their scruffy loafers ever to get any higher or the hems on those hideous uniforms to get any lower. I always want to see their bony, tight-skinned knees where scabs stay forever and Band-Aids never stick. That's *why* scabs stay forever.

Juice glass, milk glass, big plate, silverware, napkin are all piled in a bunch and brought to the sink. That's my attempt to make them totally aware they're not being waited on. Today my discipline has succeeded in making the glasses and the paper napkins stick to the syrup. And usually it causes a near collision in their "effort" for one to make the sink before the other.

"Hurry and brush your teeth and come down. Daddy's not in his room. He's gone already."

"But isn't the announcement this afternoon?" Sara asks, confused, because she knows she and Sonia are part of the big scene.

"Daddy had an early breakfast meeting. Something politicians always seem to have. And he has to rehearse what he's going to say. Now hurry and brush. And pick up your feet. And take a sweater."

A shout from a body two-timing the back stairs. "It's hot."

A yell from a kitchen mother. "It's not hot now. It's going to be later."

"But the radio—"

A scream. "*Take a sweater.*" That must have been a mother with advanced brain damage who wanted those beasts to "stay as sweet as you are . . . don't let a thing ever change you."

Down the stairs they come. With a fake fluoride smile they brush-kiss me good-by as I notice another half victory in our never ending war on wits, or is it witless war. Yes. They took their sweaters. They took them and tied them around their waists.

"Good luck on the test. And don't straggle from the bus. We have to be there before three." Luckily, Friday could work for Mark's announcement. I think it's the only time I've ever appreciated the "luxury" of private schools' early dismissals. I will never quite understand the rationale of pleasing the overvacationed child instead of the overpaying parent.

"What about dinner?" Francesca asks, knowing I haven't given it a thought. I hope one day somebody asks, "Mrs. Weldon? What's your most favorite thing in life?" Without hesitation. "A menu." Those words of Francesca's are my most unfavorite. Here's what they are. Homework. The unread Sunday *Times*. Phone calls not returned. All three? Worse.

"The girls will be home. I'm not sure about us. I don't know now." I'm thinking out loud. At least I'm thinking. Maybe we'll have dinner with some politicians. What do politicians do after their announcements? Maybe Mark will be in a big-boy huddle. I hope those big boys know there's not a chance the little woman goes home with the children. "Have spaghetti. Meat sauce. Salad. A long bread. Mr. Weldon always likes that. The girls do too. Make enough sauce. Plenty." The expandable feast, just in case. "Make brownies and cookies, too, please."

"You want to go over the list?"

If there's one thing I definitely do not want, it's to go over the list.

"It looks like much. But we haven't in a long time . . ."

"It's fine, Francesca. Don't worry." What do I look like? Some coupon clipper? After "eggs" and "½ and ½," I cross my eyes on purpose and see the list double. I don't want to read any more. I just want to hold it in front of me long enough for the proper amount of Madam-looking. When Polaroid first came out, and you had to time it before you peeled it off, I remember reading if you said the word chimpanzee after a number it equaled a second. One chimpanzee. Two chimpanzees. That's two seconds. I think about eight swinging chimps will do it. Done! "That's fine, Francesca. Make sure you get the long bread at the fish store. You know, those extra big ones with the sesame seeds. You know, those little white seeds on top of the bread that looks all twisted?" I don't know how I'm braiding my fingers, but it seems to be penetrating the Barcelona brain.

"Yes. *Sí*. Ohhhh. *Sí*."

I'm positive the bedroom clock's right so what's wrong? Is it really possible when I last looked it was only an hour ago? It wasn't ten hours ago? Ten weeks ago? Exhausted, I throw my robe on the floor and myself on the bed.

I adore this big, square room. I love all the windows. "So many windows," the decorator had said. "They are going to need so much fabric." I remember thinking, So much glass; so little wall space; unfortunately, so few paintings. I love lying here and watching the leaves wave back and forth. Fresh, young leaves with all that growing space, all that sky, between them. They almost look like an extension of the blossoming mimosa draping the windows. What a pretty pattern. How well it's lived. And I don't mean lasted. Just kept its cheer. When I do this room again, I'll use it again.

There's something so happy about yellow. What I'm not crazy about is the coral on the chaise. They call it "dusty." To me it's dirty. But at least it's not pink. I can still hear Mark's vehemence. "No pink! Don't you or that fag think you're going to get me to sleep in some powder room." I then had to make my statement and reject blue. Actually, now, I think blue on the chaise would be refreshing.

What suddenly stops the day is seeing that music box in the middle of the mantel. Early on, I had told her I was a music box freak. It was her first present. She saw it in the window of that shop on the corner of Sixty-something and Madison. "It's not old, but it looks old." I didn't say how could it be old and play the waltz from *Carousel*. Never. Ever. I'm thinking about getting up and getting it; about winding those tiny, hand-carved horses so they can bob up and down on their golden poles. No. It would make me too sad. Sad not to be able to have that day back. Ever. But that's why I'm so exhausted. It's not *this* morning. It's all these mornings. All these days filled with the draining avoidance of thinking.

In a way I want to phone her. In another, I never want to talk to her again. That call I made to cancel our day because of the Darcy thing was so miserable it still makes me weepy-sick. No wonder I couldn't erase it or think about it. And Mother, so tolerant of my getting loaded that night—"because of her excitement for Mark." Bull! Bull! Bull! Only Max knew I was strange, that my deliberate consumption was unnatural.

I couldn't have dialed sober. Yes, *of course*, she understood about the meeting. Bull! Bull! Bull! *Of course*, my voice wasn't different. A tiny too much Soave, but not different otherwise. More, much more bull.

We talked about Latham's having to dedicate the newly completed laboratory at the Tokyo Institute of Technology. The laboratory that had been donated by his father in honor of the Japanese scientists who helped him develop the original Marr transistor. I forced a joke about calling it T.I.T. But I couldn't force a laugh.

The trip was sponsored by the government. It would take about ten days. Part of the opening included a showing of her portraits. *Of course*, it wasn't a token gesture. I tried too hard. I didn't seem to have it. I would, though, when I saw her the following week. That was another reason to wait to tell her everything—I almost convinced myself.

We continued talking a lot about Tokyo, the workings of the Institute, the research they were doing. About the ghastliness of Albany. About campaigns. About everything we didn't know anything about. Then, suddenly, it was the following week.

It was Monday. When was that? Almost three, four weeks ago? It was very early when the phone rang. At first, I thought it was Mark's alarm. It was Latham. Maria's father had had a massive stroke. During the night. Michael Reese Hospital. They couldn't tell. They never thought he'd survive the first one. The one that left his left side paralyzed. And that was two years ago. Then only minutes later, it rang again. This time it was Maria. Yes. It was all over. Yes. Yes. It was a blessing.

They were going to try to make the noon flight. No. No. She thanked me anyway. But there was really nothing anybody could do. It would probably be on Wednesday or Thursday. Just as soon as everything could be arranged. No. No. And thank Mark, too. As of now, it's just family. But if anything changes. It's hard to know from here. They won't know more until they're there.

She was removed from what she was saying. She said everything with the dullness of the hundredth time. If one were to attach an intensive care monitor to her voice, the moving line would hardly peak. It wasn't forced heroics or tears pushed back. It also wasn't Maria's father who lay behind her flat, lifeless words.

It was eerie. It was almost as if one death were summoned to hasten another, by injecting the killer of time and miles. I remember wanting her to cry into my arms so I could stop the crying. And then even more than wanting it, I didn't. Most of all, I wanted her to hang up and get on the plane to Chicago.

And after the funeral, if everything hadn't snowballed with Mark, I would have definitely gone out there when her mother got so bad, when Maria knew they wouldn't be coming back before they went to Tokyo. She knew I wanted to.

And the other night, when she phoned from Tokyo, she sounded good, I thought. Very good. The connection wasn't good, but she and the trip sounded good. Otherwise, why would they be staying those extra days? Why else would the big fund raiser miss the big announcement? Again, my eyes are stopped by the music box. Tell me, dear God, why can't I just grab that box, bring it back to my bed, wind it up, and listen to it play?

"Will you turn that thing down? Sonia? Sara? Who-ever's playing it?" I yell from my door. "And close your door."

"It's the Bee Gees," responds one of the music lovers as if placating a retard.

"That's what they give me. Turn it down. Are you ready? It's almost two."

"Are you positive we have to wear dresses?"

That means they're not close to ready. One thing about my going to their rooms and screaming is, I won't need rouge. "*Positive!*" Slam. That's my door. Safe in my bath-room, I plug in my curlers and get out what I hope looks as good on my back as it did in my head when I planned today. Damn. Why doesn't the cleaner ever put the stays back in my shirts? Especially in the silk ones. Well, at least I can see the skirt has pleats. A far cry from a knife, but an improvement for the country. Boots or no? No. Too heavy. Too winter. Ah. The sling back is perfect, even sexy. Pull-ing open the two side closets, I become a three-way mir-rored glory. Not bad, anyway. A tan base. Lots of blusher. Presto! "Yes. Thank you. I had a wonderful vacation."

Jewelry. Nothing overstated, but obviously real. The Bulgari coin necklace. The gold hoop earrings. My diamond-shaped diamond ring. It may not look so big on my long finger, folks, but it could get you a village of split-levels. I extend my hand admiringly. Pang! The nail I always cut so it wouldn't hurt when it was inside her has grown as long as the others. Shit! Is it always going to be like this? Pang! Stab! Shit! And now when the thoughts come, they embarrass me.

The houndstooth jacket and shoulder bag complete my brown-beige fusion ticket. Just the perfume and plenty of it. Ears. Wrists. Neck. Thighs? Who knows? The last hurrah in the mirror. Still not a beauty, but as Mother said in an unguarded moment, after her first sessions with Mademoiselle Solange, "You have that *je ne sais quoi*."

Now to see what the other wonderful Weldon women have wrought. Actually, I'm afraid to open my door lest I'm accosted once again, by the Dee Tees attacking from wall-to-wall stereo. To my dazzlement, I hear nothing. Suddenly, two doors open and a pair of lovely young girls, about ten or eleven, stand in the hall. I believe I have seen them somewhere before, but believe me I can't remember where or when.

"What is it you want? Ten-speed bikes? Private phones? X-rated movies? Why are you doing this to Mother? Why are you making her feel kook-a-looka?" Even to the matching initialed sweaters, they are perfection. The smocked dresses I love and they hate. Shoes shined. Socks cuffed. I feel like all of us should be skipping down the yellow brick road.

The front door is answered by Pedro.

"Please tell Mrs. Weldon that Mr. Lanacola's here."

"Hello, Sandy," I call from the top of the stairs. "We're on our way down. We're all ready."

From the outset, Brad Howell had insisted on a site such as this for Mark's announcement. A site where Mark's company, Maxweld Realty, was rebuilding New York, working to house the wealth of big business he had coaxed, cajoled, and convinced to relocate in the Empire State.

The old MGM lot couldn't have created a better set. The derricks and cranes, the bulldozers and dump trucks and the acres and acres of beams and girders in midair

construction seem almost alive under the mammoth flood-
light of the burning sun. All this bigness not only stresses
the scale of Mark's achievement, but its giant size also
masks Mark's personal power. People see it more as a public project, a New York accomplishment, than a private
enterprise.

As Sandy cleaves our way through the crowd I can see
Mark standing and talking in the middle of the jerry-built
platform. Camouflaging the front and sides of the large
square are red-white-and-blue swags, the kind that drape
the front tier boxes at World Series games. Rising directly
behind the high platform is Max's symbolic brainchild
recreated in monolithic proportions. There, in living Olympic color, is Mark's face framed in the oversized middle
ring smiling out from under huge blockbuster letters:

FOR GOVERNOR
MIRACLE MARK WELDON

The "Olympic Park" is out. That had been Brad's change. It
always seems to me people like Brad, who know themselves
to be nobody's fool, always take everyone else for dummies.
"You've got to get Weldon on there," he said. "That's the
name that's on the ballot, that's in the booth when they pull
the curtain. With 'Miracle Mark of Olympic Park' they'd be
looking for the name Park."

Sandy leads us along like a string of mountaineers. He
holds Sara, who is holding Sonia, who is holding me. Finally, we make it to the steps at the side of the platform.
Darcy, already aboard, gives us a healthy tug. After the
children's easy ascent, I feel like some clumsy water skier
incapable of the slightest semblance of grace upon reenter-
ing the boat.

"It's not live," Brad Howell says. "So they'll start whenever we're set. But by God, it's network. And it's evening news. And fifteen seconds of evening news is a half million in campaign spots. All the morning papers will grab it too. There's plenty of coverage here," he says pointing at the cameras.

How about my coverage? How do I look? How do the girls look?

Brad continues. "We were hoping for the goddamn borough president to show. I don't know what he's thinking about. This project is big stuff for the Bronx. Likewise for him."

What the hell are you thinking about? The Bronx? Only the Bronx? Screw the Bronx. Boo! Boo! Boo! Know what that is? That's my Bronx cheer. Want to hear it again? "Are we dressed all right? How do you think we'll be captured as a family unit?"

Brad checks his watch. "Fine. Fine. Perfect."

The girls go to hug Mark. He blows me a kiss. He's talking to Bailey. I must say it's impressive. The gang's all here. Directly in front of us, six television cameras are semicircling the platform. The NBC N, the CBS eye, all the big logos read loud and clear on the sides of their snouted black boxes. Earphoned men keep swinging them around, adjusting their sights, making sure they can close up, pan around. Suddenly, a blackboard screech rips the air, followed by a booming voice testing for a loudness level. "Testing. Testing. One. Two." Getting better. "Testing. Testing. Three. Four." Perfect. The man at the mike is looking at the men at the amplifiers.

Sandy comes over and checks something off his clipboard. "Darcy's going to introduce Mark. Mark will be behind him. Not right behind. The cameras can't catch him there. You'll be on one side. The girls on the other. Keep smiling. Applaud before he goes to the mike. Again when he finishes. Then join him at the mike. I've told the same to the kids."

Flashing through me is what I remember I forgot to tell Sara and Sonia. It's what they once told all the baseball players when baseball was first on television. And they had to keep telling them. "Don't pick." "Don't scratch." "Don't arrange yourself." "The audience can lip read 'sonovabitch' and 'fuck-you.' " I better get to the girls.

"No whispering. No pointing. Don't pick. Don't scratch. And for God's sake don't pull at the elastic no matter how tightly it's pinching you there. Are you listening to me?"

"Uh hmm." Between the giggling and the poking, they can't get the words out.

"This. What you're doing now. That's exactly what I mean."

They contort their mouths into a strained, almost grotesque no-laugh. "We won't," Sara says. Sonia agrees. Obviously, this is one of the times I shouldn't have bothered. But what kind of a normal mother would I be if I had any faith in the behavior of my children?

Brad Howell rushes over. While talking to me, he's looking into the group surrounding Mark. "The man in the light brown suit? The one talking to Max? See? The short one?" Brad is so into them, he's unaware his arm is into my face, blocking my view. "That guy is Jack Wallenberg. Important. Very."

I move to look. I can't believe what I'm looking at. "You mean that fine figure of a fellow squashed into that double knit?"

Brad gives me an unexpected but nice clasp at the wrist. "Funny. Very funny. Did I mention you look good too? Even better than Wallenberg? But I don't have time for that now. Or, at least, now's not the time." His voice is nice too.

"All right. Yes. I can just barely make him out." We both laugh.

"He's Gotbaum's second man. Public Workers Union?"

Ohhh. A Union Jack. Does Union Jack jack—? Now is not the time. Later. "I'll go over and weave my magic spell."

"Good girl, Amanda. Give him the class act. No better bait for a slob."

I like the way Brad thinks. I like the pat, too, as I start to move. No, Max. It wasn't a shove. Too low. Much too low.

No sooner am I into my glorification of Wallenberg's wardrobe, than Darcy makes his move to the mike. While he waves his arms for quiet, I manage some icing. Nodding admiringly, I corner Wallenberg's eyes with sincerity. "Courage in clothes, I always say, is directly related to one's courage in life." If he had any idea of what I really meant by that he would probably move more toward an uppercut than the flex he's attempting.

God. I wish I could catch Brad's eye. I wish he could see how purposely close to me the people's sex symbol is standing. Brad? Maybe I'll take off his jacket, pants, and tie. Then I'll point to all three. And then I'll ask the audience to join me in just one chorus of "Look for the union label. . . ."

Is Darcy still talking? And what's he talking about? Do candidates ever feel what their wives feel? Or do they really believe what all the Darcys say? Is it true that even if it's not true, after they hear it they believe it? Is Mark really just another Wallenberg?

". . . not only selflessly brought the Olympics, but

brought back big business. Not only has he convinced major companies to stay in our great state, but he's harnessed new corporate horsepower to relocate here. What you see on this site are not promises. They are machines in action, seeding our soil with giant industries to balance a broken budget. All our taxes have succeeded in doing is robbing Peter to pay Paul. Mark Weldon is not only putting New York back on the map, but he's transfusing its anemic fiscal count with the healthy, red blood of a growing economy. Ladies and gentlemen, I'm honored to give you your next governor of New York State. Mark Weldon."

The applause gets louder. I'm applauding. I'm applauding hard. My ring has twisted around and it hurts me to applaud on it, but I don't stop. Not until the crowd eases. Even from the back, Mark looks calm and confident. The only other person I've watched perform from the back is a conductor.

A lot of hard hats are joining the crowd, ringing the perimeter. It must be their quitting time. Is it my imagination or are hard hats a group who are always smoking? Don't I always see them in cigarette ads that read strictly for taste? I'm sure the poor smoke more than the rich. An affordable pastime? I know the poor are fatter than the rich. It's junk foods. Fast foods. Foods they don't have time to prepare.

I'm thinking of Brad's "musts" for his clients. His most must. "Lose weight . . . before the camera finds it." Even Mark, Air Force Exercises' perfect passenger, dropped five for the lenses. Brad's other. "Never read a speech." I must admit, looking at Mark now, it's confidence-making seeing him talk from knowledge, not notes.

"The days are gone when candidates can ride elephants or donkeys to Albany. With independents up from twenty-five to forty percent, they must ride issues. And they must ride the ones that touch the most people. The death penalty is not one: Ten or fifteen people executed this year will not stop mass crime. And whether I am for or against abortion won't make your decision easier when an unwanted pregnancy occurs." Scattered applause.

"But negotiating to keep teachers in the classrooms touches you. Keeping transportation above a standstill moves you. And how about having the legislature cut capital gains to add incentive for you to start your *own* businesses? And what about putting more women into that legislature? And onto our benches? If forever is too long, then it's been far too long that women have been living solely by laws created by men. Old men." Big applause. Hurrahs. By women and men.

Brad Howell scribbles something on the inside of a matchbook and pushes it into Mark's palm. Like an old pro familiar with the ploys of politics, Mark glances at it quickly but never misses a beat. "And when businesses are willing to move, let's keep moving them into the high pocket of unemployment, just like we're doing here in the Bronx. I'm so proud of this project that rain or shine I was determined my candidacy would be announced from this site. And that is why it's especially gratifying for me to see your great borough president out there among you. He's the kind of people who are putting the word 'Empire' back into our state."

During the applause, Mark motions him up to the platform. Together, they shake hands, slap backs, and smile into the cameras. At precisely the right moment, Brad moves him away so Mark can finish.

"Although Aristotle said 'man by nature is a political animal,' the variety of species of this animal couldn't be housed in all the world's zoos, although many of them would do us more service behind bars. In conclusion, let me promise never to need the luxury of criticizing the misrule of my most ferocious opponents. My platform is, and always will be, performance. I am not now, and never will be, a missionary waiting for God to do man's work." The voice is strong, swelling, sure.

"I am a realist steeped in the structure of business. And what else is a state but a network of businesses more staggering and complicated than any other architecture? And now let me introduce the keystones and foundations around whom I have built my life. My wife, Amanda, and our daughters, Sara and Sonia."

Mark turns as we join him. I go to one side. The children stand on the other. The crowd is not only applauding, but yelling. They're not stopping either. It's louder and louder and *louder*. I feel my arm going up. My hand begins to wave.

9

"Listen to them yell. I can't believe it. I was so into it there, I didn't hear it like here." Walking up and down in the middle of our library, Sandy Lanacola is a mess of delirium. If possible, his black curly hair is even curlier. His face is dripping with excitement, and the knot on his tie has been tugged so constantly it's now resting midway between his wilted collar and his belt.

"Would you, or *more* to the point, could you stand still a minute?" Max twists impatiently in his chair. "Every time you fly into one of your fucking fits you manage to block the goddamn screen. Move! And stay moved!" Taking an extra long puff, Max tries to wave the smoke in Lanacola's direction.

Brad and Mark are hunched on the floor watching two small portables, one tuned to ABC, the other to NBC. The rest of us are eyeball-to-eyeball with CBS on the big screen inside the cabinet. Suddenly, Darcy gets the full twenty-four-inch coverage. "You know, Darcy," Brad says happily, "those cameras even make you look good." Though far and away the most distinguished of the group with those old-family looks and rich gray hair, there *was* something uniquely commanding about him up there today.

Darcy shakes his head as if he's seen it all but this is special. "Whoever's responsible for hanging that sun certainly chose the best angle." He's right about that sun. Its afternoon lights and darks worked wonders, from making the shabby flags look brisk and patriotic to creating a glow that seems to bathe each head in instant Breck.

As the cameras close in on Mark, he takes a determined, thoughtful breath. "Churchill said, 'Business is too often regarded as a wolf to be killed or a cow to be milked. Rarely is it seen as the horse that pulls the carriage.' " Another breath. "Business *is* our best friend. But to keep it like that, we must be that to business."

I remember Aristotle, but when did he do Churchill and the farm? God, Mark's teeth look white. He's the perfect poster for prosperity. "The day of the billion-dollar corporate walkout is done. Over! Finished!"

More yells. Hard applause. Hey! That's me. There I am. Shhhhh. Listen. I put myself almost into the set. "Concluding Weldon's announcement, he asked his wife, Amanda . . ." Did you hear Walter Cronkite say my name? Mother? Amawalks? World? ". . . and their two daughters to share in his obvious popularity. Could we be watching the beginning of another Camelot? Could be. But first, miles of 'Blood, toil, tears and sweat.' And that's the way it is. Friday, May 24th. This is Walter Cronkite, CBS News. Good night."

I'm in a trance. I want more. I want to see all the other stations I didn't see. We should have taped them. Why didn't we? Brad is on his feet. "With the Olympic coup, I expected good local coverage, but this running time outdistanced anything I could have predicted. And the network pickup is something fantastic. Unheard of. At least as long as I've been in the media. You're news, Mark. Big news. What you do from now on is headlines. Everything your family does from now on is headlines."

Lanacola breaks in. "And what you do is what you're gonna see. But what you say is only what you might hear." His voice holds a warning. "From now on, every missed shot will be reloaded by the opposition and returned ten times. A hundred times. Every off-the-record quote will be misquoted, hoping you'll deny it, fight it, give it even bigger space."

Brad goes over to Bailey. "Joe. You've been in this arena a long time, but today was different. Special. Something really got to them. Something ran through that crowd that was crazy. It was like fire. You know as well as I do that whole Bronx battalion wouldn't give this kind of a damn if *Fortune's* five hundred squatted right in the middle of the goddamn zoo! But there was something special in the air. Everybody caught it. Cronkite caught it. He said it right. It is a kind of Camelot. It's class. It's quality. People don't want to be led by cardigan sweaters, feet on the table, one of the boys. They like the idea of their state having its own empire. Especially one that's young. They think if they touch it, it'll rub off. A motorcade feel. A podium pull. A grab at the top and they're up there."

Bailey nodded. "Today, people's ideas are refined, or maybe the right word is polluted, by anybody wearing the labels, money—youth—looks. Those are the payoffs. But the sell needs lightning. We've got to hook them on speed. They don't have time for more anymore. The feed's too thick. TV, the press, the quadraphonic misfits. They're coming at them too heavy. Somewhere in between, but fast, we've got to grab them."

"And don't make the mistake," Max says knowingly, "of giving them too much. Too much class. Too many bullshit quotes." He looks at Brad. "Or too much Princeton, Howell. Yeah. Sure. They want to reach. But for something they can reach. Otherwise, bye-bye. And once bye-bye, forever bye-bye."

Drinks come in. The children go out. Spaghetti comes in. It was a good choice. The children come back. But behind the screen they must've exchanged places with two other girls for the weekend. The one in the engineer's overalls has caked meat sauce on the neck of her turtleneck. The other vision, the one in the sawed-off, still-unraveling jeans is either half in the bag or high on Mother's clogs.

There it is, fellas. The classy youth of Camelot. Although we have no napkins on our round table, feel free to snap us any time. We have no guard, because we are truly a class act. Why are the children back in here anyway? I think they're mesmerized by so many people who don't sound anything like Mattingale Hill.

The action of the voices, jumping from one idea to another, is exhilarating. The rat-a-tat plans, decisions, conclusions are nonstop. Everyone is stating. Nobody's asking. Everything's a bottom line.

"We got to have the rest of the staff like us. First rate. We need the best in the business for scheduling. That's top priority. And we need lots of digging advance men. Every district must be canvassed, every off-the-cuff comment researched."

I don't know how one knows when the other one is finished with his number.

"And a couple of days before the big day, we break the telephone banks wide open. Most voters don't even know *when* to vote. We need statewide dialers, calling the last-second command, 'Vote Weldon!'"

"Most of all, the invisible power does it. The old pols, whose consultant firms 'handle' the unions. The county leaders, whose law firms happen to employ the loudest lobbyists."

"And then there's the money 'no-see-ems.' The surrogates who play catch with the city's clubhouse 'lawyers.' That? Coming from Joe Bailey? Mister Patronage, himself? That's not a statement. It's an admission. But we need those letter-of-the-law lawyers, because their letter is always the big S with two long lines through it. We want part of that letter, part of that legality from their guardianships, receiverships."

Max sees I'm lost in a sea of clues. He holds up his hands. "Time out, please. The coach must review the last play for the new player. Where were we? Oh. Yes. The lovable lawyers." Max looks like the village bard about to weave a forbidden tale for innocent children.

"Let's say a very little girl is suddenly left an orphan, but has a few million to wipe her tears. A kindly old surrogate is given her guardianship by a lovable old lawyer. With the best paternal instincts, he safeguards her money in the bank. In the bank of a good, old, reliable friend. No, the account does not happen to bear any interest. Yes, the bank does have full use of the money. And yes. The good, old friend shows his gratitude to the surrogate for the use of that money. And yes. The surrogate shows his gratitude to the lawyer. Now, when the poorer, dear orphan is finally old enough not to need her warmhearted guardian anymore, she becomes interested in how much interest isn't there. If she happens to ungratefully compound what might have been and tries to do something about it, she'll soon discover that her inheritance was legally abducted by that lovable old guardian-law. The law of no return."

Mark steps forward. "Moral. Conscience doth *not* make cowards of politicians. Nor real estate men, for that matter, Max."

Max doesn't even acknowledge Mark with a look. "Anyway, Pretty Polly, that's a legal lesson in pretty politics."

Brad takes his encore. "Pretty Polly is going to be more than pretty. She's going to be beautiful." In complete discrepancy with the world-weary, past-imperfect tone of Max, Brad's voice is leaping. "You heard it today. Again tonight. The way the crowd picked up when Amanda joined Mark. There was something on top of the air. A new electricity. A new kind of current and we're plugged into it. But we need to keep it going. Starting now."

Me. Isn't it? Is it? Does it matter nobody ever looks at me? Still, even after today?

"And those people were poor people." Sandy Lanacola comes from where he speaks. "But she's what they see when they're out shopping, out buying the pink satin dress for the daughter that doesn't look anything like Amanda. She's what they see their son bringing home. Even *my* mother might see her share the oilcloth on our kitchen table." Sandy winks at me. "Maybe. Don't get all your hopes up. Maybe."

If only he didn't perspire so much. . . . I'm sorry, Sandy.

But why don't you carry a towel in your attaché case? A face towel would do.

"What about Mazurski? Is she a threat?" Mark asks. "She's good-looking. Not Amanda good-looking," he adds quickly, more to assuage them than me, "but she has an appeal."

"As we've said, people don't want what they are." Brad is impatient. "They want what they want to be. That's what we are all about. The everything else is just that. Everything else."

"You can't rule her out, Brad." Darcy is thoughtful. "You can get her out, but you can't discount her. Every candidate is a factor. She's got a helluva Liberal following."

"Hold it. Hold it. Wait just a goddamn minute." Joe Bailey raises his hands. His voice claims the authority of a thousand times in the ring, of enough fights to split each and every political planet. "Number one. Mazurski doesn't know her ass from third base about running. Two. She hasn't the dough for a team. More to the point, even if she could get a team, the team she could get couldn't get the dough. She'll need cooling, but that'll come with a guarantee from us. And believe me, the first feel of your heat and she'll accept. And for three through a hundred? Two million New York Jews are never going to vault a Pole into Albany. No matter what blessing she gets from Saint Peter's, there's not a Jew alive who doesn't know Warsaw had a ghetto long before Hitler."

I'm wondering if John Paul II would pardon Roman Polanski if he made a really great movie on his life and gave the money to the Church. With that generous a thought, a shot of terror shoots through me. All I have to do is say that any time, any place, and the whole thing is dead. For Mark. For Me. Oh, God. Father? Your Holiness.

Remove that Polish, whatever the opposite of joke is, from this poor unfortunate brain. And Father? I know I have sinned. Again, it was in a crude, disrespectful manner. But I shall sin no more. I shall never again, O Holiest of Fathers, refer to your Vatican Eminence as THE PEEP.

God must know I'm sincere, because the sun's sky-splitting afterglow is as glorious as I've ever seen. Wild pinks and oranges seem to be defending all that says day against the onslaught of dark. Actually, I can't believe there's still daylight after all that's happened. It's as if today has been predestined to be extended in time, as if it has drifted into a no-time, a no-space dimension.

I wonder if they are all thinking the same. That this morning, ten years ago, they were balancing the same coffee cups on the same knees or in the same midair. Do they always have their coffee like that? Quick stops. Fast talks. Fast coffee.

I better not have to organize any coffees up here. Up anywhere. The thought of those "I'll just have one more before I go" horrors inspecting my furniture, the bottoms of my saucers, and my medicine cabinets makes me crazed. Of course, I could always leave a little something in the bathroom. And not just in the guest bathroom so they'd think a careless child forgot to flush. All the bathrooms. Ah! The ultimate dirty trick. But maybe, as word got around, disbelievers would swarm just to see. Ugh! I'm gagging myself right out of that open touring car, as I accept the screams and waves from well-wishers lining the avenue on our way to the mansion.

"Over the Fourth, we'll hit the beaches. That's when you drop the big one." Brad Howell sounds like some map-pointing general briefing his men for Hiroshima. "The people would storm Albany if they knew the Wilcox deficit since he's been governor."

"Christ. They'd storm Albany for cock-sucking privileges at the Y. They'd burn it down for a billion," Max says. "Mention a billion and they'll think you're talking the whole country. Then hit them with wiping it out, making a surplus that makes a tax cut, and they'll come as they count."

"You'll go from Coney right to the tip of Montauk Point." Lanacola is already en route. As he talks, he keeps writing in a small loose-leaf book with a black plastic cover. "With Coney Island and Jones Beach so close, they'll be filled first. Anyway, it's too cold early in the morning for the Hamptons and Montauk." He looks up. "Latham's got a big chopper, hasn't he? I mean his company?"

"One?" Max's voice is incredulous. "That test-tube titan wouldn't be satisfied with one. Especially, now, as our finance chairman. Two choppers to go! On rye. Lotsa rye. And for God's sake, hold the water!"

Is it far to the Fourth? When is it? What is it now? I'm all hazy.

"When's Latham coming back?"

"I don't know."

"Mark? When's Latham due back?"

"I'm not sure. Amanda? When are they due back? When did Maria say they were coming home? Amanda?"

I hear you, Mark.

"Amanda? When did Maria say she'd be home?"

Again the feeling of distortion, but different. Now I'm into phasing out. I'm not with them anymore. They are like strangers. Why are they all pointing and jabbing at me for answers? Why me? Why do they know I know? I hear my disembodied voice answer. "Soon."

"When soon?"

Mark. Stop whittling away. Stop looking at me that way. I'm not focusing but I feel eyes. "I spoke to her . . . let's see when it was . . . it was yesterday. What was yesterday? No. It wasn't yesterday. It was Wednesday and she said Thursday. Obviously, not yesterday Thursday." I'll pull myself together. If I look straighter, I'll sound clearer. "A week from yesterday. That's right. That's next Thursday." I have the feeling if I don't stop now, there's a chance I might stop forever.

"He's got to get those fund raisers going. Big ones."

Would *you* get going. All of you. Now. *Get out! Go home! You do have homes, don't you?* I know I'm all right. Nobody's moving. I kept my screaming to me.

"Before we all get out of here . . ."

I did. Didn't I?

". . . I want to set up a meeting with Amanda."

Who's Amanda, Brad? Which Amanda?

"Tomorrow? At my office? My office in town?"

Aren't those questions answers?

"It'll be quiet. No phones. We can plan which shows. What stands to take. Sandy? See if something's available at the top of the week." Sandy makes more notes. His handwriting is so little. But, then again, it has to be to fit between those close blue lines.

Tomorrow? "Isn't tomorrow Saturday?" See, gang? I do know the days.

"That's all right," Mark says generously about me to me. "Brads wants to hit them hot. He's right."

"Ten? How's that? Is that good with you?" Brad asks.

Are those more answers? Obviously. He's continuing.

"Seven-four-seven Fifth Avenue. We're the twenty-ninth floor. I'll let the garage know you're coming so you won't have any problems. It's right on the side of the building."

Sandy closes his book and shakes it at the group. He seems about to present us with some great revelation from its scripture.

"*Good Morning America* could have the slot we want."
He nods his head in agreement with himself. "They were
supposed to do Princess Grace, but she has a kid graduat-
ing. Anyway, she canceled. It was for Monday or Tuesday.
I'll check." Again he scribbles.

Me? Replace Princess Grace? Dahling? I don't really
know. The notice is teddibly short. But then, she'd do it for
me. Has.

What? Is it really happening? Are they really going?
Thank goodness each "good-by" and every "really great
day" are all together. I don't know how much more togetherness I could handle before becoming unglued. Finally, locking the door, I'm not quite sure if it's I who am
locked in or they who are locked out.

I'm going to keep my eye on the red glow until it changes
again. If the next sound you hear is the sound you just
heard . . . ! Can anybody else hear a digital clock? The
minute is flashing away and the sound you hear is the
sound you heard. You must be wound up. Who asked you?

Getting out of bed in the dark, the thought hits me that
if I were struck blind, it wouldn't matter in this room. Like
now, I would unerringly make my way between the two
small ottomans, around the corner of the huge mattress,
past the bench holding the spread, with not so much as a
toe touching the overflowing heap. Avoiding the needlepoint wastebasket jutting from the corner of Mark's bureau,
I go through the low arch to my bathroom door. With the
tried touch of a two-story man, I achieve a one-try feel for
the knob.

Medicine cabinet open. Short, fat container in hand.
Push top down. Turn left. To be sure I'm right, I feel for
the crease bisecting the flat tranquilizer. Now, a vitamin C

for good measure. No confusing that giant. Faucet on. Let it cool while I find the glass. Always slowly for the glass. Too often it has slipped and fallen into the sink, onto the floor. That's when we're both smashed.

All set? Pills back! Water front! TENshun! RrrrreVERSE!

I was gone just long enough for the electric blanket to feel good. Where are those death-saving sermons I give Sara and Sonia?

> "*Never if the temperature's over fifty use electric . . .*"
> "*Never take vitamins. I don't care who . . .*"
> "*Never take any pills unless a doctor . . .*"
> "*Never a glass glass. Lucite is . . .*"

Amazing how Mark never wakes when I get up. Even more amazing how he doesn't snore with his face smothered in the pillow. That's the best part about you in bed, Mark. But then you don't smoke. You don't really drink. Your passages are clear. So are mine, Mark. Mark? Do you really think you'll be governor? Do you think the governor's headboard has a seal in the middle of it? The orange and blue seal with the Indian on one side of the scales, and the pilgrim on the other?

I can't wait for Christmas cards. "Governor and Mrs. . . . " I hope they don't have to be the same every year. It could be the seal again, only spruced up with holly. I'd like a Currier and Ives skating scene of Central Park, showing boys in a racing crouch, their high black skates laced tightly and their red wool scarves flying, while couples with arms entwined glide as if alone on the ice.

I reach across the bed and poke Mark's leg with my foot. Still asleep, he pulls it back with a jerk. I stretch some

more and do it again. "Mark? He turns and buries the other
side of his head. "Mark? Mark?" I flatten my foot against
his hip.

Slowly, he rolls on his back. "What time is it?"

What difference what time it is? What does the time
mean? Maybe I don't feel well. "It's ten to."

"Ten to what?" He's squeezing his eyes. I can't see
them, but I know.

"Ten to your own business. Ha. Ha."

"Are you crazy?"

"Yes. About you. It's almost three. 'There's no one in the
place except you and me.' Mark? Do I sing good Sinatra? I
mean, I wouldn't want to be a threat to him, but I would
like him to know there's someone else. Would you care,
Mark, if there were someone else?"

Maybe I'll tell Joe after he sets 'em up. Anyway, in these
wee small hours (stop worrying, Frank) Joe's got to be hep
to what I want. Why else would I be here?

I nuzzle close to Mark who's drifted back. Everything's
whirry. Do I really need him? Or do I need him, extra-
needingly, to want me? Or am I as my children might say,
"A little hyper, now, aren't you, Mom?" No. I'm not.

Softly, into his ear. "Mark? Do you really think you'll be
governor?" The word sounds like shiny boots, a bicycle
mustache, and lots of medals. He's reviewing her majesty's
troops on the first day of his new command. That's from the
movie of the same time when the map was either blue with
water, or pink with the empire.

"Amanda. Please sleep. I'm exhausted." It's the "I beg
you don't say any more" voice. It's the "I'm still, thank God,
not awake" voice—"Let me fall away before I am."

"You have all tomorrow. I, but these wee hours that
mock me with madness. Tomorrow, I have an engagement

in New York. An important appointment about my husband's appointment. Appointment by the people for the people . . . I'm one of the people."

"Amanda. You are crazy. For God's sake." He pulls away to the unopinionated comfort of his pillow.

"Mark. I'm sorry. Just one thing. Really just one. Do you love me, Mark?"

Muffled. "Of course."

" 'So set 'em up Joe. I got this little story I want you to know. . . .' "

10

As the door starts to close, Brad presses his palm against the elevator's rubber stripping. Angling my way out, I can't believe I'm facing the big gold letters HOWELL ASSOCIATES so soon again. It's only three days since Brad and I were here planning what's already over. Everything was so different then, so empty, so people-bare. I hate offices on weekends. You feel if you scream it's going to echo. I like it like now with all the hustle. I like a cast and crew and *"Action!"*

The receptionist and I smile to each other. She is long and decorative. She reminds me of all those boyish-bodied name-takers who go back to their emery boards after their bosses pass. I see the magazines are still rigidly rowed to reveal just their titles as they top the tables between the Naugahyde sofas. The tall plants, "watered, pruned and replaced by this fantastic service," are still here, spreading their life into dead corners.

But most important, live bodies are here, hurrying through corridors, pushing carts with mail and memos, Danish and doughnuts. By the way, everybody, just a little while ago, I was live on the *Good Morning America* show. Did any of you fast-passing people happen to see me on that show? Maybe you're passing too fast to recognize me. You were where? The subway? Whatever were you doing on the subway?

Again, Brad leads me around the perimeter of window offices, but this time the trip is punctuated by a nod here, a "hello" there. But no introductions. Not one. He stops at the high-piled desk outside his door.

"Good morning, Mr. Howell. And a special *Good Morning America* to you, Mrs. Weldon. You were wonderful. Just wonderful." Getting up, she reaches over the stacked clutter for my hand.

"Amanda. Meet Cathy Cormack. Cathy's not only both my arms, but *all* my girls. Life without Cathy . . . ah, even the thought makes me shudder." Brad's mock dramatics are probably more meant than mock.

I always wonder why people like Cathy don't write exposés about famous clients. Otherwise, their futures seem so futureless. Unless, of course, the idyll of the bachelor boss and the girl secretary sustains her. "Hello, Cathy. I'm very glad to know you." But she couldn't believe that, especially since there's just about no girl left to Cathy. Or is the bulk of her problem too much girl? Part of the misfortune is certainly due to all those peasant pleats around all that peasant waist.

"You also looked beautiful, Mrs. Weldon."

My one rotten thought followed by her nice words and that fatso has me into guilt. "Thank you, Cathy. Thank you so much." Perhaps if I vulnerable myself to her, it will help us both. "Cathy? Did I seem nervous to you? Did my voice seem strained or come across funny?" As I speak, Brad gathers some papers from Cathy's desk and goes into his office. He's answered enough me-questions while riding through Central Park, on our way back from ABC's Sixty-seventh Street studio.

"You didn't seem at all nervous. You looked relaxed, too, like you didn't even know the cameras were there. Did Mr. Howell tell you not to look into the cameras? That real actors never do? And you know he's right. When you're at the movies, just look at the stars never looking into the camera.

Actually, Brad did tell me that, but I never thought of it until now. "Yes. He did tell me, but it must've been my subconscious that remembered. I don't remember thinking about it on the show."

"You're a natural." She rubs her hands together excitedly. "But even naturals get nervous. Sometimes the most. Tell me. Were you really scared?"

I'm sorry she couldn't see me collapse in twenty-six-inch solid-state splendor. "Well, for your ears only, I was terrified. But the worst terror was before going on."

"Go on. Go on."

"What's really horrible is just sitting there, watching everyone else go on while you wait your turn. That's when the terror has time to build up. But the worst was when the director said I wouldn't go on for another half hour after he'd just told me it would only be another five minutes. I knew right then I'd never make it, that I'd be deathly sick. Once you're primed for one time and they say later, every minute's an ulcer."

"Oh. I can feel it."

Grabbing her stomach, Cathy looks hopelessly ill as she starts sublimating my pain. Whoa! Hold it, Cathy. Please

hold it, girl. Old girl. I'll tell her it only lasted a second.
"But the sick part only lasted a second. Really, only a second. Then I was great. Great." Go, Cathy. Go from sick to
smile. See my smile? Now let's see your smile. Good girl.

"You know, Mr. Howell works mostly with men," Cathy
said smilingly. "The few women he uses, I mean works with,
are much older. Working with you is a treat. Finally, someone *I* can relate to." Cathy reads and rereads my body as if
she's memorizing a speech. Across. Back. Across. Back. Whoa
again! Don't you know it yet? "Mrs. Weldon? Did the studio
tell you what to wear?"

I hate to disappoint Cathy. I know it would help her if I
said down to the reinforced toe of my tummy-control panty
hose. But I've done my act of contrition. "All they said was
that catch-nothing 'country casual.' But the studio's big
deals are hair and makeup. Especially makeup. In fact,
women arrive an hour earlier just for the Dorian Gray
treatment."

"What do they do first?" Cathy's leering interest is just
that.

"First comes the makeup buildup. The hair's always
after since there's usually some wisps on the face." Involuntarily, Cathy's fingers slide over her forehead. "Using oozing
sponges, they apply thick globs of pancake with all the
delicacy of boys whitewashing a picket fence."

Her face is a question mark. I gather *Tom Sawyer* was
never required reading in her section.

"Not being used to heavy layers of pancake, it feels
weird as they keep slopping it on. But suddenly, as it starts
to shadow, smooth, and deline, you see why they use it. But
just forget the lengths they go with the mascara." We both
feel our lashes. "No doubt I'm permanently stuck with
these match sticks."

Cathy gives makeup one final scan. Reverting to wardrobe, she stands for an even better look. "Would you believe, Mrs. Weldon, that I've been looking for just the sort of paisley skirt you're—"

"Last year's."

"My luck," she says without disappointment, having established that we obviously have the same taste. Tugging the slipping sweater back on her shoulders, she takes a deep breath. "They'll have to tear down and rebuild this building before they ever get the air conditioning right. Either it's freezing like today or it's breaking the outside heat record. You're smart to wear that jacket."

The sound of the buzzer saves me. Picking up the phone, Cathy nods into the receiver and hangs up. "The Howell of Howell Associates wants you in his office. See you later."

"Right. Thanks."

"Want any coffee? If yes, with what?" she calls.

Without turning. "Black. Please. Thank you."

The sunshine is surging through the corner windows, onto the leaves of the sprawling Ficus trees. If I had an office I would want it to be this high, with just this view of the Palisades, the George Washington Bridge, and the terraced tops of buildings along the way to the Hudson River. As glamorous as the outside view, the inside view is certainly incongruous for anybody but a Brad Howell.

There are no pictures of Brad with his world-famous clients thanking him for everything. And in most instances, "everything" would not be overstated. On every continent, in every important country, people are in power because of the Howell handiwork. Instead, Brad's office is a mass of memorabilia. Little things. Fun things to delight and amuse him. Prewar toys, like the windup ferris wheel with the tiny, sunsuited bears swinging in tiny tin seats; garish bicentennial hoopla but only if it includes the cracked bell;

137

and lots of snow globes, but only if they include Christmas, like the one he's just turned upside down. It's almost as if the one thing he doesn't want to think about at work is work.

Putting the globe right side up, the silent snow falls ever so gently over the low little houses and the high hill-top church. "Every Swiss village, even in summer, always seems gift wrapped for Christmas," Brad says. His voice is far away, somewhere near December. He looks soft and relaxed. His unshined brown shoes are on the edge of his desk. His ankles are crossed and his head is resting on inter-locking fingers while he leans back until the last flake falls. Now, facing me, he says, "I just hung up from talking with Blausteen. The guy with the red vest? The director?"

"And the beard? And the shaved head?"

"Remind me about your memory." He laughs. "They've already had a big response to your segment. Lanacola's confirmed it with the ABC switchboard. That's a pretty fair start, Amanda." He takes the globe and shakes it again. "I like you, Amanda. I like you a lot. Don't change." I hear him, but barely. Again, his voice is in December.

I like you too, Brad. Underneath, are you this nice? Do you know what I want to do now? More than anything? I want to take your skinny-framed glasses and clean them. Maybe the crystal of the snowball makes the smudges clearer. As I get up, I'm thinking how I'm not going to pull them off so they get stuck on an ear or poke you in the cheek. Good girl, Amanda. You did it good. See Brad? I'm still okay. Okay?

"Now you'll see the steeple from the people." I let my monogram show as I rub first one lens, then the other.

"That's going to stain your handkerchief," Brad says, as I redip a corner into my coffee.

"I don't care." I don't. I know if Mark wore glasses he'd carry those cleaners with him. On second thought, he wouldn't. The packet would bulge in his pocket. I can hear him now about my lipstick. "Yes. I love you. Love has nothing to do with it, Amanda. I don't happen to have my suits tailored for lipsticks."

Brad's chair springs forward as he lifts his feet from the desk. He stretches for his glasses. "Aha," he says widening his eyes over the rims. "Much the better to see you with, my dear. Thank you." He pushes them on properly. "My God! They must've been a good eighty/eighty. But now that I can see you so clearly, I want you to tell me what I am looking at. Whom I am looking at. Better still, at whom am I looking." Looking so young, so simple, so ingenuous, I can't believe he's done whatever all he's done.

His elbows are on the desk. His chin is resting in his hands. If I cleaned his glasses so well, why is he squinting at me? "First Amanda Weldon, tell me who *is* Amanda Weldon? That all the swains adore her. Is she what she wants to be? Does she think she's something different from the Amanda Weldon she sees? From the one she lets be seen?"

I want to answer him, but I don't want to rattle stupids. I want to tell trues, but I can't tell all trues. "Who am I when? When I'm alone? When I'm unencumbered? When I'm mistress of all I yell at?" I feel as though I'm swaying somewhere between a personnel form and an analyst's couch.

"I can create people from all kinds of people." Brad manipulates his hand like a magician. "I can create a real person from a fake person or an imposter from an impossible reality. It depends what's needed. What image the public doesn't know it wants. The creation's not tough. It's guessing the public that's tough. I can't write off the Edsel and bring out the Mustang. I've only got one shot. Somehow, looking at you, I think they want you. Muted or magnified, I think they'll buy you."

Ordinarily all my years with Mark would make me charge at the word "buy." Don't ask me why, but when I hear it from Brad it doesn't make me feel like some carload of soybean futures.

"Amanda, you've got something for every one of them. I don't give a damn if she's a suburban communicant to a tennis court or a motel. Or the new Ms. with electroshock hair."

"Kind of a rat-pack den mother. I like it. I like it." I like it a lot.

"Since you know you so well, the image will come alive fast. And as I said last Saturday, once they're into you a little, they'll want more. Immediately." Brad's words are tight and close together. He doesn't pause. When does he think? "But just remember, it's the blots they want to see too. Not just the escutcheon. It's the flaws in the lady that enable them to be the lady. Then, as night unto day, your strengths become theirs. And once that idiotic syllogism gets them, you've got them. Understand?"

"I've been there."

"Who hasn't? But now it's you who's the high priestess out there. It's your lowdown on your frictions back home, on God's little acre, that's going to make every car pooler content. They'll weep endless words for you. They'll thank God for the life-style you've made them reject without their ever realizing they could never come near it. They'll commiserate at the horrid responsibility of running so large a home, supervising so many servants. They'll share the panic of private jets and yawn at the dreary details of dais dinners with world leaders. Oh, what a sympathy vote. And it's not really because they're sorry. It's that they are thrilled the book's not the cover."

I love the energy in Brad's voice. He enjoys his mind, his words. Me too. And while he talks, all during his plans, he doodles stars on a long yellow pad. Sometimes he makes them without even looking. At this point, he's drawn so many they're starting to collide in not enough sky.

Suddenly he breaks into a laugh. "What'll really grab them is if you publicly confide your longtime hang-up to make up dirty Latin-sounding names for those garden club stiffs who love cutting people like you for not knowing this-and-that-plant."

"I am so crazy for that idea I wish it were tomorrow."

Brad crumples the first starry night and throws it into the basket. Starting smack in the middle of a new page, he begins again. I must look up the significance of celestial scribbles. Wow! Especially that one with the eyes and nose in it. I'd like to say it's heaven, but he might hate me forever.

"Actually, Amanda, you emerge as a kind of mixture of feminist and femininity."

"Why has the word feminist become so masculine?"

He leaves his yellow sky. "The wrong women push it. You're the real blend of PTA and ERA. The believable both whose following from both could be enormous. And the bigger it gets, the more activist asses and country club asses will try to kiss yours. Not that they love you or want Mark to win. Their kisses are strictly precautionary. They live by the fear of what might be. Who might be. 'Fear *Omnia Vincit.*' The motto of the middle mind."

I'm thinking of Boop and Muffie. Activists after the fact. Of all the Boops and Muffies, driven by that negative force, the terror of not being counted as they helplessly organize "Women for Weldon." I wonder who'll first acknowledge Mark's candidacy is only Mark's money. Otherwise, of course, their husb—

"Amanda. You were a playwright. A good one. You gave it up. Why?"

"I don't know. Why?"

"You were sick of cause crusades. Exit anger. Enter marriage and children. Now you're sick of years of silence, years of no time for you. But don't think those years were unproductive. Those years have fashioned that mind with enough material to dress as many theaters as you would want to fill. So, exit silence. Reenter anger. Just make sure this new anger doesn't use you. Anger's an atom. It destroys and creates. With you it must create."

"Should I demand my name above the title?" I smile at Brad. "First you tell me I'm great as me. Then you tell me I'm really a different me. Will the real me please try and stay in tune. *Mi! Mi! Mi! Do-re-mimimimi!*"

Brad is giving me one of those why-don't-you-know-what-I-know looks. I guess there's nothing more frustrating than not getting across the obvious. "What I'm trying to do," Brad continues slowly, "is try and extract the best you. What I see, what I want to stop, what I guess I'm saying badly is that you seem to be suffering from you instead of exhilarating in you. You need success in you."

I need you in me, Brad, but that's one of the trues I can't tell you. I can't ask you if you would be nice in me. Close and warm and patient. Cozy and fingering and kissing. I'm thinking about your bed and if it's made now. If you leave a note for the maid to change the sheets after you've been with a girl. Are there a lot of girls? Are you in love now? Have you had a homosexual experience?

"Amanda, have you seen the television show *In Your Own Right?* About successful men married to successful women and vice versa?"

"No." But more important, Brad, if you fell asleep with your glasses on, I'd take them off and clean them for the morning. Why do I picture your falling asleep reading rather than making love? Ah! That proves your theory and mine. I need success and you in me. Brad? Did you like *Love Story?* I wanted desperately to go to Radcliffe, but my mother thought it was too far away. Not that she ever came to Poughkeepsie.

"It illustrates how successfully married people can independently pursue careers without identity loss, role reversal, or any of those other out-of-order signs people hang on marriages. The basic trouble with marriage is marriage."

If Mark said what Brad just said it would have to come from somebody else. Even if he originated it, he would quote somebody. That's sad. It makes me sorry. Sorry or guilty? Guilty or angry? Angry at whom? Mark? Me?

Maybe that anger will make me a great playwright. Didn't the war produce penicillin? Sadly, I can see it all. Right after the final curtain, I'll be reluctantly dragged to the stage by my grateful cast. Then 'midst strewn bouquets and lone roses, I'll curtsy deeply and scatter hand-blown kisses into the swelling chant of "Author! Author!" Then the real-life players, those ingrates of my lean and fattening years, will drag me from the stage to the landmark weeping willow, weeping away, far away, in the middle of the village green.

Brad, I'm still tuned into you about that TV show, but you started me thinking of me. I'll be right out of me. I just want to witness my successful opening night because it closes with my death—dealt by loving hands at home, neighbors, hell-wishers.

Hey! Hold it, neighbors! Stop! That play wasn't about you. You're making a terrible mistake. Worse. You're making a shocking admission. The play had nothing to do with you. Craig! Stop looping that knot. You have to conserve that beautiful branch. What would your Road Review Board say when they rode and reviewed the merits of a broken branch against a broken neck? You know you'd lose. It's always the branch that bears the laurels, dumbbell. And what about you, big little Whitethorn? Kick that stool away. Now! Too late, later. The boy in the play who fucked the tavern tart wasn't you. What makes you think . . .? And Muffie? The tavern tart wasn't you. What makes *you* think . . .?

And you, Father. Father? Stop pacing and mumbling into your little book. Go away and stay away. Don't just come around for my soul. What about my body? Aren't you supposed to keep them together? Why do you always separate them? That's the trouble with you. None of you work with what is. You work for the life that isn't. The one in the womb. Or the one on the way to the hereafter. Why do the nonliving get the right to life? What about us live ones?

"Amanda? Are you still with me?" Brad cups his hand, microphone-style, to his mouth. "Come in, Amanda."

"I was just thinking about what you said. You're right. I am angry. I'm really angry."

"But that's only half of it, Amanda. The flip side is making it work *for* you."

The abrupt sound of the buzzer is intrusive. "Put him on," Brad says. While holding the phone and waiting, he smiles and starts to tell me something, but the other end is on too fast. "Well? What did *you* think?" Brad asks. His brow wrinkles as he listens. "No. That's definitely something I think you should say." He presses the earpiece even closer to his ear. "No. That wasn't at all unusual. Actually, you'll discover it's much more typical than not. Someone's always late, or has a plane to catch, or another appointment. It doesn't take much. True. But in this business, you've got to be flexible. Where did you say you went again?"

Brad's tone is like the parent to the selfish child. What he's really saying is, "Yes. You did tell me, but it was so relatively unimportant to what I wanted you to do, that I forgot." Sonia and Sara have made me an expert on that particular variety of impatience.

Brad's eyes flash on mine and just as quickly move away. But in that flash I saw it. I don't know how or why but I caught it. Extracting a supersharp Black Wing pencil from the crowded cup, I print my message in the remaining bits of yellow sky. "I KNOW WHO IT IS. I SWEAR I DON'T CARE."

He reads it and looks up. He keeps looking at me as he talks. "Yes. Really great. No. Not one thing in particular. Sort of all the particulars in one."

I add four more letters. I put one letter in the center pentagon of each of the biggest stars. First letter *M*. Second letter *A*. Third letter *R*. Fourth letter *K*.

"Well, Mark, if you're sure about my telling her, I will." Brad looks at me. "Anyway, I'll try and get a tape so you can see it. And I'll get the transcript over today. At least you can read what was said. You can be very proud. Yes. Leave it to me. I'll know how. Right. What did you say the name was again? She will? Good. Good, Mark. Right. Good. Good-by."

Brad squeezes my shoulder as he walks to the cabinet

on the other side of his office. Not only do the high folding doors open to two large TV screens, but to a mirror-backed bar that could pass for professional.

"It's not an arsenal," he says, catching my surprise. "It's more like a gym. Sort of a limbering and loosening up place for tight campaign contributors. I'll take it to parallel bars anytime. How about a Bloody Mark?" Listening to what he just said, Brad shakes his head in a double take and can't stop laughing. "Amanda. As God is my judge, that just slipped out."

"I love it. But isn't it a little early?"

"That's when it's fun. Only alcoholics stay sober until noon. That's how they know they're not alcoholics." Brad drops some ice-maker cubes into two thin-stemmed bubble glasses.

"Spicy for me, please. Do you use lemon?"

"Do you like it with lemon?"

"I like it like you do."

"I hate that kind of question answered by that kind of answer. Why can't you say, 'No lemon'? Lesson number one. Honesty." I watch him squeeze lots of lesson number one into both our glasses.

"I'm glad you include the pits in the course." I sink into the corner of the soft leather sofa and watch as he opens the little refrigerator. Removing two leafless stalks of celery, he holds them under the faucet before putting them into the glasses. With a tiny cocktail napkin covering his wrist, he bows and hands me the glass. "In case you're concerned, madam, let me assure you that there is no extra charge for the pits."

God. He's nice. So easy. So unfascinated with himself. "Brad?"

He takes a big swallow and shakes his head at the spiciness. "Oh. I almost forgot. Mark thought you'd want to know the Parkhursts called to say you were wonderful."

"Mark must be kidding. The real joke is he isn't. By the way, why didn't Mark watch?"

"He thought you were replaced or displaced or I don't know what when you weren't on schedule, so he tuned off."

"He'd be more flattering to Amtrak. Brad? Have you ever been married?"

"Why do people always say 'ever' as if your life is already lived? But without further detour, no. It's all quite simple, really. I'm in love with my mother, who's in love with my sister. My sister Lavinia. Not Lascivia, as most people tend to believe."

"I guess you'll be just as direct with this one. Is there anyone now?"

He comes and sits by me on the sofa, but on the very edge. His look is thoughtful. "Not so anyone would notice." His tone is overly confidential. He moves his head closer to me. "Every morning before I leave for work, I push her back in the wall with the bed."

"You're crazy."

"You bet. It's the only thing that keeps me sane."

"I'd love to see an old Abbott and Costello with you."

"Tough to see a new one."

"Do you hurt laughing when people run in and out of bathhouse doors bumping into people they're avoiding?" He's laughing now. I raise what's left in my glass. "T'us! To hell with the enemy. That girl in the wall."

11

Brad waves good-bye from the taxi as it starts its broken field run through the downtown traffic. I like being with Brad. He's a warm climate where everything grows, so different from the cool indifference I'm too used to.

I would like to buy him something. Something special. I remember Hammacher Schlemmer always has those snow globes in their Christmas catalog. What's a mere six months ago? Maybe there's a new shipment for people to give people if they're going to Peru. Because in summertime it's wintertime there. Right? Right. God, I hate the cold weather. Why can't it always be like today? Even the smell on Fifty-sixth Street and Fifth Avenue smells good.

One thing I'll never understand is why all these people are always going in and out of Steuben. Don't they know glass should be delicate? Doesn't even the word sound fragile? People who buy it must be desperate to serve financial statements along with the vintage. I even read someone bought a vase—a vase?—yes, a vase, and of course a thick one, for a thicker (yes, I'm lisping) ninety-five thousand dollars. A South American. Maybe he took it to Lima with the snow globes.

Wow, the coins in that fountain are shiny. Who do you suppose takes them home each night and what do you think the take is? It would be good if that black blind man who's always in front of Tiffany's trained his dog to push them to a neutral corner so he could fish them out. Of course, he'd work in the dark. And, yes, his cup would—

God. There he is. Sandwich sign and all, for all to see

he's blind and deaf. Why is that German shepherd always lying down? Business should be good today. A lot of folk are out. In all the times I've passed him, I have never given him anything. He gives me the creeps. I don't even like to look near him. The only street people I've ever given to are the Salvation Army Santas. I love their lopsided beards and hearty yells of "Merry Christmas." I don't like the Salvation Army women, though, with their black pioneer bonnets and tambourines. They're too uncheery for Christmas.

"Giving to beggars only encourages their begging and discourages their learning." From Mother's lips to child's ear. I think the only guilt she ever spared me was the giving-to-beggar-guilt which was also reinforced by her mother, who told me about the legless man on the rolling dolly who she swore got up and walked away after she gave him a dollar. He might have walked away. That part could be true. But it was never my grandmother's dollar that gave him the legs.

I love to watch the very rich getting out of limousines, like this woman now, sliding across the back seat of her special-body Lincoln. I like that she's young and expensively dressed. It's crazy how the rich clothes in *Vogue* are modeled by girls in their twenties, yet bought by women who need forty more years to afford them.

I like the way she's waiting for the chauffeur to open the door. I'd have been in the store before he'd been out of the car. She has a European poise. It's different. She's not embarrassed. She's not flaunting. She's accustomed. She speaks quickly as the chauffeur walks with her, past the blind man, to the large, revolving door. As she speaks, he nods and nods and nods. So many instructions?

Government drivers never wear livery. The President's driver and that dark-suited security man next to him don't even wear hats. With their close-cut hair, motionless faces, and straight-ahead eyes, they look like a brace of Thorazine addicts. I'm sure the governor must have a special limousine. He needs those special extra seats for those meetings between meetings. I wonder what the license plate is. Just N Y or just the number 1? I think I'll make it into an apple. I hope it doesn't always stay in Albany. But there must be one for here, too, but not with the same license. Although, as guv, he could take that license. Right? Right. In fact, my dear, you haven't been wrong all day.

Should I go into Tiffany and spell it out for Brad? Buy him something too much? I'll bet the only too much gifts he gets are *after* the junta. What about a before bonus for nothing? Not a payoff. An "I like you."

I wonder how many young, hand-squeezing couples that salesman tells, "It's top quality. Yes, you can get a bigger stone for less money, but not Tiffany quality. It's D flawless." In my class "D" wasn't so good. He hands them his loupe. Each takes a turn squinting into the tubular monocle. "See the clarity? Not an imperfection anywhere." She doesn't want the high-pronged setting sized to fit. "I want to wear it out." She's torn. But the salesman persuades her. "If you don't leave it you'll lose it." Although they've just bought a Tiffany diamond and they're so much in love, they walk away disappointed.

It's always the old Brooks Brother whose eyes press through the constantly chamoised vitrines for "something she can wear on a suit," completely unaware pins have passed. It's still the circle of rubies or the floral spray they have gift boxed. I see them safety-deposit boxed, lying lifeless, uninsured, waiting for reincarnation.

Do you think a calligrapher at two dollars and fifty cents an envelope writes the governor's invitations? Waste!

Waste! *Aux armes, citoyens!* I'm sure they never send re-
minders. Once is a command. Thick vellum? Thin vellum?
Script or Bodoni bold? Embossed or engraved seal? But no
stamp. It's a free ride on the pony express. How lucky can
we be? Birthday party invitations too? Never. That's what
they'd get us on. Right? Right. But again, my dear . . .

How many of you know that stationery makes the most
money of any department in the store? It's part of the incidental intelligence I needed with new fellas. Brad, I also
know how the martini got its name.

"It used to be Tiffany never carried anything they
didn't make. Now they carry anything." Guess who says
that dismissingly? And guess who still places her jewelry
piece by piece, on the vanilla velvet insides of the blue "old
Tiffany leather boxes, when Tiffany really cared. Everything changed after the war." Everything in my parents'
existence seemed bisected by World War II. The only war.
The most calamitous war. The war when their friends got
killed. Successive wars existed, but not for them.

Their war was in the forties when they were young and
wanted to be carefree-young. It spoiled that. Daddy in
naval intelligence. Mother hating Washington. And "How
selfish Daddy was. He wanted to see action. What did he
want me to see? A flag-draped coffin?"

Cuff links? Brad would never take the time. Gold stays?
He'd never remember to take them out. Slowly, I edge
along the glass. Nobody is asking me if I want help. I always have the feeling there's something a little too high
class about these summer-jobbed salespeople, especially if
one rates their arrogance against their ignorance: this
dying breed of vacation debs and their dance-card coun-
terparts, talking together, abrupt at any intrusion. Like the
way that vested-suit prick just said, "Sterling is a second-

floor item." Does he really feel in, helping her out like that?

"All of Elsa Peretti's things, and they're almost *all* sterling, are on this floor." I'm talking very loudly, snidely. He turns his head, much too bored for a complete body swing. "Yes." I continue, glaring. "I'm talking to you." His surprise becomes scrutiny. He's judging. I see the waves transmitting that I could know his family. He turns completely but doesn't move forward. He thinks I shall. I'm staying put, prick! You move. He moves. The lips part. "The second floor has always—" I shake my head, do a one eighty on the open mouth, and cross the aisle to another counter.

Watches. Good. Too good? No. His crystal is so scratched and the dial is so faceless. I just hope it's not anything sentimental. I hope it's an "I never get around to buying myself anything."

"Would you like help, madam?"

I don't even have to look to know he's older, nicer, here for years. "Not yet, but I hope soon. Thank you."

"Not at all."

Past the pocket watches, the chronographs, and the Cartier clones with their Roman dials and sapphire stems. Stopping, I point to the case and not to the salesman. He looks up questioningly as he reaches into the display.

"No. The one to the left."

He hands me the watch without mentioning price. Already a plus. I show him my own Rolex. Now I can avoid any sell.

"Then you know." No more. How nice.

I like the stainless steel for Brad. Also, it's as expensive as I should go without going gone. I hand it back. "Will you please set it and gift wrap it?"

"Certainly. Is this a charge?" he asks, removing the thin-stringed price tag.

My God, no. "No."

"Do you wish to enclose a card?"

"No. Thank you."

He turns towards the big round clock high above the double elevators, the ones that ride to sterling, as he puts today into motion. Then with a coin, he tap-tap-taps on the counter. Immediately, a smocked, back-room Tiffany clerk whips the watch to an even farther-back-room Tiffany wrapper who will fold just the right amount of tissue, before pulling just the right size box that she'll tie with the perfect length of satin ribbon.

Flipping past earlier sales in his book, he now documents my purchase. I like his pointing where to sign, since every store has its "X" somewhere else. When salespeople just stand there, with their books outstretched, I feel challenged to sign fast, to show them my credit card is mine.

"It will be a few minutes." He smiles as he rips away triplicate.

I once had pearls restrung here. There's a lady on the mezzanine who's spent her life tying knots between pearls. And you have to sit there while she threads and ties, threads and ties. "It's for your protection as well as for ours, dear. We want you to see we don't change any of your pearls." Luckily, stomachers were out then. Lucky, pearls are out now. Their string was long enough, even long before Matthew and the swine routine.

"Would you like a small shopping bag?" he asks as the smocked drone returns with the package.

When will I give it to him? Why will I give it to him? Should I write a card? What if he doesn't take it? Why do the words "out of proportion" come into my head? It isn't. I'm rich. I'm very rich. He knows that. Not money-out-of-proportion, but relationship-out?

Why am I forcing me to feel this? Relax, wreck. Float through those layers of biofeedback. Enjoy. Have you really become a creature of your husband's acceptance? Is that what you're always fighting against? Or is it for? And what about identity? Is it easier when he accepts you? Or easier when you think you've earned it because he doesn't?

Stop lurking, Mark. Why is my response conditioned to think Mark when I look at the box in my purse? Why? Hey! Sartre, Buber, Castaneda, Chomsky—clue me in. Don't bother. I've bothered with you so I know you can't. Mark? You clue me in. I need your feedback, Mark. Put me on the super highway to me.

Where the hell are you, Mark? Time-study man. Television segment time-study man. You said you would be at the apartment by six. It's seven. The ice in the bucket is probably stuck together, all stuck into one misshapen ball. I even shined the bucket, Mark.

I love this apartment, Mark. Even though your deal was unfair, I love it. It was your concession, your "ridiculous indulgence of my insecurity" for moving forty miles into what you promised would be dreamland. A land that would protect me from muggers, murderers, and those "gun-cocked, cock-cocked cooneroonies." *And people, Mark. People who talk, Mark.*

Whoever sold exurbia as paradise should be sentenced for land swindle. And as he sold, so shall he be raped. Sentence? Lifetime imprisonment. Where else? Paradise.

Ex.ur.bia (eks-ur'-bi-a), n. 1. Rural hinterlands; differentiating itself from suburbia by distances and lack of civilization. 2. Sparsely populated pastureland on the outskirts of the brain. Wow! That's the real devil in you, Mr. Webster. Would you like me to give it to you unabridged? How many volumes am I allowed?

Sitting here, stupidly, angrily, I'm unable to concentrate on the paper or the television. I'm thinking instead of the times I've fucked in this beige and orange library, in the coral and white bedroom, in the yellow-yellow living room. The kitchen's too small. And I've fucked much, much, much, much more with others than with you, Mark. I didn't plan it that way. You set the pace by not having one. And you know, they were all really crazy about me. That's really what I was telling you when I fucked them. One of them, Alex, introduced me to Soho. His loft was next to Radner's. Radner couldn't even get into a gallery then. Now he's at MOMA, Mark. And one of his canvases that we own, one you've never even asked about, is worth over twenty thousand dollars.

And Alex, my friend, is having his first one-man show next week. I don't think you would like him, though. Too messy-arty. But you would like Paul, Mark. Paul was graduated from the Yale School of Music. And right tonight his musical is playing at the American Place Theater. It's in its second week of previews, and word of mouth has it a hit. I don't fuck old fuckees, Mark, but we keep in the other kind of touch. Paul told me if it's a hit, it's coming to Broadway.

Mark? Do you know Alex lives near us? In paradise? Wrong, Amanda. You mean escapes near us. He's weekends. Aha! Now you've got it, girl. A place for everything and everything in its place. Snakes eat mosquitoes. Right? Please! Let's not start that again. Anyway, we've unearthed exurbia's reason for being. Weekend head clearing. Just don't even confuse it with head filling. Forget the unabridged. We got the whole thing here in one line. Got the whole thing—

"Amanda? Amanda? You home? Amanda?"

You see the lights, dummy. "I'm in here, Mark," I call, walking out of here.

"I'm late. I know. It's their fault. I'm sorry," he says, not sorry.

I stand frozen as Mark, Sandy, Max, Darcy, and whoever she is come in like they're supposed to be coming in. "Did they turn off Con Ed where you were?" No one answers. How can anyone answer? They're too busy piling their shit on the fifty-dollar fabric that covers the foyer bench.

"Amanda. This is Ann Mazurski. Ann, my wife, Amanda."

Did you hear the one about . . . "So nice to know you, Ann."

Why isn't Brad here? What kind of job did he do to get her already? And how did he do it? Actually, she's attractive. I don't know why I expect people in government to look poor. Maybe because most of them do. But I like her looks. Maybe because she looks a little like me. Although her hair is browner and she's not quite as tall, she has my same kind of build, yet she's way off on her browns and beiges. But I still don't understand. Why the fuck are they all here?

"We're celebrating," Max says uncannily, surpassing Mach anything in his jet scan of my brain. "Mazurski believes it's better to join. She's sick of promises."

Mazurski smiles. She offers to help me with drinks. She has a subtle femininity, an undemanding decor. I can see her wielding a quiet kind of power. The kind that acts only after careful reviewing, only after she's considered all counties. And when or if she gets married, it will be from making up her mind, never from falling in love.

I guess she must believe in Mark. She must think he's

hot. She's here. I wonder what she'll want when it's down to the nitty-gritty, or as Max would say, the "nut cutting." Owwww! Whatever, it's sure to be something she'll demand more than something anyone'll offer.

"With Robinson's hat in the ring, it's a different ball game," Lanacola says, wiping his palms on his pants pockets. "Robinson's also from upstate. And as minority leader, he commands a lot of territory."

"First things from the beginning," Darcy says, leaning against the antiqued-orange desk, addressing the upturned kingmakers. "Any elected anybody with a voting record is always hostage to that voting record." His words are sure and strong and time-proven. He looks around to be certain we're all with him. "And nobody's ever voted all good. No matter what Robinson promises for the future, he's already half hung by his past."

Mazurski pushes her tinted glasses from her hair to her nose, brushing the wayward wisps from her forehead. The furrows between her eyes deepen as she shakes her finger into the group. "Never once did Robinson use his old White House buddy to boost this city's bankroll when the city seemed finished. And not once did he back the governor when the governor tried to help. First he vetoed the bridge bonds and then he put the flaps on emergency financing. And take my word, once you go out to lunch on this town, there's no coming back for dinner."

Max sighs a deep, it's all so obvious, sigh. "Why are we wasting time? We're all agreed. You can't fuck the city and find love! Next."

Mark looks at Mazurski, then at Max. He seems embarrassed. He looks back at Mazurski. "Max may not be delicate, but he's direct."

"Thanks for explaining my charm, Marcus. I wish you had some to explain."

"As George Bernard Shaw said, 'What really flatters a man is that you think him worth flattering.' And I can always count on you, Max, for the instant buildup." Mark's smile is so genuine he appears convinced Max meant to make a joke.

"My favorite Shaw is naturally political," Mazurski says confidently. "'Democracy substitutes election by the incompetent many for appointment by the corrupt few.'"

"What is this?" Max asks, flicking no tobacco from his tongue. "Some high-school scrimmage between man and superman? If it is, fuck. I've got more important things to do. Like fuck."

The laughs are nervous. Even calling home would be better than sitting here. Shutting the bedroom door, I dial the house. The great house. The one in paradise.

Two voices, on two extensions high and shrill, are going at once. It doesn't take long for the inevitable.

"Shut up!"

"No. You shut up."

"I was on first."

"Get off. Creep. Nurd!"

"Double nurd. You get off!"

I hold the receiver at arm's length. Is it really possible that with the receiver even farther away, the voices are even louder? Not only possible, but happening. Putting the mouthpiece to my lips, I start to blast through those tiny, dainty holes, but instead I decide to slam them both out of earshot.

Although they are out of sound, they're sadly not out of sight. I see it all. They're meeting in the upstairs hall, having run from their extensions. Quickly, they're talking strategy about their callback. They know "Mom is really furious." They're deciding what to say and who's going to be the first to say it. When they call this time, they'll both be hugging the same phone. This time they're allies. In fact, their allegiance of fear is dialing this number this very second.

Rrrrrinnng.

"Hi, Mom?"

One is talking. One is breathing. Actually, I guess both are breathing. "No. It's not Mom. It's the head of Child Abuse. And I don't blame you for calling. I hear your mother not only uses foul language, but is going to beat the living shit out of you."

"I made honors, Mom." The voice is sweet, expectant, palliating.

"It's because Daddy's rich. 'Twas ever thus. 'The appointment of the corrupt few.' Shaw, you know."

"Mom?" The amount of syllables placed on those three letters obviates her adding that perhaps I'm a little kookalooka.

"I told you. I'm not—"

"Mom. I'm sorry. Sonia's sorry, too. But I have something important to tell you. Guess what? Elizabeth and me made honors."

"Are you and Elizabeth both in an English-speaking school? Elizabeth and *me*? Me made honors? Is that how they say it?"

"Only seven of us, in the three sections put together, made it. Here's Sonia, Mom. Sonia? Take it. Talk."

I feel the push. No pull from Sonia. Just Sara's push. Poor Sonia. Obviously, she doesn't even have honors to pave the way. She must really dread talking to me. Or as we say in the eloquent upper case of Amawalk Country Day, to "I."

"Hi. Mom. I'm sorry, too. Our grades aren't all in so I'm not sure about honors. I have a feeling Mrs. Foster might give me a C or C plus in math. If that nurd does, it's going to keep me off. Everybody hates her. She's not coming back next year."

Who cares for honors when you can say all that without an inhale. We must think in terms of opera. I wonder when Sonia learned Mrs. Foster was definitely giving her a C.

"My dear Sonia. If Mrs. Foster did that to you with merit, of course she won't be reappointed next year. She hasn't made it among 'the corrupt few.'"

"Mom?" There it is again. All those syllables.

"Didn't your sister tell you that I'm not Mom. I'm the lady from Child Abuse?" I can just see Sara's big, wonderful eyes rolling around at Sonia while pointing to the phone. I'll bet it's not easy to control the giggles until they get off. I want to giggle with them. I haven't giggled in so long. "Seriously, sweetheart. All I want to say to you both is that I hate it when you two argue when I call."

"We know. We're—"

"I know. Sorry." And I also know you're children, which none of us ever seems to know. "Tell that other monster that I love her equally with the other half of the hate I have in my heart." I hear her tell her while I'm still on. We all laugh. God! Is that the front door opening?

"Amanda?"

"Mark?" As I go out of the bedroom, I can't believe they're all actually going out of the door, each reclaiming his shit from my fabric. I not only press for their elevator, but hold it for them. "It's here! Hail, gang. It's here." A handshake. A hug. An air kiss. Max's tongue and they're gone.

Mark returns to the library and starts to write. He writes hurriedly. It's his get-it-down-before-I-forget writing.

"Want a refresher?" I ask.

"No. No. Mine's still a virgin. It was a good meeting. Don't you think?" No pause. "She'll be good. Don't you think?" No pause. "And Robinson, just like Shakespeare's Roman fool, will die on his own sword."

Darcy is too nothing for Mark to credit.

"Mark? I still don't see why they were all here. Just to decide Robinson isn't a factor or to see if Mazurski is?"

"Both. Sort of." He doesn't stop writing. "It doesn't matter."

"What does matter is that I don't matter enough for you to explain." Turning my back on his, I walk to a drink.

I hear the chair move. "Good Lord, Amanda. Dilute that drink. That's just pure neutral grain spirits."

"For a first cousin to Carry Nation, you sound more like a distiller, Mark. Don't worry. The ice'll poison the proof, especially this nice, holy ice. I wonder if the bagman from Lipton's got the patent for the flow-through cube?"

"Amanda. You've got the damnedest mind."

"So do you, Mark."

"We're going to need our minds, Amanda. We've got a lot of people to convince, almost a million in Westchester County alone."

That's what I mean about your mind, Mark. It can't help spoutin' that sweet talk. "No. I did not know that. Did you know there are forty-two hundred species of plant life in Westchester County?"

Mark looks startled. Maybe even stunned. "That's exactly what I mean about your mind, Amanda. Why would you remember that? How would you even know it?"

"I read it in *The New Yorker*. I collect trivia. You never can tell when you'll have to use it. Do you remember when I used to use it?"

Mark smiles. "The martini! Named for the man who invented the gun whose kick was as strong as his concoction of gin and vermouth." He shakes his head. "*Plus que ça change.*"

"Is that Shaw in French?"

"What?" Now *he's* into all those syllables.

"Mark? Where were your eyes this morning when twenty-three percent of viewing America saw me say how wonderful you are?"

At this moment, Mark looks as wrested from himself as I've ever seen him. Too bad he hasn't any people's mannerisms to ease his discomfort. Clear your throat, Mark. Go ahem. Crack your knuckles. Scratch! Itch! Pick! Are you some kind of weirdo? Draw stars!

"I'm sorry, Amanda. When you weren't on time, I thought they'd canceled you, especially since you were there on a cancellation. I know it doesn't sound logical, but it seemed so this morning. I'm sorry."

"Sorry you missed it? Sorry I'm upset? Sorry to have to explain? Why didn't you tune to your *Wall Street Journal* and wait at your office? Where else was so important?" Taking a long, piercing swallow I close my eyes on some tears while the swallow travels and burns. This may just be the best drink I ever made.

"I had an aberration, Amanda. I don't know television. I thought their timing was better. But I see it's like mine. I'm dumb about a lot of things, Amanda. Remember how you used to call me 'gappy'?"

He's trying to catch hold, advance by retreating to the old woo bit, the old self-depreciation pitch. But so far, Mark, your pitch is low and outside. But please, Mark, try again.

"Mark? Maybe we should try and fill in some of those gaps, especially some between us."

He looks bewildered. "Tell me one couple who's got more going for them than we do. Tell me one wife who's in on more than you are. Included in more or needed more. Name anyone."

"I want to be more like a mate, Mark. A mate mate. Not a running mate. You know?" He doesn't.

"I don't. Not really."

The ice is hitting my nose and not because there's too much ice in the glass. It's all that's left. I've drained all the neutral grain spirits. Disappear, Mark. I'm going back for more. Well, since you're not disappearing, at least disapprove. Why aren't you saying anything? Is nothing always better than encounter?

"Mark? I love you. I want to love you."

"Amanda. What are you trying to get into? You're being absurd. I love you."

"Would you care if other people made love to me?"

"You're better than that question."

"Good escape, Mark." Maybe he's right. Why should he fight for something he's convinced he can't lose?

"We've got a big goal ahead of us, Amanda. And I mean 'we.' You're as important as I to me."

At least public schools grammared him good.

"Amanda? Didn't we discuss about political wives not being ornaments anymore?"

"Don't confuse me with some ERA lobby, Mark. When I wanted to go back to work, didn't you call married women's careers time-filling hobbies? Don't narrow your eyes. You did, Mark."

"That was long ago, Amanda, and you've taken it completely out of context. I need you, Amanda. I couldn't make it alone."

"Say it straight, Mark. Make what? Make life or make Albany?"

"Whatever you say." Nothing *is* better.

"Mark? Are you an illusion? Did I fall in love with an illusion? Am I another victim of what never is? Do you see me as another Emma Bovary? Do you know you can make the name 'Mame' out of 'Emma'? You know the same man wrote *Dolly* and *Mame?*

You coaxed the blues right out of the horn, Maaaaaaaame.

I guess you didn't get my lyric. God, I'm pissed! "Mark? You know Latham's a lush, don't you?" I try not to sound too thick. "The worst kind of lush. The worst kind of white goods lush. Gin! Mark? Do you know when a quickie before dinner's a martini, the honeymoon's over? That's not like my old martini trivia, though. You know what I mean? . . .

Mean to me—why must you be mean to me? . . .

"We need Latham, Amanda," Mark says quietly. I watch Mark watching the air, fixing on Latham's whirly-bird chop-chop-chopping his way to stardom. My visibility may not be a hundred, but there's enough clearance for that "red-red-robin, to go bob-bobbin'-along—along."

"And when we don't need Latham anymore, will we shoot him?"

"Amanda!"

"Mark!" Why don't you hit me? Or kiss me? Or smash my drink and pull me to bed? Oh, Emma. You are a fool. *Tais-toi, Emma! Tu es vraiment une bête!*

"Amanda. Please listen. I want to say something important. I am very, very proud of you. In every way."

"My bartending? Is proud the same as love?"

"I said I loved you."

"Oh. That's right. You did. Sorry. Just one to a customer, folks." I get up and kneel beside Mark. "Mark? Are you sure about what we're doing? Are you sure it's right? Albany and everything? Do you think we're reshapable enough? Sometimes, Mark, I, too, can be Evita Perón, but mostly, Mark, I'm the people from the hills.

Mark laughs. He laughs his fucking, fraud-freaked salesman's laugh. His deal-doing, game-host, piano-tooth laugh. The sound of that laugh slices through me with bloodless clarity. The haze of a minute ago is gone. What you want, Mark, is clear. *But,* "Do I want what you want, my dear?" Sing it, baby. Wow! It could be a great number with a new arrangement.

Anyhow, Mark, I tried. It didn't work, but the try was real. Let's try what you want and see if that works, my dear. Insincerely, I bounce back the bogus smile.

"You're wonderful," he says, relieved at the demise of my insanity.

"You are, too. Shake."

Mark shakes into the air.

"No. A real shake. People always shake after deals. And for some people a shake is all they have. We're lucky, because we have it in writing, too. Can you believe it's been almost twelve years?"

Lest my madness return, Mark shakes. I hold onto his hand and press hard. I feel a slight pullaway. "Mark? Look at me. Look right into my eyes. Listen. I want to say something important." Still a bit wary, he keeps humoring me by looking right into me. "Mark. To tell me you love me is horseshit. To tell me you need me is true."

I release his hand. It's easy to let go knowing we're together, and knowing where we're going together.

"I told you, Amanda, I'm sorry about the program. I don't know what to say anymore. I did hear you were wonderful. And I thank you. Thank you."

"No. Mark. Thank you."

Thank you for submitting to this productive encounter session. If you suddenly flattened me and fucked me, I would have to come to the next meeting to tell this group I was wrong. But I don't think I'll be coming to that meeting or, for that matter, any meetings ever again.

With a passive hostility, I double-pat Mark's shoulder. "I think I'll go inside for a while." Before going, I take a small box of stationery from the side drawer of the desk.

Lying on my bed, I draw a diagonal through my name on the crisp parchment card.

For Brad,

When it's clear as crystal, is it better?

Amanda

12

Dearest Amanda,

Always read me into your future. I love you soooo,

M———

Oh, my God. She's home from Tokyo.

There have been so many cards and letters between us, saved, hidden, read and reread. But now, looking at this one, I feel completely alien to its existence. And we never did have our talk. The one where I was going to tell her how she really feels. But she's got to feel like me. And the trip—all the weeks away—she probably even wants to have my talk with me. It's called how to make two friends of lovers. Right, Mr. Hart? Okay, Mr. Rodgers? What d'ya mean it's bassackward! Those once wonderful "oooos" seem silly and mocking, the bold red lettering immature. I want to tear the card to tiny pieces and watch them fly into a Humpty Dumpty ending. I want it never to have come taped to this small square package that seems almost devoured by the sealing wax seals of Cartier's overexhausted double C. Give me the Pharaohs' double falcon. The Hapsburgs' double eagle. Bill Blass' double B?

I know what's inside is expensive and I know I don't want it. She's dropped it here on her way to her apartment. I see it all. While at the airport, waiting for luggage, she phoned the country. The country said I was in the city. Fabulous. I'd get it right away. I'd be excited. I'd know she was back. She'd wait for me to open it. Then she'd call. Then the thin voice. Then what?

The "John" on her card jumps at me like the isolated E on the eye chart. I'm thinking about when she wished Latham were Latham's middle name. It would look better. She said it would look like old money because old money always uses last names for middles. It made me smile, because only the unself-consciousness of old money could say that.

But now it makes me sick. And when I think of making that montage for her, actually ripping those labels out of those dresses right in the stores, I cringe. But nothing could stop me then. Nothing could make me now.

I'm trying to think of making love with you, Maria, but I can't look at my thoughts. Everything's humiliating me. Your fingers make me squirm. Don't you understand, no matter how long they're there nothing will happen again? Move them. Please, Maria.

I've got Mark's disease. Encounterphobia. Mine is the virulent, galloping type. But Maria, it's unfair for it to strike so hard. Didn't I mainline myself with a lifetime antidote when I made you into a good, maybe great photographer? You'd still be snapping Sundays in the park. I gave you somebody you never had. I exchanged her for me. I gave you somebody who can finally love you and never leave you. You.

Now is one of the times I wish I'd been a little nicer to God. Why does religion only seem to heal the conscience of return patients? I don't care what it costs, but I desperately need a prescription for my *lésion d'honneur*. Anyway, doesn't the world's greatest opiate deserve to be the world's greatest usurer?

You know I'll pay. Didn't I travel all through Italy crossing palms with every priest who showed me a link from Saint Peter's chains or a splinter from His cross? And aren't you allowing my husband to replace your turned collar for a sizable offering next Sunday?

And what a great opener Brad found for Mark. I can just hear Camelot revisited. "As President Kennedy once said, I know you all have an idea where my opponent should go, but here, in a church, I don't want to raise the religious issue." You'll pause then, Mark, because Brad told you a big pause would put you in the hands of a big applause.

Brad? Help *me*. What am *I* going to do? She'll be calling any second. Brad? Should I phone her off at the pass?

"Service."

"Hello. This is Mrs. Weldon."

"Hold on, please." Click. Muzak. Fuck you, "Born Free."

"You have no messages, Mrs. Weldon. Please hold another moment." Double fuck! Why are you leaving me to answer that? You usually let mine ring into tomorrow. Why can't you ever hire enough robots, dummy?

"Sorry, Mrs. Weldon. Today we're shorthand—"

"Just stay with me and listen. If anyone calls, I have gone to the country. Is that clear? They can reach me this evening, after five, in the country. Do you have that? I'm leaving the city now."

My God! She's repeating exactly what I said. Why the shock? That's what dummies do, dummy!

Rrrrrinnng. Rrrrrinnng. Rrrrrinnng.

I can't believe the timing. I'll bet Maria hasn't even put down her purse. The one with the double G's.

Rrrrrinnng. Rrrrrinnng. Rrrrrinnng. Rrrrrinnng.

Pick it up! You short-minded robot!

Rrrrrinnng. Rrrrrinnng.

Only Maria would be that patient. *Goddamn it! Answer it!* Finally. I'd better call to make sure it was Maria. Chinning the receiver, I realize my hand is still clinging onto Cartier.

"Service."

"This is Mrs. Weldon."

"Yes, Mrs. Weldon. We just delivered your message to a Mrs. Marr."

"Thank you."

That makes Cartier easier to open. First the crumbly seals, now the glossy white box, now the inside red one. Press. Open. God! It's really beautiful. She remembered the story of my gypsy ring. My loving it. My dropping it. My stupidly asking the waiter to look. He looked. He looked and looked and after he found it he said he couldn't find it.

How perfectly the red, white, and blue stones are set in the thick gold band. How long ago did she order it? I wish I hated it. Where to now? I'm usually so fluent with choices. Where are they? How about this symbolizing everything having gone full circle? The fitting end. It is measured for my last finger. That's an amoral enough choice. Isn't it? Wouldn't anyone call it sufficient cause for my wearing it in the best of ill health?

I know I should get dressed, but I'm still too afflicted

with morning sickness. I'll never make it out to lunch with
Brad. Why can't he phone it in? I'll obey. We know I come
over okay. Write the part. I'll play Amanda better than
Amanda. I have all the shamelessness in the world needed
for winning. Look at this ring.

Rrrrrinnng. Rrrrrinnng. Rrrrrinnng.

My God. The service actually picked up. Listening in, I
hear Brad. "Thank you. I'll take it. Brad?"

"For a minute I thought you'd gone out."

"No. No."

"Some Mexican jumping bean has a crisis! Would you
mind going over the format at your place and skipping
lunch?"

"Wow! What words. I'd have given anything to hear
that."

"A pound of flesh?"

"Would you believe a hundred and thirty?"

"Yes."

"No wonder you're single."

"Is an hour good?"

"What is it now?"

"Ten."

"Great. See you at eleven." Rushing to my closet, I get
on tiptoes and feel around the top shelf for the watch.

What to wear is harder to find. What's between liberated and moonlight? I hold the narrow beige column to the
mirror. Not bad. Not bad at all. But it needs the sash to
delineate me from the silk.

Pulling the draperies all the way open, another glorious
June morning invades the room. Even the sunshine fabrics
seem crisper under its brilliance. It's one of those mornings
the sun is so dazzling you have to look under the shades to
make sure the lamps aren't lit.

Looking down from the window onto Park Avenue, the

women are dressed, as Grandma would say, "in their figures." It's fun being low enough to use people as ther-
mometers. They're certainly more accurate than someone
who's been in the studio since five.

There's energy in a day like today. It tantalizes and
baits like a breeze not quite close enough to catch, a lust
lingering just out of reach. Grab it! Grab it before it melts
into the crumple of summer. Before it's lost to women
wearing white plastic purses, window-shopping with husbands wearing wrinkled jackets that ride up on fat behinds.
And to ugly, lagging children whose socks have wilted to
their ankles and whose FAO Schwarz shopping bags scrape
along the steamy pavement.

Brad? Do you want to walk in the zoo? Do you know I
still buy the balloons with the Mickey Mouse inside? And I
still stand there making up my mind about the color. I
don't even pretend it's for Sonia or Sara. But you know, I've
never been able to grab long ago long enough to feel it? To
know I was really holding on to it. "Once you pass its por-
tals, you may ne'er return again." Shut up!

Here's what I want to know. Who ever jumped in a
shower? Like now, I cross rather carefully over that marble
saddle. Here's what I do know. I am the best shower singer
in this shower.

> *Toyland. Toyland. Dear little girl and boy land.*
> *Once you pass its portals you may ne'er return again.*

I never was in such voice.

"Sorry, kid. Better luck next time."
"But, Mr. Ziegfeld, I've come all the way from—"
"Sorry, kid."

Boy, I bet he never treated Fanny Brice or Marilyn Miller like that. I should have had my mother here. She'd have told him a thing or three. Anyway, Mom, aren't you thrilled I'm in the shower? "The body filth doesn't run back into your parts as it does in the tub."

Rub-a-dub-dub. Three men in a tub? Roaring, degenerate faggots! Put your little soap, put your little soap, put your little soap right *there*. Rub. Scrub. Rub. Now to the back, and now back to the front. Wow! Take a fresh washcloth over those teeth. Across, up and down, underneath. "Shine 'emm, sweetarrt. Atta way, sweetarrrt." I'm definitely dropping Bogart from the act.

I'm freezing and the mirror's steaming. No doubt jealous of my singing. Really, mirror? Why, thank you. You bet I believe you.

No wens, no warts, no temple gray
No brows nor lashes gone astray.

I wish I could leap into a diagonal and click my heels twice. "Forget it, sweetarrt. You're a singer, not a hoofer." Hey. I thought I told you O-U-T. Hmmm. I think I'll try some of Mark's cologne. Go, girl, go. Once over lightly. Since he likes lemon in his Mary, here's hoping it transfers.

I think I'll lie down a minute. That audition took a lot out of me. Damn! I never noticed that face in the wallpaper. God damn him! He's all over the room. I'll never see those flowers again without seeing, if you can believe, George Washington. Why couldn't he be content with the quarter? I wonder if the designer did it on purpose. If it was his trick to put old George into even more bedrooms. Maybe the first person to recognize him will win a million dollars. But then, on the other hand, as Sonia and Sara would say, there are five fingers.

"This is WTFM on your radio dial with music around the clock." I love you, WTFM. Do you know my girls really believe WABC is going to call them while they're listening and send them a car? Do you know I'm insane from hearing WABC?

It's almost eleven. Where did the day go so soon? So soon. Who stole my pantyhose away? Where the hell are you? You were just here. Did you run away? Ha! Ha! Oh, there you are. Who said you could go to the bathroom? Amanda. Please remember, you must make allowances. They're Siamese twins. Oh, yes. Sorry, girls.

No. Never! That sash that way is a great error. It looks like it's linking hot dogs. Of course, "all beef" Mother. Let's see. Now try looping it over once and pull it through. Perfect. Flat and square. No. Not you. Never you, my pet.

Somebody ought to do an article on the stupid things people do while waiting for the bell. Like me, now. Here I am, purposely sitting in a certain position, listening for the bell that will disarrange my position. My particular inconsistency even goes so far as my underlining a *Commentary* I'm not reading.

The bell. The bell? The bell. I heard you. I'm coming. I just hate to leave my contrivance so soon.

"Good morning, ma'am. May I have a minute of your time?"

I'm holding the door open, but I'm not moving. My only thought is why I didn't notice the worn corners on his attaché case and buy him that instead.

"Err. Ummm. Excuse me. Ma'am? Would you mind if I took a few minutes of your time? I'm from the Early-For-

Christmas-Snow-Globe Company." Brad brings his hand from behind his back. "This is but a sample of our extensive line."

My eyes move from the frayed leather to the snow-filled Alpine village.

"If you'll just let me in, ma'am, I'd be more than delighted to show you others. We have angel globes, snowman globes, Mother-and-Ch——"

"Excuse my keeping you out here." I look from the falling flakes to the soft smile. "Please come in."

"Thank you. And this sample is for you. Please accept it as there are obligations that go with it."

Moving it slowly, I feel as light as the flakes settling atop the tiny village. "I love it, Brad. I truly love it. Thank you."

"It's fun. That's all it is. No less. No more. But then again, there is no more."

The similarity to what I'm thinking catches me off balance. It's as if he's showing me my way without seeing my map. Is he reading me? Is he saying him? Both?

"Brad? I have something for you, too." It's hard for me to look at him straight. I'm caught between the brown belt and the tightly knotted tie. But any looser and it wouldn't fit in the narrowness of his button-down.

"It *bitter* be lemon." He pauses for our horrible, together funny. My eyes are at his eyes now. Whatever I wanted to hide is wide open. "Amanda, we haven't much time to prove we're not alcoholics." He pushes the scratched crystal in front of me.

"How do you read that?"

"With difficulty."

Whatever's in the air is closing in on me. Its excitement is making me crazy. It's following me into the kitchen. Brad is too.

"Here's the ice. And for me, please, since I learned my lesson, less bitter's better. Everything else you'll find on the bar." *Go, Brad, go!*

I rush to my room for the package. Looking in the mirror, I shake my hair until some sexy ends fall on my forehead. Taking the Binaca, I squirt the sharp sprays into my mouth. Back in the library, the encircling flurry is making me ding-a-ling. It's bouncing and building into a blizzard. As calmly as possible, I exchange my slim blue box for Brad's bloody victory over AA.

"To you, our most learned Lady of the Garden Club. May you serve your ladies well. For to serve is to rule. *'Cui servire est regnare.'* But then a Latin scholar like you knows the old Groton motto, just like all your ladies do. They pass it daily, framed beside the faded picture of the squash racquets team. Up theirs!"

How Mark would love to throw away those lines, toss them from his background to the back room. But then, he wouldn't be running for governor. Would we?

"Now, let me think. What could be in here?" Brad shakes his present from side to side. "Just what I need. A telescopic umbrella."

"That's not fair. You can see through." God, I wish we were in one of those chalets in the globe.

Brad pockets the card and tears through the paper. Thank goodness. I hate people who try to save wrappings while explaining poor backgrounds. Who gives a shit? And they never use it again, anyway.

"How does it look?" Little boy proud, Brad extends his wrist.

"Wonderful."

"Feel free to replace anything you want. I'll try and wear worse and worse to make it easy."

Brad? Do you know there's going to be an avalanche in

the village? You couldn't not know. Maybe you're just cataclysmically calmer than I am. Right? I mean, you know it's coming, you just don't think it's imminent. Right?

Brad opens his attaché case. While sifting through periodicals, pamphlets, and papers, he intermittently adjusts his glasses and drinks his Bloody Mary. Neither action diverts his sorting. After scribbling some fast notes, he closes his case and looks up. Removing his glasses, he rubs the hollows of his eyes with his palms.

"Don't do that, Brad. It'll only make it blurrier. It's the lenses that need wiping." He nods his head and extends his glasses for me. I was already on my way.

"Thanks," he says. "Never, ever have I had vodka and tomato juice make me see better. Now, sit down a minute, Amanda. I want your full attention." He takes a deep breath during which he seems to be studying me, evaluating me, slotting me. It's almost as if he's passing judgment on my readiness to be shoved through the chute.

"You're going to sway this election, Amanda. In a strange, unique way it's you who holds the high hand. No matter how powerful the conservative swing, labor can topple the ante of any establishment king. But you've got the breeding and the credibility to keep them in the game. Class attracts the classless. And your issues will be completely different from Mark's. There'll be no trace of mimic in the independent Amanda. And when the believability's built to fever pitch, you'll side with Mark for the really high stakes. By that time, you'll have them all. I saw you work Wallenberg at Mark's announcement. You think that kind have any at home like you?"

Brad's voice is direct, measured, uninflected. "Our winning depends on labor's knowing their needs are our burning issues. The Democrats' death doesn't mean they're without a torchbearer. In 1564 Michelangelo died. In 1564 Shakespeare was born. There's always better and brighter. And as Caesar's wife, my dear Amanda, you're even beyond reproach."

Amanda who? Which Amanda? The governor's cooze? The television tart? The country cunt who holds garage sales of sex?

"Brad? Do you like me?"

"I like you. I respect you. I know you."

"Same."

"I know that."

"What else do you know, Brad?"

"Your bargain."

"What bargain? The one with Mark?"

"No. That came after the real one. The one you really made is the one with you."

"What for what?" I ask, watching his eyes travel my face.

"Today for tomorrow. Lots of todays for the big to-morrow."

"Am I that tough? That obvious?" Again, I see that maplike tracing.

"By whose standards? I can read you. And you're not really tough. Not yet. Not yet, at all."

"What about Mark?"

"You passed Mark before you joined him at the altar. And now you're leading the way you both want. And don't ever be misled by the "happiness" of those husband-fuck-ing, car-pooling, charity-slaving superslobs. Their inevitable divorce is God's revenge on their not admitting their misery."

It's odd sitting here defenselessly answering this almost complete stranger's naked probes. Odder still that I welcome the exposure.

"Were there a lot before Mark?"

"Enough."

"More after Mark?"

"Not right away."

"After you thought you could have it all?"

"I never thought that."

A disbelieving grin curves his mouth. "Anyway, *Candidates' Wives* is a big show." Brad slaps some notes on his hand and gives them to me. "Here are some of the issues likely to be raised. Mostly, they're bullshit. You can make your own issues. And since you're not lacking in looks, the camera will swing to them right away. But you'll only hold it there if your mouth does more than smile. It does, doesn't it? Doesn't it? Show me, Amanda. Show me what else your mouth can do. Make your lips talk without words. Do you know the best single fucks come from the people who make up the couples who are public envy number one? The ones everyone knows are so devoted. I'll help you, Amanda. Now where do you suppose your lips should start to thank me?"

I'd do anything. Suck. Fuck. Faint. But I can't move. I'm pinned beneath the trembling and the pounding. The jacket just missed my head. I hear the swoosh of leather being pulled through loops. One. Two. Never unlaced a shoe.

Brad pushes me to the floor and spreads my lips with his tongue. Softly, with moonlight, he kisses me for the first time. I knew the trembles were more than tremors. I knew I didn't want to be evacuated. God! Suddenly, the whole town's under water and it's ripping through my silk, tearing through the nylon. But why is Brad so rough, pushing me on my stomach, forcing me upside down?

"Come on and put that fucking mouth where it belongs. Open those starved lips. Open them on this. Open them! Here! Put them on this!" He's trying to pull his shirt from

around his thighs. "Goddamn it! Help me! Pull it away! Do
you hear? Or do you come sucking shirts?" He maneuvers
his fingers between our bodies and rips away.

As much as I try, as rough as I let him continue, nothing happens to him there. Gasping, gagging, moaning, I try
anything, everything to make him hard. Just a little, just a
tiny hard, please, Brad. Then I promise I'll make it work.
I know I will. But what I really down-deep know is the
futility. We both do. That's the real horror as we continue.

Suddenly, his body stiffens as my fingers and my words
try for tenderness. Breaking loose, Brad gets up fast.
"What's that noise, Amanda?"

I play along. "I don't know." I'm not angry.

"Don't give me that tone. I heard something." Within
seconds, Brad's stuffing the blue broadcloth into his trousers and buckling the leather. Like a discarded doll, I lie
watching his stupid speed.

"Get up, Amanda. I heard a latch. What the fuck are
you proving?"

Suddenly, balefully, the most unholy scream is filling
every inch of space around and inside me. Whirring keys
shatter a half-emptied glass, while Maria's purse catches
Brad's ear.

Nightmare, don't fail me now. Continue on if you have
to. I'll even feel pain. But do wake me. *Wake me!* Let me
tremble out of you. But please, *Let me out!*

I've never felt nakedness like this. Even more than there
is to show is showing. It's tamping me into a fetal hug,
forcing me to fold into myself.

"Whore! Whore-ass whore!"

Stupid, piss-ant words. Not the wild words of a real
person. And the screams. The screams aren't a real person's
screams. Thank God. At least I know I'm still okay. Still
asleep.

My God! What insanity is twisting and pulling my little finger?

"She wore this when she loved with you?"

I see three bright, crazy eyes, wild with fright, being torn from my pinky.

"Owwwwwwwwww!" Almighty God! I heard that scream. It was a real scream. From a real person. Me! From pain. Excruciating pain. Why didn't it wake me? God knows it was loud enough to wake me. *Wake me! It's over!* You did it all. The pain. The terror. Everything. You did it all. *Let me go!* "Owwwwwwwwww!" My God! Again, the pain. It's Maria's heel spiking my ribs.

"Maria! You're insane!" Brad's voice is unbelieving. "What the fuck's going on? Maria? Are you crazy?" Desperately, Brad tries to subdue Maria.

"Let go! Let me go! You whore-lover, whore-fucker, dyke-doer!"

From my crouch, I see brown shoes kicking high heels. I see the high heels kicking, attacking, fighting the air. I hear the thuds of shoving.

The slap and the wail are almost simultaneous. The sobs are heavy, groping gasps. Suddenly, the filled lungs empty into everywhere with unbroken wails. Rising to a semi-stoop, I go past the bizarre reality of what is. I go for cover. To my bedroom for a robe. Shell-shocked victims must stumble the same way. The voices they hear must be in the same distance, with the same far impact, screaming the same pinched sentences.

"Get your filthy hands off . . ." (Maria)

"Don't you kick me, you sick . . ." (Brad)

"Amanda! Amanda! Please, Amanda . . ." (Maria)

"Drop that ashtray before I . . ." (Brad)

"Did she ever tell you we were lovers? Longtime lovers? You know I have letters and she also gave . . ." (Maria)

"If you don't get those fucking teeth . . ." (Brad)

Another slap. Now nothing. No noise. No sound. I never saw so many George Washingtons in my life. I can't stop seeing them. I'm counting them. Did I do that row? I better start again. One. Two. Three. Four. . . .

"I'm taking you home, Maria. Now!" No answer. No sobs. Nothing.

There's someone at the bedroom door. It's Brad. He looks cruel.

"Look. Whatever turns you on. But on your time, Mrs. Weldon."

Now nobody's at the bedroom door. I hear feet shuffling on the foyer parquet. The front door's opening. Slowly, it latches shut.

Fifty-eight. Fifty-nine. Sixty. Sixty-one.

13

"Sixty-two percent recognition factor is gigantic after only three weeks on the ballot. You can thank the Olympics for that. But remember, Marcus, you can sink as well as soar with the primary not until the middle of September. Ten weeks is a lot of rope."

Somehow, Max's yelling, even his choking Havana smokescreen, gives me a kind of security. His supreme belief in him is an anchor to windward. No matter how rough it is, Max can get it together.

"Max. Stop worrying. I swear nobody will ever know."

"Swearing in front of me, Marcus, doesn't matter. I want to stop it from being in front of the grand jury."

"No way, Max. It's as clean as—"

"A barrel of pig shit."

"Max. There's no trace. Nowhere. Nothing. Don't you know what I mean?"

"Who doesn't know what you mean? What you don't know is the whole meaning. You don't know what they could do to you, to Amanda, to everybody if anybody traced even an inch of Olympic Park to you."

Just short of the library, I find myself stopping, holding back, holding breath. I can't be seen or heard. I need to overhear everything. All I've heard before are crazy clues. I flatten against the wall like they do in movies when they're on the outside of high buildings, ledging it to the next apartment.

"Max. Anybody could have bought the land. We've been through all that."

"Anybody wasn't fucking well sure Times Square would become Olympic Park. Anybody isn't running for the state's highest office, an office that can as easily be a springboard to Dannemora as to Washington."

"There's no way it can be traced."

"Not now, Marcus."

"What's that supposed to mean?"

I want to look out of the window to see if Pedro's taken the station wagon to pick up the girls, but I don't want to move. Where were they? Oh, yes. The round robin. Hopefully, I'll hear the crunch in the driveway.

"I've changed the names of everything and moved it all to Lausanne. Leases, mortgages, everything. So, Marcus, you'll just have to spend it over there. Next year you can charter the Guinness yacht. We can berth together at Monte for the Grand Prix." Max sounds pleased and mocking.

"It's all there?" Mark's voice is incredulous.

"We had to run, Marcus. Far and fast."

Now I know why the fastest animal in the world is called a cheetah. It goes seventy miles per hour. Compared with you, Mark, at only twenty-seven point eighty-nine, think of the mileage he'd make on your deals. How do I know such things? Keep listening to my mind, Mark. There's more. The garden snail is point zero three miles per hour, Mark. Now, don't ask me any more. That's enough. If you want to know any more look it up in the Guinness Book of Records. They'll obviously have one on the yacht. Right? Oh, please.

"What we've got to do now, Marcus, is throw Maxweld behind the city, behind the Olympics. We've got to take a major stake in it, show how much we believe in it, how much we want it to work. For the city. For the state. Not us. Country before cash."

"I'm with you, Max. And the sooner the healthier."

I hear the crunch. But now it doesn't matter. Now I can go in. They'll welcome me, be overjoyed it wasn't earlier. They'll think how lucky can they be. But, wow, isn't timing usually lucky? Just ask me.

"Hi. Max." My tone is light. I grab the "thank God" look between them.

"Surprised?" Max asks.

"Not too, since I happened to have choked all the way from the top of the stairs on your far-reaching calling card."

I'm glad, at least, before slipping his tongue between my lips, he flicked what may or may not have been a touch of tobacco.

"Max. Meet my wife, the politician, the charmer. As James M. Barrie said, 'If a woman has charm she need have nothing else. If she doesn't have charm, it matters not what else she has.' "

"She is most definitely charming. Charming. A great

asset." Max raises his brows as he lowers his eyes and pats my asset with the most indelicate of pats.

"Ours should be a great hotel, Max. After fifty years of no New York luxury hotels, just look at those sky-scraping projections for the Palace and the new Hilton. Times Square can't even boast a flophouse. And what a market to draw on. The theater, the Garden, the garment center, Penn Central, the Port Authority. And no one's been near there since Astor."

"And, Marcus, on a site where we *don't* own the land. It's just too bad it was all bought before us." Max puffs and leans way back, sinking into the corner pillows, watching for his words to sink into Mark. Again, a fast look stretches between them.

"It'll be a hell of a price, Max. By the time we break ground, costs will be unreal. Thirty, forty, maybe even fifty dollars a square foot." Mark is talking to a crowded scratch pad.

"It can all be done." Max opens his mouth and pushes out five circles of smoke. "I must learn to connect those into the Olympic logo. That would be what I would call an accomplishment. First they'd appear, then they'd meet, then intertwine, then disappear. Like people do. The success would all depend on timing. Like life does."

Max the mentor is into one of his finest hours. What does he care about a Hawaiian shirt over suit pants when he puts rings around life? "Maybe I should perfect the act before we hit the beaches next weekend."

Mark looks up from his tote board. "Where's our schedule for the Fourth?"

"Lanacola's rerouting it. Lucky for us Brad checked Robinson's advance team. Otherwise, you'd both be noshing at Nathan's at the same time."

"When will Brad be here?"

"Now. He's coming from Greenwich and going straight from here to the city to beat the traffic."

Here? Brad? Now? I don't want him here now. I'm not ready for him here. It isn't long enough yet to see him. It was awful enough on the phone. But when he's here in person, he'll translate every look, and he'll be looking. I'm still not far enough from crouching naked and praying that I'll wake from the wails. I'm still an air raid victim waiting for the all clear of the elevator to open and swallow Brad and Maria. "Down. Please." Way down. *Please!*

He'll stare to see what he didn't see in the beginning, to see why he didn't see it. It'll be technical, clinical, lablike. And silently he'll be saying that I was his fault, but I'll hear those words "emasculating cunt" screaming into my skull. Oh, God. There's such a fat fear ball growing in my stomach. It's bouncing around and making me shake. I want to pull the covers high until there's no light at all. Fuck. Shit. There's one growing in my throat, too.

"Is the chopper all ready?"

"Set to go." Max rescues his leaning cigar with all the agility of a juggler reaching behind his back for the last falling pin.

"They traded in the Bell Ranger. This one's Italian. Anda the gooda news is, itsa seats seven and doesa one eighty. The bada news is the pilot's name isa Pontius." Max pauses and puffs. "Heya Marcus. Youa no laugh. Youa take offense atta me?"

"No offense, Max." All that lands on Mark's pad is numbers.

"Anyhow, it's a timed-to-order swap. Of course if they'd ever let Marr call the shots at Marr, that Bell Ranger, my son, today would be a Frisbee. By the way, Marcus, how goes the loafing legacy since Tokyo taught him he wasn't ever the rising son."

"Max, please. You know. We all know. We need
Latham. When hate springs eternal, can't you simply say,
Latham Marr is millions, more millions, more even than
millions? Why do you think Amanda cozies with Maria? To
pick her brain? We're a team. Everybody plays a position."

Mark's laugh is not export, not salesman's, not anything
I've ever heard before. What is he laughing at? What is he
saying in that laugh? Something. Mark?

"Am I right, Amanda?"

Something's going on that I'm in on, yet outside of. I'm
outside of an inside thing about me. My fear ball has just
reached baby size. It's kicking. It's kicking hard. I feel a
determined foot pushing and pounding. I can hear it thump-
ing. Faster and faster. Faster and louder.

"Maria's nice and all that, but Amanda's investment in
time is just too much not to be an investment. Maria is not
that compelling. Her main attraction is our future." Mark
shakes his head dismissingly. "Look. It's foolish to follow
this any further. I merely mention it, Max, because you've
got to do some of that with Latham."

"Okay, Marcus. Latham Marr. Millions. Latham Marr.
More millions. Latham Marr. Even more millions than that.
Latham Marr. A drunken, pol-fucking prick who's just
slightly lucky he's got millions." Max winks at me as he
chews his raveling stub.

Why do I suddenly feel funny in what I'm wearing? I
wear it all the time. But now it feels bare and skimpy. My
arms could goose-pimple from bareness. Even my thonged
feet seem bare and awkward. It's almost as if this isn't my
house and it isn't a Sunday in the summer. It's an any-day
city-day, and we're in a board room where what I wear has
everything to do with everything I am. But doesn't the
board understand if the slits on the sides weren't so high I
couldn't walk? I'd have to Japanese step?

But doesn't the bareness also boast a country-class campaign? Where summer tans glisten and peroxide can hibernate? Right, Mark? Right?

"Right, Amanda? Right? Answer me." Mark presses. Did I hear voices through my thinking?

Who? Me Amanda?

"Amanda? All right? The girls are coming next Saturday?"

"Yes. Next Saturday. Where?"

"She's a charmer, Marcus." Max is laughing. "A real charmer. Hangs on to your every word."

"The beaches." Mark is enraged. "What in the hell do you think we've been talking about?"

I knew I heard voices. "The beaches. Of course. I know. But we decided that a long time ago. The girls know they're going next Saturday." Or they will as soon as I tell them.

"Girls? Did I hear somebody mention girls? Bring on the girls! But make sure they're on the feminine side." It's Brad. How did he get in? My God! I don't believe him. He's even carrying a drink. "Hello. One and all. I've just decided, on my easy way in, to write the definitive piece on the air-conditioning noise, entitled, 'The Burglar's Boom Is the Hummm-Drum.' "

Mark is glaring. Please, Mark. Don't be your fuck-ass self and start to polemicize about Pedro's expert training. Mark? I never knew your eyes could get so narrow.

"Is everyone aware that when you have charm you don't have to train servants? Just ask my wife, Amanda."

After patting Mark and Max on the back, Brad slowly comes toward me and befriends my shoulder. His hand makes me feel like a porcupine, hyped and ready to quill out.

"Hello, Amanda. How go tricks?" Brad asks.

"They're gone. All gone."

Brad slants his head like some smart-ass bird. I hate it. "Are you crystal clear?" Notching his thumb into his belt, he looks at that watch.

"Are we boring you so soon?" Max asks. "Or are you squeezing us between those two juntas you're planning for the Third World.

"Right on, Max. However, you omitted what I'm planning for my mother. She wants to belt hard rock and live in a lavender Rolls."

Brad's concession to country clothes is rolling the sleeves of his button-down up. Yet somehow, he can get away with wearing the same things in dissimilar surroundings. I wonder if he's ever owned any black shoes. No. Of course, dancing pumps don't count. Oh, God. There's that ball again. Just seeing those brown shoes . . .

"Amanda! Amanda! Are you deaf?"

"Yes, Mark. Why are you screaming at me?"

"My normal tone seems incapable of traveling the distance."

"Must be the refractions, Mark."

"What refractions?"

"How should I know? Somebody once told me everything in the air has to do with refractions."

Mark's exhale must have reached the highest refraction of exasperation, because it's reaching me very loud. But that's not what I want to hear. Again, I want the all clear.

"Amanda, don't be cute. Brad's right about Flora Robinson. She's extremely bright. And with the first big polls due the day before the show, she'll try anything. She has to. *She* has nothing to lose."

Flora Robinson? I know her. She's the one who plays

the haggard wife and the no makeup mom in the old movies. No. No, dummy. That's Flora Robson. Oh, Robson.
Right.

"The third candidate's wife is Jane Cruckshank," Brad
says. "Wife of Ted Cruckshank, the Socialist Party's pick no
matter what the office. The program's scheduled for the
Thursday after the Fourth." Taking off his glasses, he twirls
them in the air. "We've got to think where they'll get you.
We've got to plan our answers before their questions."

"When do we do that?" Do I dare take those glasses and
do them right? He's smearing them more trying to clean
them.

"One day when you're in town. We can do it at your
place. Like we did last time."

There is absolutely no inflection in Brad's tone. In fact,
it's that goddamn matter-of-factness that makes me crazy.
I've got to do something. I've got to get up, be busy, move.
Mark is showing Max the numerology on his pad. Brad is
still polishing.

"Give me those, Brad," I say tightly. "You're not getting
them cleaner. You're only spreading the smudges."

Looking quickly toward Mark and Max, he grabs my
hand and leans very close. "And next time, Mrs. Weldon, I
want to hear everything you and Mrs. Marr did to each
other. Everything. Every loving detail. I want you to tell
me exactly how you fucked with Maria. Do you hear me?"
His fingers are into mine. "Is that crystal clear?"

"Yes. Yes." Mostly I hear my pulse. It's about to break
out and splatter.

"And don't leave out so much as a finger. Understand?"
he asks, bending my pinky into pain.

"Whatever turns you on, Brad."

Brad smiles and nods. "Right on, Amanda." Although

he's let go of my hand, it doesn't feel released. You hurt me, Brad. You rotten bully. You really hurt me. I'd like to throw these rotten glasses right across the room. Instead, I take the cocktail napkin, dip it in into my Tab, and rub the lenses clean, thinking every second of what Brad said.

"If we get the weather," Max says, "we can count on those beaches being wall-to-wall chicken fat with millions of greased communicants making their annual pilgrimage."

Brad doesn't even bother to put his glasses back on. "Jones Beach will get the top coverage. That's where our grab 'em speech will . . ."

". . . and in continuing, let me say, what we need is vision. The vision to see not only *what* we pay to taxes, but where that *what* goes. [Pause—applause]

"I, like you, am disillusioned and disenchanted with the state of our state, with its wanton, willful waste on welfare. Imagine our frugal forefathers giving millions of people billions of unearned dollars, people capable of filling their own pockets without pocketing from ours.

"Why don't we, instead, hand them what our fore-fathers fought for? Let's really be generous. Let's hand them true independence, by making them useful to them-selves, happy with themselves. As George Bernard Shaw so wisely said: 'We have no more right to consume happiness without producing it than to consume wealth without pro-ducing it.' "

Mark? Am I hearing right? What the hell is this Shaw bit? Is that more Mazurski? It's the Fourth of July. Not the fucking Coronation.

"What more appropriate time than the Fourth of July . . ."

That's better.

". . . for us to declare our own declaration against those who are constantly selling us out and therefore enabling others to sell us short. Let us return to the truths of Mr. Jefferson. For now, more than ever, the course of human events makes it necessary to dissolve these enslaving bonds. The alternative must result in a monetary and moral bankruptcy for us all.

"Our ancestors fought the tyranny of a king so they could be endowed with the inalienable rights to life, liberty, and the pursuit of happiness. And so must we fight the tyranny of society's scavengers to maintain these rights. We must once and forever bid a farewell to the breaking burdens of welfare. [Pause—applause]

"And when I become governor, these words will become self-evident truths. I pledge my life, my fortune, and my honor to bring independence to indigence and prosperity to we the people."

The way Mark is lifting his arms is almost spiritual. As Sonia, Sara, and I move close to him, the revival-type response seems uncontrollable. So intense is the fervor, I again feel tears falling into my smile as Mark raises my hand with his while the cameras move in and in and in.

WELDON 46%–ROBINSON 27%
MIRACLE MARK GALLOPS AWAY

The Gallup Poll's first results for the Republican gubernatorial candidate puts former Olympic chairman . . .

NEWS POLLS WELDON 51%–ROBINSON 25%

If these candidates are running to save New York, the *Daily News* proposes the primary be held immediately with the unspent campaign millions donated to the state. An upset possibility with Weldon's unheard-of . . .

ROBINSON CLAIMS
WELDON'S OLYMPIC FEEDBACK
CARRIES NO GRAIN OF POLITICS

Responding to disastrous showings in the polls, John W. Robinson, liberal candidate for the Republican gubernatorial nomination, told the *New York Post* Weldon's wide margin was purely Olympic feedback. "Politics is a different game. I am confident by September . . ."

G-A-P IN GOP CONFIRMED
BY GANNETT AND NEWHOUSE

Canvassing by the Gannett and Newhouse chains confirmed the incredible gap between a truly Miracle Mark Weldon and his opponent, John . . .

14

The full summer sun, gushing through the high corner windows, sparkles like a dance hall ball on top of Brad's sleeping snow worlds. But it would never dare to get inside them, dare to melt Christmas, no matter what the month. Yet somehow, today, among these proplike people sitting in his office, the tiny Swiss villages and ferris-wheel bears seem out of place.

Signatured show-off pictures of important clients would seem more appropriate with row after row smiling from inside narrow black wood frames. Some of the glossies should be puckered or cracked from age, catching the sun at an angle where one would have to move to see who was in the picture.

"Anybody for more coffee?" Cathy Cormack is standing at the door. She's addressing me. How nice. It's the first time anyone's addressed me this morning. I shake my head no and smile. What I'd really like is to pull open those high cabinet doors and make myself a Bloody Mary.

Max turns to Cathy. "More for me and remember, no sugar." Why is Max's voice always tinged with distrust?

"We only have sugar substitutes, Mr. Mandell."

As if she's a spy, Max waits for Cathy to leave before continuing. "I don't care what we're ahead, it's impossible to control the ball till the final gun. It's a matter of how low can we lie until the primary. How many waves can't we make." Max crosses his feet on the edge of Brad's desk.

"We'll have to become experts in the power of negative thinking." Mark, per usual, is glued onto outer space. "I think we can safely put Max in charge of that division."

"Funny, Marcus. Really funny. The only time it won't be funny is when there isn't a Max."

Looking at Latham, slouched in the corner of the sofa, I'm wondering why he's around or why he even got up. Or did he? The only thing saving him is that the red of his tie is minimizing the glow of his eyes. I'm sure it's coincidence. That kind of thinking is too big a sweep for a vacuum like Latham. I'm still not sure why *I'm* here. Why did Max change Brad's coming to my apartment to my coming to Brad's office? To be mesmerized by these masterminds? Whatever, thank God.

"The reason I wanted us all here instead of just Brad and Amanda . . ."

Max? Were you and I ever one person in another galaxy? I don't believe how you come in on me. It's more nervous making than if you really came in on me anywhere. No. I guess not *any*where.

"... is that tomorrow's show needs everybody's thinking. We need the near geniuses"—Max stops and focuses on Latham, who luckily can't quite focus—"as well as the authentic geniuses."

Lanacola, less sweaty than usual, looks up from his notes and pushes his pen in the air for attention. "I know the reporters that'll be on the panel."

"How do you know?" Max closes his eyes. It's not the sun. It's the skepticism.

"The producer's a buddy of mine. One reporter's a UPI guy named McKnight. Smart and tough, but decent. The other's an uptight broad from *Newsday*, Tina St. John." Sandy points his pen at me. "St. John's dream of the second coming would be to have the whole world look and act like her."

I wonder if "her" is better or worse than "the cat's mother." Best of all would be the "meow." I wonder how you get to be the "meow." Maybe it happens when you're called a "she-person" instead of a "her." I must say it's constantly fascinating being decided about while I'm here. It's like how "her" should be slipcovered. They'll choose and cut the fabric today so they can be sure it'll fit "her" tomorrow.

Brad gets up from his chair. "That's a big break for us. I've known St. John for years. We couldn't have picked better." He takes off his glasses and squints into a thinking look. Can he think better by not seeing clearly? But more important, why do I always have to see he can't see?

Pacing behind his desk, Brad is exhilarated, confident. "I know her every lead-in. I know exactly what she'll ask. How she'll react. Christ. It's a setup. Duck soup. Home free."

"Did all those gems really fall from the media maestro of the western world?" I say in my most syrupy juleps and grits, but Brad is nowhere near my wysteria.

"Lanacola? You're sure about those names?" Max asks. "Who's your producer friend? Whose mouth would come that close to your dago ear?"

I turn to Max. "Max, lovey. You do have the darlin'est ethnic patter in your phrasin'." Again, no notice of honey-chile.

"Who is he, Lanacola? Does he own a name?"

"You're a trusting son-of-a-bitch, Max. By saying Tom Carbona, does it say I really know? Remind me, from now on, to tape my calls for you."

Max puffs high to the ceiling. "Videotape, Lanacola. I've gotta be sure. Think of all the warped wops that could sound like you." His exhale is so hard that his shirt spans to reveal a not insignificant amount of flesh above his belt.

"Nothing like a team." Mark is angry. Very. Not so much by his tone, but by the lips not opening. "Nothing like one for one and none for all. What the hell's going on?"

"I'll find out who's going on," Latham answers as usual, only half-getting the question. "We pour enough dough into those networks to get what we want. Which network is it? It doesn't matter. Our clout's everywhere. We talk big money."

Clout. Money. *Big* money. You make me sick, Latham Marr. Poor Maria. Really. Poor, poor Maria. Millions. More millions. All I can say is *"Iccccchhhhh!"* My God. They're all facing me. Each and every one. I feel like E. F. Hutton.

Max laughs loudly. "Hey, Mrs. Weldon. You're quite eloquent yourself for a southern belle. Could you repeat that for the northern establishment?"

"Sorry, Max. It's strictly for local consumption."

"She's a charmer, Marcus." Max comes over and puts his arm around my shoulder. At least his getting up closes the gap in his shirt. "What a lovely, ladylike sound," Max whispers, while his hand drops down from my shoulder. "Remember," he says, fingering the top of my breast, "millions. More millions. Even more than that."

"Yes. Max. Sorry. I remember now. What could I have been thinking of? *Millions! More millions! Even more millions than that!*" I'm not only network, I'm satellite.

"Amanda!" Mark is wild.

"I'm not a quick study, Mark. I needed Max with my cue card. But once he cued me, I said it right. Didn't I?"

"Amanda's right," says Latham, oblivious to any interchange between Mark and me. "We do spend even more millions than that. God knows how many more Marr millions. But first things first. I'll get advertising to check those fellows, even though that St. John fellow's a woman." Latham's loud and lonely laugh is always more hysterical than hearty. And the way he's taught himself to say "first," like all those Long Island fucklings who believe omitting the *r* establishes class, is a total travesty.

Impatiently, Brad taps the top of his desk. "Let's get to tomorrow. After all, isn't that what we're all about?" He looks at me knowing he must do something with me, as if I represent some blank form he has to fill. His head is traveling fast. His mouth is half open so it can start immediately. "Amanda, the most important thing you have to create about you is a kind of amorphic quality, a nothingness. You've got to be here, but not strongly here. As we said before, no waves. Middle it. No right. No left. No controversy."

Max takes my chin and turns it toward him. "Stick to how you look. Class. Rich. That's what they want, not how you're going to change the world. Don't disappoint them. Give them Vassar. The uniforms your kids wear to school. The Cézanne show. George Bernard Shaw." Max rolls his eyes at Shaw. "You get the picture. And don't forget to drop a lot of that incidental shit you know."

Brad puts his glasses back on and zooms in. "Mc-Knight's not too used to interviewing women like you, Amanda. You know what I mean. So, he'll probably generalize with something like 'What are your interests?' "

I loathe Brad. I smile warmly at him. "A perfect question for a nothing person." I smile again so he certainly knows I'm intelligent enough not to have taken offense. "I have the perfect answer, too. Ready?"

"You're on."

"Mr. McKnight? You asked about my special interests. History is one of them. I believe most Americans know much too little about their country. In fact, just the other day I asked the members of the garden club—"

"Great reference," Brad interrupts.

"—if anyone knew how New York was named. Not one knew it was for the double-titled Duke of York and Albany, who in 1664 captured and renamed what was then called the New Netherlands."

Max secures his cigar stump between his teeth, risking asphyxiation to start off the applause. I nod politely as would any millet-making maiden from the New Netherlands. The energy of my falseness amazes me.

"Boy. What an image." Lanacola wipes his forehead with his crumpled handkerchief.

"Thank you, one and all." My insincerest smile circles the room. "It's not exactly how I see me, but then one can't really be one's own image maker, especially if the image is sort of nothing."

"My mother's really gonna go crazy at me not finding somebody like you."

"Lanacola. Sometimes I think you are crazy," Max says, finally putting his cigar out of everybody's misery.

Now what's happening? Why isn't anybody looking at me again? It's as if they've all closed ranks. It's like those birthday parties when I was little, when the music would jerk to a fast stop. We'd all hurry for a chair and I couldn't find one. But why are they still talking about me? Because, nothing, they're pulling and pushing and hauling you into your no-image.

I have a feeling I ought to perform. It'll be part of my act for my new no-image. May I have a little soft-shoe music, please. Very light and very soft. Good. Thank you. Now, let me begin by saying, There are two me's to my act. There's my me, here. And there's their me, there. From the outside, it's impossible to tell us apart.

Top hat, please. Thank you. Cane, please. Thank you. And now, that one big spot to follow us across the stage. Thank you. Are we both ready? Good. Smile.

Me and my image, strolling down the avenue
(tap a tap tap tap tap)
Me and my image, all alone and feeling blue
(tap a tap tap tap tap)

Is everybody happy?

"Just a little more under the eyes, Mrs. Weldon. That's better. Much better." Glen, NBC's special makeup man, pats the wet sponge onto my hollows until even my late twenties slip away.

"I thought I looked good when I came in."

"Those lights out there are murder. They even make kids look like old midgets. You ever been on television before?"

"A few times. A long time ago."

"You look like an actress. Well, not really an actress. You look like you should be somebody. Are you anybody?"

"No. I'm nobody. Nothing. What's that you're using?" With his middle finger, Glen is dabbing and smoothing something pink over most of my face.

Smiling into the wide, bulb-rimmed mirror, he says, "It's my own product. I was thinking of marketing it myself, but it takes too much money to break in. I've got a date next week with Revlon's top chemists at their lab in Jersey. If I can get the right deal, I might sell it to them."

Is it memory or imagination? Doesn't every makeup man everywhere have his own batch of beauty better than any best-seller on the market?

"See. It doesn't cake. It doesn't melt. It just gives you this glow. Saintlike. I call it Madonna."

"Good name."

"That's all going to be part of the deal with Revlon. After thirty years in this business, there's not much I don't know. They'll probably want to put out a whole Madonna line, but they'll have to pay big royalties for that name. You know I've got a lawyer?"

"I didn't."

After finishing with Madonna, which definitely sounds more maternity than makeup, Glen puts the jar in the sagging pocket of his sweater. No sharing the table with that ordinary stuff for La Madonna.

"You know the other ladies on the show?" he asks.

"Not yet."

"They're a lot older."

"Even after Madonna?"

As I get up, he pats me on the back. "It's great, isn't it? And you can always say you knew me when."

"Same to you." Looking into the bank of mirrors, I push my hands deep into my pockets and shift my skirt till it's centered. Reaching underneath, I twist the shirt till the stripes are straight. "Glen? Where are the other ladies?"

"In the living room."

"The living room?"

Moron laugh. "How should you know what that is? That's what Miss Parker, Jane Parker, the moderator, calls the set. They're there. You should be there, too. You're on soon."

"I know. I just don't want any last-minute wisdom."

"From who?"

"Some people I came with who think they can fix my mind like you did my face. Make it special for TV. Or is it a TV special?"

More moron laugh. "I know what you mean, but we better get going. Okay?"

"Okay."

"Watch for the wires where you walk. Okay?"

"Okay." He's right about these wires. They're like Con Ed's intestines.

"Why are you stopping?" Glen asks.

"I want to get a good look at the living room from where I can get it all in."

He gives me a knowing nod. "Sizing up the opposition. Right?"

"Right." In fact, powder puff, you couldn't be more wrong. I just want to absorb this whole hokey parlor. I want to size up those oversized modular chairs and sofas, snuggling into each other with all the warmth and intimacy of a factory closeout. Even more glorious are the huge rubber plants. There's no way they can be fake. They've *got* to be a hundred percent rubber. And in such a nice Irish green. Remind me to talk color fashion to Firestone. I'll get *my* lawyer, too. They could come out with a new line. "Firestone blowouts to match Fisher bodies."

Someone is coming toward me. I think it's the spider. I feel any moment my mother's going to give a shove to get me into the parlor.

"Welcome. I'm Jane Parker. Please call me Jane. I know you're Amanda Weldon. May I call you Amanda?"

My God. No. Call Me Madam. Call Me Mister. Call me irresponsible. . . . "Of course. Nice to meet you, Jane."

"Come and meet the others. We've just been going over some of the questions you're likely to be asked."

". . . back to the guests on today's edition of *Candidates' Wives.*"

I can't tell if the camera is on all of us or just on fat, lovable Mama-San Parker. I mean how wide-angle can you get? I'm surprised she hasn't taken each of our hands and made a comfy little pile in the middle of her generous lap. Ah, the word "lap" only brings to mind the wise words of my own mama-san. "Be certain, Amanda, you not only stand but sit when your coat is fitted. You need a generous lap for winter." Rough translation. Get a lot of extra mink. Why hasn't my mind ever released any memory of her?

Why is Mama-San drinking so much water? She's hardly said a word. Maybe she's trying to puff up the rice that didn't digest too well. "Miss St. John? You have a question for one of our guests?"

"Yes. Thank you. Mrs. Cruckshank? With creeping socialism already running away with our freedoms, what makes you believe a large dose of it wouldn't enslave us entirely?"

Blah-blah-blah-blah-blah-blah. I wonder if all Socialists look messy. I guess all they care about are pamphlets and leaflets and Eugene Debs.

Pamphlets and leaflets and Debs on the wings
These are a few of my favorite things.
When the Trotsky bites, when the Stalin stings . . .

"Thank you, Mrs. Cruckshank. Mr. McKnight? You have a question?"

"Yes. Thank you."

"Mrs. Weldon?"

Thatsa me, boss.

"Do you have any particular interests that you feel would help your husband's campaign for governor?"

"Yes. Indeed I do. They may be controversial ideas, but controversy is one of the reasons my husband and I get along so well. We both firmly believe that upward mobility is directly due to controversy. Unless there was controversy over what is, nothing would change."

"What are some of the things, some of the controversial things, you feel you would like to change?" Mr. McKnight is looking at me rather like a puppy who hasn't the faintest idea what "come here" means.

"First I would like to wipe out sex discrimination in employment. I would like to excise the words 'woman's work' from those sad, threatened men who imprison seventy-five percent of all working women in the lowest-level jobs. Representative democracy in our state and country is a sham."

Tina St. John is so anxious to tackle me, she's about to

tee-tee through the itchy, nubby, scratchy on Grand Rapids' best.

"Miss St. John? You have a question?" Even through her slanted slots, Mama-San sees all.

"Yes. Thank you, Jane. I would like to ask Mrs. Weldon about the millions of women who take pride in 'woman's work,' who don't find home and husband the warped world she paints."

Well, ask me, freak. Why are you asking her if you can ask me? "Miss St. John. Excuse me, but you've missed the point completely." Thank you, Mark. I never thought I'd love that line. "I'm not discussing the nursing mother or the happy homemaker. Nor am I dragging them out of their homes. I'm talking about the ones already out. The sixty million already employed. Are you aware that the majority of women are employed in only two dozen of the more than four hundred available occupations in our country? That there's about as much equality in females' futures as there is in rights for gays?"

Flora Robinson is twisting her handkerchief and shaking her head in either disbelief or palsy. She's a perfect Boop. Axed from the same gnarled stump. Even their wardrobes are cut from the same wash-dress pattern.

"Mrs. Robinson? You have a question?"

"Yes. Thank you. Mrs. Weldon? I naturally share your concern for women's rights, but are you equating their rights with those of the gay people?" Even the word is anathema. Soon, she'll wipe the distaste from her lips on that twisted piece of lace. "Do you really want them to infiltrate our children's schools, our society?"

Up until the very second of washday's challenge, I really didn't care. "Infiltrate, Mrs. Robinson? What a chilling, ominous word. No. I certainly don't think they should infiltrate. I believe they should be allowed to teach our children and enter all of society through the front door." How's that for my middling image? "We have over a half million homosexuals in New York City alone, Mrs. Robinson, who contribute greatly to—"

"Mrs. Weldon. Perhaps infiltrate was a poor choice." I think the half million got to her. Something did. Her handkerchief looks like a worm.

"Ladies. Ladies. Mr. McKnight has a question."

Mr. McKnight is so up tight, it must be a ghost he's seen

Or, *Mr. McKnight, are you so up tight, because you're a closet queen?*

"Thank you. Mrs. Weldon? Does your husband share your strong feelings for gay rights?" No doubt about it. Those pursed lips are a dead giveaway he plays whip-out at the Y.

"We have never discussed it." But I'm sure it won't be long before we do!

"It might turn out to be a strong part of your upward mobility." McKnight smiles in self-appreciation.

More blah-blah-blah. Still more blah-blah-blah. About gays in schools. About gays with the police and firemen. Should I say I'm all for the gays to help put pep in the fireman's ball? Damn. Too late. Commercial.

Oh, we're all so friendly and chatty. And Mama-San, with those teeth, is telling us how stimulating we are. And how interesting, because we're all so different yet so politically courageous. What about Boop, stupido? Her, with her security hanky.

The red light's back on. Mama-San's fat smile is back on. We're on.

"Socialized medicine." God! Blah-blah-blah.

"Women's lib." God! Blah-blah-blah.

"Abortion." Don't listen, God.

"Windup." *Thank God!*

"And now, Amanda Weldon, a windup word from you for our listeners."

Go! Amanda! Go! Sis boom blah-blah-blah. Go! Amanda! Go!

"Thank you. It was 1907 when **Dr.** Alfred Adler gave us the phrases 'inferiority complex' and 'overcompensation.' Unwittingly, he also gave us an out for not facing what's facing us. Gay rights. Equal employment. ERA. These issues and so many others are so vital to today. If my husband is elected, I want to help him meet these issues in the only possible way, straight on. I've always found the time I'm most likely to fall is when I'm running *from* something."

Not bad, Amanda. Not great. But a lot better than the Duke of York and Albany. That's for shit sure!

I feel like those pictures you see of criminals being escorted to jail. Brad is pressing on one side and Lanacola on the other. Nobody is saying anything. We're moving fast, but I still feel a little shove to move it even faster. Should I put my arm across my face for the photographers?

"Did I look okay on the monitors?"

"Wait till we're out of the studio." Brad pushes hard on the metal bar of the heavy exit door. Still holding me by the elbow, we go to the corner and he hails a taxi. A little one. Now I really feel locked in. All of us sitting ramrod straight, no air between.

"Okay, Amanda. Tell me." Brad's voice is hard. "What

the hell was that all about? What the fuck were you doing?"

"My thing." I feel tears.

"Your thing. We're a team. You're a selfish maniac. What in God's name were you trying to prove?"

"That I'm me. Not you. I can be part of a team, but my part. I never even tried my part out before you wrote it in."

"You could have. You've got a mouth. Don't we all know that? I'll tell you why you didn't. Because you didn't want to. Because you knew it was everything everyone wanted to avoid. Because you wanted to get out there and say 'fuck you.' Well, Amanda, the one you really fucked was you."

Tears. Don't drop. Please. "You wanted a shadow. Not a person. I'm not settling for nothing. Never!" Oh, God. Don't let them come.

"You've got to be the oddball in everything. Don't you, Amanda?" I can't believe Brad means to be that cruel. Doesn't he know I can give it back? Or is sex too secondary to the great Howell kingmaking? Does he plan to make me pay forever for *his* bankrupt body?

"Sandy? What do you think? Is it so off base to say what is? Answer me, Sandy. Brad won't kill you. If the truth be known, I think my performance was pretty great. I'm sure I performed better than Brad could perform. In fact, I don't believe he could perform at all." Nice low blow, Amanda. And "low" is the key, nonoperative place, old girl.

Sandy doesn't turn his head from the window. "I know what you mean. Those are hot issues. But that's the trouble. They're too hot. You don't know what pots they'll stir and, being so far ahead, that's what we don't need."

"Were, Sandy. Were." Brad is ice.

Sandy nods to the window. "And with Mark a conservative, maybe you stumped a little loud for gays. It's not our thing."

"A half million votes in the city and probably ten times more in the state isn't our thing?"

"Spare us a census, Amanda. You're not only defenseless, but pathetic." Brad takes a small leather diary from his pocket. "But don't worry about being programmed anymore, because there won't be any more programs." Flashing through the pages, he makes big crosses through advance dates.

"Do I dare ask where we're going?"

"*We're* not going anywhere. Sandy and I are going to the office. Why don't you go to your cozy apartment and wait for your fan mail or maybe just for some fans to catch you unawares." Again, the cruelty.

Would I love to jump bail and land smack in the middle of all that traffic. I want to hear the horns scream and the tires screech and have Brad think he killed me. Prick!

Leaning forward, Brad taps the driver on the shoulder. "Hold your clock at Fifty-fifth. The lady's going on." He reaches in his pants pocket and flips a five-dollar bill in my lap.

As the cab pulls to the curb and stops, Brad angrily helps the door with his foot. While getting out, I catch his cheek with the wadded five. Grabbing it before it hits the ground, he stuffs it back into his pants and slams the door without a look back.

"Where to, miss?"

"Make a right at the next corner and go up Park. Okay?" Why am I still sitting all pushed together? I'm as cramped as when I was captured. I loathe Brad. Did he really think he just had to wind me? Who is he to tell me who am I?

Now that I'm here I don't know why I'm here. I have nothing to do here. Where was I thinking of being before Brad said my apartment? I guess back to Brad's. Back to wait for the hurrahs.

Rrrrrring. Rrrrrring. Rrrrrring. Who knows I'm here? It's obviously not Brad or Sandy. "Hello. Hello." Whoever it was gives up fast. No. There it goes again. Maybe whoever it was thought he dialed wrong. Maybe it's Cathy. She's my fan. Maybe she's a you-know-what and will be an even bigger fan now.

"Hello."

"Amanda?"

Thatsa me, boss. Bigga boss. "Hello, Mark."

"Darcy, Max, and I just had the pleasure of watching you race for the opposition ticket."

Why did I ever pick it up?

"That was quite a performance, Amanda. Is that how you picture helping me? By being some self-styled cheerleader for gays?"

"I'm for anybody who's equal but not treated equal. I can identify with that."

"And what's that supposed to mean?"

"That I won't be force-fed formulas. That *I'll* be the last word on me. I've got a mouth, Mark, but it's attached to a mind, not a string."

"Did you ever hear of waiting till you've got the job before saying what's wrong with the company?"

I hear mumbling in the background. The coaches must be calling the plays. "If you'd listened, Mark, to what I said instead of what your seers said, I said you'd know I was after the woman's vote mostly. You do know, Mark, women vote? It was August 26, 1920, that the Nineteenth Amendment was ratified, stating the right to vote shall not be denied on account of sex."

"You've always been glib, Amanda. But don't get too carried away by your own hot air. A few more todays and nobody'll have a tomorrow."

I slam the phone so hard that the plastic casing comes loose from the works.

Wow! Wow! Wow! Fellas. An awful lot over the goddamn since I've played that tape in this car. I guess that's why I can play it again. God, how those little, tiny comes used to swim over me when I heard it. What's a better feeling? But Maria, we knew we were never what we wanted for always. That's why we were so desperate about always saying it was for always.

What the hell's that granny goose honking at? Would he like me to go through the guy's trunk? I look in my mirror to be sure I can give him the finger. I never give it to blacks or cars ready for the wrecker. Being a nature lover, my pets are beetles and rabbits. And if I'm not lucky enough to see a bright blue bunny who's about to get my whole treatment up his li'l hole cottontail. Aha! More horn. And so a little more finger to you and also for those back home in the euphoria of your split-level warren.

No. I'm not going to turn it. This time I'm letting the tape finish. But it's nothing to be sad about, Maria.

I've decided people who really love driving either have big problems or they don't want thoughts. Yes, you know I'll certainly submit these findings to the *Analysts Annual.*

THESIS ONE: People who constantly find driving relaxing have deep and constant problems.

THESIS TWO: People who sometimes find driving relaxing have problems sometimes.

CONCLUSION: The seriousness of the patient's problem is in direct proportion to his wish for the wheel.

"Amanda. Always be careful at this turn. Railroad crossings are known deathtraps." Guess who? Right! "Your father and I never trusted those switches. We looked for ourselves. I've always read how unreliable they are." Mother's idea of emphasis is saying she read it. To her, when in print, never in doubt.

"Where did you read it, Mother?"

"All over. So many, many times. Why, Amanda? Do you want to trip me up or save your life?"

Here I am, at the *Reader's Digest* exit, standing before the crossing. The untrustworthy light is on, the misleading barricade is down, and here comes the Orient Express carrying Agatha Christie to Istanbul.

"Pedro? Any calls?"

He points to the list. "This lady call two times. She wants you to call. P-a-r-k-e-r. This is her office until five. The others call later."

"Thank you, Pedro." Whatever could fatso want? My body? "Pedro? Ask Francesca to make me an iced tea, please."

"Yes, Mrs. Weldon."

"And bring it upstairs." Suddenly, I'm exhausted. Anyway, I need to take Mama-San lying down. Either I really am gone or they've added more steps to these stairs since I've been to the city. Whew! Like a dead weight, I hit the extra-firm, extra-long, extra! extra! Read all about it. Fuck the spreads being on. They're mine.

"Hello. Ms. Parker, please." I hate Ms. I don't know why I even said it. Even on paper it looks dykey.

"May I ask who's calling."

You may not, you presumptuous bitch. "It's Amanda Weldon. I'm returning her calls." I make sure I enunciate the *s*.

"Amanda? Jane Parker."

"Yes. Hello."

"You sound so far away, my dear."

"I drove back to the country to be able to pick up the children." That even makes me sick.

"You're lucky they're still small."

Not luck, Parker House roly-poly. It's a matter of age. Remember? "Have you any children?"

"Long since flown."

How'd they get airborne? "Rill-y?"

"Oh. Thank you. But yes. It's true."

You mean you really thought I thought *rill-y*? "I called the minute I got home and got your messages." Let's hear it.

"Firstly, Amanda, I want to say that in behalf of myself and the producers, we feel today's program was the finest we've had since our series began. Not only was our live audience enthusiastic, but there was a fire and an electricity among our staff. And a very positive response is coming in over the switchboard. We feel most of these reactions were due to you. It's not that everyone shared your opinions, but everyone admired your courage. Your husband is fortunate, Amanda."

Usually when things are this crazy, I want to wake up, but now I want it all to continue. I *must've* been exhausted, because the last thing I remember was flopping on the un-opened bed. Shoes and all, Mother!

"In fact, Amanda, we would like you to return next week for our special, 'Topics Candidates Won't Face.' And don't worry about its being so soon. A knowledge like yours is enough preparation, dear."

There are times when I've come in my sleep. And sometimes I've raked in the blue chips at Cannes and Biarritz. I've even been with Mother when she wasn't teaching me. But this has to be the best. Granted, it's a one-shot, but what timing.

"It's next Thursday from seven-thirty to eight. Is that good?"

Well, there's the Charcoal Fantasy at the club. Maybe I better think about it. Charcoal Fantasy, you know, only comes during the summer. And we have a table with the Whitethorns and the Van Sandts. I am definitely going to have to think about it. I've thought. *Yes.*

"Amanda? Are you there? Is Thursday all right? Amanda?"

"This is Amanda."

"Did something happen to our connection?"

"Were you speaking all this time?"

"Yes. About Thursday evening. How much did you hear?"

Sitting upright, I dig my nail into the fat flesh beneath my thumb. My God. It hurts and dents. "I guess the connection did go bad a minute. Could you just repeat a little?"

I don't believe it. I do believe it. I believe in me. Yes, I believe in me. "Definitely, *yes.*"

"I'm so happy, Amanda. I knew you would."

"Jane? Would you do me a favor please, because I must pick up my daughters at ballet this very second." Even they'd crack up at that. The gawks.

"Of course."

"Please call my husband at his office and make sure it's fine with him. And then call Mr. Brad Howell of Howell Associates and tell him what you just told me to see if he has any reservations, or perhaps ideas. He's so sensitive to audience response and to the feel of things. It would mean so much if you . . ."

"Consider it done. I'll be in touch. And congratulations on this morning."

"Thank you. Good-by." You know, I can tell by her voice she's gotten thinner and younger. And do you also know I feel there's an ever increasing possibility that these giant think tanks might have to wrestle with my instincts instead of their expertise. As for finding what to say, is there such a thing as a natural? What do you think, team? Here's what I think.

> *Bailey and Darcy and Maxie and Sandy*
> *Marcus and Brad-y and Latham the dandy*
> *You're only with me when your words I do sing*
> *That's why myself is my favorite thing.*

When I think of their toughness and your softness, Maria, I'm sad. I'm sad for me and I'm sad for you, too, Maria. I was sad for you when I heard Latham at that meeting, heard him counting his money. But I don't want you to be sad. I wanted to tell you that as I played the tape

in the car. But I will tell you. And you will listen, won't
you? Please?

We'll have lunch. Like old friends. Even like old lovers,
because I can picture us together now and not feel those
funny feelings anymore. And Maria, you're going to find so
many people to love you. But make sure you find them on
Latham's time and on his money. It's no different from
looking for a better job while you're in one. It's fair. It's
more than fair. What isn't fair is for him to have you at
all.

I've been wanting to call, Maria. I just haven't been
able to. And now that I can, I don't know what to say.
Maybe just, "Let's have lunch, Maria. Please?"

15

I hate going into dark restaurants for lunch like I hate
coming out of matinees into the afternoon. The saloon
squalor is just as disorienting as that first shock of daylight.
That's why I love it here with all the sunshine and flowers.
But where is Henri? I did say the corner table, though,
didn't I?

"Yes? May I help you?"

"Is Henri on vacation?" That's letting him know, big
girl.

"Yes. In France with his family. I am Charles."

"I'm Mrs. Weldon. I have a reservation for two. And I
asked—"

"I know. For the table by the window." Leaving the
lectern of reservations, Charles leads me to the far corner.

"Thank you, Charles."

"Would you care for something while you wait?"

"Yes. I think so. If the white wine is really chilled, I'd like a glass without ice. And please, Charles, remove the bread sticks."

"Thank you, madam," he says, smiling and backing away.

Hurry, Maria, before I begin to believe I don't have anything to say. Or what I have to say isn't really anything.

"Oh. Thank you, Charles. Just the right temperature. Thank you." God, I don't believe it, but she's here again. She has a lot in common with the Scarlet Pimpernel. "Never, dear, order bar wine if you're in a restaurant early. Chances are it's a bottle from the previous evening. You know, it's never the same as just opened." I don't think she ever read that one.

I hate to sit staring while waiting. Taking out my agenda, I do what I always do when I have nothing to do. Make lists. Lists of whom I have to call, of menus for the weekend, of guests we're having, of doctors to see, of people I've fucked. Taking the unopened rose from its vase, I put it to my nose. No smell at all. Why do only some roses smell? Everything else that's supposed to smell smells. Why only some roses? You see, Gertie, a rose is not a rose.

"No more now. Thank you." I put my palm over the top of my glass. "I'll wait."

There's not a chance she wouldn't. No. There couldn't be. Anyway, it's only a little after one. What other lists can I make now? I know. I'll write down a number and then look up and see how close it comes to how many men are in the room. Then I'll do hats. Then Bloody Marys.

"Pardon me, madam." It's Charles. He's pulling the table for Maria. She looks beautiful. I can't believe how

beautiful. She's tan, her hair's tied back in chiffon. She reminds me of that first time in Mexico.

"Maria. You look beautiful." I go to squeeze her arm,
but stop in the middle. I hope she didn't notice.

"Hello, Amanda. You look well, too."

"Have some wine. It's cold and crisp. I've already had
some," I say, rolling the stem of my glass between my fingers.

"I'm not late. Am I?" Maria looks at her Cartier Piaget
buckle-strap watch.

"No. Not at all. I was early. I wanted to make sure to
get this table so we'd be alone." Now why did I say that?
It's not some tryst we're having or some horrible scene
we're going to have. Damn!

"It's so beautiful out that I walked. That's why I
thought I was late."

"No. No. You're on the dot. I love you in coral, Maria. I
never saw you in coral before. It's a marvelous color for
you."

"I wasn't sure. I'm glad you like it." Maria is looking at
me, but our eyes never seem to meet. "You were wonderful
on the show, Amanda. You came over wonderfully. The
makeup and everything was great."

"Glen, the makeup man at NBC, takes years off you. It's
amazing to sit at the mirror and watch him wipe them
away."

"Oh."

"I'm doing another show, Thursday." I'm twirling so
fast, my glass careens into the vase. As the water streams
across the table, I try to stop the flow with my napkin.

"Let me, madam." Luckily, Charles has brought wine as
well as napkins.

"Did any get on you, Maria?"

"No."

"You sure?"

"Yes. None."

"Good."

After Charles leaves, we both sit with our glasses full. What now? Happy days? Good health? Prosit? Down the hatch? Up yours?

"To tomorrow, Maria." I swear to God I don't know where those words came from and I haven't a clue what they mean. I only know we're both drinking, not crying.

"Latham says Mark is a cinch for the primary. Are you glad?"

"I don't know. I guess I'm mostly glad. If this is what we really want, I want to win. I'm not always sure it is, though."

"It's all Latham can talk about when he can talk."

Again, my reaction is to reach out. But I catch it sooner this time. "How's the photography?"

"I definitely have a show at the Whitney in October. It sounds crazy, but it's on the architecture of highways and freeways seen from all angles. Helicopters, cars, trains, flat on your stomach." Our eyes meet and she looks happy.

"Congratulations."

"Thank you, Amanda. Thank you. It's due to you."

"You can only lead a horse, Maria. What's Taylor doing this summer?"

"Again thanks to you. He's gone to Mexico with the experiment. He's living with a family of eight in Guadalajara."

"Good. He'll be able to help us all with all our help." We both laugh. I suddenly remember her fluent Spanish. How nice of her to laugh, anyway. How typical.

"Amanda? I was so afraid to see you. I almost didn't

come so many times. That's really why I walked. I could turn back easier. I still can't believe you want to see me again." Maria is looking into her wine. Her voice is small, like the tiny child with the big "I'm sorry."

And here *I* am again cast in the "Don't worry. Everything will be all right" part. "Don't worry, Maria. Everything's all right. Your reaction would have been mine. Anybody's." As soother and salver, I can reach out. And do. What I don't do is linger.

"Thank you, Amanda. How many times do you think I've said 'thank you' to you?"

"Too many. Let's have another glass and we'll order if you're hungry."

"I'm not, really, but I'd like some more wine."

"Perfect. Waiter? Some more wine, please." He tries to take my glass, but I'm not giving that swallow to anyone but me. I have to nurse it until he returns.

"It's so pretty here, Amanda. How are Sonia and Sara?"

"Horrible. Showing off. Telling their good friends their father is going to be governor. Keeping them from camp to campaign was a big mistake. Screw the candy-box images. The best thing for them would be not to be in the middle of all this bogus bull."

"Why don't you take them away?"

"I might. I very well might."

The waiter reaches down and exchanges our now empty glasses. "Waste not want not," I say through a sickly smile. His smile back is worse.

"Amanda? I don't want to dwell on it or anything, but what was your first thought about what I did?"

Must you go over it? It's making me all naked again. "You'll admit, Maria, I didn't have much time to think and when I did, I didn't want to. I pushed it away until I could live with it. And after living with it for a while, as I said I decided it would have been anybody's reaction." Why did I tell that ass to take the bread sticks? I'd even settle for picking off the sesame seeds.

"What were the repercussions?" Maria's intensity is almost morbid.

"Some snide cracks. Nothing not handleable. But that's all over and maybe the speedy exit was the best out. I should thank you now. Is your mother coming east? Do you have any plans to visit her? How is she?"

"No. Fine. Amanda? The very first time you saw Mark afterward, what did he say?"

"Mark? You mean Brad. Just the snide cracks. But he's not exactly all missionary position, either."

Maria gulps the last of her wine. "Should we have one more?"

"Fine." I nod to the waiter who by now understands it's not for food.

"Amanda? If we talk about it for a minute more, I promise not to mention it again. Believe me, it's as horrible for me, but I have to know what Mark did with them. God, I'm sorry. I'm so very sorry."

Maria and I are obviously not watching the same movie. Or something is drastically wrong with the sound.

"It was the only thing I had to lash out with. And only that moment was real to me. For weeks, I've wanted to call you." Maria digs into her Vuitton sack for a handkerchief and glasses. "It's not the wine, Amanda. I'm not high. I'm really hot."

What are you? Who are you? What are you trying to put into words that you know I know, but I don't know anything about? "I don't think, Maria, we're talking about the same thing."

"Why are we here?"

"To be friends. I'm as much to blame. Maybe more."

"Not true. Never. You never would have given Latham *my* letters, Amanda. Never. I hate myself. And Mark is so cold and clever. You always said how cold he is. What's he doing with them? Holding them over you? Is that why the girls aren't in camp? Did he threaten you unless they campaigned? Amanda? I hate myself." Tears are streaming from beneath the YSL lenses.

A drench of perspiration covers my body. I can feel the beads popping on my forehead and under my hair. I don't want to say anything right this second. I first have to synchronize the action and sound. I have to put it in reverse, then run it again. Okay. Forward. Maria. Letters. Mark. My letters to Maria. My letters to Maria to Mark.

"I couldn't get there fast enough, Amanda. I raced from your apartment to my apartment to Mark's office. Did he say when I threw them on his desk, the ribbon tore, and they fell all over?"

"No, Maria. He didn't. He never said anything about the ribbon." What in God's name is *he* playing? What is he doing or wanting? It's not natural not to explode. No matter how he hates encounter. When did we last sleep together? Since the letters? Yes. Anything different? God forbid.

"Amanda? What did he say? You can't torture me any more than I've tortured me. And how can't you hate me? It's not natural."

That's why, Maria. Nothing about any of this is natural.

"Please, Amanda. Tell me what he said."

"Not much, Maria, really nothing. Since you threw the letters in such fury, he knew it was over between you and me. Right? And since it was your fury, he knew I must've called

it over. Right? So he couldn't plead with me to break it up."
But why didn't he care if there were others? Another one
now? What's he after?

I'm glad no one's here I know. I'm glad Henri's not here.
Is that superficial enough? It's real, though.

"He never tried to hit you, Amanda?"

"Mark's not physical, Maria." That's the century's under-
statement.

"Did he show you the letters?"

"No. I'm sure they're in the vault next to our marriage
certificate."

"I'm so sorry, Amanda."

"Can we see a menu?" I ask the waiter who's been cruis-
ing our table and staring so hard he must be undercover for
Robinson. Wait till he sees I only want to fan myself.
"Thank you. Sorry to do this, Maria, but I'm dying."

"Never say sorry to me, Amanda. You could never do
anything that—"

"Maria. Stop it!" I can't stand any more tears or
choked words. "I didn't ask you here to be sorry or sad.
Enough guilt. And remember, what happened took two." I
smile at her with a great feeling of sadness and sorrow.
"Friends?"

"Friends. Can you, will you ever trust me?"

I tear today's dated page from my agenda.

> Dear Maria,
> I trust you. I love you.
> You friends for always,
> Amanda

Oh, God. Back into the Vuitton. Here they come.
Handkerchief. Glasses. I hold her small, warm hand between

mine and suddenly feel a soft, small friendly kiss on my cheek.

Thank goodness Maria had to go to a meeting at the Whitney. Otherwise, she'd have gone with me to my nonexistent dentist appointment. Being alone will help me get my breath. I'm going to need it when I get to Mark's office.

Why do I imagine there are envelopes in every store window I pass? Envelopes with matching letter paper and small engraved cards to go with gifts, all appliquéd with love and longing, desire and destruction. I wonder if Mark told Max about the letters. In Mark's mind, this would definitely be classified under business. Big business! Maybe he's burned them all. After all, he knows I'll never know he knows and so it's better just to abrogate the aberration. Transient, as it was, of course. Of course, that's exactly what he did.

Never, Amanda! Not Mark Weldon. Not your Mark. Actually, isn't his thesis "the principles of harmony and proportion are never in the architecture of buildings, but in the structure of their deals"? But just what is your deal for me, Mark?

How should I begin with him? Lead from strength? Wait for him to play his hand? Then trump his ace? Now you've got it, dummy.

You've got the whole deck here in your hand.
You've got the whole deck stacked in your hand . . .

How often I've heard Max say, "If you're big in building and your buildings are big, be on a high floor. Then you can point out your successes to the dunces who think you're there for the river view." Now, on my way up to that river view, I'm not sure if it's the elevator's jolts or my meeting with Mark that's ousting my insides.

How like Mark to have his Manhattan office in Rockefeller Plaza. Just Mark and Max and those other brothers. And Mark, as much a part of their rock, as I am of his. Some crock o' rock, Mark!

Right before I get to the door, I brush my hair for the closed-circuit TV. I wouldn't want Marcie to see anything but a star on her set. After all, I have a reputation to maintain.

"Hello, Mrs. Weldon," Marcie calls from the end of the hall. And I must admit an impressive hall with all those models of Maxweld monoliths that can be pointed out from the long wrap-around windows.

"Hello, Marcie. Hot enough?" If there weren't such a thing as weather, what would people talk about to people they didn't want to talk to?

"The air conditioning here is perfect. I guess I'm lucky."

You sure are. A secretary for twenty-seven years, spending each night with a dying brother, each vacation with a crippled mother, each day working for Miracle Mark, and never having been married. Well, maybe the last does make up for the rest.

"I'll tell Mr. Weldon you're here. He's with Miss Mazurski. I think she looks a little like you. Not much. But a little."

Thanks for explaining "little," lucky.

"What a surprise," Mark says, opening the door.

"Well, hardly," I answer cheerily. "I did call."

"I mean just your being here. You remember Ann."

Just Ann? "Of course." I extend my hand. "We met at my apartment."

"Right."

Hey. That's my word.

"I saw you on television, Amanda. You were very brave. Very."

Brave? What kind of a fucking adjective is brave? I think I know what it is, Annie, but Mark's not going to know. No way. "Oh. Thank you so much, Ann. Really, thank you. Coming from you, that's such a compliment. I'm so flattered you thought that. Thank you." If I continue I might be quarantined for being rabid.

"Ann was just leaving," Mark says too quickly, like some obvious oaf in a sit-com.

My God. As she passes the window, I notice my blond wisps have really streaked through her hair. "I hope not on my account."

"No. No. I really must go. I have a meeting with a ridiculous group of anti-gay landlords." She smiles at me.

Got it again, Annie. Oh, wow. Did I. Wiping up after me, hmmm? What a nice girl you are, little Annie. "Well, I'm sure you'll be very convincing and refocus those short-sighted views." My smile is all outdoors and hopefully pushing her in that direction.

After she leaves, I try to appear relaxed as I settle into the sofa. My eyes are riveted to the top of Mark's desk, the desk where all the letters spilled when the ribbon tore. After Maria ran out, did he calmly sit there and read them? One by one by a hundred?

"Well, Amanda. To what do I owe this?" Mark is almost regal in his stiff voice and high-back chair.

"I know you'll be away for a few days campaigning upstate and you know me, when I have something on my mind it has to come right off." I try a casual grimace. "I think it would do everybody good if I took the girls to

Europe for what's left of the summer." Mark is looking at me as if I've just flown in through the window with a scheme even more preposterous than my entrance. "What do you think, Mark?"

"As you know, Amanda, I'm a quoter. And to answer you in the words of a very famous woman, 'No way.'"

"Mark. It's no good for the children here. They're being carried away by your fame, my television, even their own miniprincess press. I hate to see them change. I mean that, Mark."

"How selfless."

"Maybe it isn't completely. I need some cooling off, too. But what's wrong with a mother spending time alone with her daughters? It'll even read good, Mark."

"Who are you, Amanda? What are you? One day a star. The next a feminist. Today a mother. And yesterday, lots and lots of yesterdays, Maria's lover." Every word slices the air with the same steel edge. And the phrases run together like some wild watercolor caught in the rain. And all the while his eyes are digging and digging into the mixed media of my mind.

Was that his ace? Maria? Has he really played it or only lifted it from his hand? I don't want to go out of turn. This late in the game, I could never make up the penalty.

"I see, Amanda, you're intelligent enough, or rather not fool enough, to deny it."

Not yet, Amanda. He's still only pulled the card. Only pulled, not played.

"Remember, sweetheart, our old dictum? Never write a letter? Never tear one up? Were you that carried away?"

"How long have you known?"

"Long enough to know a moment like this would happen."

"What I did didn't matter. Right? But what I might do

was what you were waiting for. Right? Just a weapon in war. All is fair in war, Mark, but not in love. Never in love. Right, Mark? Tell me. The truth is always easy to say when you're not in love, Mark."

"Right on all counts, Amanda."

"You were probably even pleased with the disclosure. It's like banking blackmail until you need to cash it. But how nice to know it's there. And how nice we have such a nice relationship."

"Those were my sentiments exactly when Maria let it all fly. And now that you know where you're at, let me tell you where you're staying. Here! Right here, Amanda! You and Sara and Sonia are going to be my devoted bookends, hugging me all the way to the primary." Mark gets up as if the interview's over and the interviewee may also rise and get the hell out.

It's time, Amanda. He's made his play. For God's sake, don't miss yours. He's leaving the table. He thinks you'll throw in your hand. Hurry. "Just a minute, Mark. Can you grant the prisoner a little ear time, please?"

Mark entwines his fingers and stretches his arms tiredly before him. "Hopefully, it will be short."

"But not sweet, Mark. Are you sure you don't want to sit?"

Mark unclenches his fingers and leans against his desk. "Go on, Amanda."

"What I adore is the true hypocrisy of it all. You're beginning to believe you really *are* Miracle Mark, that you really *are* working for the good of the people. What people, Mark? You, the people?"

Mark's exhale and glazed eyes have just the right amount of disdain for my explosion. "Maybe, Amanda, I should *lie* down."

"No. No. I'm almost there. I just love the foreplay. It excites me. That's one thing you never did learn about me, Mark. Anyway, don't worry. I'm used to doing it myself."

"I've got a plane to catch."

"I've got a bomb to drop."

Mark's hand pats a feigned yawn.

"Don't buy a mortgage or a lease until you're sure of a tenant for that mortgage or that lease. Right, Mark?"

"About what?"

"That dictum?"

"Isn't that enough foreplay? You must be ready by now."

God, how I would hate to deal with Mark without a stacked deck. "I just want to ask you, Mark. Hadn't you and Max nailed down the fact that the Olympics would be played on the garbage fields of Times Square before you so generously cleaned them up by buying out all the Forty-second Street real estate you could? Yes, my darling husband, before you invested one dirty dollar you knew that what the owners believed were worthless slums would soon be prime property. And Mark, please don't bank on its not being traceable to your untraceable European account. Because, for your information, it is. Your whole sweetly charitable Maxweld maneuver can still nail you to the wall."

Mark's disbelieving eyes don't leave me as he walks backward, in a slight crouch, to the chair behind his desk.

"I don't know, Mark, why you're sitting down now. I'm about through. We'll drop you a card from London."

16

"TWA flight six seventeen for New York. Last call. TWA flight six seventeen boarding for New York."

"Come on, girls. Sonia. Sara. Please. We'll miss the plane. You should have thought about Pedro's present for the last six weeks, not the last six minutes. Come on."

"Place your parcels and your purse here, please, madam. Thank you. Girls! Girls! Please don't pass through the monitor together. One at a time, please. Thank you. My, aren't they sweet. Proper English dresses on them, too."

They do look good with that little-girl smocking and crisp collars. Certainly, two damn sights better than the cut-off rags they'll unearth the minute we get home. Why can't they ever walk with me? Why are they always lagging?

"Will you hurry along? Good grief. Why must you always be dawdling?" Were those words I? Ekchewly, yes. Jolly good, that. I rahthah liked it myself.

"How many people can fit in this jet?" Sara asks.

"More than any other."

"No one's asking you, Sonia. Mommy?"

"Three hundred and sixty." Now that's the kind of important emotional question Mommy's so good at.

"Can we go into the bump?"

" 'Bump,' Sara, is ultimately crude. It's a bar, not a bump, stupid."

"We had such a nice trip, Sonia, Sara. Why is all this starting now? Anyway, the bar is only for first class."

"Why are we always tourist?"

"When I was your age I'd never even—"

"Been to Europe!" In chorus, yet.

"Mrs. Weldon? Yours is the bulkhead seat on the aisle and the girls are six rows back."

"Can we see the movie from there?" Sonia asks.

"That's why we're there, dummy."

"What's the movie?"

The stewardess already seems weary. "I'm sorry. I'm afraid I haven't checked. There should be a program in the pocket in front of your seat."

"Can we go upstairs?"

I shake my head at this poor girl who, on our return and on our account, will undoubtedly leave flying for a career in planned parenthood. "Sonia and Sara, will you please sit so others can do the same? And hold on to your own sweaters. Just sit." Children should positively be double fare, not half.

Thank goodness I'm up here. Not so much for my size as for my sanity. Although it certainly isn't crowded. I guess everybody's home by now, by Labor Day. But wasn't it just yesterday we flew over these same gray cliffs of Dover? And weren't the girls just feeding the pigeons in Trafalgar Square while not listening to a word about Lord Nelson and Lady Hamilton? I kept wondering if it was the fate of all Emmas to suffer and they kept wondering how much pigeon-pooh would drop on Nelson's head.

Did I really think I could get away by being away? That miles would mean removal? Maybe I did. But ever since I did, I've become so devout a Muslim, I can give certified proof that mountains do move. Ekchewly!

"This *is* Mrs. Weldon. . . . The what? . . . Paris *Tribune?* Here in the lobby? We just got. . . . How did they. . . . No.

I don't want them to come up. . . .Yes. I'll come down. . . .
Yes. Right away."

"Can we come, Mommy?"

"May we."

"May we?"

"No."

The succession of flashbulbs as the elevator cage opens
activates my arm to such a degree that it propels my purse
across the lobby to the popping paparazzi. But in a miracle
of one-arm banditry, the flasher makes such a stupendous
catch that I know he's used to being tossed at and out. The
clincher is the way he hands it back, with all the gallantry
of returning a dropped hanky.

While noting the *mon Dieu* horror of the concierge, I
suddenly feel a keeper-type push on my arm, maneuvering
me away from the scene of my madness.

"I'm so sorry for the stupidity of that camera. I had told
him no." Even the calm of his voice makes him sound white-
suited. White-suited, but tricolor-accented.

"Who are you?"

"You must excuse me, Mrs. Weldon."

"Why?" I pull my arm back.

"I know what you feel. I am Paul LaFoure of the Paris
Tribune. I am sorry, but I would have thought your Mr.
Lanacola had—"

"If he would have, Mr. LaFoure, I wouldn't be here.
And that's why he didn't."

"I understand. Believe me, I do. And please forgive me.
Come. Let us have a coffee together."

Again, the push. But why am I going with him? And
look at him, with his typically thin bony face, the kind so
many Americans so often mistake for aristocracy. Yet there
does seem to be some coziness underneath that sharp Hu-
guenot heritage.

"You already have your uncooperative, terror-stricken pictures. What else do you want?"

"Not those. I promise you." LaFuck's eyes cut right through my anger with their "I don't blame you, but I am really sorry" appeal.

"Then what do you want?"

"France wants desperately to host the Olympic Centennial. You see, it was in Paris in 1895 that a committee met and decided to reestablish the games after a lapse of more than a thousand years. And due to that Paris meeting, the Olympics returned to Athens the very next year."

That's good, fuckface. Right up my incidental shot put.

"Personally, Mr. LaFoure, I believe the Centennial belongs in Greece."

"So do I." The hand is now pushing from the middle of my back. "Since we finally agree on something, will you have some coffee with me and give me a quote on how you and your husband believe the Olympics should be in France?"

"Of course."

The total scene is so absurd that as he laces my coffee with Pernod, I smile like the finally subdued patient.

"Aphrodisiacs are best at breakfast. In the evening, they suffer from too much competition," he says, taking a long sip.

The heaviness of his suit is making me hot all over. What is it with Europeans? Do they think "summer weight" is slang for bourgeois? *Mon Dieu!* But I do like the way the cuff isn't all buttoned, exposing the extravagance of custom-made. I like it, too, because it's classy. Maybe even aristocratic. "Are you married, Mr. LaFoure?"

"It took you slightly longer than most. At least you

know my occupation so that didn't come first." Although he means what he says, he looks amused.

"Have you ever timed how long it takes the average American to be ugly? That could add a new dimension to your old disgust."

"No. No. No. Do not get me wrong. I find it charming, not ugly. Just like you look and laugh at my heavy suit. I know. I can see." He cups my hand and smiles. "And please, my name is Paul. I shall be thirty-eight tomorrow. My wife is Jeanne. We are married for twelve years and have three, of course brilliant, boys. I give Jeanne the privilege of taking them every summer to her parents' home in Vence. In August, I join them for three family-filled weeks. More would be intolerable. I can never understand why, after one is grown up, he should be forced to take on other parents just as he has become free from his own."

"You must call me Amanda. I have two girls. One is ten and one is eleven. They are upstairs. They are, of course, prodigies. I think I adore them." God, the coffee's good that way. Paul, don't ask me if I want another. Just order it. If you ask me, I'll have to say no. I'll have to go back and adore my two daughters.

"What have you planned for them today?"

To lock them up and give them tranquilizers. "We are going to Versailles."

"Ah, but you should go at night when they have the *son et lumière*, the glorious lights that spring from the fountains. It is extraordinary."

"I would love to. But the car is set and our lunch is arranged. And since the girls don't really listen to the guide when they're awake, imagine at night. So far, what's thrilled them most is that Marie Antoinette became queen at fifteen. And what's disappointed them most is that they couldn't see her guillotined."

What a great laugh he has. It's closer than cozy. "When I took my boys to Washington, first they insisted on seeing Kennedy's grave and then where Lincoln was shot. They are all little ghouls." Paul turns to the approaching waiter. "*Merci. Oui. Merci.* I took the liberty, Amanda, of ordering another. If you cannot . . ."

I look at my watch, not noticing the time. "No. No. One more is fine." I love how he says my name, Ahmondah.

"I have a sister in Paris with a girl your girls' age. I know she would love to have your daughters for dinner tomorrow. And that will free you to celebrate my becoming thirty-eight. The very same age that Marie Antoinette lost her head."

Monsieur, I might very well do the same.

"What a lovely picture, Paul. Is this your wife?" No, genius. It's really the wolf, but this time instead of a granny gown, it's a wedding gown. And instead of in bed, it's in church. And instead of alone, she's on Paul's arm. Keep quiet! "She's lovely, Paul. Really lovely. But you look so serious."

"Amanda. When a man exchanges the adoration of many for the complaints of one, it's a grave step."

"Or maybe even omit 'step.' "

I just love Paul's laugh. I love it. He smiles and holds my chin between his fingers. Close, close, close to his lips. "Do you have any doubt about my illustrious past? Or our future?" He takes my scarf and slowly unwraps it from my shoulders. "Amanda. Have a look around the apartment while I fix a drink."

At least I'm improving. I'm not asking if the three boys skiing with his wife are his sons. And I'm not asking him if this is he golfing and riding. Anyway all these sports are exhausting me, yet I should evince some interest. "Paul? Where was this riding picture taken? The one with you leading the group?"

"Oh, that. That's at my mother's in the country. It's only an hour from Paris. It was before the hunt. Do you ride?"

"I did. But I don't." It hurts Mark's gonads.

"Pity."

I feel almost on tour walking through these big old rooms with their high ceilings and intricate moldings. Just perfect for the worn tapestry rugs, the deep bombé commodes and elaborate boulle tables. Yet somehow, now, it all looks lonely, as if it's waiting for the season to start and for tanned, back-from-summer bodies to gossip from the over-cushioned chairs.

"Amanda? Amanda? Where are you?"

"In here. I'm coming." Why aren't the rooms numbered so I can find my way back to admissions?

"Amanda. Where did you go?"

"I don't know. I lost the tour."

"But not your guide. Amanda, I know you don't care especially for champagne, but it is my birthday and a grand occasion." After pouring two glasses, he takes my chin until our lips touch and touch and touch.

"Paul? Shouldn't we call your sister?"

"Are you worried about the girls? I promise they will sleep very well. I shall not promise the same for you." That smile. That everything smile. *Wow!*

At first, the linen of the sheets feels rough and harsh. But don't worry, Mother, I would never, never . . . and have him think I'm not used to the best? Really! Why don't you ever trust me?

Paul. Please hurry. Cover me. I feel extra naked under this soaring canopy. It's so far away. God! I think I put on too much perfume. I can smell it all over. That was dumb. Furiously, I wave the sheet up and down over my body.

"Amanda? Are you sending smoke signals?"

I didn't mean hurry that fast. Damn. "No. No. I thought maybe there was too much perfume. I mean it suddenly seemed so strong." I don't know what the hell I mean. Now I feel even more naked, and I don't know why this comes to me, but I feel American. God. I wish I were back at the Ritz.

"I think it's just right." Paul puppy-sniffs my ears and neck in a way that immediately sets me in motion. "Amanda. I want to look at you," he says, pulling down the sheet.

And you thought you did feel naked?

"You are so long and so lovely." Ever so lightly, his hand moves from my head to my feet and back again. "I want to see everything. Everything."

I cross my arms over my eyes so I won't see anything. As if rippling a keyboard, he starts again at my feet and moves up between my legs. While one hand circles above my waist, the other strays between my thighs, at first softly caressing, then harder, then faster. Never stopping. Plunging his fingers inside me, he pushes them in and out. Easily, slowly, harder, faster. Never stopping. Shamelessly, I spread my legs as far as I can while I twist and writhe. But Paul's fingers stay with me.

Abruptly, he pulls my arm from my eyes and pins it at my side. "I want to see your eyes, Amanda. Now! Your eyes. Look at me. I want your eyes to tell me exactly when."

I open my eyes and watch his body cover mine. It is

exactly when. "Oh, God, Paul." His lips, his tongue, they're over my eyes, my nose, my tears. Maybe when wasn't then. Now is more. "Paul. Paul. Oh, God, *Paul!*"

"This is Captain Andrews speaking. We have reached our cruising altitude of thirty-three thousand feet and we anticipate a smooth flight over the Atlantic. Our stewardesses should be serving . . ."

The drive along the Moyen Corniche from the Nice airport throws off so much diesel smoke that it looks more like the Long Island Expressway than anything resembling the Gold Coast. Thank goodness, though, Cannes is near Vence so it won't take too long from our hotel. If the pension is really halfway, it shouldn't be over twenty minutes. And since Vence is high up, I won't have to drive through this bumper-to-bumper crop.

I wonder if we'll have an aperitif first. Pernod and coffee? Will our bedroom have a lock on the door? Or will the maid come in and out with as much concern as if it were empty? I hope so. There's something exciting about it.

Taking each girl's hand, I squeeze them tightly. I'm so very happy. For them and for me. I'm so glad to be with them. How I love, love, love them. And how happy I am I met Paul.

"Ouch, Mom. Those are my knuckles."

"Sonia. You're such a brat. Mom is just saying she loves you."

"But it hurts."

Of course love hurts, but never fear, Mommy won't guilt you with anything that dramatic.

"Mom? What was the name of the cheese market in Holland?" Sara asks.

"Alkmaar," Sonia blurts, overjoyed.

The horns of a mother's dilemma. Should she say good memory to one and zilch to two? Why isn't anything ever simple? How do we get to simple? One child for one trip? One man at one time? Never polygamy, always monogamy. *But,* continuous monogamy? Simple. The continuum of one-after-one-after-one equals the square root of a rounded life.

"Alkmaar. Oh, yeah," Sara answers flatly.

" 'Yeah' is not a word." I have no doubt that sentence is my sentence for life. Somewhere, sometime, I must have somehow done something to have it continuously intercepted before it ever reaches either one of my progeny's brains.

"Okay, Sonia," Sara continues. "Name the painting of the Dutchmen in the ruffled collars."

"Which one?"

"The wide one."

Any curator would love their phrasing.

"Let me think."

"Give up?"

"No. I'm thinking."

"Still?"

"Still," Sonia says.

" 'The Night Watch.' " I guess Sara felt she was getting close.

"I never gave up."

"Oh, yeah?"

See what I mean, world? "Ladies. Ladies. Would it be too boring for Mother to point out the Mediterranean on our left and peeking high above the walls on our right, some of the most glorious homes in the world? People from every corner of the globe crave to come here."

"Are they all rich in those homes?" Sara is now interested.

"Obviously. Dumbo!"

"Could we buy one, Mommy?"

"Obviously," Sonia chides.

"Obviously not. No way." I'm talking as much for the driver as for the disenchanted. Miraculously, he seems to be closing in on our next suitcase sticker.

And what a glorious suite. Windows all facing the sea and so many fat, squooshy pillows that they alone could make the goose an endangered species.

"Look what we found," Sara yells, as she and Sonia trip over their giant-sized terry robes. "Can we keep them?"

"While you're here only," I say as they turn to each other with a "Don't tell her we'll pack them" look.

"Can we wear them to the beach?"

"You don't think you'll trip on your trains?"

"Can we go?"

May we. *May! May! May!* I guess if I really screamed, they'd remember with, "Oh, yeah."

"Can we get one of those pedal boats?" Sonia asks, her tiny hand pointing to the beach.

"I'll go with you. Then I'll come back here, make some calls, then come back for you. And where I'll say we'll meet, you be!"

"There is a message for you, Mrs. Weldon," the concierge says as we trail through the lobby.

"Thank you. I'm just taking my daughters to the beach. I'll be back in a moment." I smile extra pleasantly.

On my return, I catch his trying to look like he's not looking at a tip before putting it into his pocket. As he slobbers all over the slob, I wonder how much he over-tipped.

"Aha. Mrs. Weldon. Here is your message. It arrived only minutes before you. I'm sorry we did not have time to have it in your room."

"That's all right. Thank you." Ripping open the en-velope, I rush to the elevator. What?

"Call overseas operator #5. New York City. Urgent."

How odd to feel disappointment and even anger at an unknown urgency at home. No fear. No anxiety. No panic. Just an angry letdown.

"This *is* Mrs. Weldon. Is this operator five? . . . No. I'll hold. I don't mind. . . . Hello? . . . Marcie? . . . Hello? . . . Fine. Couldn't be better, thanks. . . . Just as if you're next door. . . . Is everything all right? . . . What? . . . They're what? . . . When did they decide that? . . . They left when? . . . When do they arrive? . . . Is that my time or yours? . . . For how long? . . . Yes. Of course, I am. Naturally. . . . I'm sure he is. Of course. . . . Yes. Wonderful, Marcie. They're wonderful. . . . Yes. I certainly shall. Thank you. . . . Yes. We've been lucky. It's been perfect. . . . Yes. I'm very excited. Very. Good-by. . . . Thank you. . . . Yes. Good-by, Marcie."

Merci, Marcie. You affable asshole. Or rather. Mercy! Marcie. Mercy, *pour moi!* For that wonderful news. You asked if I'm excited. I'm lathering, shaking, heaving excited. What could be more thrilling? Mark and Max, the gold medal swindlers, the tandem Swiss Frankensteins, arriving this very afternoon in Nice? Nice, but not nice. Not nice at all. Paul. Paul!

"Paul. Paul! I can't believe it either, but what can we do? Thank goodness you called. . . . No. She didn't know how long. . . . Me too. . . . What's even more than desperate? . . . I can call you there? . . . I'll call as soon as I know. . . . Oh, God. . . . Me too. Three, four, five, a million, a million trillion." I can just see and feel that everything smile, everywhere.

The thick Cinzano ashtrays, the faded umbrellas, and the preponderance of Americans staring at other tables, not talking at their own, never vary. But still, there's something compelling about this cafe. Whatever action is around is here. And is it ever now.

"Amanda? Did you hear me?"

"Yes, Mark."

"Remember, Amanda, you were the one, in that wonderfully selfless way of yours, who said the trip would read well. You were right. It was a great story. And what I'm planning will be even greater."

"That LaFoure sure did one hell of a job," Max says, frowning from the sun and the smoke.

With all the years Max spent on yachts in the south of France, I can't believe he's sitting here looking like some tired salesman stranded on his way to a used car convention. His short socks, loose tie, and now permanently pleated pinstripes make me want to shove him through some door that will revolve into "Resort."

"You're looking very fit, Amanda," Mark says. "The European air obviously works wonders for the harried housewife."

"I hope an heir with dough." Max does a Groucho with his cigar and eyebrows.

"Impossible," Mark says, smiling. "Amanda's all for girls. Excuse me. For the girls. It's her selfless maternal instinct."

From the way Max is flicking, he must have finally found some tobacco. "Maybe, Marcus, her health hails from lack of contamination. But what's your excuse for honeymoon pallor?"

I think I'm hearing something that isn't being said. Why do I always listen so closely?

"Mark? Where do we film this togetherness idyll? And would you like the last hurrah to be of Mommy being buried in sand?"

In one of his more endearing gestures, Max tweaks the end of my breast. "You should never be his. He deserves—"

"Who?" Mark asks defiantly.

"Whom, Marcus. Whom."

Mark must be nervous. He's squeezed the whole lemon into his Perrier. "Amanda. The camera crew's coming early tomorrow. They'll shoot three scenes and add the voice-over later. One scene sailing, another at a picnic, and the last at the Matisse Chapel during a special mass to grant me guidance."

"On that nauseating note, grant me another Pernod and coffee. Please, God."

"Marcus. I don't know what, but I think Amanda's telling you something with that Pernod. Four weeks is a long time alone. You agree, Marcus? I mean, I know how lonely you were."

I get what you're painting, Max. But who's it of? Okay. Whom?

Mark gulps his Perrier. "You know, Max, someday that fat mouth will get that even fatter body of yours in big trouble."

"Say. That's good, Marcus. Where'd you steal it?"

"Max? Without me, where would you go for jollies?"

"Whom would I have to kick around?" Even outdoors, Max blows perfect rings.

I love the sensuous way Pernod travels through me. Even the smallest sip is hot and lingering.

"Anyhow, Amanda. This commercial is to show that Marcus Weldon is really uncommercial, that he didn't spend his whole summer politicking, that his family came first."

Of course it does. Hey! Hey! Farmer Gray. Took another load of hay away! I'll bet that pension serves only wine. I'd better bring the Pernod. I can't wait.

"Mark? Are you staying until the end of our trip?" I hope I've infused a confusing amount of hope in my voice.

"You know that's impossible. You don't get back till the primary. I can play it cool, but not crazy."

I know. I'm hep. But when, for God's sake, are you leaving? Hurry.

"I'll go at the end of the week. I need that long in case of retakes."

"How romantic." I feel tears, but only because that's when I leave.

I have only fucked twice in the south of France. Once was on my anniversary, when I pretended Mark was Max. And now again, tonight, when we are both pretending each other is someone else.

"You know, girls, we didn't have to travel to Venice for you to feed pigeons. We could have summered in Central Park."

"I've never seen so many," Sonia says, balancing them on her hands and arms.

"How come there're so many?" Sara asks, showering them with peanuts.

"That's why. What you're doing."

"Everybody's doing it."

"That's more why."

"I guess so, but they're better than museums. I mean for a change."

"And churches. I mean, like Sara, for a change."

"Mommy? How come you said the one who painted 'The Last Supper' invented the airplane?"

The one. What wonderful references they have. How gratifying to have children take so to culture. "I said he made sketches of inventions, including the airplane, almost five hundred years before anybody else. I was calling your attention to genius." Something I don't think will ever worry you.

"Did they ever get the person who stole the thing off the Marini horse?" Sonia asks, looking at Sara.

That did it. That completely set their nervous disorder into a seriously convulsive stage. Nothing like a stolen cock to recall a work of art. Perhaps only perversion can create the true cultural environment for the truly gifted.

Looking at the people in this square, it might be good if Venice does sink. Or maybe just stays under long enough to drown the damage. Then like some enchanted Disney creation, it will rise for its second coming.

"Come on, girls. Enough pigeons. Enough people. We're just in time to see some glass being blown."

Again the looks. Again the hysteria. Again the sound of those delicious know-everything, know-nothing years.

Never have I packed so fast.

"Why are we leaving Venice for London when we've been there already?"

"It's Daddy's brilliant idea that before we go home, Mommy does another interview with that nice man we met in Paris. But now he's in London."

"What'll we do there?"

"We only have a day and a night." But what a day and a night. "I've arranged for you to visit a boys' school in the country and stay overnight with friends of Mr. LaFoure's. The school is so strict you'll probably see teachers paddling boys' bare bottoms when they misbehave." Nothing like a mother appealing to her children's sadistic sensitivity.

What a way to end a trip. And to have it happen as close as tomorrow makes me feel as if I've just swallowed a giant bolt of delirium.

Wow! Wow! Wow, fellas!—No! One fella's enough.

"Ladies and gentlemen. This is Captain Andrews. Since there doesn't seem to be any delay in the metropolitan area, we will momentarily be making our descent into JFK International Airport. Please have your customs forms completed before deplaning. Make sure your seat belts are fastened and observe the no smoking signs. On behalf of myself and the entire TWA crew, it was a pleasure serving you today and we hope you'll fly TWA soon again."

The grinding of the landing gear and the click of seat belts begin to reset my clock. As the silvery skyline closes in across Long Island Sound, I feel that anything's-possible excitement I always feel when I near New York.

I wonder who'll be at the airport. Wouldn't it be fun if they still rolled stairways to the doors for cheesecake exits? Now it's ram the ramp and into the chute. They certainly don't do that on Air Force One. Not only do they have stairs, but a long red carpet and a bunch of long red roses. So what if they're flattened by the cellophane?

"Mrs. Weldon? Mrs. Weldon? Right this way. May we get just a few pictures with your husband, please? Stand right there. Good."

"Now. One more like that. Great."

"How about with the girls? Girls? Get on either side. Right. Good. Perfect."

"Let's have some of all of you and we'll put Mrs. Weldon's mother in the middle. Closer. Closer still. All together now. Beautiful. Stay like that. Don't move. Super."

"Excuse me a minute, Mrs. Weldon. Would you look over here, please? Thank you. I'm Alan Harper. CBS News. Was your arrival planned for today in order to vote for your husband in the primary tomorrow?"

17

"It certainly was. And I urge every registered Republican to do the same. Only by your getting out to vote can Mark Weldon get in."

"Our viewers must have heeded Amanda Weldon's plea. Now, forty-eight hours later, Mark Weldon *is* the Republican candidate for governor. Although victory was predicted, the wide Weldon margin left even the savviest pollsters gaping."

Hail! Hail! Here we are again, gang. Chained to the same screens, in the same room, clinking the same crystal. But instead of watching Mark's living color candidacy, we're glued to his prime time victory.

"And now to last night's victory headquarters where, after Robinson's concession, Weldon told reporters, 'In the early twenties, Scott Fitzgerald wrote that the Jazz Age produced "a new generation, grown to find all gods dead, all wars fought, and all faiths shaken." Not too dissimilar from the corrosive situation we find, but don't face, right here today. When I become governor, I pledge to lead all generations out of the torpor of yesterday's politics and into rebuilding man's faith not only in man, but in mankind.' "

Fitzgerald? How primary-puberty can you get? Wow.

Incidentally, do any of you know our star-spangled anthem was penned by his ancestor, one Francis Scott Key Fitzgerald? No shit. Of course, the song is.

"Speaking from his Albany office, incumbent Matthew Wilcox told our newsman, 'My opponent's salvo of promises will be little match for my twenty years of accomplishments. I am eager for debate and confident that when issues get down to specifics, my opponent won't come up with answers.'"

Darcy smiles at the set. "He's sure old school with that first rule. Always 'my opponent.' Never a name."

"I'll say more than his name," Max yells. "Do you know what you are? You're a cocky-cock, Wilcox sonovabitch."

"Goooooo, Max!" Brad cheers. "Keep stringing those pearls tighter and tighter. Goooooo!"

"Shut up, Princeton. Your job is to put the king's tongue into Marcus' mouth, not mine."

"Max!" I say. "I have told you time and again. When will you ever learn? The king will never put his tongue into Mark's mouth until he becomes a queen."

"We'll hear from the unions now," Darcy says, more to himself than the gang. "With that lead, the Teamsters and Carpenters are sure to break. Being the building boys, they're the ones who'll *suggest* the contractors for Olympic Village. And believe me, we'll listen hard to their suggestions. Their money has a mouth we can't afford to shut."

"With over three million gone in the primary, we're going to need at least three times that till we're through," Latham says. "Make that till Wilcox is through." He laughs at himself by himself.

"We'll be getting shift money, too," Bailey adds. "There'll be lots of shooters liking the odds after this primary. The everyones who don't back hunches anymore."

"We can also count on out-of-state money," Brad says. "The minute they see this coup could one day mean a national sweep, we'll be pushing them off the bandwagon."

Great show, *Bandwagon*. Great score. Of course, "Dancing in the Dark" isn't any "rockets' red glare."

"Nothing's for free," Bailey, the patronage padrone says, with a why-should-I-even-have-to-say-this look. "When generosity explodes, it's from a pride that's got to show and tell. It's one of our uncomplicated childhood hangovers."

Mark paces in front of the window, squinting into his own thoughts. "We're lucky with our ticket," he says. "Damn lucky. To inherit Merebaum's win for lieutenant governor and Ortega's for comptroller gives us the perfect ethnic balance. Schenectady and Spanish Harlem. Even the geography works."

"Even! Are you aware," I hear myself ask, "geography freed the slaves? Abe never would have made President if they hadn't needed a southern candidate to challenge Stephen Douglas for the Senate."

"Which brings us to debates," Brad says, smiling at me for the first time in a long time. Maybe he sees me now where it really counts for him, close to the winner's circle. I've lost my sex, but gained power. A power that to Brad spells win. A power he senses is behind Mark's seeming strength. He's still smiling at me as he goes on. "Let's stop scratching ourselves with how great it's going to be. Never forget, an incumbent is always a tough adversary. And since today's elections are won on the tube, debates are crucial."

Lanacola stops riffling his notes and looks at Brad. "We've gotta plan our schedules and make them tight. Make security tight, too. And we need to get a top, trustworthy double-dealer in Wilcox's camp."

"What about Mazurski?" Bailey asks. "She's not above a little give for a big take."

"You're crazy." Mark is irate.

"Take it easy, Marcus. This isn't Joe's first lap around that track."

"I like your vocabulary, Max," Bailey says.

As Mark glares from Bailey to Max and back again, the dots on Max's painting begin to connect.

Dancing in the dark
Till the dots end, I'm dancing in the dark
But they now end
And I'm waltzing to the wonder of . . .

You shouldn't be waltzing, stupido. You should be doing the Mazurski. Never fear, my dear. I shall be. But in my own give-no-quarter-time.

"A penny for your thoughts, Amanda," Max says, getting up to get a match.

"A penny! For *my* thoughts?"

"Should I pay more for what I know you're thinking?"

"Thanks for letting me know, Max, but why did you wait so long?"

"Max! Amanda!" Mark is still wild. "What the hell are you two doing?"

"Whispering. Should we shout?" Max pretends to whisper again. Instead, the tip of his tongue touches my ear which seems to touch me all over.

"Can you finish, Max?" Mark asks.

Like a cherubic menace, Max tilts his head. "Not here, Marcus."

As Brad walks toward me, I don't see how he can. No way his glasses can make it this far. "Amanda? What we need is a whopping Women for Weldon kick-off. Immediately. While the weather's still good, open the house, the grounds, the closets. Get them with influence and affluence and make sure you get enough of them with enough insecurity to fold and lick and stamp. And, also, see what liberal Republicans you can enlist."

"Liberal Republicans?" Max throws me a look.

Mark punches his fist in and out of his open palm. Pow! Pow! Hard. Harder. "Yes, Max. 'Liberal Republicans.' Do you have trouble hearing?" Mark looks at me, too, but from him it's more like sighting through a rifle. "I'm sure I can get Ann Mazurski to help. With her persuasive powers, there's no telling *whom* she may sway. I've been told it's really the man more than the party."

I was right. He was sighting. But what a rotten, over-the-heads, scare 'em shot.

"Mark's not far from base about the man and the party," Bailey concedes. "Especially with so many swing independents."

Maybe not from your base. But way away from Mark's mark. Maybe, Annie, you better get your gun. Then, you, too, can be a big shot at the Women for Weldon shoot-out.

And—
We can face the music together . . .

Although the day is hot and crowded with sunshine, the leaves are already beginning to flee. Overnight the long summer days seem to turn into long winter evenings. If spring is too late, autumn certainly is too early. Those fat Corot trees, splashed with feverish reds and yellows, like children, will soon plant their own seeds and grow away. As dazzling as fall may be, its forecast leaves me joyless.

"What a beautiful day," Ann Mazurski says, realigning the coffee cups outside the poolhouse. "We're lucky." She adds, "If two hundred women had to be in the house, we'd have havoc."

How would you know what causes havoc in my house? "You're so right. I'm just ecstatic they're able to walk through these glorious colors."

"I love fall."

I prefer autumn. "It's my favorite season. How I long for the snug, early darkness and the wonderful wildness of the bare trees. And what could be cozier than a freezing winter with plenty of wood to split?" She must be thrilled that we're more and more alike. Except her hair is a little too streaked, her skirts a little too long, and her frame a little too thin. Maybe her thin frame is why her skirts are long.

"Amanda. I see some people coming."

"They'll be quite a while from the house to here."

"Why?"

"Watch."

"Watch what?"

"They'll stop and mentally price every bush, blade, and begonia. Excuse me a minute, Ann." Going into the poolhouse, I dial the kitchen.

"Pedro. As soon as about fifty ladies are here, bring the food. And remember, both silver services. And send some extra waiters down now. But first please remind them never to pass a drink without a tray. Thank you, Pedro." I can't wait to hear the pings of crystal testing.

Next, the superintendent. "Mike? It's all right if the men work near the pool. Just not on top of it. (Ha! Ha!) And let the tree pruners finish, too. And when about fifty or more women have arrived, bring down the giant baskets of dahlias." I wish I could hear their exaggerated servant count. "You give to a person, not to a cause." Right? Right. But only a person you want to feel in with.

"You were right, Amanda," Mazurski says, surprised. "They're not here yet."

I've got lots of surprises for you, blondie.

Suddenly, the place is swarming with more Women for Weldon than Weldon could handle in a lifetime of servicing. With their eyes stretching far farther than their imaginations, they're all computing waiters and gardeners between running platitudes.

"You're so *lucky* to have all of this, Mrs. Weldon." My very unfailing favorite.

"My grandparents lived like this, but real people just don't anymore." My second favorite, although very close to number one.

"You must let me have the label from that wine." In the top ten.

"Do you and your husband do the place yourselves?" In a class by itself!

"Hi. Amanda. I don't think you've met Jay Van Sandt's sister, my sister-in-law, Penny. Amanda's my oldest and best friend."

Amanda who? "Hello, Penny. I'm glad you could come."

"Amanda. Guess where Penny comes from?" Muffie asks.

"Now don't tell me." I know. Doctor Caligari's cabinet. Without waiting. "Van Sandt copper. Penny? Get it?"

Get it? I just pray it's not contagious. "How about changing it to Fuzzy?" Sort of updating it. Copper? Police? Fuzz-y? Get it?" Oh. Wow. I've definitely caught it, but I don't think Penny did. Although she is smiling a little. Maybe she's a mute.

"Anything we can do to help?" Muffie asks, looking blindly at the extra eight waiters.

Leave! "If I need you to pass a few things, I'll ask. Thanks."

"Boop is definitely coming. I spoke to her this morning," Muffie says, not so much to allay my anxiety as to illustrate her community standing. She turns to Fuzzypenny. No, dummy, Moneypenny. Oh. Right. "You met Boop at the club. She's Junior's wife?"

She's only shaking her head. My God. I think she is a mute. Put 'er on fold, lick, and seal, boys!

"Amanda? Is Lucy here? She's supposed to be here. With Brownie."

I turn to Moneyfuzzy. "Brownie is a Whitethorn, which really means a redskin. The redskins fought the redcoats, one of whom was a Mattingale, who is now a MacIntosh. Get it?" She looks as if she never gets it, not even so much as a mercy fuck.

I back up, watching carefully that this mutation doesn't follow me. I must be cautious, though, not to bump into Boop. I wonder if there's a *Reader's Digest* staffer around for an unforgettable character. One profile could write off the whole group.

I doubt if by now too many have missed turning a saucer or checking a hallmark. I do think, however, before the shadows lengthen any farther and before the "girls" are completely swacked on just the thought of my putting a name brand into their Bloody Marys, they should remember they're not here only because they're my nearest and dearest.

As I see them sitting in clusters around the lawn, listening to Mazurski, it somehow would seem more appropriate if they were dressed in bloomers and middies and headbands.

And standing in the rear, two of the tallest in the group would be holding the very old, very worn class banner. Maybe it's just their humidity hair, their eaten-off lipstick, their catalog clothes.

"Being with the city government these past years, let me tell all you Women for Weldon, that I, Ann Mazurski, am one hundred percent against government's interfering with our social and economic life. That isn't being liberal the way I think liberal. That's being foolhardy. That's why I say, look at my record. You will all see how I . . ."

With all those "I's," I'm not sure they're not sure she's not running. But those scattered hands won't get her past Poughkeepsie.

"That was great, Ann. They loved you. Wonderful. Too bad Mark couldn't have heard their response." Wow.

"Thanks. You better go on while the crowd's hot."

Have you flown even the cuckoo's nest?

"Maybe before you start, I'll ask the waiters to ask if anyone wants anything," Mazurski says.

Now you're running my house? "I don't think we should give the crowd a chance to cool."

"You're right."

You're catching on. But first, I'll do my hair, put some moistener over my lips, and make sure I'm positioned where my ring can catch the sun's most blinding rays. If there's one thing they don't want standing here, it's what's sitting next to them there.

". . . and it's not only the wealth of what you see around you that's associated with the name Weldon, it's the wealth of ideas, of integrity, of industry. Those are the 'I's' that spell 'it' for you. With the limitless business incentives Weldon tax cuts propose, people will be able not only to make money, but to keep the money they make. Mark

Weldon knows the way to riches. And what he wants, when he wins, is to pave that way for you."

I can't believe the applause. They're getting up and still applauding. I wish I had more to say so I could hear it more. They're circling me like some series pitcher.

"Bravo! Bravo! It's my firm belief the wrong Weldon's running." I'd know that subtle hand, meaning to miss my waist, anywhere.

"Max. I'm so glad you're here."

"How'd you know?"

"A certain touch," I say, not moving.

His hand strays over my back and stops at my backside. "Of class, Amanda?"

"Rhymes with it. How long have you been here? I never saw you sneak in."

"Long enough to hear Mazurski ice the crowd. But you revived them like Billy Sunday. Marcus got so carried away he thought he was up there."

"Where is he?"

"Letting the people touch him."

There, blazer perfect, his arctic eyes flashing, I watch him surge through the group unleashing his best export laugh. I hope he's happy gathering my rosebuds. I feel like some "as told to" writer who gets all the work and gives all the glory.

"Max? Are you going to Ithaca with Mark tonight?"

Far above Cayuga's waters. There's an awful smell.
Some say it's Cayuga's waters. Others say Cornell.

"Am I in voice?"

"You're incorrigible."

"Why should I fool with more political science geniuses? I have enough with one know-it-all," Max says.

"They expect thousands. Not only from the university."

"I can think of better time-wasters than hearing Marcus
recite Howell's Phi Beta bullshit, then sticking around
while the mob goes crazy and he stays cool."

I must say that's Mark's life. Even these cloying harri-
dans don't make him lose that cool. I guess if it's part-play-
ing, you don't. Maybe I'll go with him to Ithaca, watch him
hook the new hordes.

"Amanda," Mark says. "You were sensational." He looks
at Mazurski. "We know this group. To get them going is
like lighting a wet wick." Mazurski just smiles.

"What time do you go to Ithaca?" I'm already planning
what to cancel.

"I think about—"

"Five thirty," Mazurski says to Mark.

The tiniest tightening of the muscle in Mark's cheek
makes me unplan and uncancel. Goddamn my always seeing so closely.

"I better go and throw a few things in a bag," Mark
says.

The day you, Mark Weldon, just throw a few things
into a bag, I'll know the trip you're on, you better get off.

"Come up with me, Max."

"Hold on, Marcus," Max says, hoisting his pants. Each
year, the belt falls farther and farther below the waist.

"You were really very good, Amanda," Mazurski says
as Mark and Max climb the hill to the house.

"Thank you." I smile warmly and ingenuously. "I'm
amazed, frankly, but thrilled because I know how important it is. Don't ask me why, but I guess there's something
in me people feel close to, want to be like." I love watching
her. She's like a turtle on its back.

"It looks as if they're all going, Amanda. Should we say good-by?"

"Good idea. And after they go, let us have a quiet drink together." I have a good-by to say myself.

As the guests leave newly filled platters, waiters still waiting, and a hostess who has money do her work, I can just hear their "discussions" when the old boy gets home and starts icing the glass for his first martini. But then what's a great party without those kinds of souvenirs?

I don't believe what I'm seeing. The turtle righted itself and is scurrying up the hill. "Ann. Ann! Wait. You forgot our drink." Why is the step down slower?

"What'll you have, Ann?"

"What are you having?" Is that copying or cautious?

"Pimm's Cup, number one. No. I'm kidding. I think I'll have some vodka with soda and lime."

"If you don't mind, Amanda, I think I'll just have the soda and lime."

"I don't mind." Keep your wits, Annie. Anyway, you'll be drinking later. Maybe, Cayuga's waters.

"I think you boys can go," I say to the waiters. "You were wonderful. Thank you. All of you."

"They were wonderful."

How would you know? "Why don't we take our drinks to the other side of the pool? It's a fabulous view. The sun sets directly between the copper beech and the pin oak. Mark and I love sitting there watching the other side of the earth swallow the sun behind those far hills. Did you know Mark was a nature lover?"

"No. I don't think I did."

"Do you know the average large tree has a million leaves on it? Just think of the energy God needs to push them out and the strength man needs to rake them in."

"Really?"

No between the brook and the stream for her. "Sit back, Ann. Relax. It's so peaceful with the people gone. Stretch your legs. Do you think these lounges need new webbing? I'm afraid over the years they've gotten quite loose."

"No. They seem comfortable."

"I'm glad you're comfortable. I am, too. But then you and I are pretty much the same size and weight. A rather different story with Mark." I laugh insincerely.

"That's a good point." She laughs insincerely.

"Ann? Who streaks your hair?"

"Excuse me?"

Never. "Who streaks your hair? I think it's a little too streaked compared to mine. If all the brown is gone, none of the interest is left. You want it like mine, don't you?"

She's back on her back. "What are you doing, Amanda?"

"Playing?"

"What?"

"War. It's sort of like baseball. There's always a winner, no matter how many innings."

"I don't understand."

"I'm well aware of that, Ann. But certainly you understand evolution. Getting somewhere? Survival? Or let me say, too many of one species can't survive. And two wives is one too many for Mark. But he might need a lot of fucks. And you might need a good appointment. Stay useful, but don't mistake useful for irreplaceable. Remember, I am as much the candidate as Mark. You've seen it on the air, and in the air. Mark would kill for me. And I for Mark. Don't bother to put us to the test. And I also wouldn't bother mentioning this."

How peaceful to have them all gone, especially since it all went so well. Suddenly, I feel supergreat. Why *can't* I jump

in the air and kick my heels twice? Why do you always
want that? You can't do everything. Right? Wrong. What in
God's name do I hear? The peaceable kingdom certainly
didn't have a long reign.

"Amanda?"

"Here, Mother. On the porch."

"Hello, darling." She half kisses me so the eyes can look
around without my seeing them. "Although I hated missing
this afternoon, it was such a good idea for me to take Sonia
and Sara from what Andro tells me was three hundred
women?"

"Not quite."

"You look so tired, dear." She sits directly across from
me, frowning, taking a deep, troubled breath.

"I feel wonderful." So far.

"Is that what you wore? Pants?" She sits directly across
from me, frowning, taking a deep, troubled breath.

"Would I? I wore a new wool dress and jacket. So
pretty and practical." I wouldn't own a dress and jacket.

"Wasn't I right, Amanda, about people being more comfortable helping themselves than having waiters wandering
among them?"

"Completely." The moment you said it, I hired more.

"As I mentioned, I'm so sorry I missed it. Sometimes, I
wish I could break my heart. Not the way you break it, my
darling. Divide, I guess, is a more appropriate word. But I
did feel it was totally unnecessary for the girls to be exposed to those questioning women."

"Where are the girls?"

"They have a surprise for you. But be surprised. Don't
make them hate me by saying I said one word."

How did you know I want to make them hate you?
"You know, Mother, you look just wonderful?"

"I don't know how. And I certainly don't know why."

Taking out her mirror, she smiles weakly into it. "Now, let me hear about today. Tell me everything. Did you enunciate clearly? Who came? By the way, did I tell you I think Sara is going to need braces?"

"No, Mother." She can't even hear about my afternoon, no less have been here for it.

"Well, she will. I don't think because of the spaces. It's the overbite. Now, please don't go and say Grandma wants her to have braces. Amanda? Come here a minute. Over here where it's light."

Possibly she's spotted an early but irreversible stage of leprosy. "Whoever is streaking your hair is putting red into the formula. *I* don't like it. I don't like that brassy look. You never tell Mark you color your hair, do you?"

I just tell Mark's mistress, whom I have to my home quite often. "Would your daughter be a fool?"

"I would hope not. And I would hope her daughters won't be either. And they won't be if they're brought up correctly. Where is Andro, dear? I feel like a Scotch."

"Pedro's resting. I'll get it."

"I didn't mean for you to get it, darling," she says, staying seated. "How come when I'm here they're always resting?"

"He had a rather full afternoon."

"Of course. I forgot. Amanda? Do you remember this suit I'm wearing?"

Since college. "Vaguely."

"I can see you don't. Anyway, MacGregor removed the old lining and made this new blouse and lining to match. She's clever, she is. Clever about charging, too. But you know the Scotch? Speaking of which."

"Oh. Yes. I forgot."

"Don't apologize after your exhausting day."

I won't. But I'd better get something for me, too. Something white and straight and strong. As I carry them out, I seem to hear familiar giggles getting louder. Suddenly, they've stopped. Control time.

"Goodness, Amanda. What a heavy hand."

"Would you like more water?" There's none in it. We both know it's exactly as she wants it.

"No. No. Don't get up again. Well. Well. If it isn't the girls. I mean whoever or whatever you are." Mother turns to me and rolls her eyes as if I'm supposed to faint. Thank God for the girls, they're wearing masks over their hysterics. "I know, Amanda, I'm a little early for Halloween, but I couldn't resist these outfits. But why do you think the legs are so short?"

The legs are short, Mother, because they don't make these misfits over toddler four. "I can imagine," I say, "how the girls must adore them. I can't decide if *I* prefer the skeleton or Mickey Mouse. Maybe Mickey Mouse because it's not strictly Halloween."

"Promise me, Amanda, you'll take pictures of them ringing doorbells."

"Do you want them to smile?"

"What's that supposed to mean, Amanda? I'm sure something denigrating."

"Just a joke, Mother, because of the masks."

"Everything in life with you is just a joke."

"Or a bowl of cherries."

"Or a fresh answer."

Aren't you glad? It's a good excuse for your gulps. I hear a muffled, "We'll take them off now so we can save them."

Following them out, I two-step the stairs. Shutting the door, we fall on the bed. We laugh and roll so stupidly that

Sonia falls on the floor. Laughs you have to hide are always the funniest. "We're all so very lucky," I say, my eyes filling.

"Mom. I don't believe you," Sonia says, watching my eyes fill up.

"Why not? She's always like that when she's like this."

"I hope you're both embarrassed."

"It's not so bad, at least, when you do it at home," Sara says, kissing me.

"Sara's right," Sonia says.

"Just don't forget, girls," I say sternly. "Send Grandma pictures. I certainly know you won't be the slightest embarrassed to wear these." Now they are so convulsed, the break-away seams have left.

Back on the porch, I notice Mother's drink is quite a bit higher than when I left. "Where's Mark?" she asks as if he should be here when she is.

"In Ithaca. Making a speech."

"Ithaca?"

"Ithaca."

"Why aren't you with him? You should always be with him. I never left your father. What do you want to be? A woman alone? I know what it means to be a woman alone."

Please. I'll give you anything not to discuss Daddy's dying.

"You think you're smart? Leaving a man like that, in his position, alone?"

"Thanks, Mother. Your faith is reassuring."

"Of course, if I had known Mark were away I'd have stayed for dinner. But knowing you, you've probably given the couple off."

"I'm not even having dinner. I'm going straight to bed."

"You look ready to collapse. I wish you would take better care of yourself, Amanda. I'm sorry nobody else cares

enough to tell you. Of course, why should they as long as
you're still strong enough to do things for them. Nobody's
like your mother."

Tell me about it.

If my mother hadn't left when she did, I *would* have
collapsed, right into the Emergency Room. Even now, as I
watch Joan Fontaine catching her first, faraway glimpse of
Manderley, my stomach is still not normal. Whatever that
is.

The jangle of the phone, so late, is always jarring.
Quickly, I press off the TV sound. "Hello," I say, as dazed as
I can in case I want to hang up. "Max? . . . Of course, I know
it's you. . . . Say that again. How many thousand? . . . I
can't believe it. . . . The cheering was how long? . . . I don't
care what kind of advance team, he can't get them like that
unless he's got. . . . Thanks, Max. I was thrilled with today,
too. . . . Forget it, Max. Do you think I'd be here if I weren't
sure what'll turn him on for the long run? And it'll be a
very long run, Max. . . . I adore you, too, and thank you,
Max."

18

"Politics is a slippery pole, Mark," Bailey says, twisting his
pinky ring straight. "No matter how long it takes to go up,
the downslide is overnight. I've had to switch my deepest
loyalties just when everything seemed sewn up. Sure, we're
front-running now, but with the election still four weeks
away, we have plenty of time to make underdog." He looks
at Brad and Darcy. They both nod agreement.

I feel weird sitting here, in this overframed living room,

without Maria. Not that we were in here a lot, but I seem to be straining to find her perfume. Like Latham's frames, it belongs all over. I wonder where Latham will put the picture of Mark and himself. I guess he'll do what he usually does, push another "out" to the back and put another "in" out front.

"I don't get the gloom," Mark says, moving his arms as if to wave it away. "We could start another Peace Corps the way we won the colleges. The majority of the unions are already fellow workers, not to mention Gannett and Harris showing up breezing past Wilcox."

"It's caution, not gloom," Brad says. "You're passing Wilcox with the Olympics, with your energy, with the images of youth."

"Also," Darcy adds, "Wilcox didn't pack too many guns for that first round. But since our audiences have tripled, momentum has mounted, and *Newsday* gave us an early endorsement, Wilcox will call on his whole damn arsenal for the second debate."

"For Christ's sake," Mark shouts, "we should expect weapons from an enemy. Maybe everybody's used to taking everything too easy."

"Just you take it a little easy, Mark." Brad's words are slow and hard. "Preparing for any enemy when you don't know its position isn't simple. However, your best shot'll be not to refute or rebut what Wilcox says. By even acknowledging Wilcox, you double his point as well as his time. And fuck any idea about thoughtful pauses. Snap out your answers."

"Well, which is it, folks?" I interrupt. "Is it 'He who hesitates is lost'? Or, 'Act in haste, repent in leisure'?"

Brad throws me a look. No. I don't think it was of love. He turns back to Mark. "All I'm saying is, project confidence as well as energy."

I'll bet if there were only radio, Mark would have more than a struggle, whatever more than a struggle is. Because you can't hear a smile, a richness, a crop of thick hair, a mind that never needs a note. I can't believe the quantum leaps in crowds for a man who's never even held office. Why not? He got you, didn't he?

"Was that a bell?" Max asks, as if from sleep.

"It's Lanacola," Darcy says. "I had him check the rumor."

"What rumor?" Mark asks.

"Some dumb rumor," Darcy answers.

"I wasn't wrong. There is gloom. What the hell's going on here?"

Lanacola rushes in, tossing his case on the pale velvet sofa. Thank goodness he wipes his brow before shaking it.

"What'd you find out?" Darcy asks.

"It's true," Lanacola says, looking down at the carpet.

"What's true?" Mark sends a saucer flying as he bangs his fist on the table.

Bailey adjusts his tie pin. "Crane, Wallenberg, and Brooklyn's Councilman Klein have deserted the dais the night of the fund raiser."

"What's that supposed to mean?" Helplessly, Mark looks from one to the other.

"Nobody knows," Brad says.

"What is this nobody knows? Trouble comes and everybody turns idiot? What about our contact in Wilcox headquarters? I thought he could talk his way into God's confidence. You said he'd know Wilcox's strategy before Wilcox."

"I just spoke to him," Lanacola says. "He doesn't know anything. But at least he got Wilcox believing you're not marching Columbus Day. That means he'll stay in Albany so you can walk away with us paisanos." Sandy manages a very weak smile.

"Want me to call the senator?" Latham asks. "I got Crane on Capitol Hill, I'd better be able to get him on the phone." Latham's stupid laugh, trying to be one of the fellas, only seems to isolate him more.

"Call him, big shot." Max sneers. "Pick up your million-dollar-due bill. If you get him to talk, I'll autograph my bar mitzvah picture for you."

Wow! Is this air sulky. The first friction. The first time heroics aren't bouncing off the walls. It must be something massive to have them all defect. It couldn't be Switzerland or Mark and Max would know. Anyhow, I'm sure Max already has that pinned on Wilcox in case of emergency.

"I wish we had some clue about what they're up to," Darcy says. "We know we're clean. And we know our pulling together has pulled them in by the hundreds of thousands. We also know four years of their pulling together only managed to tear the goddamn state apart."

"What could they have?" Mark asks. "What could they have for all three to walk away?" As upset as Mark is, he still looks cool.

Latham returns with what looks like straight bourbon in a tumbler-size glass. It's so full, he leans to sip from the top before it spills on his shaky hand. "Anybody like to join me?"

"Is there an AA meeting?" Max asks.

"Shut up, Mandell." Mark goes over to Latham. "Well? Did you get Crane? What the hell's it about?"

"He's out to lunch." Latham can now raise his glass to his lips.

"You've been out to lunch since I've known you," Max shouts. "Who's at lunch at four thirty except some drunk

who can't see they're setting up for dinner? I guess you also
believed his secretary saying he wouldn't be in till tomorrow."

"He'll call me this afternoon, Max. As soon as he gets
back, Max. He's planning to run again, Max. You know
what I mean? You know, Max?"

"I know you know my name."

I can't believe what I'm seeing. Max is watching his
cigar fall and keeps watching it burn through the burl of
the table. It's the first time I've seen a trace of happiness
on anyone's face. He catches me staring and the happiness
even breaks into a smile. God!

Latham sprawls into a corner of the pale velvet. "Find a
mob and you'll find power. There's always a mob around
power. And now they're deserting."

"You want to go with the rats, fink?" Max asks. "Maybe
it would be better than your constructive cheeriness."

"I'll call campaign headquarters," Darcy says. "Sometimes, anonymous tip-offs come in when something hot's
about to hit."

"I've checked our key press guys. Nobody knows anything," Lanacola says.

"That's obvious." Mark fumes. "Nobody knows a goddamn thing. Or, everybody does but us."

"If it were as simple as forged hate pamphlets, we'd
already have counterattacks at every corner," Brad says,
doodling stars.

I guess now's not the time for me to mention that Lyn-
don Johnson saved all his doodles for posterity. That he'd
grab them off Air Force One when no one was looking.
Obviously, someone was looking.

"And nobody I know can be angry yet," Bailey says

bewilderedly. "So far, I've promised everybody everything."

"Money's all laundered," Latham mumbles.

"We're all saying the same thing," Max says, flattening the burn with his finger. "Nothing."

"Who's that?" Latham asks, at the heavy sound of the front door.

"In case you're not seeing so good, it's your wife," Max answers.

The men stand as Maria enters into the somber summit. "I hope I'm not disturbing anything, but I didn't know you'd all be here." There's that perfume and yet, almost not.

"No. No," Latham says, pressing his arm on the arm of his chair, just enough to make a pretense of standing. "I'm waiting for a call from Washington. From Crane. Very important. Urgent."

I'm so glad she looks so good. "How's the show going? You got fabulous reviews."

"The attendance has been fantastic. You look beautiful, Amanda."

I look at Mark, but he's so settled into his own discomfort, he's not thinking of making any for me. "Thanks, Maria. You too."

"Saint Laurent." She says, only half jokingly.

"He's at least as good as Saint Paul and Saint Louis." Max says.

"Max!" I say as if he's Sonia or Sara.

"Amanda!"

He's hopeless. "Forget it, Max."

"Sorry, Amanda, I thought you called."

"I did call," Latham intercepts. His selective hearing is beautiful. "Now I'm waiting for him to call back."

"There he is," Lanacola says, as Latham hustles to the phone.

"Why all the gloom?" Maria asks.

"See! See!" Mark says wildly. "She caught it right away. Why was everyone trying to fool me?"

Wow! It's tense time in the old town, all right. Nobody so much as whispers until Latham returns. "That was Crane." He slurs directly at Max.

"Well?" Again, Mark bangs the table.

Latham stares into the group. "He says it's true. He's not coming. And what Wilcox has is dynamite. He says it's going to be a big scandal. A sex thing that'll break in tomorrow's papers. He couldn't say what exactly. He wasn't alone."

Mark glares right through me. Looking away, I watch Maria's deep, sad eyes fill with fear. In one panic spurt, I become soaking wet. I hope I go quickly. I can understand people begging for death. As I scan the frozen room, all that's moving is the constant smoke from Max's nervous puffing.

"And you've got key press guys?" Mark walks over to Lanacola and flips his tie into his face.

"The best," Lanacola answers, his eyes angry.

"They wouldn't know yet," Brad says. "Writers are always told the last second so they won't have time to use any muscle on the press, no matter what their pull."

"You mean threat," Max says.

"Mark, no matter what you've done we'll prove you haven't," Darcy says. "Anyway, sex is in. Show me a national neuter."

"Hoover," Latham manages.

"He's dead like you," Max says.

I wish I were. Again, Mark stares at me. Never has he engaged in such forceful eye contact. "No matter what we hear," Mark says, "what they print will be worse. We might as well wait till this evening, till the bulldog editions come out."

"They're out!" Lanacola yells.

So are the open sandwiches. Dry and thin and untouched, they look like some still life that was born deceased. So do the ice-melted drinks, the people. Suddenly, I see a whole group of these walking dead, erecting a scaffold, knotting the noose, and listening for the bell to toll, to toll for me.

"There it is," Lanacola says, his voice piercing reality.

All at once, a pile of papers is thrown in the middle of the floor. Wow! Look at that close-up.

CAMERAS CATCH WELDON
REGISTERING FOR SEX

Mark Weldon, Republican candidate for governor, pictured registering Mr. and Mrs. while wife in Europe. (Register card enlarged. Signature verified.)

Story, page 3

Even the *Times.*

WELDON SIGNS MR. AND MRS.
BUT MRS. NOT MRS.

Republican gubernatorial candidate signs in wife but wife out of country with children.

My first feeling is relief, almost more for Maria than for me. I don't know why I still think of her as fragile. Maybe I just think of me as responsible. A fragment of a smile breaks her lips, but it's sufficient to shatter the scaffolding forever.

"What's going on here?" Ironically, it's Mark who asks the question everyone's waiting for him to answer.

"If you can't remember, you can read, can't you?" Max asks disgustedly.

Mark flings the papers against the wall, their pages unfolding and flying everywhere. "Whore! Whore! Whore! Damn whore!" Grabbing a big batch from the piled stack, he rips them as if they were a telephone book and heaves them around in a frenzy. "Goddamn whore-mongering whore!"

It's the least self-contained Mark's ever been. Even his hair is flying. And he's got the audience panting for more. Goddamn right we want more! We don't know anything.

"Get me a drink," Mark orders.

"What?" Darcy asks.

"What d'ya mean, what? Straight. That's what."

Raising my brows at Darcy, I show that "what" doesn't matter. It's medicinal. As he swallows, Mark squeezes his whole face shut.

Slowly, very slowly, he sits down and looks at everyone in the room. Not as a group. One at a time. "Here's your story. My story. All there is. Firstly, I don't know how they got that picture."

"It's a new thing in motels," Lanacola says. "A hidden camera takes all the registrants in case they skip or their credit cards are fake."

Mark continues. "Anyway, that picture was taken in Rochester in early September, right before Amanda and the girls came home. I spoke at the Civic Center that afternoon and at the Kiwanis Convention that evening. That night I stayed at my mother's. Forget the wisecracks. Sandy had a top advance team working. I flew there with just one aide. I mistakenly thought I didn't need a guide where I grew up.

"First stop was the Travelway Motel. My aide, a female, asked me to sign Mr. and Mrs. She said a woman registering alone often gets unwelcome callers. Not motel guests, but maintenance men and owners. The ones with keys. It made sense. What doesn't make sense is this." Mark picks up the *News* and slaps his hand across his paper face. Crushed, he lets the paper fall and rubs his palms into his eyes.

I can't see what his eyes are doing, but mine are tearing with fire and anger and hatred and vengeance. I know what Mark said is true. We all know. It's too stupid simple.

"Who was the aide who did it on you?" Darcy asks, almost as an afterthought.

His hands still to his face, Mark answers. "Ann Mazurski."

19

I never thought I'd be happy to have drizzle and winds for this morning, but wow was that weather welcome. Not only did it help thin the reviewing stand, but it emptied the would-be mobs from crowding the miles of barricades. No telling how many jeers we were spared as we marched up the Avenue.

"Lanacola was great at placing the cameras," Max says, looking out of the window in Mark's office. "While the mayor was cheering the fat Sons of Salerno, Sandy had it angled like the mayor was waving to you. He even synched it with the crippled kid we planted to throw the flowers.

Sandy should get an award." Max is really giving his gut to sound up.

"He should get it in the papers," Mark says tiredly.

"Marcus. Stop hitting yourself on the head with those lousy polls. What are polls, anyway?"

"People, Max," Mark says. "You know? Voters? And as Bailey so elegantly understated, polls can be very slippery. Ours must have been greased with lightning."

"Mark," I snap, trying to pull him from his own jaws. "Keep your doubts to you. Give the public 'damn the torpedoes!'"

"I'm glad you can sound so confident," Mark says.

"She already won me, Marcus."

"How was it possible to slip so far on such nothing slime?" Mark asks disbelievingly.

"All anybody has time for is circumstantial dirt," Max answers.

God, if we don't reach Mark, he won't reach anybody. "Mark. Right this very minute, your timing is perfect for a colossal comeback. Everybody's pet is always the once-up, once-down, up-again underdog. Just you and them and your flea collar against the whole machine."

Mark walks over to the scale model of the Bronx complex and shakes his head. "With millions already milked from Friends of Weldon, how many friends do you think Weldon will have after the first Tuesday in November? How many buildings do you think we'll be able to build without the unions?"

Max taps his ash in the last unused ashtray. "Marcus! You're not real. You've already lost the election and now our business too?"

It's impossible for Mark to deal with the unknown. And unknown to Mark is adversity.

"The AF of L and the CIO are still neutral," Mark says.

"How long do you think it'll take them to declare for Wilcox?"

"How many times have you heard Darcy say that the pros discount the dirt the public seems to buy?" Max asks.

"They can't discount the polls, goddamn it!" Mark yells.

"We've already started our own polls, Marcus. They're rigged just right. But if you don't cool it, you'll blow yourself out of the box before you even give this time to blow over. Why don't you go to the series with Latham? I'll get Bailey to get you to throw the first ball."

"It's in LA today, Max. And that's what you know about what's going on."

"At least, everyone'll be glued to the game," Max says. "Nobody'll be thinking about you. Except you, of course." Max goes over to Mark and puts his arm around his shoulders. "It's bad, Marcus, but not black. You've got a great team. They're committed. And believe me, there are too many others who can't afford to let you lose."

"I don't get it. I can't get it," Mark says, pushing those fists into his palms, trying to punch reason out of emotion. "Since the goddamn primary, crowds have quadrupled. I've made fifteen stops a day, as many as five dinners a night, and gagged on enough tea and honey to fill a freighter. And now, that stinking slime is oozing me out of the state? I don't get it. I can't fight something I don't get."

"Marcus. Listen. Amanda's right. The minute you get them back, you've got them stronger than ever. Once the underdog takes over, you've got it made."

"Once! Once! What's going to make that once? What's going to make Wilcox debate again? And you think people will work for Weldon with the same fire? What do you think they think now? All this work, this far, for this?"

I look at Max and put my finger to my lips so he won't

answer. "Mark," I say, "the best thing you can do now is march into campaign headquarters with your head high and your morale smiling across your face. Joke and laugh as if the polls are only props set up to give the campaign some action." I nod to Max to agree.

"She's got a great sixth sense, Marcus. Not a lot of the other five, but I'd go with that instinct. They'll die to fight with you leading them, but never without you."

"Never. No way," I say, smiling at Mark. "Go. Please, Mark. I know I'm right." I know I am.

"It's a shot," Mark says.

"Don't go like that!" Max is screaming. "Like a leader."

I stand in front of Mark, not letting him avoid my eyes. "Don't you see, Mark? If you win this, it will be a greater triumph than if everything just kept spiraling. This is you over adversity. This is spunk, grit, stamina. This is strength under stress. Your ability to face what is."

"But it wasn't, Amanda. Not that night."

"Mark. That's not important. That's not what counts. What counts is showing them you've got the courage and the faith to be proud not apologetic. There's no way we're throwing this campaign into some motel detective story. You're not going to win by disproving Wilcox, but by proving you."

Mark smiles for real at Max. "I see what you mean, Max. She almost got to me."

"So go," Max says, sighing. "Good luck."

"Why do I need—"

"Get out, Marcus!" Max helps with a light shove.

Exhausted, I sink into the sofa. "What do you think, Max?"

"I don't know what I think. I know it's not good. I know we've got to stick to one game plan. I just don't know what it is. Darcy's worried, too. Mostly about the unions. The fact is we're fading and the incumbency is shining its shit."

"But don't you agree, Max, about not spending money on disproving Mazurski?"

"Me? I can't figure why in today's world anyone cares."

"I can, Max. People first react to conditioning. Those crippled Calvinists out there immediately pit hell and fire against original sin. They'll buy it under the counter, but they won't read it in the parlor. Everybody else is fucking but them. When they do it, they give it another name. Like, it's good for my marriage. Guilt makes me nicer. Whatever. God! Don't I live in the middle of it?"

"How do we get to those righteous fucks?" Max undoes his belt as if to loosen his brain.

"I'm not sure. I'm thinking. But I know there's got to be a way to get Mark back in that parlor."

"Forget those deadheads, Amanda. Once they lock up their minds, they lose the key."

"They're not dead, Max. Just crippled. And the crippled can still move. Their minds have already changed once. Why not again?"

"It's too much exertion." Max crumples the cellophane from another cigar and misses the basket by yards. "I should've put rocks in it. Amanda? Have you thought how happy you've made all those pigs who can feel sorry for you now? Ah! The rise and fall of the quick-rich. Think of the muscle you've put back in their sleeves. They'd do anything for you. Their kids might even rake your lawn. For money, of course."

"And they'd never mention they never rake theirs. Right? That they leave their leaves to turn to mulch. That mulch is good for the grass. I can taste the flavor of their sympathetic junk food. I can see it now.

"The platter is bare except for a double bed and a small table and lamp. A neon light, flashing Travelway, pulsates outside the thinly curtained window. A man and woman, too lustful to undress, heave to the beat. A chorus of ever faithful villagers sway and chant to the rhythm. *'Poor Amanda. Poor Amanda. Poor Amanda.'*"

Max wipes his forehead. "What is this? Are you already out of Albany, too? You sound set for your old career before the new one's begun. I swear between the both of you a person could develop a little melancholia, not to mention a severe depression."

"You mean, Max, you don't have a back-up talent?"

Leaning his head on his shoulders, a talent of perfect smoke rings, like mini life preservers sails forth until it blurs. With a flourish of his hand, Max takes a seated bow. "I have a feeling if I fall back on that, they may not pick up my option."

"Max. Listen. I'm not kidding." I'm talking quickly not to forget. "What do you really think people expect us to do? I mean, how do you think the public sees Mark's next move?"

Max looks at me funny.

"I'm not being funny, Max. Just say what you think. The first thought in your head. As strenuous as it must be for you, let the masses crowd your mind."

Max throws up his hands in a "what I'm going to say is so simple" gesture. "First, they'll expect a denial. Then they'll expect some old fart swearing he never saw Marcus at his motel. And then we'd buy some other old fart who'd say he'd known Marcus since he was a Boy Scout, delivering *The Saturday Evening Post* on a bike he bought baby-sitting."

"Great!"

"Are you as undemanding in bed?" Max asks.

"Max, you're right. That's exactly what they expect to hear. So when it comes it's already discounted. It's been too long on the back burner. It won't change their minds. They won't believe it. All they'll believe is that now he's a liar as well as a lover."

Max's new cigar is already chewed into shreds. Watching him try to pinch it together is one of life's ugliest failures. "Go on, Amanda. You asked me to listen and I'm listening. What the hell are you staring at?" Now Max licks around the pinched end and starts puffing away just in case the cigar might not be lucky enough to die.

"Your delicacy, Max."

"You want delicacy or an audience?"

"The point of my sermon, suh! Seriously, Max, don't you agree we'll lose our audience forever if we attempt reheating that garbage you threw out? We've got to feed them something hot, but also something they can swallow. We've got to tempt them in a direction they think they've discovered. And they've got to be thrilled to be there."

"How are you going to produce this miracle?"

"By mass-marketing fucking."

Max stretches his legs onto Mark's desk, and for a minute I'm sure the space between the edge of the chair and the edge of the desk is going to gulp that glorious body. Luckily, the chair and Max suddenly lurch forward.

"As you just witnessed, Amanda, I almost lost my life on the way to the market. Do you mind if I ask how you propose to popularize your product?"

"On television."

"Madam. I believe you have an acute problem. Perhaps I can be of some help since it involves something sexual. My service requires nothing to buy, nothing to hook onto your TV. You merely plug it—"

"Max. Please. Listen to me straight through."

Max shrugs and smiles. "I'm listening."

"We'll buy a chunk of air time the same date as Mark's next debate. The World Series will be over and so will the Mazurski fallout. Also, by then, Mark will have shown his class by never having squatted to that filth."

"Amanda? Do you plan to comb the massage parlors for co-hosts?" Max is looking at me as if whatever I've got could never be medically recorded.

"It's a one-person spot, Max."

"And for the nonpeople persons, do we call Clyde Beatty or the ASPCA?"

I'm tired and getting angry and again I feel tears. "Is everything always a joke, Max?" Only because I'm hearing you know who ask that are my tears canceled.

"Just when I'm frightened." He's not even smoking, but he's holding his fingers like they're holding a cigar.

"Trust me, Max."

He nods. "Who's the one person?"

"Me. Amanda Weldon. Wife of the next governor of the state of New York." As Max watches my determination, I see him refocus with eyes that don't say "crazy" anymore.

"Politics is always prey to unpredictables like Mazurski."

"That's why Amanda's shot could kill every future pledge."

"What's our choice? If it doesn't turn us around, we won't need any more."

"Almost a week and the polls haven't even leveled."

"Maybe she can pull it out. One thing's sure. It's now or never."

Again, the government gurus deciding what's already

decided. In my home, they're making up my idea and treating me like some dried arrangement only they can make bloom.

"We've dumped a hundred thousand a week since June."

"The last spot cost two hundred alone."

"Retake after retake after retake."

"For Christ's sake! You all screamed location. Why? So everybody could live in a tent and draw overtime for rain?"

"If we can cut into that margin, Mutual Life will have more ready cash than we'll need. And Metro's O'Rourke wants his brother as counsel so much, he'll not only deliver the church, but the poor box as well."

"That and secretary are the top jobs. What big shot shot his mouth off with those?"

"Rocky's percent slipped from forty-three to thirty and Goldwater soared from twenty-six to thirty-five after the divorce. Rocky could never recover."

"Who has? He's what made Nixon."

"That's exactly what we're fighting," I yell. "You give them anything but lies. Sex is a purifier compared to lies."

"How many can we reach?"

"We coul dreach six to eight million counting radio."

"There's no telling how many if it's picked up."

"It will be," I say.

I'm glad I thought to call Glen for makeup. Why not have the years fall off into innocence? His cover-up is certainly more convincing than Grandpa's Bible or "direct from our finished basement." Evidently Revlon never finalized the fine print on his Madonna contract. But for God's sake, Amanda, don't ask.

"Ready? Mrs. Weldon?"

"Give 'em hell, Mrs. Weldon," Glen says, following me with his powder puff. "Just deny all the dirt. I guess you have to be President before it doesn't matter. I guess Ike was the one who surprised me most. Although, I don't know for sure. Roosevelt did, too, but I think that was because of his wheelchair. You know?"

I know I'm sorry I thought of calling you. One more pat of that puff, while running alongside my face and . . .

"Mrs. Weldon? Sit right here, please. Good. And now if we can just test a voice level? Good. And would you just look into the camera one minute? Thank you."

I like how I look in the monitor. The lips moist, the hair lingering, the V low. Just the right statement to say what could translate into: "Obviously, he wouldn't." "Why would he, with her?" "Absurd." "Even if he did, what could it possibly mean?"

(oops . . . tally light . . . count down . . . hands in lap . . . friendly face . . . *ready! set!*)

"The following is a paid, political announcement from the Friends of Weldon for Governor Committee."

(go . . . smile . . . calm . . . the lady)

"Hello. I'm Amanda Weldon. As you know, my husband, Mark Weldon, is running for governor. But what you can't know is how he's become the victim of a vicious political smear, a deliberate setup aimed to ruin him and run him out of the race.

(sincere . . . hurt . . . the lady)

"That motel picture of my husband is a complete distortion of the truth. That's why I'm here today, preceding the debate. I am going to expose this diabolical hatchet job and show it for the cheap shot it is.

(as if unaware, twirl wedding band . . . look down at it)

"When that picture appeared, I immediately asked my husband who was his supposed partner. The name Ann Mazurski merely meant another Weldon worker to me, although I knew she was also a high-priced appointee who had eagerly switched her political loyalties to Mark when his Albany bid really took off.

(superlady)

"Mark's going to bed with another woman would never be an issue with me. Nor should it be in the campaign. Maybe you think I'm mass-marketing infidelity. Maybe that wouldn't be bad.

(ingenuous laugh . . . then determined, grim)

"But what is worse than bad is the incontestible evil and treachery in Ann Mazurski's plot to discredit my husband. Ann Mazurski knew what she wanted. However, the job she was after in the Weldon administration wasn't available. Nor would it ever be, because it was a lifetime appointment. The job she was after was mine.

(squarely into camera . . . angry)

"When realization struck, Ann Mazurski became what is known in the double-dealing, double-crossing world of slime as a double agent.

(great close-up on the monitor. Look at my eyes scream! They're wild. I really feel crazy wild right now. Just hold it, Amanda, until you completely destroy that Mr.-and-Mrs.-register-bit . . . direct . . . hard)

"Blah . . . blah . . . blah . . . blah . . . blah . . . blah . . . blah . . . blah . . . blah . . .

(not too much . . . don't lose them)

"Blah . . . blah . . . blah . . .

(enough . . . now the wham-bam-hit-'em-ma'am! . . . very first lady)

"As the saying goes, 'ridicule is only a shield, never a

weapon.' Therefore, no matter how many ridiculous as-
saults Mazurski and the incumbency unleash, my husband
will doggedly continue the fight with the weapons of
victory—truth and loyalty.

"Mark Weldon is fitter than ever to fight and to win.
Never forget, when you strike at a king you must kill him.
Mark Weldon has only been strengthened!"

20

"Jesus, God. Mary, mother-of-pearl! I can't believe what
I'm hearing," Max says, whirling around Brad's office, proving the exception to fat men being good dancers.

"Everybody knows people need more luck than brains,"
Latham says, toasting the air.

"Not people," Max says. "Just you."

"Could everybody sit and cool it or nobody'll be able to
hear anything," Bailey shouts.

Although my pores are still thick with Glen's makeup,
I didn't want to waste a minute taking it off at the studio
and take a chance on missing hearing the debate here at
Brad's.

"I can't believe a Wilcox no-show. And I'll never believe
his timing." Max now has two cigars leaning against the
ashtray. "How do you figure it?"

"Who cares?" Lanacola asks. "I mean, I don't wish him
dead or anything."

"Why not?" Max says. "Wish it. Confess it. You'll see.
You'll make heaven, anyway."

"With Wilcox pulling so far ahead, a no-show radio
debate isn't that strange," Bailey says, looking at Darcy, the

other old pol. "He didn't need the risk. And he could never predict this."

"It's incredible," Darcy says, grinning from sideburn to sideburn. "We've had over a dozen debates and to no-show this one is incredible."

"And not one fucking voter will believe it wasn't due to Amanda. In fact," Max continues, "even those who don't have coitus won't believe it." Clownlike, he puffs both cigars at once.

"That was smart of Brad to have the panel come early to see the spot," I say.

"What was smart was you came up with the spot," Darcy says. "This one-two punch is one in a million."

"Can we all just listen a minute?" Bailey turns the volume to "blare."

"Mr. Weldon? I'm Tom Corby from the Syracuse *Herald Journal*. Tell me. Do you believe Governor Wilcox was afraid to face your wife's charges and therefore didn't show?"

"Let me say, I think he became confused about this date as well as my supposed one."

Oh! Wow! Good! Right, folks? I feel as if I'm part of some old-fashioned family, huddled around some newfangled crystal set, listening to magic come out.

"Mr. Weldon? I'm Glenda Loughlin from the Syracuse *Standard*. What do you predict the ramifications will be from the governor's not appearing today?"

I hear Mark's deep breath. I can picture Brad's thumb and index finger forming the circle of "blast him."

"Ms. Loughlin," he says slowly, "I believe the governor's just run himself out of the running. Allegations are political tactics. Lies are political suicide."

Lanacola makes some marks in his book, then snaps it

shut. "I've put every advance man in the area in touch with every media man possible. This'll be front page and network before the night's half over."

I wonder how many times Mark went to bed with her, how many times he used her.

"Mr. Weldon? How do you view the governor's settling of the teachers' strike?"

"Mr. Corby. The strike can't be ascribed to the mayor or the settlement to the governor, as the governor would have you believe. Perhaps, if during his tenure, my opponent had claimed a little less credit and a little more blame, he might be in a better position to continue that tenure."

Mazurski? You, a user, didn't know you were being used? What happened to your smarts, dummy? And you should know, nobody likes an all-the-time know-it-all. You remember Poli-Sci 105? "All dictators overstay their welcome"? Of course you do. Now. But now is too late.

"Mr. Weldon? How do you read the effect of the governor's proposed welfare plan?"

"Ms. Loughlin. We can no longer raise taxes to support the idle poor. We must lower taxes to create a climate for the rich. By suppressing incentives people are forced to use their creativity dishonestly. We need tax cuts and tax credits. We have to woo major corporations, not only in but back. And once and for all we've got to confront and conquer the welfare-bought votes."

What an asshole you are, Annie. Asshole Annie. Do you like that name? Or is Annie Asshole better? Did you really think a couple of streaks, a lot of beige, and a campaign cooze could do the job?

"Mr. Weldon? Do you see the Mazurski episode as a turning point in the polls?"

"A returning point, Mr. Corby. However, I would prefer not to comment on the Mazurski matter or on how my opponent could put his faith in a former informer. But as we know, stupidity always accompanies panic."

Double *wow*! Just keep not commenting like that.

Even Bailey is applauding. "Fabulous. With less than two weeks to go, just let him keep going like that."

"Where do you think the polls will be tomorrow?" Latham asks.

"Reversing," Darcy answers. "But the momentum's got to keep building. We've got to keep getting top endorsements. The biggest national names. Union leaders. Congressmen. The President."

"And we've got to keep covering as many of those hundred and fifty districts as we can," Lanacola adds. "We need a massive media attack. The telephones, the presses, the airwaves—we've got to pull the stops out of all of them."

"We've got to have more cash pour in before we can pour it on," Latham slurs.

" 'Pour. Pour.' That would be a word you'd use," Max says. "Not only once. Twice." As spry as I've ever seen him, Max jumps up and plants himself in the middle of the room. "Out of the twenty administrative departments in our state, governor, attorney general, and comptroller are the only ones we elect. Okay?" He smiles at Darcy and Bailey, acknowledging he knows that's obvious. "So now we've got to get those seventeen appointed pricks to believe we'll reappoint them. And, at the same time, line up big-giver replacements. Whether those commissioners are sitting on liquor, small business, motor vehicles, whatever, they're in more positions to do favors than a whore in heat."

Darcy sits at the desk, race-writing on Brad's long yellow pad. "We've got to set a stiff schedule," he says. "Amanda, you and Merebaum will go with Mark. You're especially important, Amanda. Together, you and Mark are media dynamite. You don't double together, you quintuple. We'll rework the heavy metro areas. Buffalo, Utica, Syracuse, Saratoga, Binghamton . . ."

"Being in Binghamton today, where your great Democratic mayor has arranged this overwhelming turnout for me, my wife, Amanda, and our two daughters, is the real payoff in politics. As we stand on the platform of this train, listening to the band play and watching parents hoist children onto their shoulders, I feel as if I'm part of some Lincolnesque tintype, during the days when our media *was* whistle-stop, and when the magic wasn't from the makeup but from the man."

My smile isn't quite frozen, but my earlobes are. The charm of where the Chenango meets the Susquehanna leaves me . . . right? Right . . . cold.

"In 1848 when these steel rails finally replaced the old Chenango Canal and Binghamton became Broome County's largest and . . ."

They're wearing parkas, gloves, and scarves, and I've got to stand here freezing my flue?

"Although my roots are Rochester, I certainly know the country's second largest producer of film, the giant GAF, was only part of Binghamton's significant industrial heritage, including such leaders as . . ."

At least when Mary stood on the ole caboose with Abe she had that nice long skirt and that sweet, ear-lapping bonnet.

"So let me conclude by saying that the strongest force

you have to free yourselves from the ties of taxes and make yourselves ripe for the riches of prosperity is a vote for Mark Weldon on November fifth. As Abraham Lincoln said, and probably from just such a spot, 'The ballot is far stronger than the bullet.' I thank you."

Listen to them. Now my chill is from them. They're going crazy. And the way the band's whipping it up is wild. They can't all be Lanacola plants.

"Faster! Faster!" Brad yells. "Get those engines going. Amanda, you and the girls and Merebaum close in on Mark. Hurry! Wave, kids! Wave up high so they can see you. More! And don't stop until we're way past the station, until there's smoke between you and the tiny dots."

". . . and with everybody flying over and past everything today, nobody has the time to spend overnight on a train, to really meet the people along the way. And for our girls, Sonia and Sara, to be able to be here in Elmira, and visit the home where Mark Twain lived and wrote *Life on the Mississippi*, is something they'll never forget."

They sure won't. I've seen them bored, but today's reaction makes me think they're a Wilcox payoff.

"And what a sad commentary that they are the only children in their entire school who have ever slept on a train. When we think a train is what pulled America together, glued us into one nation indivisible, it's criminal to bear witness to another pleasure passing for progress."

I wonder how I would kill myself if my husband suddenly said we were moving to Elmira.

"The beauty of this river-straddling city, with our country's largest fire engine factory still clanging to the . . ."

I think I'd get a state map and shoot myself right through the little black dot next to "Elmira."

"And as far as the raging storm of my opponent's harangue against me goes, as Mark Twain stated in *Life on the Mississippi*, 'I scratch my head with the lightning and purr myself to sleep with the thunder.' Thank you."

Thank God we can finally get off this "passing pleasure."

"There'd better be more people at the auditorium tonight," Mark snarls at two of Lanacola's advance team. "What the hell's going on? I'll tell you one thing. It won't be me without a crowd."

"That was a crowd for Elmira," Brad says.

"Did you see the mob for Wilcox in Utica last Sunday?" Mark asks.

Brad rubs his eye under his glasses. "Mark. Elmira is a working town. Today's Tuesday."

"Then why are we here?"

"The train ends here."

"So could the momentum." Mark shoves his fists into his pockets looking as cool as before he whistled through these twelve handshaking horror hamlets.

"Take it easy, Mark," Brad says quietly. "Every candidate always thinks the other guy's ten feet tall when the end closes in. That his crowd's bigger, his team's tougher, and the media's making more room for his heat. It's normal paranoia."

"Where do the polls stand now? The CIO? The AF of L? What about dough? What am I? The last to know too late?"

"Mark. Easy. I'm waiting now on something that should break in Buffalo."

"Don't bother to let me in on it."

"If we get those million and a half bison to line the streets, will you feel better?"

". . . and as we circled Niagara Falls only minutes ago, before landing at Buffalo's International Airport, we received word that *The New York Times*, obviously following the farsighted lead of the Buffalo *Courier*, endorsed my husband, Mark Weldon, for governor of New York.

"As any responsible organization or individual knows, our state needs, demands, begs for leadership. And for me, the definition of a leader is not only someone who is going somewhere, but someone who can persuade others, like you, to go with him. Like he did me, a long, exciting time ago.

(they're really applauding and yelling . . . they're screaming my name . . . I can't believe it . . . I love it . . . they're not stopping . . . but I better before their hands do . . .)

"Thank you. Thank you. Please. Let me conclude. Not that I want to end here, because I love you. I love your warmth, your sincerity. But it won't end here, because I want you to know when you vote for Mark Weldon, you'll also be voting for me. We are a team. A team of public people who are also private people with regular lives, who can feel as you feel and who know what you want. We're not afraid of hard work or the hard truth. We need them both to provide us with the atmosphere that will bring salvation to our state.

"No matter what the challenge, the name Weldon will fight to uphold the moral principles of decency and compassion without relaxing the cudgels of combat. And only with your support can we crumble the crises ahead while making the name Weldon the mark (smile . . . look around

. . . a more self-effacing smile), and sometimes the Amanda, of achievement. God bless you all!"

Am I hearing okay? Is that hysterical hoopla for me? Even when Mark joins me and holds our hands up, it doesn't get any louder. It can't. Now they're joining our names. Both our names are being chanted to us. Throw kisses, Amanda. Smile and mouth "Thank you." Now, let go of Mark and walk to the edge, to all those reaching, grasping hands. Keep going. *Wow! Wow! Wow! Fellas.*

"With little more than twenty-four hours to go until the last voting booth closes, gubernatorial campaigning reached its peak today. Early this morning, Martha Morrison and our CBS cameras caught up with Amanda Weldon as she blitzkrieged her way through the minority sections of the Bronx and Brooklyn."

"This is Martha Morrison, working the rush-hour subways with Amanda Weldon and her continuous commuter cast of thousands. When we asked Ms. Weldon what she thought of her husband's chances tomorrow, her answer was to throw the question to the crowd.

"Well, viewers. Well, Walter. Those roars may not be the final results, but if they're any kind of indicator, the Weldons and the Wilcoxes better start packing. Martha Morrison. CBS News. Bruckner Boulevard. The Bronx."

Max "bravos" so loudly that Pedro looks down at the glasses on his tray to make sure they're not shattered, only shaking. "Christ, Marcus. Did you hear that? And from a Wilcox stronghold?"

"Typical Howell brilliance," Darcy says. "Using only that last name, whenever possible, is brilliant. And take it from me, the woman's vote grows every second."

"The women! Fuck the women. Or should that go without saying? What about the men?" Max asks, looking at Darcy like he's a fool.

Lanacola slaps his black book across his palm. "Do both you Weldons know, between the two of you, you made over fifty stops today?" Sandy wipes his forehead as if he were at every one.

I wouldn't say it out loud, but I'm not even tired. My feet may kill, but my head is running through the crowds and cries, the cameras and the mikes. Everywhere I left, I really didn't want to leave.

"These last ten days cost more than the last ten weeks," Latham says. "But it's coming in big now. We should end up only two or three million in debt."

"Hot damn. 'Only.' 'Only,'" Max says. "If two or three million is 'only' to you, why don't you take it from Marr petty cash?"

"Max! Don't you ever let up?" Mark asks, staring into the spitting logs in the fireplace. "Money is the least of our home-free worries."

"Now what?" Max asks, blowing out the match, then looking at the end of his cigar.

"I'm worried about the President." Mark walks over and slides his index finger over the leather books on the bottom shelf.

"What more could he say, Marcus? He's a Democrat, for Christ's sake. He said he knew you two could work together. He didn't say shit for Wilcox. Are you nuts?"

Mark looks at his finger and moves it to another shelf. "Don't try making me the moron, Max. Not me, Max. Ever."

"Easy," Darcy says. "We've only got one more day."

"If you mean Mandell's days are numbered, you could be right," Mark says.

"Fuck you." Max leans back and blows the most perfect rings of his career. "All you wanted was the President. We bought you the President. I think you're crazy."

Waving his arms, Mark breaks every one of Max's rings. "Forty-eight percent of the people think the President's doing a lousy job. Only twenty-one percent would vote for him again. Did you see that today? He needs me."

"Not for another two years, Marcus. All the public really understands is that the President endorsed Weldon. But more important," Max says, in a fag voice, "if ever you touch my rings again, I'll smash your face."

Thank goodness Mark is smiling. Not so anyone normal would notice, but he knows Max notices. Mark turns to the TV. "There's Wilcox," he says. "Let's listen."

"As Governor Wilcox emerged from his Gulf Stream One, Bob Peterson was on hand at Albany County Airport. Looking tired, yet smiling to the crowd, Wilcox retorted to Peterson's questions about Weldon's presidential endorsement with:

"The President would have been better advised to stay in Washington and combat inflation. By this time tomorrow, the President will regret reacting to the trumped-up polls and hyped-up crowds of my opponent."

"He's got some balls to claim any victory, no less an early one," Max says.

"Look at that crowd. Listen to them yell." Mark's tone is shrill.

"What's that? A couple of hundred people behind a gate?" Lanacola says. "When you were with the President it looked like Red Square on May Day."

"Bullshit. Where's Howell?" Mark asks, just managing to hold control.

"Behind every TV spot that's plastering every program

pause," Max says. "And his last people endorsement had so many colors, it looked like the UN Christmas card."

"Where's Howell now?"

"He's with Bailey figuring tomorrow, deciding the best places for the hot money," Darcy says. "Unless the blacks and Chicanos are bought big, they'll never pull the levers. We also need the Delivery Unions to pay newsstand dealers to poster Mark's face on the sides of their stalls and to push the name Weldon every time anyone plunks a quarter for a paper."

Mark's knuckles are white as he bangs them into his palm. "I'm not going to win with the fucking blacks and spics," Mark says. "Not that I blame Howell for a TV blizzard. Since it nets him a sweet slice of channel time as well as his fee."

"Mark." I want him to stop. Fast. "Brad's got the public so turned on that—"

"Are you that public, Amanda? Does he turn you on?"

He could, Mark. He sure could if I thought I could make him come the way you will when you win.

"Brad! Brad! I'm so sick of hearing what a genius he is. A genius to fire the drunken speech writer or a fool to hire him? A genius to capitalize on the no-show or an idiot to have trusted Mazurski? I know you're each a fucking brain pulling the strings on a lucky slob. Well, now hear this. And stick it up your masterminds. If I win, and by the way that's a big *if*, just remember *I* won." Mark goes to the bar, takes any bottle, and pours it over some ice.

"I've seen this a million times," Darcy says, his arm around my shoulders. "Why don't you get some rest. We'll stay with Mark. Tomorrow's a big day."

"Stay tuned tomorrow when CBS News will carry complete coverage of the election returns starting at . . ."

21

Even through the closed draperies, I can feel the cold gray of coming winter. Each year it seems to intrude earlier and earlier on autumn's lease. It's sad to know those lifeless leaves, still clinging to the world, need but the slightest nudge to fall from their branches. Curled and crisp, soon all the hold-ons will spin slowly back to dust.

Was it only last spring the mood of the mimosa on the draperies matched the tender unfurling of young buds? Only five months since Miracle Mark stood among the cranes and derricks announcing his plans for today?

I wish before creeping out of bed, showing me his quiet thoughtfulness, he had given me a good luck fuck. I like occasion fucks. Christmas, anniversaries, birthdays. I don't care about Easter or public birthdays. Children's birthdays are the best occasion fucks. Anyway, I feel they're cementing to house and home.

Certainly, Election Day is an occasion. And before this day is over, it'll be too late. We'll be way into tomorrow. And it won't be the same tomorrow. It's unreal to think that tomorrow at this time will take the same as it did from yesterday until now. Although everybody's certain about today, nobody's sure. "Variables." "Variables." I'm so tired of people hiding behind "variables." They can't say, "I don't know," because they're being paid to know. Well, I'm not paid and I know. Goddamn it.

And, wow, am I going to dress like a winner. Smart, expensive, jeweled.

I'd better open the draperies and give a hearty welcome

to this first Tuesday in November and shut my mind to variables and unknowns. My God! The courtyard's already crowded with cars. Poor Francesca and Pedro. Well, look at it this way. If Mark doesn't win, the crowds will go and Francesca and Pedro will stay. And if he does become governor, they'll stay. And that's the kind of variable I like. Right? Right. You just better be that today, big girl!

Even the hot tub doesn't ease the raw excitement. My whole soapy body seems saturated with Dexamil. I remember when I was little thinking when I became very important, I'd get even with Janet. She was so mean to me. Doesn't even the name Janet sound mean? Very important meant inviting three girls, none of them Janet, to the circus and buying them a lot of souvenirs without my mother making their mothers pay back. Then they would like me much better than Janet. Before sex, that was my favorite fantasy.

Now, "Please God," as you know who would say, I'll be important. But now there's nobody I hate like Janet. Not one person I want to have get sick, move away, or fail. That's not really a hundred true. There is definitely one person I want to have fail. Please God.

Does Mommy hear the sweet thunder of angels running through her bedroom? Indeed, she does. And, of course, when one stops the other crashes into her.

"Watch it, Sara!"

"You stopped on purpose. Toad!"

"Good morning, lovely ladies." I'm so used to this smile, I'll bet even my children are beginning to think they do no wrong.

"Mom. You look so pretty so early," Sonia says, patting my arm gently, as if she's touching a miracle.

"Daddy and I are voting early."

"Do you think he'll win? Do you think he'll win?" Sara asks, jumping to the rhythm of her questions.

"I think so."

"I can't stand it. I can't stand it," Sonia shrieks.

"Why's everybody saying things in twos? Is this some wonderful new Amawalk ritual?"

Sonia nods twice at Sara, who does the same to her.

"Right. Right. Mother. Mother," Sara says.

"Enough. Enough," I answer, feeling a loss of smile. "And when Pedro and Francesca bring you to the city, don't give them a hard time about a nap. You're going to be up all night. Please, promise."

"I promise promise," Sonia says hysterically.

"I'm serious," I say without so much as a grin.

"Mom? I don't want to live in Albany," Sonia says.

God! Who could live in Albany? "What's the matter with Albany? A fine, historical city, founded in 1609, when Henry Hudson terminated his voyage on the *Half Moon*. You could go to one of twenty-four elementary schools, watch all five television channels, or listen to at least eleven—"

"Mom's kidding you, Sonia. Aren't you, Mom?"

"Albany, girls, has a disease called location that makes it completely uninhabitable."

"I knew you were kidding. I knew you were kid—" Sara says, catching herself. "Honestly, I didn't mean to say that twice."

"You two are too much. Get it? And in case you haven't noticed, I'm crazy for you. And don't yell about the dresses you're wearing tonight. There's something about painter's pants and basketball shorts that doesn't televise too well."

"I love you, Mom," Sara says, hugging.

"Me too," Sonia says, pushing her away.

"I adore you both. Now go and wish Daddy good luck. I'll see you later and—"

"We promise," they say chorally, without turning around.

It really is a gray lady out. I'd better wear something heavy over this thin wool. But Amanda? Why in God's name are you pulling out cloth? Cloth is for losers. Wilcox's wife is the one who's got to push poor to tell all those "loans" that their future mobility is permanent. As the "they" might say, "Rather owe it to you than cheat you out of it."

"Hurry up, Amanda!" Mark yells. "We've got to move."

"You said Sandy said not to hurry. That the morning's so dark, the cameras had to wait for it to lighten."

"It's lightened. Come on." I hear Mark unlocking the front door, but I don't hear it close. His trick. Leaving it open, knowing the incoming cold will make me rush.

The coat I'd really like to freak them out with today should be one sewn from every ugly ferret that this league of women cunts feels so virtuous protecting. They do more for them than for their children. Well, it's easier. And haven't they given their all to their kids? After all, they've given them the school, the church, and the club. Anyway, my coat of many coons would also contain squirrel, groundhog, hedgehog, mouse, mole, and muskrat. And right after their "ooohs" and "aaaahs," I'd tell them how I lovingly skinned each pelt myself. And do you know what? They'll still "oooh" and "aaah." And do you know why? Of course. Mark Weldon will be governor.

"Get off that horn. I'm coming. I'm here."

"Isn't mink a little dressy?" Mark asks, revving for the Indy 500, as Sandy helps me in.

"Not for a winner. Mark? Are you still worried about these frauds?"

"Just a reflex."

"Then hit the other knee." At least Sandy laughs.

"What's the school routine?" Mark asks Sandy.

"Very casual. Very natural. Just don't look directly into any camera. Keep shaking hands and saying 'Thank you' to everyone. It comes across that everyone is saying 'Good luck' to you. And don't be afraid to get close to the people. They've got to look like warm friends, even if you've never seen them before. And don't talk to separate mikes. Today's togetherness. Let the cameras get you both in. And remember, they'll start the second you roll up."

Wow! What a mob. It's Andy Hardy in *Hometown Boy Makes Good*. They're sure all here. Every Amawalk sicky wishing us well. Oh, how sweet it is. God! Is that really Junior Parkhurst on the steps with our Country Day's own Mr. Chips? It's all so glorious and insincere.

"Where do we go from school?" I ask Sandy through my camera smile.

"The church."

"God! Then where?"

"The club. For the Westchester Workers' breakfast."

"Right. I forgot." Forgot, your ass! You pushed that into a recess you don't even have.

"Thank you." "Thank you." "Thanks so much." "Thank you." "Thanks." "Thank . . ."

Junior almost trips over Boop's tassels as he "helps" me to the top step. "We made no mistake the day Boop and I brought you into Amawalk," Junior says, regaining his balance. "Not that we needed this to know you're both winners." At this moment, Peter the goat is so TV tuned, he wouldn't notice my tit if it were turquoise. And all I can notice is his crest. Actually, it might be quite useful in target practice. Rill-y? Rill-y!

God, Mark looks good as the wind takes up that corner of his hair. I'm glad hats are out. I wonder what it was about overcoats that made them out also. Was that Kennedy too? Looking at Mark's perfectly polished shoes, I can just see his taking them from Pedro, thanking him for the good shine, then wiping them again the minute Pedro left. I bet I could even make up in the mirror of those toes.

"We're certainly proud of *all* the Weldons," says Chips, claiming complete responsibility for Sonia and Sara. "You know, when I was a tad at Amawalk Country Day, I actually believed that no one could make our little community any bett—"

"This way, Amanda," Sandy says instinctively.

"Thank you," I say to Mr. Chips, the goat, and the Boop. I wonder if I'm the only mother who doesn't know the inside of this school. I mean I've been here. Uncomfortably, for sure. Will somebody once and forever tell me why parents sit on children's chairs for those illuminating conferences? To make us feel little? Oh. I get it. Not nice-little. Be-little.

"Sign here, please, Mrs. Weldon, and good luck."

"Thank you." If it isn't one of my league of women coon collectors. No! *Never* that kind.

"Mrs. Weldon? You're number twenty-one to vote."

"Our audit number at the club." I smile. I hope its only significance is related to the salute.

"In here, please, Mrs. Weldon."

> *Curtain up! Light the lights*
> *We've got nothing to reach but the heights*
> *Starting here, starting now . . .*

. . .

"... God created the heaven and the earth. And the earth was without form and void; and darkness was ..."

I wonder how much each of these stained glass windows cost. People are into making them again. I really only like them in taverns or churches. The ones here are pretty, but not nearly long enough. I like them longer.

"... God said, Let there be light: and there was ..."

Will Sonia and Sara walk down this aisle? And before they do, will I undo that slipknot and pull out the piles of tissue to see how they look in what "your daughter will someday wear"? No. I know I'll never unwrap it again. I wonder which one will be the first to march past these name-plated pews; "In loving memory of. . . ." Let's see how many I can see. "Hannah Van Sandt." "Iphigene Parkhurst." "Endicott and Mathilde Mattingale"? I have to have my prescription changed.

"... and although 'they heard the voice of the Lord God walking in the garden' they did not listen. But as He showed them, we must listen to Him, for He is our only master." Close Bible. Long look at ceiling. Heaven? Long pause. Long enough!

"I chose the Book of Genesis for today's sermon, because what could be more appropriate for what we pray is the start of a bountiful new life for Mark and Amanda Weldon, than the start of life itself. No matter where they go ..."

Even the banquet room at Holiday Inn would be less depressing than this chipped-paint excuse for a club. Why can't one of their heir-tight bartenders mix some paint as well? I'd personally spring for the flat white enamel, but I know I'd never get a buyer for the brush. Anyway, what difference? They're always blind when they're here. It rill-y couldn't matter less.

"The more I think of how generous you've been to Amanda and to me, the happier I am to call this home and you my family. The Westchester Weldon work force has not only been tireless and loyal, but perceptive and caring. Therefore our promises have hit the hearts as well as the headlines.

"Although eighty percent of Westchester County's four hundred and fifty thousand square miles is wooded, the other twenty percent probably houses the most geographically democratic . . ."

When I told you to say that number, I never said say *democratic*, dummy!

". . . from blue to white to starched. From ten minutes to ten generations. That's what makes us Westchesterites . . ."

I can hear the helicopter motors coming closer. I just can't believe they're allowing it on the first tee.

"Therefore, the best way to thank you is to carry out those promises when we get to Albany. And when that time comes, I'll need you all even more. May God bless each and every one of you."

The hoots and hollers of our names are outnoising the helicopter. And look at those hands. They really just want to touch us. It's always staggering.

"The tower just told the pilot it might rain," Latham says, as we fasten our safety belts.

"Instead of preaching about all those angels pouring down Jacob's ladder, the good Father should've prayed for a downpour of rain," Mark says.

"Don't worry," Lanacola says. "You don't need it."

"What about Wilcox's new rebate bill?" Mark asks the clouds. "You don't think that'll push the city Democrats to the polls?"

"It's personalities not issues that are our real issues. You and Amanda. I've never seen anything like you two. Just don't worry," Lanacola says, wiping his brow.

"Max and Brad'll be at the heliport," Latham says. "I've arranged cars, walkie-talkies, the works."

"I'm sure you've organized everything because I'm sure everything was left for you to organize." I can't resist.

Mark gives me a look I don't take. "Where's Maria?" I ask. "Latham? Where's Maria? You remember Maria?"

"Just thinking about something. Sorry, Amanda. What'd you say about Maria?"

"I said she's wonderful." I could cry.

"She is. She'll be with us later," Latham says, incapable of having two thoughts in the same space.

"How many polling places do you think we can hit?" Mark asks.

Lanacola sighs. "A lot. We also have to go around thanking workers, union guys, headquarters people."

"Who saw that lightning?" Latham yells, slapping his big, ugly hand on my thigh. "It's going to teem. Albany, here we come!"

As I cross my leg way over, his hand flops to the side.

"That storm certainly won't hurt us," Brad says, picking up a half sandwich, then putting it down again. "And peaking right through lunchtime's going to wash out a lot of Wilcox loyalty."

I wonder if Brad is seeing me with him, remembering us on this floor of this apartment, hearing Maria scream.

"When will we know something?" Mark asks.

"You're driving me crazy," Max says, puffing double time.

"You really take this smoke-filled room shit to everyone else's heart, don't you, Mandell?" Mark asks, smacking his fist into his palm.

"Maybe, Marcus, we should watch some old army films to get our minds calm, our appetites back. How about the all-time favorite, *The Administration of the Enema?*" Nobody, thank goodness, encourages Max with so much as a grin.

"Bailey's made sure of police coverage," Darcy says. "They'll move with us most of the afternoon and tonight a patrol car will take us when we're ready."

Mark could break his hand at this rate. "Can't anybody answer? How early can we know anything? Or do you think early returns will be bad? Well, if you want to know what I think, I think late will be too!"

"The AF of L and CIO would never have switched such big dough if even their own polls hadn't shown you way out front," Darcy says.

Good he added "front."

"The city's too Democratic for an early projection," Darcy continues. "It wouldn't be accurate."

"What about the storm?" Mark asks.

"It won't keep them all home," Brad says. "When out-of-city tallies start, projections will, too."

"I think you're all crazy!" Mark yells. "You're all avoiding the question. All I'm asking is when."

I don't think I've ever jumped in and out of a car so much in my life and to such strenuous welcomes. Who says New York's Democratic? The polling places we hit were Weldon blizzards. And those workers. Those thanked-today, thankless workers. They were actually crushed the campaign was over. Slowly, I let more hot water fill the tub, trying to keep it coming at the same rate it drains.

"Amanda?"

"I'm in the tub, Mark."

"Hurry. Brad may have something."

I guess this is the prettiest silk dress I've ever seen. I can't spoil my beige image, but I can pull it more off the shoulders as the evening goes on. Now, I don't even need rouge. Whew! Easy, girl. Eye makeup? Now, but not later. Not bad, Weldon. "Wow! Wow! Wow! fellas!"

"What's the news?" I ask Brad, coming on like Bacall around Hoagy (no, not Bogey). Hoagy, at the piano.

"I've just called a pal at CBS. All the networks have a technique where they poll key districts to get a microcosm of the state, a reading on how the voting's going. Each network wants to be first with the right projection."

"And?" I'm leaning into "A sigh is just a sigh. . . ."

"The bellwether districts read Weldon."

"Why don't they announce something?" Mark asks.

"It's a leak, not a final return," Max says.

"Are the papers still planning two front pages?" Mark asks.

"They have to," Brad says.

"Why? If it's so clearly Weldon."

"Maybe you'll die from acute Weldon," Max says.

"Let's go." Brad motions. "We've got some rooms at the Carlyle where we'll hide out until we go to the VIP suite at the Statler Hilton when the results are final. Everything's set. The patrol car'll wait at the side entrance of the Carlyle for our signal to move."

"What's our signal if I'm not too mental to know?" Mark asks.

"When Wilcox says he'll concede," Darcy says.

Mark shakes his head. More like the accused than the victor, he walks the last mile.

The screeching siren and whirling lights pull to an abrupt halt at the side entrance of the Statler Hilton. Rushing past flashes and screams, our caravan piles into the extra-deep back elevators on our way to hear Wilcox.

The flowers, the food, the faces, they're all a weird blend of chaos and euphoria. The workers, pressmen, union heads, all blur into a bunch of slaps, drinks, and unpressed clothes. The televisions are soundless in the noise until somebody almost topples from a table shouting quiet, more quiet. "QUIET!"

I can't look. I hate to look. Poor Mrs. Wilcox. She looks so tired. Their two daughters are crying and smiling. The boaters, the banners, that huge picture of him in back of him; they all have to be out by tomorrow. And nobody will feel like doing it. He looks a lot older than that picture.

". . . in this time of conflicting pressures, I hope Mark Weldon's victory will symbolize more cooperation between Albany and City Hall and continue still further the balance sheet of accomplishments the Wilcox years have brought to our state. I give him my support and my blessings."

"A pol all the way," Brad says admiringly to Darcy, who shakes his head in agreement.

"Why?" I ask Brad, still sorry for Mrs. Wilcox.

"Not only did Wilcox keep praising himself, but that sonovabitch waited till after eleven, after prime time to concede. He was through at nine but at nine more viewers would see him lose. See us win."

"I like that." I do.

"Let's go!" Lanacola yells. "Now! Let's go! Move it!"

I don't know how it happened, but I'm between Maria
and Sonia as we file from the suite. I squeeze Maria's hand.
She presses mine back. We know we shall always love each
other as two people do who have given each other something each once needed desperately . . . and could find only
in each other. As we approach the Grand Ballroom, the band
grows louder and louder and louder. It's almost as loud as the
"WE WANT WELDON" rhythmically booming to the stomps
and claps. The platform is already crowded with lesser union
men, lesser press, lesser importants than the big bamboos
who followed us from the suite.

"WE WANT WELDON!" "WE WANT WELDON!" "*We want
Weldon!*" "*We want Weldon!*" "We want Weldon."
Slowly, it lowers as word gets around "They're up there."
"Look up there!" "They're here." "There!"

Mark, Merebaum, Ortega—the big sweep all join
hands. The crowd goes crazy. Merebaum and Ortega bring
up their wives and kids. Now they all leave. Mark and I are
alone with the girls. The girls leave.

Now it's just Mark and me. The mob grows manic. It's
like the Peep! Hitler! Woodstock! Wow!

No matter what sentence Mark speaks, the crowd breaks
it with yells. Every word charges the atmosphere with even
more frenzy. Sandy is right. It's not issues.

"Today marks a new era in opportunities for us all. We
now have a new leadership. One called Weldon. Or should
I say two called Weldon?

(My God! I think the ballroom will cave in.)

"Thank you. Thank you. We pledge, once and for all,
to curb instead of cause inflation, to cure the chronic ills
from governments past, and to bring forth an intensity of
purpose destined to make New York State once again the
greatest name in our nation.

(It must be solid steel.)

"All of you helped win this victory for me and my wife, Amanda. But as the Bible tells us, 'Above all things Truth beareth away the victory.' We thank you. We love you. And we pray for God to bless you."

I can't believe it's four thirty. I can't believe I'm alive. I can't believe it's Wednesday. Tuesday is over. I can't believe *it*. I can't believe *me*. But didn't Max, long ago, tell Mark, "You'll run, but she'll win?" And I heard that win last night. I hear it now. The growing roar, the screams, the hysteria. I see the clutching, grabbing hands when I joined Mark, when we stood together waving, watching our victory.

We may have cashed in our marriage, but this alliance has a power and a thrust whose bonds are tighter and more binding than any, ever. It gives me an energy that insists that anything's possible. I like it. I like it a whole lot. And I have a feeling I'm going to like it a whole lot more. From governor of New York State to—where? From the governor's wife to—what? Yes, I can even imagine "Amanda Weldon" banners and my standing up there alone, receiving those same roars. Not yet. Not now. But sometime.

I know Mark saw what I saw, heard what I heard. And he knows I know. Our balance of power is scaled just right, right now. I put my hand on top of his as we turn into our driveway, the headlights beaming.

A Note on the Type

The text of this book was set on the Linotype in Janson, a recutting made direct from type cast from matrices long thought to have been made by the Dutchman Anton Janson, who was a practicing type founder in Leipzig during the years 1668–87. However, it has been conclusively demonstrated that these types are actually the work of Nicholas Kis (1650–1702), a Hungarian, who most probably learned his trade from the master Dutch type founder Dirk Voskens. The type is an excellent example of the influential and sturdy Dutch types that prevailed in England up to the time William Caslon developed his own incomparable designs from them.

This book was composed by Maryland Linotype
Composition Co., Baltimore, Maryland.
Printed and bound by The Haddon Craftsmen,
Scranton, Pennsylvania.
Typography and binding design by Virginia Tan.